I0708723

His expression turned serious, his eyes dark and shrewd.

"Look at me, Eden." A huskiness lingered in his voice. "Let's not play games."

She cleared the knot in her throat. Slowly, she lifted her lashes from her cheeks and looked into his eyes. "I'm sure I don't know what you mean, Major."

His fingertips dug into the small of her back. "I'm quite sure you know exactly what I mean." He glided her toward an unlit corner of the room and pulled her closer. "I want more, much more than a dance from you, my dear."

The last time she heard those words were from Patrick. He had said he wanted more from her and then proposed to her right then and there. True, the major had been toying with her, but he clearly desired her. Perhaps he had marriage on his mind, too. Certainly, it would not be the first time a soldier, home from the devastating war, became infatuated with the ideals of marriage after witnessing the horrors of battle firsthand. These days, hasty proposals by lonely, war-weary soldiers were commonplace. She would wait for him to ask and take pleasure in turning him down. After all, two could play this game.

"Why, Major, what more could you *possibly* want from me?" She quivered her lashes and smiled.

"You can stop with the modest routine, Eden. You know perfectly well what I'm interested in."

"Well, I'm sorry to disappoint you, Major, but I'm not like the other belles around here. I don't wish to marry any time soon."

Thorns of Eden

by

DIANA BALLEW

TRIFECTA PUBLISHING HOUSE

Thorns of Eden

Copyright © 2011 by Diana Ballew

Trifecta Publishing House edition, 2015

All rights reserved. Except as permitted under the U.S. Copyright Act of 1976, no part of this publication may be reproduced, distributed, or transmitted in any form or by any means now known or hereafter invented, or stored in a database or retrieval system, without the prior written permission of the publisher, Trifecta Publishing House.

This book is a work of fiction Names, characters, places, and incidents are the product of the author's imagination or are used fictitiously. Any resemblance to actual persons, living or dead, business establishments, events, or locales is coincidental.

Published in the United States of America
First Printing: 2015
Print Book
ISBN -10: 1943407037
ISBN -13: 978-1-943407-03-3

Trifecta Publishing House
871 Coronado Center Drive
Suite 200
Henderson, Nevada 89052-3977

TRIFECTA PUBLISHING HOUSE
Contact Information: Info@TrifectaPublishingHouse.com

Cover Art by Rae Monet, Inc. Design.
Formatted by CyberWitch Press

To my real life heroes who keep me grounded:
John Douglas, Jason, Sean, and Conner.

To General J.E.B. Stuart, whose romantic nature
and true heroism led me to dream.

While Mars with his stentorian voice
Chimes in with dire discordant noise,
Sweet woman in angelic guise
Gives us hope and fear despise.

The maid of Saragossa still
Breathes in our cause her dauntless will
Beyond Potomac's rockbound shore
Her touch bids southern cannon roar...

General J. E. B. Stuart

Chapter 1

"Oh, Father. If we'd only known," Eden Blair whispered. A stiff poke gouged the small of her back. She turned around and glared at her stepmother, Ann. "What did you do *that* for?"

"Father? Oh, do move on, Eden. It's been a whole year, for heaven's sake."

"I thought you were going to the bakery." Eden spun on her boot tip and examined a roll of rose-colored fabric in a bright beam of sunlight illuminating the shop's counter.

"Well, I just—" Ann gasped and tugged at the material. "That color is revolting. Sometimes you're so thick-headed. I don't know what I'm going to do with you."

"And just what's wrong with this fabric?"

"What a matronly color. Are you actually trying to look unattractive for the event? Older? Ann sighed and shoved an invisible strand of ebony hair away from her forehead. "With all the nice boys off fighting, this may be the only social occasion we go to all year." She swatted her dark skirt. "I'm so happy we're finally getting out of these black dresses tomorrow,

I could dance a jig."

Eden rolled her eyes and sighed.

"I hope you're listening to me." Ann inched closer. "Considering it's next to impossible to catch a husband right now, one year of mourning is more than sufficient for both of us. So, while we're here for your brother's wedding, may I suggest you try to look your best? Perhaps one of our soldiers in gray will find you attractive. And mind you Eden, I said gray...not blue."

"Enough!" Eden grabbed the roll of fabric and shoved it at her stepmother's midsection.

Ann's blue eyes widened as she caught the fabric against her thick skirts. "Thank you for another fine display of defiance."

"Well, I certainly learned from the best."

"How dare you!"

"Ladies, please." Mr. Johnson darted in, positioning himself between the two women. He lifted the roll of fabric away from Ann's firm grasp.

Eden flushed from embarrassment. She shouldn't act in such a manner, especially in public, but Ann was deliberately provoking her with cruel comments about Patrick's betrayal. After all, it wasn't her fault he had practically left her at the altar and turned his back on the South to join the Union Army.

The elderly shopkeeper stroked his gray beard, his pale eyes brightening. "Ladies, I do apologize for my limited selection. Perhaps Miss Eden would enjoy seeing some fabric I received this morning and still have in the back." He smoothed the jumbled material, his gaze darting between the two women, awaiting a prompt answer.

Eden and Ann glared at each other like a pair of Siamese cats before a tussle. Just then, the bells on the shop door behind her jingled.

"Oh, Ann, my dear girl."

Ann's face suddenly beamed with a bright smile, and she called to the older woman. "Good morning, Mrs. Radcliff. I'll be finished here in just a moment. Now, don't you go running off 'til we have a chance to chat."

"Miss Eden?" Mr. Johnson gestured toward the back of the shop.

"Pick out something real pretty, sweetheart," Ann called, then dropped her tone, "And I'll strangle you silly if you dare embarrass me in front of my friend."

Eden stuck out her tongue just as the bells jingled once more. Her stepmother's sudden rapturous gaze was not the reaction she had expected. Instead, Ann's passionate stare was aimed at the shop's entrance.

"Oh, Lord, have...mercy," Ann breathed, "Lord have mercy, look at that divine man."

Curious, Eden turned toward the morning sun flooding through the open door. The bright light embraced the tall man, obscuring his features while outlining the breadth of his shoulders and the ease and grace of his movements as he removed his hat.

"Well...hello," Mr. Johnson called to the stranger. "I didn't rightly expect you so soon, sir. I'll have your cigars in a jiffy." He walked toward the back of the shop. "You coming, Miss Eden?"

Eden watched the tall man shut the door and stroll to the counter. His wavy, jet-black hair and dark eyes were in sharp contrast to his crisp white shirt and embroidered waistcoat. The stranger looked in their direction and smiled, revealing gleaming white teeth as he set his hat on the counter and leaned casually on one elbow.

Ann's tongue darted out and moistened her bottom lip. "Stay out of my way, Eden."

Eden shook her head and frowned. "You're pathetic."

"Oh, hush up!" Ann adjusted the cameo pinned at her throat, her gaze scrolling up and down the handsome man's form.

"Miss Eden?" the shopkeeper ventured, "Do you still wish to see—"

"I'm coming." Eden brushed by the stranger, unwilling to watch her young stepmother throw her considerable charms at yet another handsome man, the same way she had once dazzled her father. Behind her, she could hear Ann's impetuous greeting.

"Ma'am," returned the stranger, in a low easy drawl.

"Now, I've got these new pretty dress goods." Mr. Johnson led her into the cool, dimly lit storage area. He placed the rose fabric on a shelf and gestured toward a table with cloth and ribbons of various colors lying in neat rows.

Eden winced. "I apologize, Mr. Johnson. Ann has a way of bringing out the worst in me."

"Oh, I don't worry about her any." He pulled out a roll of pale jade silk and shook it in a loose spill. "I imagine her bark's worse than her bite."

She ran her hands over the iridescent fabric. "So lovely."

"I believe you wouldn't be ashamed of a dress made of this." He waggled his bushy eyebrows and smiled.

"It's beautiful, indeed, but..."

He lifted the roll and brought it closer to the door entry. The fabric caught a glimmer of sunlight, and it shimmered with a delicate radiance.

"I love it — truly I do, but I'm just coming out of mourning. Perhaps something more subdued would be more appropriate." She frowned and poked a finely woven gray taffeta.

"Why, that's...what did she call it — *revolting?*" Mr. Johnson teased.

She smiled. "Well, even if I could wear the jade, I can't afford such luxury right now."

He shifted his feet and paused. "I thought a lot of your father, Miss Eden. He helped my family through some rough patches. I know many folks around here feel the same."

"What a kind thing for you to say."

"Well, I mean what I say. He was one of the best doctors around, and I wish he were still alive so I could tell him how much I appreciated his care. Lord knows, we sure could use a man like him now. I hear there's a terrible shortage of good docs on the battlefields. He was a loyal man, and I know he would have wanted—"

She bit down on her bottom lip and looked away.

He set the fabric on the table. "Why, I'm sorry. I guess what I'm trying to say is Doc Blair was a good man. I didn't mean to ramble on and upset you."

"No, it's fine." She patted his arm. "Thank you for your kind words. He thought fondly of you and your family, too."

He nodded. "I know it's been hard on you. I just want to say I admire how you stayed by him and nursed him best you could, when he took sick. I don't imagine she was much help."

He cocked his head in the direction of the front of the store. "I would like to make a gift of this—"

"Hiram."

The deep voice startled her. Eden turned and saw the stranger strolling toward them. Caught by surprise, she could not remove her gaze from his.

Mr. Johnson examined his pocket watch and gave the man a curt nod. "Excuse me, Miss Eden. You think about this fabric or...or choose something you like better."

"Yes, of course," she whispered.

The old man turned toward the stranger. "I have what you ordered in my office, sir." He patted her arm. "I'll be right back." He hurried toward his small office just off the storage room, leaving her alone with the stranger.

Eden watched the slow appraisal in the stranger's eyes with dawning comprehension. The man stared in a way none of the boys ever would have dared while her father had been alive. She had rarely left Oak Hill during her year in mourning, but country life had certainly not dulled her senses.

She wrenched her gaze from his and realized her fingers were crushing the soft material. She smoothed it to hide her trembling hands.

"Mr. Johnson. I believe I do want this," she called. "Can you send it down to Miss Annette's, and I'll go pick out a dress pattern? Mr. Johnson?"

"Excellent choice."

She flinched. The man stood close behind her — too close. She hugged the roll of fabric against her chest and turned toward his voice without looking into his face. "Thank you, sir," she replied, though her voice barely rose above a whisper.

She cleared her throat and called toward the closed door. "Mr. Johnson? I'll...I'll just take it with me—"

"May I ask what you plan to wear with it?" the man asked, blocking the exit. He reached out to stroke the fabric near her cheek.

Towering over her by at least a foot, the stranger's commanding energy made her feel off balance. She sensed his dark eyes boring down, urging her to look up.

If he touches me, I'll faint!

"I don't know," she responded in the direction of his square jaw. "Please pardon me, sir."

He did not move.

"Diamonds would be far too strong with this color. I saw an exquisite emerald necklace at a shop down in New Orleans that would complement your eyes. Perhaps your husband could find something similar."

"I...I have no husband, sir. Pardon me." She stepped forward, but he remained in place. She contemplated pushing him aside, a prospect that seemed as likely as moving a mountain. *Where is Mr. Johnson?*

"Ah..." the stranger mused, "my sympathies on your loss, then."

She sighed and finally looked up at him. His expression appeared solemn, but rich brown eyes, hinting of amusement, stared back.

"Well, you certainly don't look very sorry," she blurted. "It was my father. Now, will you please excuse me?"

"Then perhaps I could take you to New Orleans."

Stunned by his forwardness, she forgot to be frightened. An unknown man speaking in such a manner is beyond contempt — particularly one who appears to be enjoying it.

"I've had all of this I can stand. Let me by."

He flashed an audacious grin and folded his arms across his chest.

She tilted her chin high. "You're an utter cad, sir. In your defense, I can only assume you've been away from polite society too long and have forgotten how to speak to a lady."

He raised a raven brow. "I daresay, you do have me there."

She smoothed the pleats of her skirt. "Just where you've been I won't venture to guess since..." Her gaze shot up and down the length of his long form. "Well, since you aren't even decent enough to be in uniform like all of the other brave men. There's a war going on, in case you haven't noticed."

He frowned and tilted his chin. "Is this your way of telling me I appear, shall we say, able-bodied? If so,–"

"Oh, for pity's sake!" A flush warmed her cheeks. "How dare you make fun of me. I want nothing more to do with you, and I'd bet my boots the army wants nothing to do with you, either. Now, let me out of here!" She stomped her leather boot on the wood floor.

He laughed, and she caught the sweet hint of brandy upon his breath as she attempted to pass him.

"Then, it's only my lack of suitable military attire you find offensive?" He grinned. "In that case, perhaps you would like to accompany me back to my room where I could remove these wretched garments and–"

"Oh, if you aren't the most ill-bred man!" She narrowed her gaze, took a step forward, and stared at him dead-on. "How dare you insult me with your lewd comments."

"Oh, calm down, now." He sighed and slowly moved

aside. "You can smooth those ruffled feathers. I'm not in the habit of deflowering unwilling young maidens, my dear."

Eden took another step and paused, unable to think clearly. Something about him made her feel unsteady, as though the secure flooring beneath her feet could rip out from under her at any moment.

Just don't look at him.

She toyed with a loose thread of fabric on the roll. "Well, I don't know who you think you are, waltzing into this shop with your fancy clothes, ordering your fancy cigars. Haven't you heard about sacrificing such luxuries for the sake of our fine men and the Cause?"

Before she knew it, he extended his arm and drew her close. With a firm hand, he nudged her chin up and bent down, his bronzed face only inches from her own.

She held her breath, unable to speak — unable to move! *Oh, Lord above, he's going to kiss me!* She slammed her eyes shut.

"I sacrifice far more than you know, madam," he whispered.

She inhaled the brandy upon his lips and the invisible veil of cigar smoke resting upon his collar. His mouth was a whisper away from her lips. Her heart hammered, fierce as wild thunder, causing her to gasp. She contemplated slapping him — slapping him hard across his arrogant face, but there she stood in front of him, frozen in place with her eyes scrunched shut.

The moment his hand dropped from her chin, she opened her eyes. Trying to hide the crimson flush heating her cheeks, she took a deep breath and turned away. As much as the man unnerved her, even frightened her, there was something wickedly attractive about him. The problem was, he knew it, too.

With trembling fingers, she toyed with the collar of her dress. "Sir, I sincerely hope in the future you acquaint yourself with proper etiquette before addressing a lady, especially a lady in mourning. Good day."

"If you and your sister are any indication, then it's the ladies who've changed while I've been away."

"Excuse me?" Not willing to allow the vulgar rat the last word, she spun around to face him. "Well, she's not my sister, if you must know. She's my stepmother, so why don't you just resume your conversation with her and leave me alone. No doubt she threw herself at you."

Judging by the fiery green eyes glaring at him, Rayce Hampton knew he'd hit a sore spot. "How perceptive. You're exactly right."

The blonde pursed her lips and looked into his eyes. "Well, I'm sure she's your kind of woman."

He shook his head slowly, meeting her challenging gaze. "Not even close."

The sweet scent of magnolia filled the small room, assaulting his senses. He inhaled deeply, savoring the enticing aroma. He imagined pulling the hairpins from her sleek, tawny hair swept under the demure, black bonnet and combing it into a loose spill with his fingers.

He reached up to brush an errant tendril from her cheek. "I think you would prove more interesting. Or must I sacrifice the thought of having you and my cigars...for the Cause, of course?"

She jerked the fabric roll back and smacked him with it as hard as she could. "Oh, if you're not the most vile rat!"

He caught the blow on his shoulder and took a step back, laughing. She stormed out through the storage room door into the bright shop.

He laughed and called after her. "I'll take that as a 'no!'"

Hiram Johnson emerged from his office and saw the blonde retreating. "Where's she—"

Rayce watched the slender woman walk away, her body curving gently in all the right places, defying the dreary black garb. "I believe she'll take the jade fabric, Hiram." He took the wrapped bundle the older man extended. "Thanks."

Hiram frowned and waved a finger. "Now, don't you go toyin' with her. I've known her family for years. She's a sweet, young woman."

"Toy...who me?" He combed a hand through his hair and sighed. "Come now, Hiram, you know me well enough...who is she?"

Hiram raised an eyebrow. "You're right — I do, and that's exactly why I—"

"Mr. Johnson?" Eleanor Radcliff rang the front desk bell.

"Come now, Hiram. I haven't much time. Her name?"

The older man's eyes narrowed. "I'll tell you her name, but you stay away from her just the same. Poor girl's had enough trouble without you—"

"Hiram!"

"All right! Her name is Eden. Miss Eden Blair. Now, I have to go." He coughed and lowered his voice. "Leave through the back door." He smoothed his thick mustache and hurried through the doorway.

Rayce tapped his fingers on the table. "Eden...Miss Eden Blair...Blair." He frowned, trying to make the connection between the little blonde with the ferocious temper and the familiar name. His fingers stopped in place.

Miss Eden Blair.

He tossed the small packet into the air and caught it deftly as he headed toward the back. Whistling a cheerful ditty, he replaced his hat at a rakish tilt and strode out the alley door.

Chapter 2

Like a small hurricane, Eden entered the front of the shop, halting Ann's discussion with Mrs. Radcliff.

"Mrs. Radcliff." Eden nodded and spun on her heel to face Ann. "Let's go."

"Good heavens!" Ann snapped, "Oh, tell me that's not what you chose, is it?"

Eden shouldered the roll of fabric like a rifle. "It is. Now hurry up; we have to go."

Ann sighed and rolled her eyes. She pulled a delicate handkerchief from her beaded black bag and pressed it lightly to her throat.

"Don't be so hasty, Eden," Mrs. Radcliff reprimanded. "It would suit you well if you listened to Ann's advice. Naturally, she only wants you to look your most attractive."

Ann returned the handkerchief to her bag and pulled the tasseled drawstring taut. "Yes, I do want her to have a lovely dress, poor thing. It's not easy to be young and pretty and in mourning. Believe me, I know."

Mrs. Radcliff patted Ann's arm. "Yes, dear, I can imagine."

Ann sniffed. "And as these boys ride off to war, her prospects grow thinner by the day. Eden simply must have a new dress for her brother's wedding. Of course, I'll be fine in my old blue gown. After all, I've already had my chance at happiness."

If you only knew. "May we go now?" Eden interrupted, "I'm suddenly feeling ill." She shifted the roll of fabric to her other shoulder and stared at Ann.

Mrs. Radcliff smiled. "Oh, sugar, are you talking about the cornflower blue gown you wore to your engagement party to Eden's father? Why, I adore that color on you."

Ann sighed. "Yes, that's the one."

Eden tapped her toe on the smooth floor planks.

Eleanor frowned and heaved a heavy sigh. "You know, Eden, it would be wise to show Ann a little kindness. Remember, dear, you attract more flies with honey than vinegar."

"Well, I'm having that ol' blue dress remade, of course. My Fifi is a wonder with the needle." Ann waved a spool of blue thread in her hand as proof.

"Why, what happened to your girl, Sarah?" Eleanor asked.

"Oh, it is Sarah, but I decided to change her name."

"Now, what have I said?" Mrs. Radcliff chuckled, quizzing Eden. "I have always said our Ann surely has a romantic nature."

Ann smiled and flushed. "Oh, now, stop."

Eden couldn't help but wonder what prudish Eleanor Radcliff would say if she knew Ann's 'romantic nature' had led her to divest herself of her virginity in the carriage house with her second cousin. Apparently, the romance came to light shortly thereafter, and he had been sent, without ceremony, to Charleston, South Carolina, and Ann instructed to find a husband.

Her father had met Ann at a garden party and somehow found her charming. He had been a well-respected doctor, known for his practical sense, but also a lonely widower, thereby ripe for her picking. Eden had tried to talk sense into her enamored father, but it was too late. Ann had sunk her claws in deep, and without the blessing of his children, they married after only a few weeks of courtship.

"Let's go," Eden repeated, "Lucy will be waiting. I'm sure the train has already arrived."

"Oh, and how is Lucy?" asked Mrs. Radcliff. "Is she excited?"

"Thrilled as she can be," Ann replied. "Just think, Lucy will be a member of our little family. I do hope Isaac's furlough isn't cancelled at the last minute." Ann sniffed, searching for her handkerchief again. "I simply can't believe how grown up my stepson is—"

"Stepmother," Eden interrupted.

"Oh, fine, then." Ann sighed. "Let's go." She turned to Mrs. Radcliff. "Goodbye, dear. I'll see you at the Ladies' Society meeting tonight. I do hope you're bringing some of your divine strawberry rhubarb jam. We can have it delivered to the soldiers camped out on the hill tomorrow. Why, it's simply the best ever."

After the goodbye, Ann made a big fuss out of shoving the blue thread into her beaded bag. Finally, she straightened. "Would you mind telling me where the fire is? You have absolutely ruined my outing in town, so I hope you're proud of yourself."

"I need to get this to Miss Annette's before we meet Lucy and her cousin at the station. They're probably waiting for us." Eden headed down the walkway. "Did I really ruin your day? I'm so pleased."

"Oh! Your father would roll over in his grave if he heard the way you talk to me," Ann said, hurrying to keep up.

Eden shook her head, refusing to get into another argument with her today despite Ann's ramblings.

By the time they had walked the two blocks to Miss Annette's, Ann had thoroughly catalogued the miseries of living at Oak Hill.

"...and I woke up drenched in perspiration, *drenched*, because I dreamed twenty years had passed, and you were still living at Oak Hill, and all these wonderful men were lined up to ask my hand in marriage and, of course, I couldn't do a thing since I still had you to contend with. Are you listening to me?"

Eden stood, staring at the glistening jet black-and-gold pinstriped brougham at Miss Annette's walkway. A pair of the finest horses she had seen since the war started stood waiting; manes like smooth ebony silk, their coats brushed to a slick sheen. A liveried negro man stood with them.

"How beautiful." Eden sighed. She slowed in front of the shop and drank in the sight of the handsome animals, wishing she could stroke their velvety noses. Only a few swayback nags remained at Oak Hill. Her father's prized thoroughbreds were the first horses to go with the local militia when they enlisted in the Confederate Army at the beginning of the war.

Ann nudged Eden with her elbow and whispered. "Who do you suppose owns such a fine carriage?"

"Someone with money," Eden whispered back, "and influence to have kept them. Even Jefferson Davis doesn't have a carriage as fine."

Ann straightened like a shot and hurried into Miss Annette's.

The black man stood watching her appraisal of the animals. She flushed, embarrassed to be caught staring. "These horses are...well, they're quite lovely."

"Yes, ma'am, they surely are." He patted one on the neck affectionately and smiled back.

The door to Miss Annette's opened a crack. "Get in here!" Ann squealed, "You're not going to believe this."

"I'm coming," Eden muttered, turning toward the shop.

Following voices, she parted the curtains separating the small parlor from the fitting room. "Lucy!"

On a stool, her future sister-in-law stood smiling amid froths of white satin and tulle cascading to the floor, burying Miss Annette, who knelt glaring at the hem.

Eden grinned back and set the heavy roll of fabric on the end of the horsehair divan, opposite of Ann who occupied the other end.

"I thought you were at the train station," Eden said.

"I was, but I received a message there that my cousin, Rayce, arrived late last night—"

"Turn a bit to the left, dear, that's it," Miss Annette ordered.

"I ran into my aunt, and she told me you were coming here first. So, I thought I would wait for you," Lucy said, her hazel eyes sparkling. "Miss Annette simply forced me to put on my wedding dress so she could check one last time."

"Yes, a veritable knife to the throat," Miss Annette murmured. "But we're fortunate we had this chance. I just found a large gap on the hem. I'll have this finished in a jiffy."

"Lucy." Ann squirmed on the divan. "Lucy, for pity's sake, get on with it."

"Oh, yes." Lucy stepped gingerly from the stool and disappeared with Miss Annette behind the dressing screen. "Rayce sent his carriage for us."

"Her cousin Rayce," Ann whispered, leaning forward, her face drawn in feral excitement. "I can't wait to meet him. And you stay away from him."

Ann shook her finger, and Eden slapped it in a flash.

Ann swallowed a cry of pain and jerked her injured hand back just as Miss Annette emerged from behind the screen.

"Now, Miss Eden, we must get busy on your gown. Let me get the pattern book. I'll be right back."

The process took longer than anticipated. Ann insisted on a scandalously low neckline while Lucy expressed opposition to such a revealing dress. Miss Annette finally chimed in, explaining to Ann the significance of Eden's first large social event since coming out of mourning; appearance and decorum were especially important.

Having listened to the bantering for far too long, the seamstress presented her fourth and final pattern book and ordered the women to pick something out while there would still be time to make the dress.

While Ann pouted and flipped through an old issue of *Harper's Monthly*, Eden and Lucy agreed on the perfect gown. The twelve yards of pale jade silk would be fashioned into a wide, sweeping crinoline with gentle pleats radiating from the pointed waistline. Guided by the expertise of the stylish Miss Annette, they all agreed an elegant final touch to such a graceful dress would be required. The tasteful neckline and full sleeve bodice would exude style and grace, trimmed to perfection with shimmering gold and cream silk brocade.

"My heavens, I thought that would take all day." Ann tugged the shop door closed. "Finding something for your figure, Eden, does prove challenging."

Lucy glanced at Eden, encouraging her to disregard Ann's comment.

The negro driver, his face stoic and chin held high, ushered each woman into the carriage. Eden sank back against the plush crimson cushions, rubbing her hand across the smooth velvet. She closed her eyes while Ann and Lucy busied themselves discussing the evening's charity events at the hospital and Saint Paul's Church.

What a luxurious ride. Had it not been for the cobbled road on Broad Street, Eden would have fallen asleep. They certainly never had such a well-appointed carriage at Oak Hill.

When she closed her eyes and thought of her home, she could still smell the fire burning in the hearth, and the pungent, earthy aroma of freshly turned red dirt awaiting new crops. What she missed most was the cozy sense of security the small plantation offered, covering her like a warm, protective blanket. With the Union Army threatening closer to Richmond, she realized she had taken her comfortable, peaceful existence at Oak Hill, for granted.

"I still say the dress will look ridiculous considering—"

"Hush," Lucy cut Ann's words short, "She's going to be beautiful, and that's the end of it."

"Well, considering—"

"Ann," Lucy warned, "let's not discuss this again."

Ann pressed her lips together in a thin line and fidgeted with the tiny beads on her bag.

"Where is your cousin staying, Lucy?" Eden yawned. "What's his name, Roy?"

"It's Rayce, dear. Rayce Hampton." Lucy pulled a folded piece of paper from her pocket. "Joseph, his coachman, gave this to me at the station." She cleared her throat and read softly. "Dearest Lucy, forgive my failure to appear at the station this morning as planned, but unanticipated matters hurried me to Richmond late last evening. Perhaps you will forgive me if I leave the carriage at your disposal, and you will see your errant cousin when I am able to free myself from these affairs. My love to you and Aunt Martha, Rayce," she concluded.

"He sounds nice." Eden stifled another yawn.

"Joseph said we may use the carriage all day if we wish, but it has to be back at the Spotswood Hotel by six o'clock sharp." Lucy flashed a playful smile. "He said he has to take Rayce and yet another one of his lady friends to some grand charity ball at Laurel Grove."

Lucy moved in closer and looped her arm within Eden's. "Have I told you how warm and wonderful he is? It's been several years since I last saw him. I think it was at his granddaddy's funeral, if I remember correctly, but he still sends me letters and little gifts. I guess we feel close because we both love our Aunt Martha so much."

"And now you'll be part of our family, too." Eden squeezed Lucy's gloved hand.

"Maybe we can visit his home while you're here, honey."

Lucy's eyes widened. "It's down along the James River, and it's positively a mansion. I doubt he'll ever be there as busy as he is, but I know you'd just adore him." Lucy cupped her hand and whispered in Eden's ear, "He does have a scandalous side to him I'll—"

"CON-SID-ER-ING Eden has no bosom to speak of!" Ann blurted. "There, I said it."

"My *bosom*," Eden snarled, suddenly wide awake, "is none of your business!"

"I don't know why the two of you get so upset about it." Ann pushed her back against the seat and stuck her chin out. "You know it's the truth, Lucy."

"Hush," Lucy interrupted in a whisper, gesturing toward the front of the carriage. "All of Richmond does not need to hear about the state of Eden's bosom."

"Well, she had better look like she has one if she's going to catch a husband. I swear, Eden, you would stay unmarried just to spite me."

"I just might," Eden rejoined, "but that would entail living with you the rest of my life, and even marriage couldn't be worse than that!" She twisted in her seat, planning to signal the driver to stop and let her out.

Lucy seized Eden's hand. "Oh, Eden, please don't make a scene. Not with half of Richmond coming to my reception. It would upset Isaac."

Lucy turned to Ann. "You should be ashamed of yourself. Eden has a lovely bosom, and I won't hear another word about it."

At the mention of her brother's name, Eden settled down. Isaac's opinion mattered to her more than anyone else's in the entire world. She turned away from the two women and gazed out the carriage window. *My bosom, indeed!*

She thought of the stranger she had met earlier at Mr. Johnson's shop. He certainly seemed quite interested in her...charms. Nevertheless, he was an arrogant cad. What woman could ever know what truly occupied his mind? She recalled the amused look on his face as his deep brown eyes appraised her body. As much as she hated to admit it, he was incredibly handsome in a dark and mischievous sort of way. She wondered what it would have felt like had he kissed her and wrapped his strong arms around her in a passionate embrace.

She shifted uncomfortably in her seat, hoping the flush in her face did not reveal her ridiculous fantasy. "The arrogant skunk," she muttered.

"Did you say something, dear?" Lucy asked.

"Ah...no...I mean, yes — look!" Eden pointed outside, relieved at the chance to divert their attention.

They turned onto Franklin Street and came to a sudden standstill. Up ahead, a cavalry regiment in the midst of a drill filled the road in front of an excited crowd. Carriages, civilians, and swarms of soldiers blocked their way, and the sounds of "Dixie" and the "Bonnie Blue Flag" echoed through the street. A mass of women and children stood tall, waving colorful handkerchiefs and scarves at the cavalrymen. To their left, a group of men raised their hats, chanting "On to Washington!" and the crowd roared and rumbled in applause.

"What a lovely gathering," Lucy whispered, her eyes misting.

Eden nodded. She noticed the handsome cavalry leader,

General J. E. B. Stuart, at the head of his men, looking particularly striking in his high boots. His attractive smile and dark reddish-brown beard gleamed under his famous wide-brimmed hat.

She bolted up to get a better look at the general who had been a long-standing family friend. Years had passed since she last laid eyes on him, but he was certainly not an easy man to forget. Rugged and dashingly handsome, women were drawn to him like bees to honey. If she remembered correctly, he was also an incredible flirt...

Ann and Lucy flinched at Eden's sudden movement.

"Oh, Jeb ...General Stuart! Yoooo hooooo!" Eden called.

Shocked at her sudden overzealous appeal for the general's attention, Ann and Lucy gasped and stared wide-eyed at each other.

Eden managed to catch his eye. General Stuart looked toward her for a brief moment, and then a smile of recognition lit his face. He pulled the reins of his mount and trotted over to the side of the carriage.

His blue eyes sparkled. "My very dear Miss Blair, what an unexpected pleasure to see you here, and looking as beautiful as ever."

After a lacy flutter of her lashes and a teasing bite upon her bottom lip, she summoned up a demure performance worthy of the finest Southern belle. "Oh, how you do run on, General. I must say, when I saw you looking so dashingly handsome riding through town with your men, I just knew I had to stop and say hello. It simply has been too long."

He nodded, his gaze wandering over her, clearly taking appreciative notice of her Southern charms.

Eden blotted her neck with a handkerchief and smiled. "Isaac wrote me you would try to come to the reception. I know with the war and all, it's hard to make any plans these days, but it just wouldn't be a party without you. Please say you'll come."

He lifted an eyebrow and smiled. "Although your charming company is enough to save any man from the miseries of war, Miss Eden, I'm afraid I'm unable to give a definitive answer at this time. There's much going on now, as I'm sure you've heard."

A young girl appeared from the crowd and timidly held out a crisp daffodil. "Mr. General, sir. I mean, Mr. General Stuart, I would be honored if you would accept this flower for your hat."

"Thank you, young miss. I surely appreciate your thoughtfulness and patriotism. Call me Jeb." He flashed a generous smile.

"Why, thank you, Mr. Jeb!" The child blushed and skipped away.

"General Stuart!" a cheerful officer called out.

"Oh, General," Eden chimed in, "I can see you're a terribly busy man. We won't keep you any longer. Please give Mrs. Stuart our kindest regards from the Blair family."

"I certainly will, Miss Eden." His gaze shifted between his troops and her. "I wish I had more time—"

Ann rose from her seat and stuck her head out of Eden's window, almost knocking her over. "Hello, General — remember me?"

"Oh...yes, ma'am, I believe I do." He nodded. "Well, safe passage, ladies. I must get back to my men." He bent down, peered into the carriage, and tipped the brim of his hat. "Miss Lucy, best wishes to you and Isaac. It's indeed been a pleasure seeing you all again." With a kick to his mount, he trotted off to rejoin his troops.

Lucy giggled. "Why, Miss Eden, did I see General Stuart stare in the direction of your bosoms?"

"Why, Miss Lucy," Eden smiled, "we all know I have no bosom to speak of."

The two laughed and settled back in their seats.

"Oh, laugh if you will." Ann pouted. "I wash my hands of both of you. Unlike you, Eden, I'll have no trouble attracting male attention at the reception."

"Well, that's obvious, considering the display I was forced to witness at Mr. Johnson's shop."

"You two stop, for pity's sake," Lucy pleaded, squirming to see if the street had finally cleared.

"What? He was a very nice man," Ann defended. "He was quite enamored and extremely cultured. He even complimented me in French."

"French!" Eden sneered. "Why, you wouldn't know French if a waiter read it to you from a wine label."

"I most certainly would know French if I heard it. I'll have you know, the husband of my mother's cousin spoke fluent French."

"Then tell me, what did he say?" Eden prodded.

"He said," Ann paused, then continued triumphantly, "he said I was *obtuse*."

"Oh, my goodness...are we there yet?" Lucy muttered.

Eden sat mute as a church mouse for fear she would burst into uncontrollable laughter.

Chapter 3

"They're getting closer. Can you imagine – Yankees taking Richmond? I can't bear the thought." Lucy bit down on her bottom lip.

"You know as well as I do, our soldiers won't go down without a fight." Still, with the news that the Yankees now occupied Fort Monroe, only seventy miles away, she couldn't help but wonder the same.

Lucy's eyes welled with tears. "Oh, Isaac…"

Joseph pulled the horses to a stop in front of Aunt Martha's large, two-story brick house and stepped down. Eden leaned forward and stretched.

"Miss Lucy." Joseph opened the carriage door and held out his gloved hand to escort her to the walkway.

He turned to help Eden, and his eyes widened at the sight of Ann crammed to the opposite side of the carriage, her hands firmly planted on both sides of her skirts. "Ma'am?"

Ann shook her head, not budging an inch.

Lucy peered into the carriage. "Land sakes, Ann. What are you doing, honey?"

"Ah, well…um…you two run along inside, now." She fidgeted with her handbag, refusing to look at them. "I see no sense in wasting this fine carriage. It doesn't need to be back until later, anyway."

Lucy sighed. "But, Ann—"

"Oh, for pity's sake." Ann stuck her chin out. "You two stop lookin' at me like that!"

Eden whispered in Lucy's ear, "Let her go. We'll have more fun without her, anyway."

A gentle smile tipped the corner of Lucy's full lips. "Well, I'm sure Ann could use the carriage for her errands."

"Ah — yes," Ann said. "That's it…I have errands."

Joseph's gaze darted between Eden and Lucy.

"Take Mrs. Blair wherever she desires to go today, Joseph," Lucy commanded.

"Yes'm." He managed a graceful bow.

Eden walked arm-in-arm with Lucy up the walkway. "You're a clever girl."

"Whatever do you mean?" Lucy asked with a coy smile.

"You do realize she plans on paying unannounced calls to everyone she knows to flaunt that carriage?"

"Yes, but she won't be bothering us." Lucy opened the door and called, "Aunty? I'm here."

Aunt Martha's servant, Eliza, scurried from the back of the house. "Lawdy, lawd, Miss Lucy. It sure is nice to see your smiling face again." She reached for Lucy's satchel, "Let me get this upstairs for you."

Lucy handed the leather bag to Eliza. "I'm guessing Aunty's out and about today?"

Eliza lifted a raven brow. "Oh, yes. She's been down at the

hospital again. You know her. Always helping those boys out best she can." The elderly negro ambled up the steps and called, "Why don't you girls go on out on the porch. It's warm and sunny out there. I'll bring you some molasses cakes soon as I finish up."

The two women headed outside to the covered veranda. Eden sat on the porch swing, and Lucy occupied the rocker next to her. After months of miserable weather, it was nice the delayed spring had finally burst forth.

Eden inhaled the lovely fragrances of a trailing honeysuckle vine embracing the scrolled iron awning, mingling peacefully with the large clay pots of jonquils, violets, and narcissuses scenting the balmy April air.

Eliza emerged from the house with plates of freshly baked molasses cakes and tall glasses filled with herbal tea and a large shopping bag dangling from her arm. A soft, sensibility radiated within the older woman's dark eyes. "I'm off to market. Now, you two mind yourselves. There's more of them cakes if you real hungry, but remember, you need to fit in them pretty dresses soon enough."

"Thank you for the reminder, Eliza." Lucy took another bite and set her plate on the thick iron railing.

Eliza marched down the steps. "Miss Martha'll be back soon, I reckon, so don't you two get in any mischief. Oh, and if you need anything..." She cocked her head toward the front door. "...just ask Sarah, or...ah — Fifi, or whatever her name is now. Lawd have mercy."

"We surely will," Lucy called back.

Lucy sighed and rubbed at her waistline. "I don't know about you, Eden, but I think I'm going to have to squeeze the living breath out of my lungs to get back into my stays after these sinful cakes." She sniffed at a wild honeysuckle flower trailing up the porch column next to her. "Look around us. I hope the weather is this nice on my wedding day."

"Even if it rains, you're going to be marrying one of the finest men ever. He loves you so much, Lucy, and I'm happy to gain a sister."

She really did like Lucy. With her own family so small, she had grown eager to welcome Lucy as a sister. A nice, even-flowing chemistry existed between the two of them, and a quiet confidence embraced their friendship. Of course, the fact that she would soon replace Ann as mistress at Oak Hill gave her the most pleasure. No wonder Ann treated Lucy as sweet as apple-pie; she knew all too well, one wrong move and she could be turned out on her pointy, *obtuse* nose.

Lucy dabbed her lips with her napkin. "You know, I need to say something."

Eden furrowed her brow at the sober tone in Lucy's voice. "Isaac told me what a wonderful job you've done at Oak Hill since your daddy's death. He is...well, I mean, we are so proud of you — and grateful, too."

"You're being too kind. I'm just—"

"No, it's the truth." Lucy fiddled with her fingernails and her eyes grew moist. "I have a confession to make. I've always wanted to be more like you. Lord above, Eden, I know absolutely nothing about running a family business or becoming a mistress of a plantation. I mean, here you are, already an accomplished nurse and midwife, and after your daddy died, it turned out you had a head for business, too. And me...well, I'm just a plain girl. I'm afraid of being a disappointment."

Her heart went out to Lucy. Although quiet and rather timid, Lucy truly was one of the kindest people she had ever known, but she lacked confidence in herself and her abilities.

"Nonsense. You're a wonderful governess, and children absolutely adore you. Don't be silly, honey. You could never be a disappointment. Not ever—"

"Joseph!" A screeching voice echoed from around the corner.

Both women swung their heads just in time to catch a glimpse of Ann hanging her head out the carriage window, yelling at poor Joseph as they passed by the intersection, her dark hair spilling from her twisted chignon.

"Sakes alive!" Lucy placed a hand to her mouth. "That's Ann."

"No matter where I go, the woman insists on embarrassing me to death." Eden snatched her plate and glass and headed inside the house, with Lucy following close behind.

Eden barely noticed the hours tick by as she sat with Lucy in the well-appointed parlor. The door opened, and in walked Eliza.

"Mm Mmm. Got some oysters and rockfish for supper for you girls. I just saw your aunt coming up the street, Miss Lucy. Let me get this bag to the kitchen. I'll be back in a jiffy."

Lucy rose from the divan and parted the lace curtains at the front window. "I can't wait to see her." She craned her long neck. "Here she comes."

The elderly woman entered the door with a bright smile. "Hello, Lucy." She extended her chubby arms as she approached her niece. "Come give me a big ol' hug. I've missed you."

"I've missed you, too." Lucy slid into her aunt's embrace.

She pushed Lucy forward at arm's length, gripping both her hands, and smiled. "I'll bet my boots you two have enjoyed yourselves while I was out. Ann's not here?"

Eden shifted her feet and sighed, blowing a loose strand of hair clear over the top of her head.

Eliza entered the room. Aunt Martha sat on the divan and gestured to the servant for her afternoon tea. Her gaze snapped toward Lucy and Eden, who sat opposite her. "Oh, before I forget. I saw Rayce a bit ago. Eden, I'm so anxious for you to meet him. I think you'll find him special."

Likely, a special bore.

"I've been trying to tell her that, Aunty," Lucy chimed in. "Where did you see him? He said he wouldn't be free this afternoon."

"Actually, he did look busy. I was walking with my friend, Fanny, near Capitol Square this afternoon, and I spotted this handsome fellow, and I said, 'Fanny, I think that's my nephew, Rayce Hampton, talking with the governor.' Then, I called his name, and he looked over at us and smiled. Well, Fanny saw him and got the vapors. Heaven help her, she all but fainted right there."

"The vapors?" Lucy giggled, "Well, my, oh my."

Aunt Martha sighed, and her full cheeks took on a rosy hue. "Ah...the effect that man has on women."

"Is Fanny all right?" Eden quizzed, taking note Lucy's cousin now had "handsome" to add to his growing list of fine attributes.

Lucy's aunt gestured dismissively, "Oh, yes, Fanny's really a tough old thing. Luckily, I had a little something with me."

She lifted her thick collage of taffeta skirts and pulled out a small flask, strapped to her meaty calf. "I just sat her down on a bench and poured a little from this baby down her throat. Soon, she was singin' like a magpie." She shook the silver flask. "I guess it's a good thing I'd been at the hospital today, or I wouldn't have had it with me."

Eden choked back a giggle. Lucy's aunt was a character. There she sat, waving her flask as proudly as if it were the Confederate flag, her gray hair piled high on her head and her big blue eyes gleaming with joy.

During her stay the past week, it had become obvious everyone knew Aunty swiggled at her flask on a regular basis. Her secret sips and minor topples into the furniture every so often were considered only small indiscretions by all who loved her, for the generous woman had a heart of gold.

"You never know when one of those poor wounded soldiers of ours is going to ask for some spirits, and I want to be there for him." She slid the flask back into her garter with a snap, just as Eliza entered with the sterling tea server.

"You're so thoughtful, Aunty." Lucy yawned and patted her aunt's forearm. "If you ladies will excuse me, I'd like to go lie down a spell — mind?"

"Don't be silly, dear, of course we don't mind. Do we Eden?...Eden?"

This cousin of Lucy's — rich and handsome. Just who is this man? Her thoughts trailed back to the attractive rascal she had met earlier at Mr. Johnson's. *What a cad.* Perhaps she would have the chance to stroll with this good-looking cousin of Lucy's in front of his arrogant face. Oh, how that would please her!

RAYCE tossed down the copy of the *Richmond Daily Dispatch* he had grabbed on the way back to the hotel room. He removed his coat and walked to the window. The general was late, which always gave him cause for concern.

He pushed the thick drapes aside and saw a group of women dressed in black heading toward the church. The sight brought back the memory of the fiery blonde he had wanted to ravish earlier at Hiram's shop. If more pressing issues had not been at hand, perhaps he just might have done so.

There was something unique and fascinating about Eden Blair, making him want her more than the others — and want her, he most certainly did. The entire time he had met with the governor, his mind kept wandering back to the depths of her emerald eyes, the curve of her full lips, and...

"Dammit!" He snapped the drapes closed with a firm flick of his wrists. The last thing he needed right now was a woman on his mind. *Just enjoy 'em and get the hell out of there,* he reminded himself.

He paced the room, determined to keep focused on more important matters. He sat and picked up the newspaper.

"*McClellan Advances! Richmond Must Be Saved!*" With the advancement of McClellan's massive forces, there was no doubt the Confederate capital was in peril. President Davis and his advisors had been meeting behind closed doors the entire day. Barring any unanticipated delay, the general would soon bring him word of his involvement in the plans.

Heavy footsteps hurried through the corridor, pausing at his door, followed by a quiet knock. He got up, tossed the paper aside, and opened the door.

"Sorry to have kept you waiting, Rayce." The general

removed his hat and entered the room.

Rayce shook his hand. "You're becoming quite the gallant Southern hero these days. I trust you kept the ladies captivated with the cavalry drill?"

General J. E. B. Stuart tossed his hat on the walnut end table and sat on the upholstered chair, his spurs spinning as he crossed his heavy cavalry boots at the ankles.

"Well, my friend, we all must do our part. I'm sure you understand that." The general fingered through a fruit bowl next to him and picked up a peach. "Where did you find a peach this time of year? Never mind." He snickered. "Don't answer that." He held up the peach and inspected it as though he were staring down the barrel of a gun. "Good looking piece of fruit, mind?"

Rayce raked his hands through is hair and sat on the settee across from the general. "Help yourself."

Judging by the suspicious look in Jeb's eyes as he took a healthy bite of the fruit, Rayce suspected his own pensive disposition had not gone unnoticed. The situation would appeal to Jeb's romantic nature, but now was certainly not the time to be discussing such matters.

"Did you make the pickup at Hiram's?"

Rayce nodded. "I did."

"Does the contact think Pinkerton is suspicious?"

"No. In fact, everything appears to be going according to plan."

"Good. I heard Pinkerton's men never suspected who you were, and they left Richmond this afternoon empty handed. I was hoping you had the same impression."

"What about McClellan?" Rayce grabbed the newspaper

and dropped it on the table in front of them. "Time seems to be of the essence more than ever. I know Johnston is rushing reinforcements from the Rappahannock, but if they don't arrive soon, the few men Magruder has holding Yorktown won't be enough. Lord help us all if McClellan finds out how vulnerable we really are."

"Ah." The general smiled and set the half-eaten peach on a cloth napkin. "Thankfully, Magruder has a flair for theatrics. He's been doing a fine job deceiving the Yanks, but you're right, we're running out of time."

"What is it you want me to do?"

General Stuart leaned forward. "We need you, Major, more than ever, and that's what we need to discuss."

Rayce nodded. "Go on, I'm listening."

"General McClellan knows you're out there. He also knows where your loyalties lie, and I'm sure he remembers all too well your abilities in these matters. After all, you saved his hide in Mexico a time or two, if I remember correctly."

Rayce smiled. "True, but what's your point?"

"You know the area better than any man I have. Lee and I, along with President Davis, have come up with a plan. Let me just begin by saying, the Ghost shall ride again."

ELIZA took Eden and Lucy to Chimborazo Hospital in Aunt Martha's buggy. The local hospitals had grown overcrowded these days, and there were never enough hands to help. Having worked by her father's side as a nurse, Eden's presence was especially welcome by the overworked staff. While Lucy spent the hours penning letters home for the wounded soldiers, she changed bandages, cleaned wounds, and assisted the fatigued surgeons.

Exhausted after the full day, she pulled the pins from her hair and slid between the smooth sheets of the four-poster bed, tucking the goose-down quilt under her chin. While her body felt worn and tired, her mind raced in all directions.

She rolled to her side and hugged a soft pillow. A gentle night wind stirred, drifting through her cracked window, carrying the earthy scent of the nearby James River. She watched as the thin lace curtains billowed lazily with each small gust...

She stood near the banks of the river, dressed in her new satin gown. Her hair hung loose, cascading down her back, blowing in the temperate evening wind.

Patrick slipped in behind her, wrapped his strong arms around her waist, and pulled her tightly against his chest. She tried to remember the last time she felt so warm and safe.

She listened to the small boats gliding across the river, their paddles treading rhythmically through the water. He nudged her around and bent down to kiss her. She closed her eyes, arching into his embrace, welcoming his mouth upon her own.

The kiss felt different; deeply passionate, demanding, arousing. He parted her lips with the tip of his tongue, searching their depths, invoking a fire in her never experienced before. Was it she who softly moaned as he pulled away and trailed his lips down the slender column of her throat?

The feel of his coarse mustache grazing the skin of her bare neck ignited a flame, like the scratch of a match, deep within her core.

He spoke in a hoarse whisper, warming her earlobe, "Eden, my sweet."

His invigorating, masculine scent filled her senses. She kissed him; savoring the taste of fine brandy on his lips and tongue. Her breath hitched, catching deep in her throat, as he kissed her passionately in return, his large hands roaming intimately over her bodice.

Slowly, she pulled away, resting her head on his broad chest, while the spicy aroma of cigars stirred against his crisp shirt.

Brandy...cigars?

"Patrick?" she whispered, pulling away to look in his eyes. A thick cloud veiled the moonlight, masking the lines on his face. "Patrick?"

A rush of wind blew the cloud away in a single warm gust, and there he stood, smiling, his dark eyes boring down upon her. A chill traveled down the column of her back as he trailed a finger from the hollow of her neck to the tip of her bodice.

"Remember me, Sweetness. Remember me."

She watched in silence as he slowly turned and walked away, enveloped by the light of the crescent moon.

"Damn him!" Eden bolted up, flushed, and drenched in moisture. She folded her arms across her chest and sighed heavily.

With restful sleep clearly eluding her and the disturbing dream invading her waking thoughts, she tossed back the blanket, lit the bedside candle, and shimmied out of bed. Clad in only a thin chemise and carrying the flickering candle, she paced the length of the room.

The dream troubled her on many levels. Obviously, she must still feel something for the less than honorable Patrick, but the man who penetrated her dream was none other than the lout she had met at Mr. Johnson's store.

She walked to the window, pushing the lace curtains aside, and set the candle on the windowsill. She stood tall, absorbing the moonlit darkness, while the light wind cooled her flushed skin. She pulled her hair back to cool her neck and listened to the steady sound of an approaching train churning in the distance. The occasional clomping of iron-hoofed horses echoed as they passed down the nearly deserted streets. Suddenly, her eyes caught sight of a small amber glow radiating from across the street...

Rayce leaned against the lamppost, his gaze narrowing, following her every move. He slowly rolled the lit cigar between his fingers.

She moved toward the window and set the candle on the sill. A sliver of moonlight slanted through the glass, highlighting her sensually tossed hair.

He inhaled the thin cheroot, allowing the spicy smoke to linger against his tongue before exhaling.

He watched as she swept her hair away from her neck with an unhurried hand and pulled it back in a long golden rope. Slowly, she leaned in toward the window and fanned her face.

"Now, what have we here?" he muttered, reaching into his coat pocket. He pulled out his flask and unscrewed the cap, his gaze fixed upon her image above. She leaned in further, and the candlelight illuminated her breasts barely concealed under the revealing white nightdress.

"Damn." He took a healthy swig of the amber liquid. Then another.

When she first looked into his eyes at the shop, her emerald gaze had hit him like a solid physical blow; his gut curling into a tight knot, knocking the breath from his lungs. The conversation with her lively stepmother moments later only aggravated the discomfort. But when he neared the small storage room, the sweet scent of fragrant magnolia invaded his senses, drawing him in like a wayward ship into homeport. And when he stood in the small room studying her, taking in the delicate features of her face and listened to the tenor of her engaging voice, it was as though a haunting tune from long ago had been summoned from somewhere deep within his mind.

Tonight felt no different.

Perhaps he had been too harsh with her when she had haughtily accused him of being a coward; as though he had no regard for the soldiers, the war, or its outcome. Somehow, she had managed to hurl him off balance and compromise his ability to keep cool in the heat of the moment. When he firmly grabbed her chin in the flash of anger and forced her full lips to within a breath of his own, God, how he had wanted to take her in his arms and kiss her, regardless of her tempered, accusatory charge.

Christ almighty. This is dangerous territory. This woman has a way of getting inside of him.

He sighed and stared at the window. The imported cheroot tasted fine; the expensive brandy, even better. As for the unexpected candlelit show appearing in the window above...Damn — was there anything better?

He inhaled the cheroot and exhaled heavily. *Wait.* He frowned. *But what the hell is she doing dressed so provocatively...and for anyone outside to see?*

A sudden blaze of heat gripped his torso at the sight of her shapely bottom and breasts silhouetted against the flickering candlelight. His heart missed a beat, and a surge of energy streamed through his limbs. Every muscle in his body tightened until it hurt.

He took a swig of the brandy, his gaze focused on the seductress above. He slowly ran his finger along the rim of the flask, replaced the cap, and stuffed the sterling container into his coat pocket.

In a world torn apart by war and destruction, nothing could be certain. Yet, as he gazed upon the woman standing at the window above, he knew with unwavering certainty, it would only be a matter of time before he claimed the lovely Miss Eden Blair.

Eden snuffed the candle in a single panicked breath. "It's him!" She twisted away from the window and slipped below the windowsill.

Slowly, she peered up, her eyes just above the window ledge. There he stood, his tall, muscular form leaning casually against the lamppost; the burning glow of his cigar bathing his bronzed face in a soft amber hue. She watched as he extinguished the cigar and folded his arms across his chest, a smile etched upon his face.

"What is he doing here?" she whispered in a strangled voice. She flushed, realizing he must have been standing there, staring up at her half-naked body, the entire time she tried to unravel her perplexing dream. "I know...I'm still dreaming!"

She rubbed her eyes until stars danced before them and looked again. Clad in a dark overcoat, his wavy hair blew freely as he stood below, still staring up at her window.

She slithered down the wall beneath the window, her teeth clenched in anger. "Why, that rotten, no good, arrogant cad. He's been following me!"

She shot to her feet, tossed the curtains wide, and threw open the cracked window full-force. "How dare you!" she yelled, her words echoing across the dark, barren night. "I've had enough—"

She turned her head side to side; her words stopped short. Like a ghost in the night, he had disappeared without a trace.

Chapter 4

Eden gnawed on her bottom lip as she and Lucy stood huddled together under a small parasol awaiting the arrival of the next train. Large raindrops pelted the thin fabric of the umbrella, and a chilly breeze whirled like ribbons of ice up her pantalets, making her knees quiver. News from battlefields had been pouring into Richmond all morning with harrowing tales of battles won and lost. Disturbing images filled her mind of Isaac and Jimmy — even Patrick, lying wounded or dead on a bloodied battlefield, miles from home.

"I hear a train. Please, Isaac, be on there," she whispered, between chattering teeth.

"He'll be there. I know he will — I can feel it." Lucy pulled a cotton handkerchief from her pocket and scrunched it so tight her fists turned white.

The constant pressure of worrying about Isaac's safety had made Lucy look pale and fragile. Hoping to ease her mind, Eden changed the subject. "Tell me more about this cousin of yours. You seem quite fond of him."

Lucy placed the handkerchief in her pocket and smiled.

"That's right. I can't believe you haven't met him yet. Why, most everyone has run into him except you and Ann." She shrugged. "I think you'll finally get the chance to meet the one and only Major Rayce Hampton, tomorrow."

Eden cocked her head. "He's a major?"

"Good heavens — yes!" Lucy sighed. "Silly me. I guess my mind's as thick as custard these days. Aunty didn't mention it, either?"

Eden opened her mouth to respond, but without delay, Lucy continued enumerating her cousin's glories.

"Why, Aunty just rambles on and on about him to anyone who'll listen. She once had her quilting bee on pins and needles describing his escapades as a young man during the war with Mexico. Oh, yes, and then there were those years in Texas in the wilds of the West, and with all those Indians..."

Indians. This is the man she'd assumed would be an annoying bore?

"...Then there was that little incident with Preacher Leroy's daughter. He almost had to marry the poor girl, but of course, we all knew he didn't do it."

Eden smiled. It was good to see Lucy's eyes sparkle under her chestnut hair and the rosy color rush to her cheeks.

"And if all that wasn't enough, he spent the last few years before the war down south in Charleston and New Orleans. Aunty told me he managed to capture the charms of many a Southern belle only to break their poor lil' hearts soon thereafter."

"I think I hear a train," a young private said to another, as they walked toward the depot.

Lucy glanced down the tracks before leaning closer.

"Personally, I think Rayce would make a wonderful husband if he found the right woman, even if he doesn't know it yet. Anyway, where was I? Oh, yes...he finally came back to Virginia when he inherited his grandfather's estate, Hampton Manor. You'd think a man who has experienced so much would be older than his thirty-four years."

"Yes...yes, you would think so," Eden murmured, after taking in everything Lucy had said.

Lucy clutched Eden's arm. "I'm such a ninny. I'm sorry to ramble on like I do. I just find him fascinating and charming, and every time I—"

Eden turned when the loud train whistle blew. The wood-burning locomotive moved slowly toward the depot, belching dark clouds of thick, resinous smoke high in the moist air. The engine groaned and panted, the brakes grinding in exaggerated shrieks along the rails. Finally, the clank and clatter of the link pins silenced, and like honey bees leaving their hive, swarms of people emerged from the mud-spattered cars.

The two women watched and waited. Finally, after the last person exited the train, the mountain of metal and dense smoke prepared to move on.

"I hope he's all right." Eden spoke to allay her own fears, twisting her stomach into knots. "That brother of mine has always made me fret with worry."

Lucy forced back tears. "I guess it was too much to hope for with the war going on. I don't know what to do, Eden. I can't get word to family and friends in time to stop the wedding and reception."

"Let's go. Don't worry, honey." Eden rubbed the small of Lucy's back, trying to mask her own disappointment. "Let's

44

return to the house and wait. Perhaps he sent word to Aunt Marth—"

"Oh, sweet heavens!" Lucy wailed.

At the sound of Lucy's shriek, Eden's heart skipped a beat, stopping her dead in her tracks. She spun around. There stood Isaac, trying to manage the last step of the train with his bag under one arm and her little dog, Beauregard, tucked under the other. True to his unpredictable nature, Isaac had stopped at Oak Hill before coming to Richmond. "Oh my!" she gasped.

Upon spotting Eden, Beauregard squirmed excitedly.

"Whoa, little Beau." Isaac stepped off the train and smiled. "Hello, ladies."

Lucy threw up her hands and ran toward him.

Eden took a step forward and stopped. She wanted to run to her brother, wrap her welcoming arms around him, and kiss his cheeks. But with Lucy visibly upset only moments earlier, she allowed them their privacy.

"Oh, Isaac, my darling." Lucy smothered his face with kisses. "I began to think something terrible had happened. The news coming into the city today has been dreadful. I was so worried."

Isaac handed Beau to Lucy and draped his long arm across her shoulders, drawing her to his chest. "Surely, dear, you didn't think I'd miss my own wedding."

Lucy puckered her nose and poked his shoulder. "Oh, don't tease me, Captain Blair. I was worried and with good reason. Surely, you haven't forgotten a war is going on."

He arched his eyebrows high. "And whose idea was it to plan a wedding during a war, might I ask?"

"Oh, stop." Lucy laughed. "You know it was you."

Isaac drew Lucy into an intimate kiss. An instant flush of embarrassment rushed to Eden's cheeks. She coughed and smoothed the folds of her dress, wishing she could hide.

Isaac craned his neck. "Eden, what are you waiting on, gal? Get on over here and give your big brother a hug. I brought you a little something from home."

Lucy grinned and waved the small white dog in her direction.

Unexpectedly, the reality of it all hit her. The brother she adored had arrived safely from the fighting in the Shenandoah Valley. In all the months Isaac had been gone, it had never dawned on her just how much she really missed him. He looked gallant in his uniform with his new sandy blonde whiskers, but noticeably thinner, too. While his blue eyes still sparkled with the playfulness Isaac was so well known for, there was a new look — a look she couldn't quite explain — etched deep within the small lines of his face.

Tears pooled in her eyes, and she swallowed the lump forming in her throat. Brimming with emotion, she ran to her brother and buried her head against his chest.

"Come now, Sis," he whispered, resting his chin on top of her bonnet. "I've never known you to cry for no reason. I'm in one piece, honey."

Eden wasn't sure why she stood there blubbering. She had been an emotional ninny ever since she spotted the obscene cad spying on her in the bedroom window. She looked into Isaac's face.

Really looked at him.

There were no visible wounds or scars; it was obvious he was safe. Without warning, her words and tears came spilling out. "Oh, Isaac…Isaac, I've just missed you so much, and I thought I might never see you again. And—"

"There you are."

Eden's hands turned to clenched fists the moment she heard that familiar shrilled voice. All eyes turned toward Ann, scurrying out of Aunt Martha's buggy.

"My dear Isaac." Ann reached up to tidy her chignon with freshly manicured fingertips. "I just knew I'd be late, but Eleanor Radcliff had me rolling bandages at that smelly hospital earlier."

"Why Ann…" Isaac raised a single eyebrow and smiled. "I mean, Stepmother, how wonderful to see you, too." He released Eden and placed an obligatory peck on Ann's cheek.

Ann snapped her fan open with a flick of her wrist and stuck her bottom lip out. "Oh, don't be mean, Isaac. You know how much I hate it when you call me that. No one needs to remind me you're older than I am. Surely, you appreciate the delicate position I've been put in with your father's unfortunate death."

Eden heaved a dramatic sigh. Yes, Ann was indeed younger than Isaac, and only three paltry years older than she was, but she had never been placed in any sort of delicate position. Isaac was in charge of Oak Hill, and with him away at war, the job thankfully fell to her — not Ann.

The spring rain had stopped, and a sliver of sun now poked through the gray clouds. Eden snapped the parasol shut, scooped Beau from Lucy's arms, and turned away from the others.

"Why, you look like an ol' white rat, Beau. What have you been messing in to look so scruffy? I'll most certainly need to give you a good bath when we get back to the house."

Beau replied with a yawn and snuggled against her body.

Ann chattered like a wild chipmunk while Isaac and Lucy stood listening, each displaying the patience of Job.

As Eden stood on the walkway with little Beau in her arms, she thought about Patrick. What would her life be like now had they married; had he stayed loyal to her and to Virginia? Would she be meeting him at a train depot, greeting him with loving kisses? Would she be living at the large McDowell plantation, perhaps with a baby? Or, would he have been one of the early casualties of war and she a young widow?

She had lost count of all the hours spent lying in bed crying, wondering what had gone wrong. He had never let on — not even once — he would side with the North when everyone talked of the stirring possibility of Virginia seceding from the Union. Time and time again, he had professed his undying love to her. So, why did he leave her humiliated and with a shattered heart?

She thought back to the time she had almost lost her virginity to him one warm summer evening along the riverbank. Despite her objection, Patrick had been more persistent than usual that night. Luckily, she had kept a cool head, even when her first stirrings of adolescent ardor had been exciting.

But the past was a world away now. Her life, as she had once known it, had changed in every conceivable direction.

With her composure reclaimed, she turned to join the others.

EDEN sat on the divan in Aunt Martha's parlor and looked at the joyful faces of her family. The eve of the wedding and reception was upon them, and everyone joined together to sip cider and reminisce about old times.

Eliza entered carrying a large sterling tray with more warm cider, molasses cakes, and homemade peanut brittle. "I've been busy as a bee in the kitchen. Made peanut brittle just for you, Captain Blair."

"Isaac, my boy, will your friend Jimmy be coming?" Aunt Martha asked between cooling blows to her cider.

Isaac's shoulders wilted, and the lines around his eyes grew deeper, but a small smile strained the corners of his mouth. "The men are having a rough time in the valley, and most furloughs have been cancelled. I'm blessed I got away myself, I assure you. Lucky for me, General Jackson owed me a favor. It'd be wonderful if he could come, but it's not likely."

With the mention of Jimmy McDowell, the name of his now infamous younger brother, Patrick, often came up in the conversation. Eden shifted uncomfortably in the chair, hoping no one would notice. Thankfully, not a soul in Richmond had been ill-bred enough to bring up the subject of his dishonorable behavior to her and the Confederacy.

Ann turned and glared in her direction.

Don't you dare.

Eden's heart stopped dead. Silently, she prayed the woman would not be so callous to bring Patrick up now. With an equally challenging gaze, she glared back at Ann. Luckily, Aunt Martha piped up, unwittingly breaking up the silent confrontation.

Aunt Martha's eyes brightened. "Oh, that's right; I heard

you boys are together. It surely must be of some comfort having your best friend fighting alongside you."

Isaac sighed and set his cider on the table before glancing at everyone. "You know, I was thinking about ol' Jimmy today. Seems like only yesterday we were both knee-high to a grasshopper and learning to ride and shoot like all the other country boys. People thought we were brothers because we looked so much alike." He paused and his jaw tightened. "I liked pretending we were brothers when we were young bucks, but I'll tell you this, we never knew someday we'd be fighting such a damn bloody war!"

He shot up and walked to the window. Darkness slowly crept into his eyes, and the pulsing muscles tightened in his jaw. He suddenly looked a decade older, and it frightened her.

Lucy hurried to the window next to him. "Dear, perhaps Jimmy will make it here...I mean, you know him, he likes a good surprise."

Isaac stared out the window without replying.

With Isaac's back to the others, Ann leaned in and whispered, "What's the matter with him? He sure isn't acting like a man getting hitched tomorrow, if I do say so myself."

"Oh, hush up!" Eden whispered between pursed lips. "I'll talk to him in private. You just keep your nose out of it."

Ann's face twisted. "Why, your father would roll—"

"I know...I know...would roll over in his grave — now, hush." She got up to join Lucy and Isaac.

Ann reached for her lace handkerchief and turned to Lucy's aunt. "My goodness..." she sniffed.

Aunt Martha replied with an innocent shrug and crammed another wedge of cake into her mouth.

Eden placed her hand on Isaac's shoulder. "Let's go for a stroll. It's been so long since I've seen my big brother, and Lucy will have you all to herself tomorrow." She winked at Lucy. "Mind if I borrow him for just a bit?"

"Of course I don't mind. You two catch up all you want. I have a few things to tend to anyway, don't I, Aunty...Aunty?"

Having just crammed another piece of molasses cake in her mouth, Aunt Martha sat frozen, her wide eyes darting from person to person. "Uh hmm."

Eden looked heavenward at the flickering stars as she and her brother walked silently, arm-in-arm, toward Capitol Square. His quiet demeanor for most of the day troubled her.

"I hope you know I do so approve of Lucy as your wife and the mistress of Oak Hill. She's a dream."

"She's a jewel; you're right. I'm a lucky man." He gestured toward a nearby bench.

"She adores you, Isaac. When the two of you met at the cadet dance, I think she knew right away you were the only man for her."

"Ah, the cadet dance," he mused. He combed his fingers through his hair and took a seat next to her on the bench.

"Even when she came to stay with us at Oak Hill before the war, we all fell in love with her right away. Even Mama Claire said she was an angel, remember?"

"Ah...yes, of course I do." He coughed.

"Even Ann is fond of her, and that's really saying something considering she doesn't think about anyone except herself."

Isaac rubbed the whiskers on his chin. "Ann. Lord, if she doesn't make my blood boil sometimes."

Eden bit down on her bottom lip and smiled. "Do you remember the time we saw that big ol' black snake wrapped up in the elderberry bush alongside the barn?"

"The thick, six-footer?" His brows knitted together. "Yeah, why?"

"Well, I never told you, but after we saw the snake in there, I told Ann I thought I may have seen her missing cameo under that bush."

Isaac winced. "Oh, you didn't."

"I did." Eden laughed. "Of course, she started snapping at me as to why I didn't just go pick it up myself, and how she has to do everything, which, of course, you and I know is ridiculous. But she marched out there just to prove her point, and I ran out back and hid in the barn before she got there."

"Oh, Lord, what happened?"

"Oh, Isaac, it was so funny. Ann was there tiptoeing around that bush, trying not to get any mud on her shoes. Then I saw her lean closer. She reached in and started moving the branches aside, and then, suddenly, her hair stood on end and she screamed and fell right on her backside into the water trough. 'Course, father was angry with me, and Mama Claire threatened to skin me alive if I ever did that again, but it was worth it."

Isaac watched the people walking by, birds in the trees, the boots on his feet. Everywhere except directly into her eyes. "Isaac, are you even listening?" she asked.

He cleared his throat. "Eden, there's something I need to talk to you about." His gaze shifted from the ground to meeting her eyes, dead-on.

"What...what is it?" The tone in his voice caused a shiver

to travel the length of her spine. Using the iron armrest on the bench for support, she slowly stood. Instinctively, she knew something awful had happened, and her body responded with a full flush of panic.

"Honey..." He stood to join her. "I've been thinking all damn day of the most delicate way to tell you...I mean, you've been through so much this past year with father's death and, well..." he paused, "and with Patrick."

With the mention of Patrick's name, her jaw instantly tightened. "Isaac, what is it? Please stop trying to protect me."

"And you know you're the last person in the world I would ever want to upset. In fact, I wouldn't involve you, but—"

"Upset me about what? Land sakes. You know I despise surprises — tell me!"

He held his hands up. "All right...all right. I didn't just happen to stop by Oak Hill. I went there after receiving word at camp there was going to be trouble."

Feeling as though she had just entered a dark cave, her vision thinned to shadows, and her heart beat like a fluttering bird trapped inside her chest. Then, she remembered where she had heard the same intonation in his voice...

Oh, no, no, no! She slammed her eyelids shut, remembering the dreadful moment when Isaac announced that father had passed away in the back bedroom.

"Indeed, there was trouble," he added.

"Trouble?" she croaked, opening her eyes.

He nodded. "I received word problems were developing near Oak Hill — at the Brewster Farm. Some of ol' man Brewster's negroes were planning a riot, and Oak Hill and some of the other farms might be involved."

"Involved — how? Why, our negroes are like family. Ol' Uncle Asa, Ezekiel, Jeremiah — they're more than field hands to us. And Mama Claire...why, she's been there our whole lives, and father's, too! Something's not right. We've always been good to our own, why—"

"Sweet Jesus, Eden!" Isaac paused and lowered his voice. "It wasn't our negroes. I'm talking about ol' man Brewster's negroes, and they were stirring up a hornets' nest of trouble. Mama Claire's the one who got word to me of what she'd overheard."

She shook her head. "I don't think I want to hear about this anymore."

"Eden, stop making this so damn hard." He lifted her chin, forcing her to look at him. "Father and I did our best to spare you the unpleasantness of real life. All you saw growing up was how we treated our negroes. There are people, unfortunately, too many people, who are not as kind — look at Brewster. His negroes live a wretched existence. When he's not hittin' them with a blacksnake whip, he's selling them at the auction house and even worse things. Half those slave babies there he fathered. We all knew about his behavior, and yet we turned a blind eye."

As long as Eden could remember, she never liked the bellowing neighbor with a vulgar disposition. Mr. Brewster's dark hair was always thickly plastered to his skull with greasy pomade, and his eyes looked as if they'd been pickled in corn liquor and left to dry. Originally from Richmond, he'd moved out of the city, buying land and settling near Oak Hill when she was young. She remembered overhearing gossip about a business he owned in the seedy bowels of the city near Shockoe

Creek, where prostitution boomed as well as nightly knifings, shootings, and rowdy fights. She heard talk about his fathering babies with young slave girls, but up until now, she had never accepted the gossip as truth.

Isaac searched her face. "You don't think the Yanks are fighting this war for unjust reasons, do you? These people wish to be free and are not free—"

"I've never heard you speak like this before." She swatted his arms away. "What side of this war are you on? You're no better than Patrick!"

"Eden..." his voice cracked. "You know damn good and well I side with Virginia, but war changes a man, honey. War forces a soldier to see life from different angles. I'm just trying to say, don't be blinded by...ignorance."

"Ignorance!" She jerked away from him and turned to leave.

"Eden, would you please stop making this harder than it already is?"

Still fuming at his unfair portrayal, she frowned and spun on her heels to face her brother. As she looked at him, a lump formed in her throat. The lines of his face looked etched with misery, and his blue eyes had grown dark and clouded. "Go on, I'm listening," she whispered.

He heaved a heavy sigh. "The Brewster place was torched and old man Brewster, well...he was hanged by his negroes."

Eden covered her mouth with a shaky hand.

"Then the mob hit the McDowell's—"

"Oh, no! Did Mrs. McDowell and the girls get away?"

He nodded. "They did. They hid down near the creek bed. Their foreman extinguished the fire in the barn, but the main house and most of the outbuildings and crops were torched." Isaac flicked at an imaginary speck on his sleeve. "Oak Hill was hit next."

Frozen. She couldn't move or speak.

He guided her by the elbow back to the bench. "It's a mess, honey. I only wish I had arrived in time."

The flush surging through her body only minutes earlier suddenly drained away, leaving her dizzy. She took a deep breath and whispered, "Go on. What happened?"

Tears misted his eyes. "When I got close, I saw flames consuming the Brewster and McDowell farms and the woods running between. I knew Oak Hill would not be spared. I rode as fast as I could, but by the time I got there, the fields, seedling sheds, barn, and some of the main house were already burning, including the drawing room. I knew father's ledgers and papers had already perished. I found Uncle Asa and Jeremiah, and some of the others with buckets of water putting out new fires as they started."

"And Mama Claire — where was she?" With hands shaking, she groped the arm of the bench for support. "Oh, heavens, is she...?"

"No, she's alive, but she's hurt. And it wasn't the fire that got her."

Feeling as if she'd just been kicked in the stomach, she swallowed hard. "Dear Lord, Isaac, do tell."

"Poor ol' girl was defending our property when the mob came to our gates. One of Brewster's negroes called her a traitor, and a scuffle ensued. Someone pushed her; she fell backwards and hit her head on a rock. I saw her, Eden. She's been in and out of consciousness."

"I want her here — with me, Isaac. I'll care for her — you know I will."

He shook his head. "She's pretty bad off — can't be moved right now, honey. She's with her daughter, and ol' Uncle Asa won't leave her side. He's always been sweet on her even if she pretends not to know it."

Eden forced a smile. The cat and mouse game between Mama Claire and Uncle Asa had been going on for as long as she could remember. He would take good care of her, of that she could be assured.

Isaac sighed and hung his head. "It's not a home anymore, Sis. But I promise to rebuild when this war is over. I will rebuild." He stretched his long legs out and folded his arms across his chest. "That land is ours, and nobody can take it from us."

"But...but what are we to do? Where do we go?" A mental image of Lucy wailing into her handkerchief and Ann dissolving into a state of hysteria flashed in her mind. "Lucy was so excited about living there—"

"Lucy already knows. I broke the news to her this afternoon when we stopped in town."

"You troubled her with this and didn't bother to tell me earlier? Do you think I'm still a child, unable to handle dreadful news?"

"No, it's not like that," he defended.

She sucked in her cheeks and jutted her chin out.

Isaac frowned. "Now, don't you go jerkin' your chin at me, little sister. I just wanted her advice on how to break the news to you. Don't hold that against me."

"Well, does anyone else know?" She placed a hand on her

hip. "You didn't dare tell Ann before me, did you?"

"Of course not. Don't be a ninny. But one other person does know, and that's what we need to discuss."

She tossed up her hands. "Isaac, I can't help but feel taken aback by all this!"

"Now, wait a minute. If you would just let me finish what I have to tell you, maybe you won't be so fired up."

She tempered her emotions and swallowed her pride. Since the death of their father, Oak Hill was more his home than it was hers. No doubt the loss left him with a dreadful emptiness. "I'm sorry. Go on."

He patted her hand and nodded. "Today when Lucy and I were in town, we stopped at Pizzini's for ice cream. I told her the wretched news. She was amazing about the whole thing, but worried, too. She knew how hard you'd take this. Well, no sooner had I told her when her cousin came walking into the shop."

Eden snapped her head around to face Isaac so fast the ribbons on her bonnet smacked against her cheek. "Uh, which cousin might that be?"

"Why, Major Hampton. She told me you knew of him."

"Oh, that cousin." She dismissed the cousin's name with the wave of her hand. "Yes, I believe she's mentioned him. What of him?"

"Well, he came into the shop, and Lucy appeared upset. She was sniffling and blowing her nose. I told him the whole sad story, and Eden, I must say, I'm overwhelmed by the man's generosity."

"What generosity?"

The small lines on Isaac's face softened. "The major lives

by himself at Hampton Manor. I'm sure Lucy has talked about the place."

"She may have mentioned it," she said, keeping any emotion from her answer.

"Anyway, without so much as a second thought, he absolutely insisted Lucy and her new relatives stay at his manor for as long as it's necessary. Because of the war, he's away most of the time. Frankly, Lucy is fond of him, and she was so excited about the idea, I didn't want to let her down, and I knew you and Ann would be taken care of."

Eden didn't know what to think. Her childhood home was nothing more than charred embers and scarred memories. She could dissolve into tears and wallow in pity, but at some point, she would have to face the devastating reality she was now a homeless wretch. Lord knows, the last thing she would ever want to do is burden Isaac with excess worries while he was off fighting. She looked into his eyes, and they all but pleaded for some semblance of tranquility; begging her to calm the storm gathering force all around them.

What needed to happen became as clear as the sparkling night sky. She would find the strength to rise above another painful period in her life. As soon as possible, she would send what little belongings they had left to Hampton Manor, and she would be sure to thank Lucy's generous cousin herself tomorrow at the wedding.

Chapter 5

Preparing for the evening reception, Eden stepped into her new jade gown, her fingers trailing along the silken fabric, smoothing the delicate pleats.

The wedding had been lovely. Isaac looked particularly gallant in his uniform, and Lucy appeared a vision of beauty, dressed to elegant perfection in her white dress of shimmering satin, delicate lace, and pearls. Eden recalled her disappointment when a telegram arrived from Lucy's cousin moments before the start of the ceremony. He congratulated the couple on their blissful union while extending an apology: *Because of unyielding military matters, he would not be able to arrive until the reception.*

Major Hampton had been responsible for the grand reception this evening. While he supplied the means, he had left Aunt Martha in charge of administering the funds to the appropriate parties to ensure the loveliest celebration for his favorite cousin. He, being the wealthiest of all Lucy's family, had insisted on supplying foods and beverages from Hampton Manor. All morning long, and by the carriage full, came sterling trays of beautifully decorated Virginia hams, stuffed wild pheasant, and oysters by the bushel. There were oversized dishes of colorful roasted vegetables, assorted loaves of baked breads, and elegant crockery of freshly whipped creamy butter. The largest cake Eden had ever seen had been prepared in advance and delivered by Major Hampton's personal coachman.

The major seemed too good to be true, and if everything he had been doing for the reception were not enough, he now offered his home to Lucy and her new family. She needed to meet this man and thank him for his overwhelming generosity.

With only a few minutes left to finish before the arrival of the carriage, she stood tall, looking at her reflection in the full-length mirror. She recalled Ann's spiteful comments about her petite bosom. She adjusted the silken bodice of her gown, shrugging the neckline a bit lower than she felt comfortable with, but she had to admit, the daring plunge did give her breasts more definition.

She turned her head from side to side, admiring Eliza's artistic finesse with the elegant styling of her hair. The emerald combs gathering her honey-blonde hair glimmered delicately and accentuated the curls cascading down her back.

Emeralds, she mused, remembering the stranger at Mr. Johnson's shop. A thread of heat slithered up her spine at the thought of his staring at her silhouetted, half-naked body from across the dark street. She watched in the mirror as her pale skin instantly took on a rosy hue.

Good heavens. "Don't give that man a second thought."

THE two women walked into the entry of Franklin Hall and

handed their lace shawls to the attendant.

Ann glared at Eden. "I'm glad you took my advice and managed some cleavage. Fortunately, it's nothing I've ever had to worry about."

The negro attendant hung their wraps and sniffed uncomfortably.

Eden was not the least bit surprised to see Ann's ample bosom practically spilling out of the blue gown. "No, I don't imagine it's anything you've had to worry about."

Ann patted Eden's wrist as they walked into the large room. "It's all right if you're jealous." She leaned closer. "Really, dear, I understand."

Her stepmother had always been most content when given the opportunity to talk about her fine attributes. Unable to resist temptation, Eden willingly engaged in the exchange.

"Oh, Ann, you're able to see right through me," she said, making her voice sweeter than sugar. "I have a question for you on that very subject."

Delight flashed in Ann's eyes. "I see. Do go on."

Eden gestured for her to hem in closer. "At night, when you unleash those fleshy udders you call bosoms, does it hurt when they hit the floor?"

Several seconds passed before Ann's smile faded with recognition. Her blue eyes darkened, narrowing to indigo slits. "Why, you little vicious witch — how dare you. You watch and see who captures more attention this evening, you...you flat-bosomed old maid!"

RAYCE took a drink from the crystal glass. Over the rim, he caught sight of the young blonde standing across the crowded room speaking with her stepmother. He stood watching the two finely dressed women, his gaze narrowing in on Eden Blair.

The moment he first laid eyes upon her, she had been wrapped from head to toe in lifeless black. Between the dark garments and reserved manner, she hardly appeared approachable. The second time he saw her, she had barely a stitch on. Lord, how the vision of the unpretentious woman in mourning black, her hair tucked modestly under a crisp bonnet, contradicted the image of the seductress he saw in the candlelit window dressed in scanty sheer white, her hair hanging long and wild, her pert breasts...

"...so, by tomorrow, the situation should have changed. How? I'm not sure yet." Jeb frowned and leaned forward. "Major? You still with me?"

"I'm here...I'm listening." Rayce jutted his chin forward.

The general turned around and grinned. "Ah, I see." He put his hand in his trouser pocket and cocked his head to the side. "The Blair women are looking particularly lovely tonight, wouldn't you agree?"

Rayce scanned the room, noting he and the general were not the only men to take appreciative notice of the two attractive women as they entered the room. "Indeed." He took another taste of his drink.

Jeb nudged his elbow. "So, which one of the ladies has caught your eye, Major?"

Rayce swallowed hard and coughed. "Excuse me?"

"I know that look in your eye, Rayce." Jeb laughed and stepped closer. "A certain beauty has captured your attention." His eyebrows rose. "Wait. Don't tell me they have both captured your affections."

Rayce smiled and sighed heavily. "You're never going to let me forget the mess I created courting both of Major Randall's daughters all those years ago, are you?"

"Who me?" Jeb put a hand over his heart.

"All right, perhaps I deserved that back then." Rayce turned his gaze toward Eden. "But it's not like that this time."

"Come now. Which one is it, then?" Jeb's blue eyes brightened. "Let me guess." The general cupped his chin and turned his attention to Eden and her stepmother engaged in what appeared to be a passionate discussion. "Mrs. Blair is certainly charming — a handful I hear, but charming, nonetheless. Now, her stepdaughter, Eden..." He sighed. "There's something special about her. Spirit and intellect wrapped in a lovely package." He faced Rayce. "Yes, if I had to guess I'd—"

"I should have known you'd find this thoroughly amusing—"

"Oh, my." Jeb nodded toward the front of the room.

Rayce caught a glimpse of Eden's stepmother making a direct beeline toward a group of officers conversing in a corner.

Jeb cleared his throat. "It appears as though the Widow Blair has managed to find her bearings once again."

Rayce lowered the glass, his gaze focused on Eden standing at the entrance to the room. Just as he had imagined, the jade gown accentuated the delicate curves of her body, and her long golden mane glistened like silk cascading down her flawless ivory skin. She looked every inch the lovely Southern belle as she stood smiling mischievously, her cheeks flushing pink as she lowered her hand from her lips.

He inhaled deeply and exhaled in jagged breaths as he imagined pulling her body close to his, wrapping her soft honey tresses around his hands and drawing that luscious mouth of hers to his own.

Perhaps the time grew near for an introduction.

EDEN looked around the beautifully decorated hall. On a table in the center of the room sat the tall wedding cake. In every corner, stood large vases of freshly-cut spring flowers in various shades of pink and purple, and in all directions people mingled and enjoyed themselves.

She spotted Ann off to the side, already looped arm-in-arm with some poor unsuspecting officer who stood smiling adoringly at her as if she were the only person in the room. "She sure works fast," she murmured.

"Eden! Eden — over here," rang Lucy's voice. "I'm over here, dear."

She made her way through the crowd to where Lucy stood, yards upon yards of white flowing fabric framing her petite body.

"I've been looking all over for you, where have you been?"

"I'm sorry. Ann took longer than expected."

"Oh, never mind, honey, you're here now." Lucy's eyes sparkled. "Have you been introduced to my cousin yet?"

"Who, the major? No, we truly just arrived." Eden scanned the room. "He's here?"

Lucy clutched her arm. "Oh, he's here all right, and I can't wait any longer for you to meet him." She brought a gloved finger to her chin and surveyed the room. "He's looking so forward to meeting you. I saw him a few minutes ago. Where is..." Her eyes widened. "Ah — there — talking to General Stuart."

Lucy's grip tightened, and before Eden knew it, she was moving through the crowd toward the rear of the room.

As they drew closer, she saw the two uniformed men engaged in conversation standing near the double doors leading to the Hall's famous fragrant herb and flower gardens. The leaded-glass doors stood wide open, and her head swam with the peppery scent of freshly trimmed rosemary merging with the humid breeze.

General Jeb Stuart winked as they approached, but the major's back faced them. Right away, Eden noted how his uniform fit him like a second skin as the gray fabric spanned the breadth of his broad shoulders. His dark, wavy hair hung long and contrasted sharply with his lighter collar.

The major, seemingly unaware of their approach, appeared deep in conversation with the general, for he suddenly tossed back his head and roared with laughter. The full masculine laugh warmed her cheeks, and she instantly felt shy and childlike as she desperately tried to remember the speech she had rehearsed earlier in her room to thank the man for all he had done.

Lucy reached up and placed a hand on the major's shoulder. "Rayce. Look who has finally arrived — our very own Miss Eden Blair."

General Stuart quickly intercepted Eden's hand and placed a cordial peck upon her knuckle. "Miss Blair, you look especially lovely this evening."

"It's very nice to see you again, General," she said as she turned to glance up at Lucy's elusive cousin.

Feeling as though her stomach had just hit the wooden floor below her feet, her legs buckled beneath her gown. She gulped and stared into the major's dark brown eyes, hinting with amusement.

With a firm grasp, the major took hold of her hands and bent to whisper a kiss upon each tightly clenched fist. "Miss Blair, at last we meet. I've heard so much about you."

This can't be happening! "Major," she managed to croak out.

The man stood imposingly tall and far too close. Her heart raced as she looked into his dark eyes, and the tiny hairs at the nape of her neck stood up.

"Wait..." he said, raising a dark eyebrow and stepping forward.

He wouldn't dare.

The major tilted his chin, and a subtle smirk lit the edge of his mouth. "Is it possible we've met before?"

"Of course not!" she blurted, snatching her hands from his grasp.

Lucy shot her a puzzled glance.

Eden's gaze darted between Lucy and General Stuart. The general looked all too comfortable with the situation and even appeared to be enjoying it.

Inhaling slowly, she composed herself the best she could and gazed into the major's eyes. "What I mean, sir, is, well, I've heard you have been terribly busy. I don't see how it would have been possible."

"Ah, yes." He rubbed his jaw. "That would appear the case, but there is something very familiar about you, Miss Blair. I can't help but feel we have met before." His dark gaze appraised her from head to toe.

"I...I believe you're mistaken, Major." Silently, she prayed he would not choose this untimely moment to reveal their unfortunate encounter at Mr. Johnson's store and...the window.

The hot flush of embarrassment burned her cheeks. She lowered her lashes from his piercing gaze, as a shudder of panic coursed through her veins. *I'm face to face with the perverted lout who spied on me!*

"Pardon my perseverance, Miss Blair..."

Oh, no. She held her breath and looked directly into his eyes.

"By chance, is it possible we met on Broad Street...with your sister?"

Eden swallowed her gasp of astonishment. This could not be happening. The lowdown cad planned to humiliate her in front of everyone.

Not willing to reveal her anxiety, lest he take it as a sign to continue his wicked game, she smiled, and in the coolest of manner said, "As I mentioned before, Major, you are most certainly mistaken. I have no sister."

He paused, frowning. Suddenly, his eyebrows jumped. "Window shopping – that's it."

Eden's heart thumped against her bodice. *Don't do this to me; don't you dare.*

"Perhaps I saw you admiring something from a window – yes?" he asked, a look of false innocence written on his face as he prodded her for an answer.

Her gaze bored into his. "Wrong again, Major. I haven't seen anything I have wanted from a window in a very long time."

Lucy gave General Stuart a questioning glance, and he replied with an innocent shrug.

After what felt like an eternity, the major finally smiled and bowed formally. "Well, then, let it never be said I did not take the word of a lady."

Eden sucked in her cheeks and glared at him. The sarcastic rat was genuinely enjoying her predicament.

"Oh, Eden," Lucy chimed in, "didn't I tell you how wonderful he is? Isn't he a dream?"

More like a nightmare. Eden coughed, nearly choking on her forced smile.

The major grinned and reached for his handkerchief.

"No." She waved her hand. "No, I'm fine."

He held out the silk handkerchief. "You're sure, Miss Blair?"

Eden cleared her throat. "Yes...yes, I'm fine." She turned away, pretending to look around the room. The major had an overpowering presence, and she remembered Aunt Martha's words. He does have an effect on women. Well, he had another thing coming if he thought he would include her in his games of love and deceit. She had no desire to let him use her in the same manner he did so many other women.

"Ah, at last you two have met," Isaac said as he joined the small group. He put his arm around Eden. "Did I not promise you my little sister's a beauty, Major?"

Rayce smiled, looked directly into Eden's eyes, and then back at Isaac. "You are a man of your word, Captain. She is, indeed."

As the orchestra announced the beginning of a waltz, General Stuart's aide sequestered him into an adjoining room.

"I just love this piece, dear. Can we dance?" Lucy asked Isaac.

"That's a wonderful idea, my darling wife." He turned to Rayce. "Major, I would be honored if you would escort my sister in a dance, as well."

Eden gasped. "Oh…no, I don't think—"

"What a splendid idea," Rayce piped in, and without a moment's hesitation, he whisked her to the dance floor.

Minutes passed in silence, but Eden was more than aware of his presence as his strong arms deftly glided her across the dance floor. Clearly, he had done this many times.

As they moved closer to the spectators, she noticed several of the available Richmond belles huddled together, whispering and staring, each clearly hoping for a spin on the dance floor with him. She tried to ignore the stiff stab of jealousy piercing her ribcage.

"I must say, I was offended you chose not to acknowledge our prior meetings," he said, his voice velvety smooth.

"We've never had any meetings, Major. You make it sound as though I were a willing participant." She avoided his gaze. "We merely encountered one another, nothing more."

"I have a feeling your idea of encountering one another and mine have completely different meanings, Miss Blair."

She caught the heady aroma of cigars and brandy. The masculine scent belonged to him, and she feared her head could swoon if she were not careful. As if he read her mind, he instantly pulled her closer than deemed appropriate, causing her to gasp.

"Care to learn how I envision our encounters?" His words caressed her ear.

"Stop holding me so tightly," she managed in a strangled voice. "People will talk."

His embrace remained firm. She looked into his dark eyes, sparkling with amusement. "Please stop holding me so tightly, Major, or I fear..." She searched for her most ladylike expression, "or I fear...I shall faint."

"You — faint?" His eyes grew wide. "Come now."

Judging by the grasp of his unyielding arms, her explanation apparently held no merit.

"You know, I was just thinking. After all we've been through, perhaps you could address me by my given name. Call me Rayce."

"We have not been through anything together, Major. Do not delude yourself into believing otherwise. You may address me as Miss Blair."

"Come now, Miss Blair, surely you were as aroused as I when you paraded yourself in front of your bedroom window the other night. The timely performance was for my benefit, was it not?"

She choked in a gasp of astonishment and stopped in her tracks. "Why you arrogant rat," she whispered between pursed lips. "I did no such thing."

He held her firmly, forcing her to continue with the dance.

"You mean to tell me the sultry candlelit dance I witnessed was intended for another?" He raised an eyebrow. "I assure you, I am disappointed."

"Dance!" Her face warmed. "I've had enough of this game, Major. I didn't dance for you then, and I won't dance with you now." She planted her feet on the ground, poised to toss his arms aside, when Lucy and Isaac glided next to them, their faces beaming.

"You two dance beautifully together." Lucy placed a hand over her heart. "I'm so happy you're enjoying each other's company. It means so much to me." Just as quickly as they had arrived, the newly married couple drifted away within each other's arms.

The orchestra paused after the dance. Eden slipped her hand from his broad shoulder, ready to make her escape. Without warning, the orchestra began another waltz. Before she could make her exit, the major had her in his firm clutches again, sweeping her away on the dance floor.

"You were saying, my dear?"

Oh, how she despised being in this situation. She felt like an ensnared lynx whose only option would be to chew off its own foot to escape the trap. "I'm not your dear, Major... and...and—"

"And?"

"And..." She sighed. "Well, what I'm trying to say is...I do not wish to be the object of your raging desire. Furthermore—"

He threw his head back and laughed so loudly she feared it would draw attention.

"Object of my raging desire? Where the devil did you come up with such a phrase?"

She gulped. "Well, Lucy and Aunt Martha have told me...things."

"Ah, say no more." He laughed. "I'll have to speak to them for spreading such vicious rumors."

His expression turned serious, his eyes dark and shrewd. "Look at me, Eden." A huskiness lingered in his voice. "Let's not play games."

She cleared the knot in her throat. Slowly, she lifted her

lashes from her cheeks and looked into his eyes. "I'm sure I don't know what you mean, Major."

His fingertips dug into the small of her back. "I'm quite sure you know exactly what I mean." He glided her toward an unlit corner of the room and pulled her closer. "I want more, much more than a dance from you, my dear."

The last time she heard those words were they were from Patrick. He had said he wanted more from her and then proposed to her right then and there. True, the major had been toying with her, but he clearly desired her. Perhaps he had marriage on his mind, too. Certainly, it would not be the first time a soldier, home from the devastating war, became infatuated with the ideals of marriage after witnessing the horrors of battle firsthand. These days, hasty proposals by lonely, war-weary soldiers were commonplace. She would wait for him to ask and take pleasure in turning him down. After all, two could play this game.

"Why, Major, what more could you possibly want from me?" She quivered her lashes and smiled.

"You can stop with the modest routine, Eden. You know perfectly well what I'm interested in."

"Well, I'm sorry to disappoint you, Major, but I'm not like the other belles around here. I don't wish to marry any time soon."

"Marry!" he sputtered. "Surely, you're joking." He took her hand and weaved his fingers within hers. "A wise man once said, 'Marriage is like putting your hand in a bag of snakes and pulling out an eel.' Frankly, I couldn't agree more."

Eden ripped her hand free from his. "Oh, for pity's sake. You and your games. Then what are you really hinting at?"

His eyes widened. "Hinting? I do apologize. I thought I'd made myself perfectly clear. I want you in my bedroom, Miss Blair, and I think you want that, too." He winked and flashed an audacious grin.

Eden's jaw dropped. "I'll...I'll do no such thing!" Her breath caught, and her hands trembled. With her guard down, she had given him the benefit of doubt, believing he had the intentions of a gentleman. Her instincts had been wrong, and the resulting humiliation felt like a knife against her throat.

Despite her racing pulse, she raised her chin and presented her prettiest face. "You're arrogant and conceited, Major, and I have no desire to continue this conversation."

He reached for her, but she pushed his arm aside and skirted past, leaving him in her wake of silk and magnolia oil.

Feeling as though the walls and ceiling were narrowing in, she swiftly walked away, her gaze shifting about the room for an exit. She had to get out of there, and fast. The man had a way about him; a unique and powerful presence causing her to question her sensibilities. Some private time in the gardens to calm the beat of her pounding heart was most certainly in order.

She saw the opened garden doors. *Perfect.*

Lowering her gaze, she hastened toward the back of the room, whispering pleasantries with the other guests in passing. She slipped through the leaded glass doors, entering the fragrant, torch-lit gardens, and took a deep, cleansing breath. The night air felt balmy against her skin, and the river air hung in the light breeze. Up ahead, a cobbled path disappeared within a tall laurel hedge. Curious, she followed the darkened trail.

She reached out, running a finger along the thick, glossy leaves, misted with evening dew.

How could I be so stupid?

She should have known better with a man like him. He outmaneuvered her on all accounts tonight, and it stung. Worse yet, she had nobody to blame but herself for the humiliation she felt. Tears stung the back of her eyes as she imagined him inside the hall, brandy in one hand, and a cigar in the other, basking in the glow of her embarrassment.

Perhaps she could tell Lucy the arrangement to stay at the major's home was off. Eden banished the thought as quickly as it entered her head. How could she disappoint her sweet sister-in-law, whose fears and anxiety mounted as each day passed? Of course, Isaac would demand an explanation, and she had no desire to reveal this to anyone. And Ann...*Oh, Lord.* If the witch caught wind of this situation, she'd never let her live it down. She remembered Isaac's words. *The major is far too busy with the war.*

True. Likely, she would never have to see him during her stay at Hampton Manor. Perhaps the war would be over soon, and then Isaac could come back and arrange a new plan for the family during the rebuilding of Oak Hill.

Enveloped by the tall hedge, the narrow cobblestone path appeared to wind forever in a loose maze, branching off in different directions. Peering over her shoulder, she hoped she would have no trouble finding her way back to the reception.

With her pride shattered into a million pieces, she tried to think about anything other than the scene that had just unfolded.

Impossible.

God help me. She would accept the devil himself into her heart if it would change the feelings stirring within her now, for as much a she despised the insufferable man, she had to concede, she enjoyed the way her body responded. The warmth of his hands against hers, his masculine scent, his husky voice caressing her ear; it all called to her on some primal level.

After several more twists and turns, the path ended abruptly, and she found herself on a grassy patch staring down a high bluff above the banks of the James River.

Looking around, she could see majestic old oak and maple trees guarding the surrounding hills, demanding respect from anyone below. Fragrant wild honeysuckle vines sweetened the air, reminding her of a familiar dream she had not so long ago.

She cast her gaze out toward the vast winding waters. Glowing lights flickered like dancing stars from the bobbing ships that occupied the river, always ready to protect the Confederate capital if and when the time came.

Tonight the river appeared calm, but she knew the truth to be different. Lurking like an eerie transparent mist, the constant threat of battle hung over these strong, turbulent waters filled with nearby enemy ships.

A cool wind blew above the river, slicing through the mild air. She hugged her arms across her chest, emotions suddenly getting the better of her. She thought about the war and her beloved home, Oak Hill, in ruins, and about Isaac.

Clearly, he was not the same man he had been when he left for the war. How could he be? Daily, he lived by his wits and watched men drop like flies all around him. She remembered his letter home telling in vivid detail about the bloody massacre that raged on for two days, killing thousands of men during the battle at Shiloh in Tennessee. Several of his friends had fought bravely and fallen in those terrible days. His anger and deep sorrow resonated with each penned word he wrote on the dreary paper.

Peering out toward the distance, the pooling tears stung her eyes. She dabbed each corner with her lace handkerchief. Another gust of cool wind rushed across the river, and she wished she had thought to bring her shawl.

She needed to return to the reception before Lucy and Isaac noticed her absence. Before she had time to turn around, the sound of footsteps approached her.

Her pulse quickened, but she was not frightened. She closed her eyes and inhaled his familiar scent, just as he slid in behind her and gently embraced her waist.

"It wasn't my intent to embarrass you, Eden." His warm, brandied breath caressed her ear.

She did not move — she could not move.

Like the deceptive river before her, his smooth words could not be trusted. She knew she should turn around. She knew she should turn around and slap his arrogant face, but she could not.

He reached up and gently brushed her hair to one side. He whispered a kiss against the back of her neck. "Say you'll forgive me."

Something invisible stirred between them, moved slowly, deliberately, like an unhurried fog filling every tiny crack and crevice. The last of her tears dripped down her cheek. The world felt as though it had suddenly changed course, spinning out of control. *Give me strength,* she silently pleaded. "I do...I think," she whispered.

His thick hair tickled her shoulder. She leaned back, resting her head comfortably upon his broad chest.

Slowly, he slid his hand along the gentle curve of her waist. Moving higher, his fingers trailed dangerously close to the side of her breast. She flinched, ready to object, but he held firm and kissed the flushed skin on the side of her neck. A soft sigh escaped her lips the moment his hand slid over her silken bodice and teased a taut peak in his lust-rousing mission.

This is madness!

Any self-respecting woman would rip his hands away — hit him — kick him — slap him. Instead, she allowed his wandering hand to cup her breast and coax the nipple fully erect. A low throaty moan of desire escaped his lips, sending a prickle of heat slithering up her backbone.

"Eden, sweet Eden." His breath warmed her neck. "I'm sorry if I hurt you."

It was as though Lucifer himself called her name, and yet, she could not care less. Her body responded — every inch of her skin reacting — feeling alive next to his. "Rayce."

She turned to face the man who stirred such passion within her — to face the handsome scoundrel who held the power of seducing her within his large hands. She looked into his dark eyes, gleaming in the moonlight.

"I do desire you, Eden, and deny it if you wish, you desire me as well."

Behind the flames of ardor smoldering in his eyes, she detected a hint of sorrow, making the wild rogue suddenly more human. Could it be he felt more than desire for her and unable to wear his heart upon his sleeve? She quickly banished the thought, unwilling to set herself up for more humiliation.

"Eden—"

She brought her finger to his lips to silence his words. "Not now," she whispered.

She rose on slippered toes to kiss him. Somewhere, lurking in the back of her mind, she knew her actions were not those of a proper lady, but as her lips met his, and his arms enveloped her, the thought completely vanished.

If she thought for even one second that her boldness would squelch his desire, he swiftly proved her wrong. Without hesitation, his lips descended upon hers, his mouth branding her as his tongue gently coaxed her quivering, inexperienced lips apart.

The kiss felt powerful, demanding, sensual. He kissed her with such fury and passion, she wondered if he would scoop her up and make wild love to her right there on the cliff above the James.

She lowered her arms and reluctantly withdrew her lips from his. Dizzied, she laid her head upon his chest. "Rayce...I shouldn't."

He lifted her chin and looked into her eyes. "Of course you should, Sweetness. Don't be afraid of your passion, my dear. I find you quite irresistible."

The familiar hint of amusement shown in his eyes. She smiled, and he pulled her close to his chest. They stood silently, holding one another, as they gazed out at the vast river below.

Rayce swallowed hard. Every time he looked into Eden's eyes, he was pulled in deeper. Inside the hall, when she gazed up at him with moist eyes pooling with tears, he knew he could get lost in their emerald depths if he dared let himself. There was no denying she initiated a physical response somewhere deep inside every time he saw her. It was like lifeless air forced from his lungs after a swift kick to the gut, followed by a deep breath of fresh air. Each and every time, he'd been left wanting more. Needing more.

Perhaps he'd been in the woods too long this last stretch. Holding her tonight felt so incredibly perfect, as if she had been destined to be in his arms at this very place, at that exact moment. The calm water in the distance, the lush surroundings, the luminous moon on a cloudless night lighting his path straight to her; it felt like a dream from long ago.

He inhaled the delicate scent of sweet magnolia in her hair; watched her long lashes cast small shadows on her cheeks when she blinked in the moonlight. He closed his eyes. A man could grow old and never tire of a woman like her. *Not ever.*

Lord. But now was not the time. Any distraction or diversion, no matter how lovely or tempting, could get him killed these days. With the relentless war and dangerous threats accumulating, he needed to stay alert and focused. Just as he'd expected, the war was heating up. God only knew where he'd be headed next. When he'd be back again.

If he'd make it back again.

He opened his eyes and gazed out across the water. "Fog is rolling in," he whispered.

Eden turned around and laid her head against his chest. "I'm chilled. I wish I'd brought my shawl."

She pressed against him, her firm breasts nudging his ribs, and wrapped her arms around his waist. The sound of her soft hands sliding slowly against the course fabric of his coat made him instantly harden.

God, he wanted her. Right now — right here; a good old-fashioned down and dirty romp right on the ground. Every muscle in his body felt on edge — alive — ready to pounce. What he wanted — no, what he needed — from her was to feel the swell of her warm chest against his, to run his hands along the delicate curves of her small waist, and to kiss her luscious mouth before he left again.

His instincts had managed to keep him safe all these years, and as he held her, felt her vibrant young body pressed against his, those same instincts poked and prodded at him, nagging him to stick to his guns as he drew her closer. Given the circumstances, it was too damn reckless to consider anything else with her.

No, what he wanted from Eden Blair involved pleasure — nothing more. Christ almighty, if he ever were to settle down, it sure as hell wouldn't be with someone like her, given her damn temper. No way, he reasoned, he'd like a taste of her fiery spirit all right, but only in the bedroom where the energy could be savored.

"I hope my actions haven't changed your mind about staying at Hampton Manor," he said, looking out at the distance. "I want you to know you and your family are welcome as long as you wish."

He stroked the silky mane draping down her back, wondering what it would feel like to grab a handful, wrap it around his fist, and ravish her right on the spot. The muscles in his torso tightened. Her flourishing femininity tortured his senses to the core, but experience told him Eden was innocent in matters of the flesh.

He scratched the evening stubble on his chin and sighed. *Slow it down, ol' boy.* He closed his eyes tightly shut, forcing the lovely image out of his head. "I won't ever push you into something you're not ready for."

When he opened his eyes, she was gazing up at him, smiling. "As long as you can keep your raging desire bridled, I think the living arrangement will be fine, Major."

He frowned and slowly shook his head. "Lord, woman." His voice barely rose above a hoarse whisper. "Don't you understand? Some things are easier said than done." He tilted her head back, exposing the flesh of her neck, and kissed the soft, slender column, his mouth trailing higher until he reached her mouth.

She pulled away from his lips and whispered against his cheek, "Oh, Rayce, tell me this is lunacy. Tell me, and we can stop this madness right now." She kissed his neck. Once. Twice.

He inhaled jagged breaths, his fingertips curling deeper into the small of her back with each brush of her moist lips against his throat. Hell if he could explain what was happening between them — the strange force threatening to unravel his life.

Perhaps it was madness.

"I have no rational answer for you, my dear. Maybe it's the world around us that's gone mad." He cupped her chin, tilting her face to his, and looked deeply into her eyes. "All I know is you're sending me back to the depths of hell with a memory to warm my cold nights." He bent low, his lips brushing hers. "Kiss me, Sweetness. Let me take this moment with me, and if I should be—"

The moment Rayce whispered against her lips, the sweet hint of brandy so close she could taste it, her walls of distrust crumbled. She rose on her toes and silenced him with her lips.

He instantly wrapped her in his arms, enveloping her until she felt like they disappeared from the rest of the world into a universe all their own. Her body warmed in his arms despite the chilled fog rolling in.

"Major? Major Hampton?" A man called from around the corner.

Rayce slowly pulled his lips from hers. He gripped her shoulders and looked into her eyes. "Listen to me. I knew the first time I saw you, I wanted you, Eden. Promise me you'll remember this night. Remember me...no matter what happens."

Remember me. Where had she heard that before?

She had no time to answer before his mouth sought hers once again. His demanding kiss felt desperate, and she couldn't help wonder if this kiss came from a man who desired her, or from a soldier who thought it might be his last.

His eyes remained fixed upon hers as he pulled away. "Over here!" Rayce called back.

A young soldier appeared, lowering his head when he realized he had intruded upon the major in an intimate moment.

"What is it, Lieutenant Severson?"

"Er...I'm sorry, sir—"

Rayce sighed. "That's quite all right, Jeffrey. What is it you need?"

"I have an urgent message from General Stuart, sir." The lieutenant straightened his spine, extended the lantern, and handed his superior the folded piece of paper. Rayce paused a moment after reading it, then slid the note into his pocket.

"Please tell the general I'm on my way. That will be all, Lieutenant."

"Yes, sir." He scurried off.

Eden reached out to Rayce. To her surprise, he slid his hands into his pockets and turned away. He took a step back and shook his head as if flushing cobwebs from his thoughts.

"I have to go. I'll escort you back." He took off his coat and turned around to face her. "Wear this."

She searched his face, only to find cool, dark eyes staring back. The time spent with him tonight had been an unforeseen pleasure, and she thought he felt the same way. Instead, she sensed his rejection — chilly, composed, and arrogant — as if he owned the world, as though she were nothing more than another one of his trite dalliances.

"That's it?" she asked, her voice rising. "I had fun seducing you tonight, Eden. Now, here's my coat?" She swatted at the garment he extended. "Keep it."

The chilled fog crept over the bluff, weaving slowly between their legs like an eerie ghoul in search of prey. The major looked into her eyes, took a step forward, and stopped abruptly.

She slid her trembling hands in the folds of her gown and glared at him. "How dare you, Major. How dare you take advantage of me!" Before she had time to contemplate her actions, she swung at him.

Rayce grabbed her fist and trapped her body against his. "Eden, stop it now. You don't understand."

"Oh, I understand all right," she sneered, wrangling with him. "I understand you're a no-good, low down rat!"

"Whoa, now." He held her firmly, taking hold of her

flailing hands. With her anger clearly getting the better of her, she was more than capable of landing a serious blow. He gripped her wrists, holding them tight. "Now, calm down, Eden. I told you—"

"Let go of me, you cad!" she snapped between clenched teeth. "I said, let go of me!" She stomped on his thick, leather boot with the heel of her shoe.

He couldn't help but smile at her temper. No doubt about it, he admired her vitality. He bent down and whispered in her ear. "What, no goodbye kiss?"

"A goodbye kick is what you deserve!" She frowned and narrowed her eyes. "I hope the Yankees get you, and I never have to see the likes of you ever again!" Her voice echoed across the tall bluff, sending sleeping birds fluttering from trees in all directions.

Her venomous words stung, and his body instantly went rigid. The moist fog moved in around them, chilling everything in its lifeless path.

"Be careful what you wish for, my dear." He released her arms, and they fell limply to her sides. "I really must go. Let me escort you back."

"No, Major," she said, her voice cracking and breathless. She cast her gaze toward the river. "I'm perfectly content to stay out here...alone. Goodbye."

He stepped toward the path but paused and turned around. He reached out, his fingertips just inches from her slender back, then pulled away. He couldn't look into those beautiful eyes again, full of pain and confusion, without scooping her up and kissing her lovely face. No, he reasoned, he could not — he would not do this to her.

He slowly walked the path toward the hall. Regardless of what she thought of him, he spoke the truth. He would carry the memory of their heated kisses into battle, and the lovely image of them together would warm his dark nights while he sought shelter under the damp forest canopy in the dead of night. But the government needed him now more than ever. It was as simple as that. Endless danger and persistent threats would be his constant companions in the next weeks. Any other preoccupation could mean a death sentence for him and anyone he cared about, if he were not careful. His line of work was far too dangerous and unpredictable. No way in hell would he put her in harm's way. Up until now, this had not been a problem. Up until now, he had not met Eden Blair.

He stopped to light a thin cheroot. He smiled, realizing he would never light another cigar without thinking of the fine woman who unwittingly charmed him to the point of distraction from her bedroom window.

He closed his eyes, inhaling the spicy, pungent smoke, and all he could see was Eden's beautiful face, smell the delicate hint of magnolia in her hair. How her body responded to his roving hands; her innocence, eager and willing, tempting him with the promise of more. Even the damn petty arguing with her he enjoyed. As for her raw, sensual instinct to survive she exuded when her back was against the wall...Hell, that excited him to the core.

He exhaled with a long sigh. It wasn't just her body he wanted — he wanted all of her.

Good Lord, get a hold of yourself!

With a heavy boot, he extinguished the cigar and continued on his way.

The sound of Rayce's dying footsteps sent a spike straight through her heart with each retreating step.

How could I be so amazingly stupid?

If he had not intruded on her private walk, she would not have been so vulnerable to his wicked game of seduction. At just the right moment, everything in her life had come to an emotional peak, and she had offered herself to him perfectly ripe for his picking.

She had known the brazen man gave into his desires and his reputation tarnished, stained black, with previous scandals of passion, and, yet, she had been drawn to him just like the others.

She lowered her face in humiliating disbelief, recalling his hand roaming over her bodice and how she didn't even try to stop him. Then a more terrifying thought crossed her mind.

She spun around and faced the empty wall of fog. *I acted no better than a common harlot. I behaved like Ann!*

Chapter 6

Hampton Manor,
Tidewater, Virginia

Eden awoke to a dark room, but the sliver of sun glinting between the velvet draperies hinted of a dazzling day. The thin slice of bright light danced off her perfume bottle on the tall mahogany bureau, casting whimsical rainbow spectrums fluttering across the decorated walls.

Eager to face the morning, she eased herself from the four poster-bed and opened the drapes. She pulled the ribbon from her braid, sank back in bed, and brushed her hair as she sat looking about the large room, now filled with the light spring day.

They had been at the manor more than a week, and she still viewed the place with awe. Lucy had told her the major lived in a splendid mansion. Still, the spectacular beauty and mystique surrounding the massive, well-kept plantation had come as a surprise. The manor and her grounds were reminiscent of an English lord's paradise, and as much as she had adored Oak Hill, her former home simply paled in comparison.

Hampton Manor's interior gleamed with rich heritage and

fine craftsmanship, obviously dating back many years. The dark, paneled walls and carved woodwork held beautiful oil portraits of the Hampton clan, their faces revealing pride and prosperity.

Blending with the home's beauty and elegance, a sense of mystery shrouded the old walls. She couldn't help but wonder about the faces in the hanging portraits, as she imagined them walking the sprawling grounds and long dimly lit hallways.

Framed within the heart pine mantel, the last of the warm fire lay in small glowing embers, reflecting off the cream marbled flooring. With the coverlet held snugly against her chest, she sat up tall and peered out the window.

In the distance, she could see the sweeping lawn leading to the river below and the manor's private wharf. After the rains of the last week, the weather had turned lovely again, and she looked forward to the tour of grounds.

The last days had been terribly hectic. As many had suspected, the nearby town of Yorktown was in desperate peril of invasion by General McClellan and his large Yankee army. Southerners were asked to help prepare sandbags to fortify the town. For three straight days and nights, through thick mud and rain, she, Lucy, and Ann worked alongside the servants until their hands were sore, scooping the gritty sand from the James River into thick canvas bags.

News about the war spread quickly along the river, and Eden took comfort in hearing the Rebels were doing a splendid job holding the enemy army at bay. Still, with Yorktown only a short distance away, and the Yankee army intent on seizing Richmond, a nagging uneasiness persisted. If the Yanks advanced, Hampton Manor would lay in the path of the huge army as it moved to seize the Confederate capital and all that lay in between.

Given the circumstances, she felt it wise to prepare an area in one of the outbuildings as a makeshift infirmary. The manor's private doctor had joined in the war effort a year earlier, but a few of his supplies remained in his quarters, and she quickly seized the inventory.

She located bandages and soap, a tourniquet for hemorrhages, as well as oil of turpentine for dysentery and a small supply of quinine. Elsewhere, she found whiskey, extra blankets, lanterns, and matches, and she instructed Daniel to gather hay from the barn to have stacked for extra bedding. There would be plenty of water from the creek, root vegetables, bread, and extra ham and bacon from the smokehouse.

An abrupt knock at the door startled her, and she quickly yanked the coverlet up to her neck. Every time someone knocked on her door, she expected to see Rayce. Even if he were home, with his appalling lack of decency, she doubted he would bother to knock.

"Yes?" she called out. "Who is it?"

"'Tis me, Miss," the servant said. "I've brought you hot tea and biscuits."

Eden looked at the clock over the hearth, and her eyes met with those skillfully painted in oils with the name *Captain Reginald Hampton* at the bottom, etched in gold.

The painting gave her goosebumps. No doubt about it; not only did the dark, leering eyes follow her at every point in the room, they clearly resembled those of the new master of the manor, Major Rayce Hampton. The family resemblance was striking, and it made her skin crawl with the eerie familiarity cast by the portrait.

"Do come in, Trinidad."

The tall black woman entered carrying a serving tray. The morning sun sparkled off the tasteful silver, and she noticed the large "H" within a crest, engraved into the sterling.

"I think to myself, you must be hungry, Miss. I know how hard you worked this week."

Noting Trinidad's accent, Eden questioned its origin — Cuba, West Indies, perhaps? A distinct rhythm, smooth as soft silk, accented her tone.

The mysterious woman had a way of watching others that made Eden uncomfortable. More often than not, she would spot Trinidad lurking in dim corners, tidying up, or dusting areas previously tended to. Generally, house servants were visible; anticipating the many needs of the families and guests, but Trinidad appeared vague and elusive, rarely offering assistance. However, with Rayce as master of the manor and his atrocious manners, nothing should really surprise her.

"Miss Lucy feel in poor health this morning. A touch of dyspepsia, I told." The servant set the tray next to the bedside. "She's sleeping now."

Eden reached for the extended teacup, wondering if perhaps Trinidad did not like her. The possibility bothered her. "I'll check on Lucy later, then. Thank you."

She sipped the tea, and while Trinidad spread honey on the biscuits, Eden examined her closely for the first time in the bright light.

The woman looked striking with her smooth ebony hair pulled tightly behind her head. Small golden strands weaved wildly throughout the well-formed bun, highlighting the wiry ringlets dangling from her temples. Only a few strands of gray gave away her age. What had Lucy said? *She's about forty.*

Her flawless skin glowed and reminded Eden of a rich shade of creamy cocoa. Her high cheekbones looked as though they had been deliberately carved to perfection, and she had the most unusual shade of eyes — a light brown with gold sunbursts woven throughout. She was lovely and must have been a stunning beauty in her day.

"Is anyone else awake?"

"Everyone except you and Miss Lucy, Miss."

"Hmm...where's Ann?"

The servant's full lips curved in a smile, and she cast her gaze downward. "She be in the parlor with a caller — a gentleman caller. She say she won't be touring the grounds today."

Eden cocked her head to the side. "A gentleman caller? Who?"

"The widower, Master Will Benton. He come calling to pay his respects. She was the only one awake. She downstairs with him now."

As if on cue, Ann's trumped-up laughter echoed through the large parlor below.

"Who's the widower Benton?"

"He be an old friend of Ray—" Trinidad's gaze shifted away.

"Just a friend of the major...down river."

Eden held the teacup to her lips and eyed the servant with suspicion.

Trinidad muttered, dropping a biscuit on Eden's plate. "'Tis a day for the major."

She cleared her throat, nearly choking on the last hot sip of tea. "What? Is Major Hampton home?"

The servant cleared her throat and snatched up the serving tray. "Ah, no, Miss, excuse me." She fled the room in a flurry of calico.

The woman puzzled her. She would be sure to find out more about her from Lucy. Until then, she had better freshen up to greet the day.

After breakfast, she strolled to the gazebo situated between the manor's main house and the river below. The view from the arched pergola had to be one of the most beautiful and peaceful places she had ever seen. All around stood giant tulip poplars, magnolia, oak, and black locust trees, and the steady chatter of robins, cardinals, and mockingbirds, filled the air on the well-kept grounds. She cast her attention to the plot of rose bushes surrounding the gazebo. She missed her lovely rose garden back home, and seeing the well-tended flowers on the grounds of Hampton Manor brought back childhood memories of Oak Hill.

When Eden was young, Mama Claire taught her the importance of getting one's hands dirty; to hold and feel the earth with bare hands and to tend, nurture, and wait patiently for the roses to bloom to perfection.

When the time was right, they would walk to the rose garden. The elderly negro woman would hum a tune 'from the old days,' she would say. She'd gently pull the ribbon from Eden's hair and unwind the long braid with nimble, brown fingers. Mama Claire would tell her stories about the days long since passed; the days when Eden was a baby, and her mother, a stunning beauty who had swept Doctor Blair off his feet the moment they met. She would remind Eden of the great love Mistress Rebecca had for her little daughter she liked to call "Sweet Eden." Then they would wrap a bouquet of yellow roses, her mother's favorite, with the ribbon from Eden's hair and lay them at her grave.

While memories of her mother had always been wrapped in the sweet fog of childhood, she clearly remembered running and playing hide-and-seek near the gardens with Isaac, Jimmy, and Patrick. When the boys would find her, they refused to tackle her to the ground as they did one another. Rather, they treated her as though she were made of the finest delicate porcelain.

She recalled another day, years later, when she stood in the same garden picking roses for her bedside table, when Patrick came galloping up on his Appaloosa. He looked especially handsome in his riding coat and boots, his hair windswept and wild, when he told her how lovely she looked that day. As if it were only yesterday, she remembered how he took her hands in his and told her he loved her and would always be there for her. She shook her head, refusing to let the familiar ache of shattered dreams swell within her chest.

The aroma of fresh mint, rosemary, and lavender scented the air. She strolled to the opposite side of the gazebo and spotted an herb garden several yards away. The familiar scents filled her senses, just as they had at the reception hall not long ago. She could still see Rayce's handsome face and hear his husky drawl as he spoke against her throat that night, and how his hands skillfully played with her hair and...*oh, Lord above!*

She trailed a finger along the wood railing. *If he comes home...well, I'll just be unavailable for the duration. After all, the manor is immense.*

"A smidgen' of pie for your thoughts?"

She turned to see Lucy walking toward her. "I thought you were ill. I had planned to check on you later."

Eden studied her sister-in-law. Lucy's pale skin cast a sallow hue against her dark dress. "Darling, are you unwell?"

Lucy waved her slender fingers. "It's just a touch of something. You needn't concern yourself, dear." She turned her back to Eden and faced the river. "Isn't this place spectacular? It's been years since I've been here, and I'd enjoy hearing all Daniel has to say."

"I thought Trinidad planned on giving us the tour."

"I guess she couldn't do it, so Daniel will show us."

Daniel came into view hobbling across the sweeping lawn. The old negro suffered a pronounced limp, looking like he could topple over with each step.

"Don't you two get comfortable there," he called out, "we got lots to see."

The women had seen the wharf and the river's shore days earlier, so Daniel began on the opposite side of the mansion.

"Now ova' yonda' be the soybeans and peanut fields. There's eight thousand acres here at Hampton Manor and most been put to crops. Course things a changing fast with the armies all meandering through these parts. Armies would take it all if they could, North and South. Fact is, most of the field hands been taken by the Reb army to dig trenches in Yorktown to keep the Yanks away." He shook his head and turned. "Yes'm, sure is crazy times."

Eden followed the direction of his pointed finger at what appeared to be an eternal vastness of low growing plants.

"Over there be the tobacco," he said.

She put her hand over her brow to shield her eyes from the bright sun.

"Not gonna be much of a crop this year because the Confederate Congress done told everyone to grow foodstuffs with the war, and all. But tobacco's been good as gold for the Hamptons ova' the years. Been the main cash crop for many folks around here but especially good to the Hamptons. Fact is, lands around here been declining for years now." He grinned. "Course, the major's a smart man, and he done figure out just how to fix the dirt and make it good for tobacco again."

"Really, how?" Eden wanted to know more. Every tobacco farmer knew over time the crop exhausted the fertility of the ground. She had seen it at Oak Hill after they had failed to rotate the crops and would have given just about anything for another solution. "What remedy did he find?"

"Oh, he done tried lots of things and nothing worked until he come up with a real potent mix of what he calls...sea manure."

Eden frowned. *Only he'd come up with such a crude name.*

Lucy stifled a giggle.

"See, we dredge the bottom of the tidal creeks and mix up sea clay, shells, and shellfish. I'm telling you, I never seen anything help tobacco grow in all my years. Anyways, that's why the major been doing fine while other folks been struggling."

He pointed to another area. "Ova' there is the barley, wheat, and corn fields. I'll hitch a buggy, and we can ride around."

"Just how old is this place?" Eden asked.

"Goodness, Miss Eden, Hampton's been here a long, long

time — well ova' a hundred years. Course it took longer to get more land, but they been a hard working bunch, and it paid off good."

"All this land they got over time? I never knew that," Lucy said.

Daniel nodded. "No ma'am, that be right. Master Hampton — that be, Captain Reginald Hampton, he was the first here. The ol' captain was a rich man back in England — owned a shipping company. He came here and started buying up land. He planted tobacco and sent it back to England — course that made him even richer. Then, when the captain had more money than he knew what to do with, he married a pretty, young lady in England. The daughter of a surgeon in London, if I remember rightly. Well, they came back here to settle for good. Then it was just a matter of time before the captain started buying up more land. Yes'm, this place has stayed in the family all these years, being passed to first-born sons. Last Hampton son being Master Rayce."

"You don't say," Lucy mused.

Daniel gave an exaggerated shiver and raised his bushy, gray eyebrows. "Well, Master Rayce be the last Hampton alive around here, that is. The dead don't always go away like they should."

Lucy gasped. "What an odd thing to say, Daniel. Whatever do you mean?"

"Master Rayce never told you about ol' Captain Hampton, Mrs. Blair? Lawdy Lawd." He took off his hat and wiped his brow.

Eden recalled seeing the name Captain Reginald Hampton on the portrait over her hearth. She wouldn't be able to forget those leering eyes any time soon.

Daniel leaned forward. "I hear the ol' captain, well...he haunts the third floor. It's abandoned, you know."

Lucy gasped. "Haunted! Goodness, Daniel."

His round eyes darkened. "Oh, yes, ma'am, but I hear noises myself a time or two over the years, and Trinidad says she hears him many times over. She told me she seen him looking out to sea, just-a-waitin'."

Lucy smiled and waved her hand. "Land sakes, waiting for what? Surely, you don't believe in ghosts. Why would he haunt this beautiful place?"

Daniel gathered in, dropping his voice to a whisper. "Well, after a few years here, the captain's wife, Mistress Faith Hampton, she ran away with another man. The two sailed off to sea together right in front of him, leavin' the captain and their young son behind. Poor Captain Hampton was prostrate with grief, waiting for her return. He never go nowheres or nothing for years. He just wait and wait for her, pacing around upstairs, looking from the third floor window out to sea."

He pointed at a large rectangular window facing toward the James. "Some say he just went mad."

A shiver traced Eden's spine as she cast her gaze toward the river. The winding waters of the James River flowed into the Chesapeake Bay at Hampton Roads, then out to the vast Atlantic Ocean that led to foreign places far away.

"Back in the day, people felt sorry for the ol' captain when they see him up there staring out. Tale is, poor man died from a broken heart waiting for his woman to come home to him where she belonged."

"The story truly is tragic, Daniel, you're right." Lucy's

words barely rose above a whisper.

"Yes'm, it surely is. Long before I was born here, there been tales of people seeing and hearing him upstairs. Trinidad says his spirit will stay trapped here until the man gets his woman back."

A cool gust of wind rushed across the river. Eden quickly reached up, securing the flapping taffeta bow on her braided straw bonnet. She gazed up at the window. "Well, I don't believe in ghosts."

The women spent more than an hour touring the grounds, first by foot and then by buggy to the various gardens, fields, and buildings. They passed by an open area of small wooden houses with whitewashed outer walls, lined in a row. Piles of neatly stacked wood sat beside each structure and a larger pile behind a weathered henhouse. Dozens of negroes stood outside tending to their chores, watching as they rode by.

She whispered to Lucy, "The slave quarters are very well kept."

Lucy furrowed her brow. "I thought you knew. Why, Rayce has no slaves, honey. He freed each of them when he inherited this place. These negroes here are hired servants." Lucy called out, "You're a free man, aren't you, Daniel?"

"Yes'm, Mrs. Blair, free as a bird," he replied over his shoulder with a big grin. "Master Rayce gave us our papers before the war even start. We work for him just the same, but he don't own us. Nobody own us no more."

Daniel called to his wife, Hetty, carrying water from the creek, and his two sons, William, chopping wood, and their youngest boy, Toby, who appeared too busy chasing chickens to notice.

Freeing one's slaves was not unheard of in the South, but it certainly was not commonplace. Eden had heard this talk from Isaac recently, but she had not expected it from Rayce. Both men were soldiers fighting for the Confederacy and the state of Virginia, whose livelihood and foundation were built on the institution of slavery.

Her sheltered life at Oak Hill had never prepared her for the complex issue of slavery. She dearly loved Mama Claire and thought of old Uncle Asa, Ezekial, and Jeremiah as part of her family. Her father had been a compassionate doctor and a decent man, yet he owned slaves, never freeing any of them. She felt a sudden surge of humiliation for having never considered the idea after he died. Up until now, she had thought these to be purely Yankee views.

Daniel faced them. "Well, I'd be lying if I say nobody left. There were some field hands took off when the war start up, but I think they did it because they feel they was supposed to. Some join up north, but I can say this for sure; none left because they were treated poorly. Master Rayce is a mighty good man."

Chapter 7

Now, where did he go?

Passing down the long second floor hallway, Eden could hear the dog's soft whimpers. She glanced at the locked black, iron door that led to the third floor, remembering what Daniel had said about the ol' captain's lost and tortured soul. "Good heavens, I hope I don't have to traipse up there to find Beau," she whispered.

Another whine followed by a bark rang out. "Here, boy," she called quietly, hastening her pace. "Come here, Beau."

She walked toward Lucy's room at the end of the hall and noticed the door ajar. Beau sat inside, ears folded back, and his head cocked to the side.

She poked her head inside. "Lucy?"

Nothing.

"Come here, you." She crept in and scooped Beau into her arms. Just as she rose up, prepared to slip out undetected, Lucy came barreling out of her privy, clad in only a thin nightdress, her face drenched in moisture. The wooden door slammed against the wall, echoing across the polished floor.

"Eden! I..."

Eden's jaw dropped. Beau's restless paws dug into her arms, and she bent low to set him down, her gaze fixed upon her sister-in-law. "Lucy," she mouthed.

"I knew it, you hate me. You hate me!" Lucy bawled. Her slender shoulders heaved with choked sobs. "I wanted to tell you — I did — but...but I was so ashamed."

The heavy hush of secrecy filled the room. Lucy stood before her, revealing a belly the size of a Virginia melon at picking time. "I...I don't know what to say."

Lucy's shoulders slumped, and she flung down on her featherbed, weeping into the pillow.

Eden rummaged through her skirt pocket for a handkerchief and rushed to Lucy's side. "Oh, honey, I'm sorry. I'm just...I'm just surprised." That was certainly an understatement. She wasn't just surprised, she was downright dumbstruck. "I wasn't—"

"Oh, Eden! Here I am, married only weeks, and almost seven months with child." Lucy looked up with puffy eyes. "Please don't stare at me like that, I feel bad enough already."

Eden realized her state of shock had been interpreted as disappointment, or worse, disapproval. Yes, she was stunned, but it never crossed her mind to pass judgment, nor would she ever turn her back on Lucy. "Dear, I'm just...surprised." She managed a stiff smile. "Does Isaac know?"

"Of course he knows. Look at me!"

Eden glanced at Lucy's large belly and then down at the floor.

Lucy sighed heavily. "I couldn't keep this kind of news from him. He's known for months and says he doesn't give a whip what others think. Our child was conceived in love, and that's all that should matter."

Eden faced Lucy and sighed. Her brother loved Lucy and clearly stood by her. Still, the matter was of a delicate nature. If she were to help Lucy, she would need more information.

"You don't look well today. Have you been having trouble...with the baby?"

Lucy rubbed her belly. "No, I don't think so. The babe moves each day, and lately even more, but I don't have much of an appetite and often feel terribly nauseated."

Eden's mind raced. "How...I mean, when did this—"

"Back when Stonewalls Brigade was near Winchester and I had a five-day leave from my governess duties. I knew if I caught the train, I'd be able to catch up to Isaac." She blew her nose. "I did find him, Eden, and he was in quite a state."

Eden frowned. "How so?"

Lucy slowly shook her head. "There'd been a battle days earlier. He saw some of his men die and others wounded. You must realize, with everything going on, we thought we'd never see each other again, and it happened. It just happened."

Eden had limited knowledge when it came to passionate affairs between a man and a woman, but if the way she felt in Rayce's arms the night of the reception was any indication, she knew desire could certainly overcome sensibilities. She struggled each day to keep what happened that night as far from her mind as possible.

She hugged Lucy and smoothed her chestnut braid.

Lucy closed her eyes, calming herself against Eden's shoulder. "I'm always so afraid. Sometimes I tire myself out with worry, and then I feel ill." She pulled away and looked into Eden's eyes, her gaze narrowing as though searching for something. "I know you've considered leaving. I've seen it in your eyes. I still see it. Please say you won't go, Eden, I need you. I can't bear to go through this without you and have to rely on Ann. Call me a ninny if you wish, but that's how I feel. I want you to deliver this baby when the time comes."

Eden looked at Lucy's tearstained face and knew what must be done. She would never leave Lucy's side while she was with child. Not only would Isaac never forgive her, she would not be able to forgive herself. She had delivered plenty of babies before. War or no war, she would do it again.

"I won't leave you. I promise." She rubbed Lucy's back. "Um, does your cousin know?"

Lucy tilted her head and stared off. "Well, we never discussed it, of course, but the day I'd been feeling ill at Pizzinni's, a look came over his face. Right then and there, I thought he might suspect. He had a look in his eyes — like he looked right through me, and no sooner, he offered his home."

Everything was beginning to make sense. The high waist and extra yards of satin and tulle sewn into Lucy's wedding gown; and with her small frame, a little juggling of the ol' corset strings was all that it took to pull off the appearance of a chaste bride. Isaac had been more than anxious to move the three women to the manor when Oak Hill burned, rather than find them a place in the city.

"You know, Rayce had just learned about Oak Hill's demise. Perhaps that had been the deciding factor in his offer. I don't know. It's hard to tell with him. I think he's just happy to be helping us." Wiping the last of her tears, Lucy turned to Eden. "Isn't my cousin wonderful?"

Her heart ached for Lucy. There she sat with swollen, red eyes like cherry tomatoes, a nose as bright as a pickled beet, and a belly that told it all. "Wonderful," she managed. "Just wonderful."

Surprisingly, Lucy had sensed Eden's desire to leave and return to Richmond, if for no other reason than to keep as far away from the annoying major as possible in the event he did return to Hampton Manor. His hospitality would likely come with a hefty price, and she had a good idea just how the brazen major would expect to be paid.

Without a doubt, the man was a handsome devil but also arrogant, conceited, and high-minded. She wouldn't put it past the scandalous lout to be familiar with Lucy's condition. Who knew how many women he had put with child?

He's probably an expert.

Still, no matter how angry Rayce made her, she had to concede she felt drawn to him; drawn in a way she envisioned a man and woman should feel attracted to one another. If he ever did return, she would find the time to speak with him about Lucy's condition, but she would be sure to keep her dignity intact, as well.

Lucy gasped and smiled. "Give me your hand." She snatched Eden's hand and placed it on her belly. "Here. Feel."

Eden felt the gentle movement against her palm. "Why, that's a fine kick."

"This babe wiggles all the time, and I haven't seen a doctor out of humiliation. I was hoping once we were here you could help me. I've had this baby strapped in so tight, now I'm worried, Eden. I want to make sure everything is all right. Can you help me?"

Eden smiled. "Absolutely."

She instructed Lucy to lie on the bed. With both hands, she felt the top of Lucy's belly, making out the size and position of the baby's head and backside. She fetched the stethoscope from the worn, leather, doctor's bag that had once belonged to her father and listened to the baby's heartbeat.

Fast and strong – just as it should be.

After the examination and some personal questions, she gave Lucy strict orders for more rest, a better diet, and to loosen her crushing stays to give the baby ample room to grow. Later today, she would go to the herb garden, pick mint and chamomile, and make a medicinal tea to help with the nausea and instruct Trinidad to bake hard biscuits for Lucy to nibble.

"I can't thank you enough, honey." Lucy patted her belly. "We can't thank you enough."

She stared at her sweet sister-in-law, wanting nothing more than to protect her and bring a healthy baby into this world for her and Isaac.

"Lucy? Eden? Where is everybody?"

Lucy swallowed a gasp.

Eden flinched. "What about Ann — does she know?"

"Land sakes — no!" Lucy said in a strangled voice. "Do you think I'd tell her before you? Do you think she could have kept her mouth closed about this?"

"You're right. I don't know what I was thinking." Eden rushed toward the door. "I'll meet her in the hallway and tell her you're not feeling well, and then you—"

"No...no." Lucy's eyes dulled. "It's only a matter of time before she finds out, anyway. Now's as good a time as any, I suppose."

"Are...are you sure?"

"I'm sure."

Ann knocked on the door. "Lucy. I know you're in there. I hear voices."

Lucy walked behind her dressing screen. "I'm going to freshen my face. Just let her in. Let's get this over with."

Eden cracked the door a sliver. Upon seeing Ann alone, she opened it further, pulled her in, and swiftly shut it behind her.

"Good heavens! You almost crushed my crinoline." Ann smoothed the garment as though it had just escaped the blades of the guillotine. "I've been calling you both; I have so much news."

"Perhaps this can wait a minute—"

"Nonsense," Ann replied with an impish grin. "I just received a note from Richmond. Varina Howell Davis is planning to evacuate the city if the Yankees get any closer. Of course, all polite society is deeply troubled by such traitorous behavior. Richmond is simply abuzz with the news."

Ann removed her riding gloves and looked up, her eyes filled with excitement. She stared at Eden. "What's gotten into you? Did you hear a word I said? The President of the Confederacy's wife is planning to evacuate the city." Ann scanned the room. "Where's Lucy?"

Lucy emerged in her nightdress, her head lowered.

Ann yelped and tossed her riding gloves aside. "Oh, sweet baby Jesus! What is wrong with you?" Her wide eyes scrolled up and down Lucy's rotund figure, her mouth twisting.

Eden rushed to Lucy and put her arm around her waist. "Leave her alone, you simpleton! What do you think is wrong with her?"

Lucy sighed and plopped down on the bed, clearly unable to deal with Ann's interrogation.

Eden's gaze bored into Ann's. "I swear you have the manners of a goat. If you can't be polite then just get out, but keep your mouth shut about this, you hear?" She sat next to Lucy and held her hand.

Ann stuck her chin out and sat on the opposite side of Lucy. Without pause, she positioned her splayed hands on Lucy's belly. "How revolting!" She jerked her hands away as if scorched by a hot oven. "It's as hard as a honeydew."

Eden shot up. "For pity's sake, leave her be!"

"My, my, Eden, aren't we feeling high and mighty today? I want what's best for Lucy, too, you know."

"Leave her alone, Ann. This is a serious matter and Lucy needs my...our help." The best way to keep this out of the Richmond gossip columns would be to include Ann. "She needs our help, mine and yours," she said, the words sticking like glue inside her throat.

Ann smiled and fluttered her lashes. "Me? You need me for this blessed event?"

Eden wanted to slap her silly. The woman could not be counted on for any real help. She learned that firsthand when Ann didn't lift a finger to help her own husband — a dying man. She swallowed the words forming in her mouth. *Blessed event, indeed.*

Lucy cleared her throat and smiled. "Dear, it's lovely you want to help, and I do need you very much. The best thing we can do right now is to keep this a secret, just for now." She bit down on her bottom lip and looked at the floor. "Sometimes things go wrong and—"

"You mustn't say such a thing," Eden interjected.

Lucy whispered, "But, Eden, sometimes..."

"Nothing bad is going to happen to this baby. Right, Ann?"

Ann stared at Lucy as if she belonged in the traveling carnival alongside the two-headed cows. "Oh, yes...yes, of course," she murmured.

Eden sighed. "Ann, are you paying attention?"

"Yes, I'm payin' attention." Ann looked up, her gaze darting between Eden and Lucy. "I was just thinking. If we're to guard this news, how do we keep it from that spooky servant, Trinidad? I swear the woman lurks in every corner of this place."

Eden had to agree. There was definitely something peculiar about Trinidad. But that aside, the secret needed to be kept away from family and friends until Lucy said otherwise. The servants at the manor were a different matter. If Lucy were to receive the proper care and attention, they should be informed of her condition and summon help if required.

Ann scooted closer and lowered her voice. "In fact, just last night during a bout of insomnia, I crept downstairs for a sip of brandy, and there, in the parlor, I happened upon Trinidad with lit candles all around. Her hair hung long and wild. Her feet were completely bare, and she was humming and dancing slowly. Why, I've never seen anything like it in all my days. She didn't even notice me, and I crept back upstairs to my bedroom."

Eden looked at Lucy. "Surely, you know more about her?"

"Really, I don't know much. Unlike Daniel, who's been

here since the day he was born, Trinidad's only been here since Rayce's granddaddy died. All I know is what Rayce mentioned in his letters."

Ann's eyes widened. "Come now, Lucy, think."

Lucy tapped her chin. "There once was some talk…Wait. I think I remember something."

Ann squirmed. "Do tell!"

"Yes, I remember now. He once mentioned that while traveling on family business he brought back a servant from the West Indies, Barbados, I believe. Yes, that's right. About two years ago, right after his Granddaddy Hampton died before the war."

Lucy held a hand to her mouth, stifling a giggle. "Oh, yes, I do remember. Because she was attractive and not much older than Rayce, it caused a bit of a scandal. Yes, it must have been Trinidad."

Eden's stomach tightened into a knot. *So that's it. The man's been bedding the help!*

RAYCE rubbed the tight muscles along the base of his neck. It had been a long, exhausting ride. With the poor creature beneath him looking as though he could drop dead at any moment, he slowed the horse to a slow trot and scanned the area for a nearby creek. He never rode a horse this damn hard, but the closer he got to the manor, the more he longed for a good night of sleep in his own bed.

For weeks he'd been trudging in and out of enemy camps, planting the false maps and inaccurate numbers with little sleep in between. Riding in the rain and mud, knocking back wretched coffee and hardtack; all while dodging minie balls and nobody to trust along the way. Hell, it was enough to drive any man mad.

He closed his eyes and listened to the sound of the horse's steady trot, threatening to lull him to sleep. He saw an image of himself walking into a Yankee camp in his Confederate uniform instead of the Union garb. If such a thing were to happen, it would be a death sentence for sure. They don't think twice about hanging a man for that.

He snapped his eyes open and shook his head, forcing the disturbing vision from his brain. Maybe the general was right when he called him hardheaded and gave the direct order. He remembered Jeb's words and how they bothered him.

"Look, Rayce," he'd said, "you haven't had an ounce of sleep in over a week. Take a few days' break while you're within a few miles of Hampton Manor. I order you to go spend some time with your family."

What the devil have I gotten myself into? Now I'm a family man?

He'd been a loner far too long for that kind of crazy thinking. Sure, he's helping out some stranded women, letting them stay in his home for a spell, but that's all.

The day grew dark. He dismounted the horse and took a good look at the pathetic, sway-backed creature. Too bad his own horse was shot out from under him two days earlier, and he had to find a quick replacement to complete the mission on time. Now, the old, stubborn animal he had to steal from the Yankee Army wasn't worth the trouble any longer.

He searched the horizon for military movement. As soon as he reached the open marshy tidelands, he could release the poor beast and go by foot the rest of the way.

He thought back to the beginning of the war with Mexico,

when he had first met the young West Pointer, a Second Lieutenant named George McClellan. Back then, both men fought on the same side. While McClellan spent his time working his way up the ranks of the military, Rayce had been busy undercover, acquiring the skills necessary for the dangerous scouting and reconnaissance missions the military required. The best lessons came later in Texas with the Mounted Rifles, where he and Jeb Stuart became friends, and again on the western frontier. There, in the wilds of the West, he learned the techniques of the Comanche and Apache warriors, to enter and exit enemy camps undetected. Of course, back then he had no idea the entire country would be ripped in half years later, each nation fighting and killing one another. Hell, if he had known this would happen, perhaps he wouldn't have followed those years messing about in New Orleans, gambling, drinking, and womanizing.

He smiled. Well, maybe he wouldn't have gambled and drunk so much.

With any luck, the long hours were paying off, and the numbers he'd planted for Pinkerton's men were being relayed quickly to General McClellan who had always been a meticulous planner and overestimated situations. He hoped to God he had the man pegged enough to know, if McClellan felt completely outnumbered, he would not press forward for a final siege on Richmond.

The sickening possibility of defeat had been gnawing away inside him ever since he heard the Confederates would be evacuating forces at Yorktown. McClellan would be closer to Richmond and at the very heels of Hampton Manor, as well. He wondered if Southerners really knew how close the Yanks were to seizing control of the Rebel capital. How close they all were to losing the Cause they were fighting and dying for every day. For the South to survive it was imperative the Yankee general hold off his advancement; otherwise, the war could be over in a matter of days.

Briefly, he had thought perhaps Lucy, Eden, and Ann would have been better off if he'd left well enough alone and they had stayed at Aunt Martha's, but talked circulated at the last meeting that put the thought to rest. Rather than give in to Yankee bombardment and invasion, the Confederate government was considering the dreadful possibility of having to burn Richmond to the ground themselves.

He slowly shook his head and sighed. God, how Richmond had changed. The once elegant city with her simple graces no longer existed. Widespread extortion, food scarcity, displaced refuges swelling the population to twice its size, the sorrowful trains bringing in the dead and wounded. Now it resembles a place of horrors where thieves and murderers walk the same streets with the rest of the residents.

He guided the reins through the dark, dense woods. In an attempt to forget how cold and wet his feet were, he thought about the good night's rest awaiting him at home while he waited for further instructions. He cleared the woods, slogging through the moonlit open marsh, his narrowed gaze scoping the region for any Union advancement.

"They haven't made it up this far yet," he muttered. "Good luck, ol' boy." He tucked the worn leather reins into the saddle. With a firm smack to the beast's hindquarter, he set the horse free. "Yah!"

He wiggled his numb toes against the inside of his boots.

The image of his warm bed, rather than what he had been forced to doze under lately, looked better with every mile he hiked. The very idea of Hampton Manor lying within a combat zone if the Yanks advanced, felt like a huge pit wedged in his gut. Hell, then again, with all those damned women housed together under one roof, who knew what he could be walking into?

Chapter 8

The fragrant magnolia bathwater had cooled. While it was earlier than her usual time to retire, Eden was more than ready for bed after the long day. Her arms felt heavy and weighted as she slowly eased herself from the tub and reached for the plush towel.

The large hearth held a warm fire, but the sudden rush of air cooled her damp skin. She slid on a satin chemise and pulled the tortoiseshell pins from her hair, combing the small tangles with her fingers. Welcoming sleep, she slipped between the smooth bed sheets and pulled the quilt high, tucking it beneath her chin.

Just as she felt herself drifting to sleep, she heard heavy footsteps on the front portico, just below her windows, followed by a swift slam of the front door. The footsteps advanced with determination, their movement barely stifled by the thick oriental carpets leading into the parlor.

She knew that walk. Rayce was home.

Weeks had passed since she had last seen him. With each day, the respite had lulled her into assuming she would not have to face running into him again. Despite the hot bath, an icy chill worked its way along the base of her spine.

The swift movement of footsteps stopped abruptly; replaced with exaggerated, muted words. She sat up like shot, tossing the covers aside, and listened.

More hushed tones.

She tiptoed to the bedroom door and pressed her ear against the thick wood.

Heavy boots. Pacing. Hushed whispers. More pacing. Did she hear crying?

She quickly slipped into her satin wrap and clutched it shut. The moment she nudged open the bedroom door, the voices became clearer. As she expected, the deep voice belonged to Rayce. The other soft, muted voice was harder to make out, but clearly female.

"No, Rayce, you mustn't. I beg of you," the woman pleaded, "I need you."

She inched open the door and tiptoed down the dark hallway. With each measured step, the tiny bones in her feet crackled like the snapping of small twigs on a frosty day. She inhaled short breaths, her fingertips brushing against the wood paneled wall, guiding her, until she reached the top of the staircase.

"How can you ask that?" Rayce questioned. "My God, woman, you know how much I care for you, but do not ask this of me."

The woman emitted a deeply pained sigh. "You know I cannot help it," she whimpered. "You of all people know I cannot help how I feel."

A slow thunder pounded inside her chest. With catlike

precision, she slithered down the wide steps, her heart beating like a heavy drum inside her ears with each careful step. With any luck, she would steal a peek around the corner and witness the confrontation.

As she neared the bottom step, the stairway suddenly groaned, echoing off the polished wood. The voices paused in mid-conversation, and a charge of panic swept through her, freezing her in her tracks. Her heart stopped for a moment, only to resume with a giant thud against her chest.

Common sense told her to get out of there; to flee as fast as she could up the steps and seal herself in her room — feign sleep if need be, but instinct led her to stay frozen in step.

Moments later, the voices resumed, and she breathed a shallow sigh as she tiptoed down the last remaining step.

"Please, listen to me," the woman pleaded. "You know I love you, yes?"

A heavy sigh. "Of course, dear," he replied. "But you don't understand."

Dear?

She slid her hands along the smooth wood molding keeping her balanced and slowly inched her way toward the entrance of the softly lit parlor. With trembling fingers, she gathered her long hair and craned her neck. Just then, a body came scurrying around the corner, careening right into her, practically knocking her off balance.

"Oh, Miss Blair! I..." Trinidad's moist, brown eyes widened. "Pardon, please."

The servant ran away and looked back, her long corkscrew curls flowing wildly as she offered Rayce an apologetic glance before fleeing to the back of the house.

Eden stood at the parlor entry in stunned silence, her hands falling limply to her sides, as she watched Trinidad's hasty exit. She turned to face Rayce dead-on, undaunted by his bold appraisal of her skimpy pink and white chemise, the hemline brushing the top of her thighs.

She knew she should quickly tie the wrap and cover herself, but after overhearing him with his beautiful, exotic servant only moments earlier, she chose otherwise.

Not just yet.

Rayce's dark eyes narrowed, his gaze honing in on her breasts pressed against the thin fabric, before settling at the lowermost part of her chemise teasing the tops of her legs. He slowly moistened his full bottom lip with the tip of his tongue. When he raised his glass for a drink and peered at her above the rim, only then did she pull the ends of the thin wrap together.

Silence.

He walked behind the divan to the scrolled walnut sideboard. "I take it you missed me?"

He turned his back to her. She watched as he pulled the crystal wedge from the brandy decanter and tossed it on the tabletop. He poured a drink and swirled the brandy in his glass. He took an ample swallow, paused, and then downed the glass of amber liquid.

The air instantly cooled. She hugged her arms across her chest, summoning up the courage to speak with him.

He raked a hand through his hair. "Drink?"

She took a step forward. "Um...yes, I prefer brandy," she lied, having never imbibed the liquor.

He turned and faced her. The lines on his bronzed face

looked more pronounced, deeper, his expression unreadable. Caked mud covered his boots like hardened glue, and pine needles hung out of the buttonholes and pockets of his coat. He gestured with a flick of his finger for her to have a seat and handed her a glass of the opaque liquid before turning away.

"Thank you," she responded, trying her best to sound undisturbed by the intimate encounter with his lovely servant moments earlier.

Rayce had been trying to explain something — something important — and Trinidad was pleading, weeping, and declaring her love for him. If she continued thinking about it, she would never find the nerve to speak with him about Lucy. For now, she would tuck away the troubling mental images flooding her mind.

"Major, we need to discuss some—"

"It's still 'Major,' is it?" He poured himself another glass before forcing the wedge into the decanter. "Well, Miss Blair." He poured the liquid down his throat. "You'll just have to wait. I'm much more interested in a hot bath at the moment." He walked out of the room without so much as a glance in her direction.

She stuck her chin out and stood up, hastily securing the silky wrap ties in a tight knot. All this time she had worried about running into him again, and other than admiring her skimpy clothing, he could not have cared less she was there.

She gulped her remaining glass of brandy and coughed. The liquid felt hot as it ran down her throat. She strolled to the sideboard and poured another one — a larger one — and plopped down on the divan. No, she didn't feel much like talking to him, either.

The first brandy had gone right to her belly making her warm. The second went straight to her head, causing her to feel deliciously drunk and tipsy. She sauntered back to her room, crystal glass in hand, whistling what she thought was a dandy rendition of *Dixie.*

She returned to the comfort of her bed, but regardless of her best efforts to get comfortable, sleep eluded her. She tossed and turned and fluffed at the pillows. Finally, with a loud sigh of exasperation, she reached across to the bedside table and lit the candles.

Flopping back against the pillows, she watched as the small flames danced across the walls and ceiling. The warm brandy flowed through her veins with each beat of her heart, pulsing in her neck, her face, her chest. The smooth satin sheets felt like cool liquid gliding against her bare legs. She kicked the covers off. *Even better.*

She lay there for what seemed an eternity, and each time she glanced at the mantle clock, only minutes had ticked by. The firelight leaped and licked at the walls, dancing in the eyes of Captain Reginald Hampton, who appeared to be enjoying her fall from refined grace to uncivilized drunkenness. She giggled and stuck out her tongue. "Oh, you wicked man."

The sound of heavy footsteps marching down the hallway suddenly paused at her door, followed by an abrupt knock. Before she had time to answer, the door swung open.

"I saw light under your door. Good. You're awake. So, what did you want to talk about?"

"Rayce! You can't just enter my room...unannounced!"

Like a woman gone mad, she wiggled and squirmed, seeking swift refuge under the blankets from his prying eyes;

but her big toe had managed to get tangled in the lace coverlet.

Too late. He swiftly moved to her bedside, flashing the audacious smile she had come to despise.

He reached down and clutched her ankle. "Allow me."

"Don't!" She pulled away too quickly, ripping the lace.

"Good Lord, woman, sit still."

"Don't touch me — don't ever touch me!"

"Hush." He remained calm, gently pulling the coverlet from her toe and tucking her leg under the blanket. "I'll have you know this blanket is a family heirloom."

She yanked the covers so high only her head stuck out. "I don't care."

His eyebrows arched. "Is that so?" He pulled the bedside chair closer to her bed and sat down.

Eden's jaw dropped. "What do you think you're doing?" she choked out. "Get out of that chair and out of my room!"

"You said you wanted to talk. I'll be leaving soon enough so..." He plopped his bare feet on her bed, crossed his long legs at the ankles, and continued. "...let's talk."

"Oh, for pity's sake — now?" Her eyes wandered over him. He was a handsome brute even if he had the manners of a skunk.

"Yes, now's good."

Her gaze paused at the damp, dark hair sneaking out of his dressing gown above his chest. He laughed quietly, and she realized his eyes had followed her own.

She cleared her throat. "I said to get out, and if you won't leave, well—"

"Well, what, my dear?"

"Well, I'll jus' have to make you leave," she slurred.

He smiled. "I don't think you'll do that. You obviously need to talk with me very badly, or you wouldn't have come to me dressed in—"

"I did no such thing! I didn't know you were home, I...I just couldn't get to sleep, that's all."

His eyes narrowed. "Not only did you know I was home, you heard me talking with someone — a female someone, to be exact — and you couldn't keep yourself away, isn't that right?"

With a snap of her wrist, she waved his question away. "That's silly and certainly not true."

"Don't fret, Sweetness. You know I won't hold it against you."

"Oh, hush up!" She forced herself not to smile at his incredulousness.

"So, what shall we talk about, Eden? Or..." He winked. "Or do you have something else in mind?"

"Of course I don't, you conceited fool." Her words reverberated in her head, causing her to wince. She closed her eyes, placed her index fingers to each temple, and rubbed gently. The brandy made her dizzy, slowing her ability to keep her composure.

He lit a cigar with the bedside candle. "We have all night, you know."

The man was relentless. If he would leave her alone for a moment, surely her head would clear. "That's enough. I said get out and if you won't, well, I'll..." She looked around her room and saw Beau sleeping at the foot of her bed.

"You'll what? Sic your big ol' dog on me?" He put his arms behind his head, the thin cigar hanging lazily out of the corner of his mouth.

His movement caused the slippery fabric of his dressing gown to slide off to the side, exposing a muscular, dark-haired thigh. She swallowed hard when she realized the parting of the fabric went so high the man simply could not have been wearing any drawers.

Had it not been for the brandy, she would have immediately started for the door. Instead, her gaze slowly followed the length of his long leg. She dared not look too closely for fear the large bulge threatening the opening of his dressing gown might escape from the flimsy fabric if she dared tempt it. Her breath hitched, and she quickly looked away.

He smiled, the smoldering cigar hanging between those straight, white teeth of his. "You like what you see?"

"Oh, that's it!" she snarled. "You have the manners of a goat. No, worse than goat — a pig. No. Worse than a pig, a—"

"So hostile you are tonight, my dear. I catch your meaning but—" he paused, plucked the cigar from his mouth and extinguished it. "I must confess, I have been called worse." He flashed a phony pout.

"You're impossible." She folded her arms across her chest and heaved a sigh.

"Come now. What's the matter, Eden?"

"Haven't you left yet?" She loosened an imaginary knot in her hair, causing the coverlet to slip southward.

"That's a lovely nightdress you're wearing."

She glared at him, stiffened her back, and firmly yanked the blanket up to her neck. "I think you should go."

"No, you don't."

She rolled her eyes and sighed extravagantly. "Yes, I do. I really don't want to get nasty about this, but you leave me no choice."

"Be as nasty as you wish." He crinkled his nose and smiled. "I rather prefer nasty — the nastier the better."

She gasped. "I don't even want to talk to you anymore. Forget I mentioned it."

"I didn't think you had talking on your mind, anyway."

"I'm sick to death of your disgusting innuendoes. What's it going to take to get you out of my room?"

He smiled and eased himself from the chair. With his hands clasped behind his back, he slowly paced her room. "Hmm, just what would it take, you ask?" He furrowed his brow. "Let's see..."

The tone of his voice made her pulse quicken. She watched as he rubbed his chiseled chin, his shadowy eyes appraising her covered body in the bed as he walked to the door and closed it. The muscles tightened in his jaw, his arms, his calves. Had tonight been the first time they met, she would have bet the devil himself resided within his dark eyes.

"What would it take, you ask?" He repeated and slowly walked to her bedside and glanced at the empty brandy glass she had placed on the table.

He turned to face her with a smoldering gaze that squeezed the air from her chest.

He lowered his chin, his eyes boring into hers. "Show me some skin."

"What?" Her voice cracked. "Show you some...what?"

"You heard me. Show me some of that charming ivory skin of yours."

Eden laughed louder than she had expected. "Oh, my goodness, you rat. You can't be serious." She waved him away.

His expression revealed no emotion, but his gaze hinted of amusement. She watched the candlelight flicker against his bronzed skin, softening the small lines etched around his eyes. He raised an eyebrow and thrust his hands into his pockets, his tall, threatening presence looming over her.

She turned away from his piercing stare. "You can't be serious. Oh, for pity's sake, I've had enough of your games."

Clearly, he was enjoying her predicament far too much. It would be up to her to change the rules of the game.

"Well, if you won't leave, then I will." She held her chin high and pointed at a hook on the wall near the door. "At least be a gentleman and hand me my wrap."

"No deal. You want the wrap, you get it yourself, and we'll call it even." He flopped into the chair and folded his hands behind his head. "I'm really quite comfortable right now."

The man was arrogant, conceited and the most pompous lout on the face of the Earth. Oh, how she wanted to slap the smirk from on his face and leave the red imprint of her hand on his cheek as a reminder. She'd happily do it if she thought she could get away with it.

As though he read her thoughts, he smiled and laughed quietly, his teeth gleaming like polished ivory piano keys under his trimmed mustache.

That's it!

She no longer cared what it would take to get the lewd rogue out of her bedroom. All at once, she tossed the covers aside and bolted from the bed. Her feet had barely hit the floor when the sudden movement caused her head to spin. She began scrambling like a mad woman for her wrap, her feet and hands flailing in a flurry of naked limbs. For a few split seconds, there was a feeling of nothingness, a sense of flying and then...

She knew she must have fallen. Her head spun with the spicy scents of masculine soap and cigars, and a silence so still and quiet filled the large room. Just as her eyes cleared, the hushed calm was replaced with a deep roar of laughter.

Shaking with astonished horror, she realized she had slammed right into the chair, knocking Rayce over. Now she lay sprawled on top of him.

Oh, my heavens...this can't be happening!

"My, my, Sweetness. If you wanted me on my back, why didn't you just say so?" He winked and lightly trailed a finger down the length of her spine.

"Why, you ill-bred rat. How dare you grab at me and make me lose my balance!"

"Sorry to inform you of this, but it is you, not I, responsible for our...how should I phrase this? Our mid-air grapplings."

She squirmed. "You swine! I didn't plan this — Let go of me!" She formed her hands into tight balls and beat wildly on his shoulders. "Get out, I tell you. I detest you!"

His jaw pulsed, and the shade of his eyes darkened to black. "Stop it, Eden. Do you hear me? Stop it now!"

In a flash, he seized her flailing wrists, grabbing them hard, and she let out a small cry. He spun her around so she lay beneath him, her hair falling in long tangles against the oriental carpet. The thin lace straps of her chemise fell below her shoulders, dangling precariously from her upper arms. Instantly, she felt something hard press against her thigh.

His gazed burned into her like a smoldering fire. "What is it you really wanted from me tonight?"

The brandy dulled her reflexes. She inhaled deeply, trying to steady the beat of her pounding heart. "I told you already, I needed to talk to you, but that's all."

His masculine scent stimulated her senses, and the feel of his hot, brandied words warmed her throat. Dizzy excitement flowed through her veins, racing across her chest, throbbing against the pulse in her seized wrists. The room was silent except for their jagged breaths.

She thought a delicate kiss whispered against her throat. She turned toward the wall, arching her neck to keep his lips from her bare neck. Reflections of dancing candle flames consumed the room, thrusting their shadows against the wood paneling, his body above hers, dark and menacing.

She squirmed beneath him. "Get off of me!"

Undaunted, he moaned and kissed her throat. For a moment, his lips abandoned her neck, and then ...

Heaven help me!

The tip of his tongue slid leisurely down her shoulder, his coarse mustache grazing her, feeling like liquid fire against her skin. She tugged on her wrists, but he held them firmly in place.

Through half-closed lids, he gazed into her eyes before clutching the thin strap of her chemise with his teeth. He slowly pulled down on the satiny fabric until the strap draped between the delicate fold of her elbow, exposing her breast so that only the tip of her taut peak lay beneath the sheer material.

She squeezed her eyes shut as exhilarated panic swept through her body.

He blazed a path of warm, gentle kisses from her bare shoulder to her neck and back down again until he reached the lowered neckline of her chemise. His breath taunted the tip of her nipple through the sheer garment, his mustache tickling her skin.

Desire rushed through her, and her fists unfolded as though they had a life of their own. He released his grip and gently rubbed her palms, smoothing out the tension, then laced his strong fingers with hers.

"Good Lord, woman, I do so desire you," he whispered against her breast.

His words beckoned, summoning her to a place hidden from the rest of the world. She arched into him, her body conforming to his, the tip of her nipple a mere whisper from entering his mouth.

The image of him alone in the parlor with Trinidad pierced her mind. She knew she should wish this scoundrel away and never set eyes upon him again. Instead, she reached up and wrapped her arms around his neck, clutching a thick strand of his dark hair. She looked deeply into his eyes, parted her lips, and pulled his mouth down upon her own.

A welcoming groan of pleasure escaped his lips. He pulled her closer, his bare legs tangling with hers.

Their tongues danced, and her head swam in a seductive sea of passion. Her body trembled against his, her breasts aching with fullness, and she felt a longing in her most private of areas.

She ran her hands through his hair, encircled his broad back with her arms, relishing the feel of the tangled mass of damp hair on his wide chest caressing her skin.

His breath quickened against her neck, and his manhood pushed firmly against her hip. A swell of desire rose from the depths of her plush center. She rolled her hips, slowly, pressing herself against the bulge straining the fabric of his dressing gown.

He moved his hips with her rhythm, and a small groan escaped his lips, quivering against her throat. His hands roamed urgently across her nightdress, tugging it lower until both her breasts were fully exposed, absorbing the candle's reflections.

"My God, Eden, he whispered." He trapped a firm peak between his lips, slowly encircling it with his tongue.

A jolt of heat rushed across her breasts. She gasped and raked her hands through his hair. "Rayce," she whispered."

He gripped her buttocks and pulled her hard against his manhood.

Heat radiated from somewhere deep inside. She grew warmer, wetter, the yearning so intense it almost hurt. Her nipples trembled against his tongue, her skin so hot it felt seared by his hands. She trailed her fingernails down his back, willing herself not to slice him open, while her entire body silently screamed for release from the exquisite torture. "Oh, Rayce," she groaned.

He dug his fingertips into her bottom. She gasped as the wild current swelled, an ache rising from deep within her core. "Oh, my, she breathed.

Just as his hand moved lower, his fingers maneuvering south within an inch of her warm desire, her body peaked and trembled, her womanhood pulsating with exquisitely warm, rhythmic waves. Heat streamed from deep within with each powerful surge, and she writhed against him with her silky warmth.

"Save me — Rayce!"

Rayce breathed in the delicate scent of sweet magnolia between her breasts and felt the hurried beat of her pounding pulse. His heart hammered so hard he thought it would leap right out of his chest. Every inch of his body yearned for hers. His body quivered, his mind went numb, and all he could feel was the supple skin beneath his body, the soft yielding flesh in his hands and mouth. Her vitality, her passion, her body; everything about her was beyond his wildest dreams. So smooth was her flesh, how fragrant her hair and her breasts. Christ almighty, was she aware how much she aroused him? He licked her breasts, sucked her sweet nipples, and gripped her bottom as her soft thighs moved against his throbbing shaft.

He was in his own world of ecstasy, imagining what his own physical release could be like, when he suddenly felt her quivering beneath him saying, "Save me."

He froze. *What the devil is she babbling about?*

She buried her face in his shoulder, her fingertips digging into his skin like small knives sinking in his back.

"Oh, Rayce," she moaned.

It dawned on him just how far his idea of fun had gone. Yes, he planned to enjoy her company in the bedroom this evening — just a little daisy dollop perhaps, but he hadn't planned on it going this far. Even though he would never readily admit it to her, he did consider her a lady and not one of his doxies, for God's sake. And here she was, squirming in carnal pleasure, asking to be saved. Hell, he never even touched her most intimate spot!

She wiggled and moaned against him, and all he could do was hold her.

Torture. There was no other word to describe it. He could

feel the wet heat of her ecstasy warming his thigh, and it was pure agony not to relieve himself of his own desire.

Several long minutes passed in silence with her curled up against him, her slender legs tangled with his. Her long golden mane fanned out like spun silk across his chest, and her head fit perfectly in the crook of his shoulder.

He slowly shook his head and sighed. The night had gone nothing like he had imagined.

What she was thinking. Was she quietly seething in fury? She does have a wicked temper. Maybe she's in tears, weeping silently in frustration. Perhaps she's humiliated; she had asked him to leave, after all.

"Eden?"

No reply.

"Um...Eden?"

Nothing.

"Look, Sweetness—" He reached down and tilted her chin up. Her head flopped back. "What the devil?"

By God, the woman's not only fast asleep, she's snoring!

Chapter 9

Eden woke to the quiet darkness of night with her head still buzzing from the brandy. Ever so slowly, she began to rise but was stopped short by something warm and heavy draped across her waist, followed by a snore. Her eyes flew open wide.

Oh, no!...no, no, NO!

She slammed her eyes shut and covered them with her hands, as hazy images of heated kisses and bare skin, tangled in intimate pleasure, flashed through her mind. Somehow, she had gone from despising the lout one moment, to squirming in passion in his arms the next.

Had she really had that much to drink? While she remembered enjoying the two glasses of brandy, she had absolutely no recollection of moving from the carpet to her bed, but everything else was becoming disturbingly clear.

She turned toward the gentle ticking of the clock above the hearth. With the exception of the glowing embers of the dying fire reflecting off the cream tiled floor, the room looked pitch black. She breathed a sigh of relief. The very idea of facing those dark, leering eyes, glowing with amused pleasure at his recent conquest, made her stomach turn. Still, she could not ignore the heavy arm on top of her...

"Major?"

Nothing.

"Um ...Rayce?"

"Mmm-hmm."

"You can't be here. Wake up, for pity's sake — everyone will talk!" She lifted his arm from her waist and sat up, recoiling to the headboard and tugging the coverlet to her chest.

"Let 'em talk," he said quietly.

She jiggled his pillow. "Rayce...Rayce you have to leave — now. Ann would never let me live this down. You do know she has eyes for you, right?" She heard his muffled laugh against the bedding.

"Oh, I remember all too well. The woman's like a feline on the prowl...in a dress."

Eden rolled her eyes, remembering the scene at Mr. Johnson's shop. She heard fumbling fingers sliding across her bedside table. After one gritty strike of the match, the tallow candle lit the room with a soft glimmer. Her eyes narrowed, adjusting to the light, and she quickly took the moment to assess herself. Fortunately, she had managed to keep her chemise on throughout the night. She took notice of Rayce's silky dressing gown draped across the chair.

An unexpected gasp escaped her lips, and she quickly turned toward the wall. "Oh, my Lord, you're completely nude right now, aren't you?"

He laughed softly and slid his hand along the top of the coverlet. He clutched her ankle and squeezed. "Trust me, my dear. If I had my way, you'd be stark naked right now, too."

A sudden flush warmed her body with the thought of him unclothed below the blankets next to her. She wiggled her foot, freeing her ankle from his grasp, and sighed dramatically. "You're impossible."

Rayce yawned and slowly sat up. Damn, he must have been more exhausted than he thought. He hadn't intended on spending the entire night in her bedroom. He trusted the servants, but they loved idle gossip as much as the next person.

He turned toward the window. Good. Still dark outside, but the sun would be coming up soon. Best he leave prior to the light of day before her reputation was shattered to pieces. Christ. He would never hear the end of that.

He rubbed the sleep from his eyes and looked at Eden — really looked at her. Her hair hung in a wild mane of pure seduction, and yet she looked so sweet and innocent. Flickers of candlelight danced in her green eyes with the soft laziness of blinking fireflies. The lovely idea of ravishing her rushed through his mind, and he grew hard again. Although tempting, perhaps it would be best to keep the conversation short and sweet and get the hell out.

He rose to leave, and she seized his arm.

Too late. He sat back down.

"Rayce, I almost forgot. I need to speak to you about something. Can we talk a moment?"

"Of course." He turned to face her. "What's on your mind?"

She winced. "It's Lucy."

"What? Is she all right? Is the baby...?"

Eden frowned. "You know about the baby? How?"

"It's not so hard to figure these things out, my dear." He sat up straight. "Tell me, is she all right?"

"Well, yes, she's fine." Eden fidgeted with her fingers and met his gaze. "It's just that she needs some extra care and...well, I need your help."

He inched in closer and brushed her bare shoulder with his mustache. "You don't say."

She jerked away. "Oh, stop it. You're relentless." She picked up the brush from the bedside and combed out the tangles in her hair. She paused. "Did you know she's about seven months with child?"

He yawned and stretched. "No. I had no idea she was so far along."

"Well, she is, and I've given her strict orders for extra rest and a better diet, and I want the servants to cater to her. I thought it best if you told them rather than me. And when the time comes, I'll deliver her baby."

His jaw dropped. "You?"

"Yes, me, she scoffed, "She's asked me to."

"But, have you done...*that* before?"

"Yes, of course. I thought Lucy would have mentioned it. My father had been a respected, skilled physician. He taught me everything I know. I'm a trained nurse and midwife."

"Well, well," he said, smiling. "I must say, I'm impressed." He fingered a tangled strand of her hair. "I'm quickly learning you are a woman full of surprises, Eden Blair."

"I'm glad you think so, because I took it upon myself and assembled a medical care area in one of your outbuildings."

He felt the blood slowly drain from his face. "You did what?"

"I said, I've assembled a med—"

"I know what you said." His jaw tightened. "What I mean is why would you—"

"My heavens! Don't be sour, Rayce." She stiffened her back and glared at him.

"I'm not sour. I'm just concerned." He wedged his hands through his hair and sighed.

"Given my training, I thought it would be wise. Before I found out about Lucy, I had considered going back to Richmond to nurse our wounded there."

He frowned. "Listen to me, Eden. You're not going anywhere, you hear me? It's too damn dangerous right now."

"I'm not. I'm trying to tell you I was planning to go, but I wouldn't think of it now with Lucy carrying this child and the war so close."

He sucked in his bottom lip, contemplating his next words. "This war's heating up. I can't go into details, but it's likely to get even harder — closer. You're just going to have to trust me. We're evacuating Yorktown, which means—"

"Evacuating!"

The last thing he wanted to do was frighten her. Judging by the terrified look in her eyes, it appeared he had done just that. But, if she were to stay safe, Eden had to have a good sense of what could happen.

"Yes, we're evacuating. Which means the Yanks will be on our heels, heading north up the Peninsula soon."

"The Yanks are coming here?" She yanked the coverlet up so only her head poked out. "They're coming here — to Hampton Manor?"

"Lord, I hope not right here, but certainly within a few

miles is likely as they push for Richmond. I don't want word getting out there's any kind of hospital or infirmary on these grounds. You'd be inviting anyone, from either army, to set up camp here, and we don't want that, understand?"

"But—?"

"No buts, Eden." He shook his head.

What the hell was she thinking?

He inhaled jagged breaths, trying to keep calm. He'd already frightened her enough. "Listen to me." He yanked the brush from her hands and set it on the bedside table. "I think it's fine you've prepared an area for medical care. Lord knows we may end up needing it, but it must be kept quiet."

"I understand," she said softly, her gaze shifting to the floor. "But I still need your help on another matter."

With a gentle finger, he tilted her chin toward him. "And what matter would that be, my dear?"

"I was also wondering if..."

"Go on," he prompted her.

Her gaze narrowed in on his. "I was wondering if you could speak with Trinidad and ask for her help with Lucy. I need to have an extra hand when the time comes, and Ann would rather die than get involved, trust me."

"I'll speak to her and explain everything."

She tilted her chin defiantly, her eyes deepening in color. "Honestly, Rayce, I don't know why you bother to keep that woman around here with the way she creeps like a ghoul about the house. And I have to say, I don't think she likes me much, either."

"I'll deal with her myself. I know how to handle Trinidad."

Eden swallowed a gasp and turned away. *Oh, I'd bet my*

boots he's an expert at handling ol' Trindad! Rather than give him the satisfaction of witnessing the piercing jealousy puncturing her heart at that moment, she forced herself to look into his eyes and smile.

The gaze meeting hers was not what she had expected. After discussing his beautiful servant, she imagined facing a dark, defiant glare. Instead, a soft, soulful glow radiated from the depths of his velvety eyes.

"Rayce?" she ventured.

He reached for a cheroot and lit it with the bedside candle. "Yes, Sweetness?" He inhaled and blew out a ring of smoke.

She watched as the murky sphere blew toward the Captain's portrait, disappearing into oblivion when it reached his vacant face. "Is there any chance you could find me some quinine and perhaps chloroform and bandages? I don't want to be unprepared for anything coming our way."

He shook his head. "No, no way. I can assure you, getting any of those items in areas I tend to frequent is a lot easier said than done. When the docs manage to have medical supplies in the field, they're carefully guarded."

Knowing just how to tug on his heartstrings, she sighed extravagantly. "Oh, how I wish I had chloroform. After all, poor little Lucy may need it when her time comes."

"Do you think so?" He took another puff of the cheroot and exhaled with a long sigh." Look. If I happen upon those items, I'll try, but I really have no idea when I'll be back."

The thought of his leaving and heading back into harm's way troubled her. Nevertheless, he was a soldier — an officer. What did she expect? Like all Southern women these days, she knew she had to put her fears and worries aside.

"Is it true President Davis is planning to evacuate his wife and the children from Richmond? Tell me we aren't giving up."

Rayce winced. "There have been rumors. If the Yanks get closer, he'll send them down to North Carolina." He kissed her shoulder and stood, tossing the cigar into the fireplace. "No, of course we're not giving up. It's all very complicated, my dear."

Eden couldn't help but stare as he stood stark naked, undaunted by her presence, and walked to the chair to retrieve his dressing gown. He had to be the most virile thing she had ever set her eyes upon. His shoulders were broad; his muscled chest full of thick, dark curls tapering down toward his groin, and... Sadly, he put on his dressing gown, leaving her no time to appreciate the rest of his fine physique. She liked what she had seen, but she sure wasn't going to let him know.

He tied the silky wrap and walked haughtily toward her. "Come here, Sweetness."

As if she were as light as a feather, he scooped her up in his arms and kissed her tenderly.

"Goodnight, my pet. I best get out of here." He laid her down on the bed and tucked her in. He raised an eyebrow, saying, "Now get some sleep...you've earned it."

Oh, Lord, tell me he didn't just say that!

She blushed and rolled to her side to watch him go. "Goodnight, Major."

He opened the door, paused, and looked back at her.

She blew out the candle, and like a hushed whisper in the dark, he slipped out of the door without a sound.

THE room was still dark when Eden awoke an hour later.

Through half-closed lids, she saw a fresh log had been placed amid the embers in the fireplace while she had been sleeping. A swirl of smoke rolled up the chimney as the big log caught flame. Early morning rooster called and sounds of melodic birds in nearby trees burst forth with song, beckoning daybreak.

The slam of the heavy front door caught her by surprise. She heard Rayce talking outside, below her windows. Beau, pleased his mistress was fully awake, scampered to her bedside; tail wagging at a lazy half-pace, for it was still the wee hours of the morning, even for him. She reached over and stroked his soft head. "Yes, boy, I'll be with you soon. I promise."

She eased herself from bed and sat at the window seat. Rayce stood below, next to Daniel, who attentively held a lantern. They looked like ghostly spirits with their bodies shrouded in a thick, slow-moving fog.

She thought back to her intimate encounter with Rayce only hours earlier and slipped back into bed, recoiling in flushed embarrassment. She could still see him sitting in his silken dressing gown, the cheroot hanging lazily from his mouth, challenging her from the chair as if it were his throne.

The chair!

How could she forget about the chair for a moment? What kind of idiotic maneuver had she performed to flip them over and onto the floor in her haste to snatch the wrap? She winced, thinking about the outcome her ungainly ambush had produced.

She watched as the fire grew bright, illuminating the portrait above the hearth. "So, Captain, what have I gotten myself into?" His eyes stared blankly back. "Oh, what do you know, anyway?"

The front door opened and shut again, and she bolted up to look outside. She pressed her fingers against the window. The fog had softened to a lighter shade of gray, and Trinidad had joined the men outside.

Trinidad.

Somehow, she had forgotten about the incident with her in the parlor. As she stood watching them outside, a smile replaced her earlier suspicions, as she recalled Rayce's obvious pleasure with her in the bedroom during the night. Surely, her misgivings about him and his lovely servant were unwarranted, for he had been in her bedroom last night, holding her, kissing her, and whispering her name against her throat — not Trinidad's.

Through the gray haze, the morning light dawned over the river. The opaque lace encompassed the dimly lit ships in the distance. She watched as Daniel handed the lantern to Trinidad and walked toward the stables. Trinidad stood barefoot, her dark, curly hair hanging long against her woolen cloak. The lantern illuminated her brown face, and her eyes glistened in the soft light. Eden felt a lump wedge in her throat, for Trinidad appeared consumed with love and devotion as she looked up at Rayce.

Instantly, the air squeezed from her lungs. Her fingers groped for the bedside table for support, as she watched Rayce reach for Trinidad and pull her into his arms. Clutching the lantern with a trembling hand, Trinidad buried her head into his large shoulder. He held her close, smoothing her hair, whispering something in her ear while her shoulders heaved with sobs.

Eden stood frozen, unable to turn away, her shallow

breaths fogging up the pane of glass. How could she have been so stupid? She had allowed herself to be manipulated by the scandalous major — used once again while her guard was down. He probably went straight from her bedroom to Trinidad's to finish what he had started!

"Oh, that snake in the grass," she murmured. She closed her eyes, remembering how her body welcomed his, opened to him, and how at the moment of her release she would have let the man do whatever he pleased. She could never forget how he had taken her away from all the hurt and pain in her life and into a new realm of pleasure. Thinking back on it now, wasn't it she who had been writhing in pleasure on the plush oriental carpet? Perhaps she had used him, too.

Trinidad pulled out of Rayce's arms and rushed toward the portico when Daniel came into view guiding a saddled horse toward Rayce. Instantly, a sense of relief swept through her knowing she would not have to see him today. How could she? Her face would surely give away her feelings of hurt, jealousy, and humiliation.

She dressed quickly, and the moment she opened her bedroom door, the scents of sweet rolls, bacon, and coffee filled her nose. She breathed in the intoxicating blend of aromas before descending the long stairway. With each step, her head throbbed, and she wondered how long she would have to suffer for her brandied sins of the night before.

"Morning Miss," Trinidad mumbled.

Eden replied with a curt nod and sat at the table with her chin held high.

"Well, look who's graced us with her presence, and so early in the morning, I might add." Ann entered the room with a bright smile and took a seat opposite Eden.

Trinidad brought out large plates of food and cups of coffee and quickly left the room.

"What are you doing up so early?" Eden asked.

"Did I hear tell the adorable major has returned?" Ann licked the tip of her finger and pressed a loose ebony bang back in place.

"If he were here, what would you do? Pull him into your bedroom?"

"My heavens. What's gotten into you this morning?"

"Oh, hush." Eden scowled and sank to the back of the chair. "You're out of luck. He's already gone. I saw Daniel readying his horse a little bit ago. Besides, I thought you were courting that widowed gentleman, Mr. Benton, is it?"

Ann scrunched up her nose. "Oh, I am, and he's incredibly rich, of course, but he kisses like a little ol' bullfrog." She sighed and fluttered her lashes. "But he is sweet on me."

"Good morning, ladies." Lucy entered the room appearing fully rested. "I must say, I'm positively famished."

Eden noticed Lucy had taken her advice and loosened the stays on her corset. With the way her poor baby had been strapped in, it wasn't surprising Lucy's appetite had returned.

"Your girl Fifi is just wonderful with the needle, Ann, just like you said. Why, she's busy as a little bee upstairs sewing extra fabric into my dresses as we speak."

Eden glared at Ann. "Her name is Sarah."

Ann stuck out her bottom lip. "But Fifi sounds so exotic and Sarah's just...plain."

Lucy's eyes dulled. "But you know I have a sister named Sarah, and she's anything but plain."

Ann waved her words off. "Well I once had a childhood friend named Sarah, and she was a dreadful bore. But if you must, Lucy, I'm quite sure Fifi will answer to either."

Ann's gaze shifted around the room. "Did either of you hear the noises coming from the third floor last night?"

Lucy's brow knitted together. "No. Not that I recall."

Eden blushed, recalling how she had been rather tipsy and far too occupied to notice. "I didn't hear anything, either."

"Well, I suppose I can't be certain, but I think I heard walking up there. At one point I thought I even heard voices."

The front door opened, and Daniel entered out of breath. "Lawd, all mighty, ladies. Rebs done moved outta Yorktown and heading toward Williamsburg, and some close to the river not far from here. I was down near the fields, and I saw Reb stragglers come by saying we gotta hold 'em off at Williamsburg or they gonna take Richmond for sure. I told the major. He got on his horse and went to check on things even though the general told him to rest. Lawd, Lawd, he just don't listen!"

As if on cue, cannon shells echoed in the distance, and all Eden could think about was the man she opened herself up to was riding straight for it.

GIVEN the uneven number of troops on each side, Rayce knew General Johnston and his Confederates had no choice but to evacuate Yorktown. McClellan and his massive Yankee army would be right on their heels once they figured it out, following them right up toward Williamsburg. He had fulfilled each and every mission, so he knew McClellan was working under the false assumption the "immense numbers of men" and the "impregnable nature of their defenses" outclassed him. The very idea the Rebels would evacuate with such massive numbers would never enter his mind.

He couldn't help but laugh, picturing the dumbfounded look bound to seize McClellan's face when he found out there would be no massive assault at Yorktown like he had meticulously planned. Given he had finally prepared for the battle he had promised President Lincoln, the idea the enemy would dare evacuate would likely hit him as hard as a bodily blow. "Little Mac" would now be forced to improvise, putting his strategic plans for the grand siege as well as his reputation at risk.

Rayce had been riding for hours. Spotting a smooth flowing creek in the dense woods, he stopped to allow the horse a cool drink. The rumble in his stomach reminded him of the sweet rolls and bacon Trinidad packed hours earlier in his haversack.

He crouched on the creek bank, cupped a handful of water, and doused the dust from his face and neck. He sat, stretched out his legs, and rifled through the canvas bag for the food.

Trinidad. He had never seen her act up like this before. When she came to him with tears in her eyes, barefoot, her lovely face begging him not to leave her, it damn near broke his heart. But she of all people knew just how important these missions were. None of her begging and pleading for him to stay could change the fact he had to go.

He shook his head and sighed. A few months ago, he hadn't a care in the world. He was fighting in the war — yes, but he had grown accustomed to such a life, as a man must do these days. Now, he had all these damn women to contend with.

Eden. What to do about her?

He knew what he wanted to do to her; that part was easy. When he was away from her, he could think clearly; knew just what he had to do and how to stay in control. But, when he's with her, damn if that woman didn't have some kind of control over him. And it's not just that body of hers, either; the kind of body a man wants to curl up with every night, he conceded. He wanted all of her, body, mind, and soul, and that could only mean trouble for a man like him.

In the past, many of his women had fine qualities, some more than others. Nevertheless, there was always something missing in the package. God knows, he never understood them and their inclination to rein him into domestic oblivion. They certainly never understood him, either, and it had been like pulling teeth trying to convince any of them his lack of commitment stemmed from bad timing. In part, much of what he had told them had been the truth. He didn't have the time, energy, or the inclination to pursue a long relationship. Now, with the war going on, timing couldn't possibly be worse, and yet, it all felt different with Eden. He thought about her nonstop. The woman was smart and beautiful — pure fire and ice, and the play between the two piqued his interest as no other women ever had. Somehow, she had managed to fill the void — the empty vessel of darkness consuming him for so long, and he had never seen it coming. At times, he could see himself being with her — really being with her. She was the package he'd been waiting for.

He lowered his head.

Bad timing.

A sudden noise rustled in the brush. He wedged the remaining bite of bacon in his mouth and slid like a snake on his belly behind a thick oak tree.

"So, what a we got here? Come here, you big horsy. Come to ol' George," the man said.

Rayce peered around the trunk and saw a Yankee private slowly reaching for the reins of his horse. Without a sound, he scanned the area, noting the private appeared to be alone.

Damn Yank deserter. He pulled his Colt revolver from the holster, cocked it, and aimed.

The man grabbed hold of the leather reins. "That there's a good horse. Good boy," he said in a low, soothing tone.

As fast as a shot, Rayce came from behind the tree and planted the gun at the Yankee's skull. "Hey, you Yankee son of a bitch!"

The wide-eyed Yank flinched. "Where the hell did you come from?"

"Never mind that, you son of a bitch. Give me back my damn horse, or I promise, you're a dead man."

Chapter 10

Ann stormed into the manor and tossed her riding gloves on the entry table. "Eden! Lucy! Where are you?"

Eden slammed her book shut and scrambled up from the divan "My goodness, *hush.* Lucy's sleeping."

Ann turned toward her voice and marched into the parlor, out of breath. "Thank heavens — there you are. I'm just beside myself! "

"For pity's sake. What's all the fuss about?"

"Oh, Eden, Mr. Benton received a letter today, and the news is simply awful."

"All right...All right." Eden guided her breathless stepmother to the divan. "Now, just calm yourself and tell me what's happening."

Ann sniffed into her handkerchief and sank into the divan. "I just knew when President Davis sent his family to North Carolina more bad news would follow. I just knew it."

Eden frowned and sat next to her. "What have you heard?"

"Well, I was out riding with Mr. Benton, and he told me

our wonderful General Johnston had to retreat within three miles of Richmond. They're getting closer. The Yankees are coming Eden, I just know it!"

Three miles. Eden's stomach flip-flopped. Hearing about Yorktown's evacuation earlier had been troubling enough, and Lord knows her heart broke when the Rebels scuttled their beloved ironclad warship, *Virginia*, and ran her aground. But this demoralizing news put everything into perspective, shedding new light on the very real threat to their survival.

She bit on her bottom lip, staring at her stepmother, trying to absorb the news without dissolving into a puddle of tears.

"Oh, Eden. Will said that nasty Yankee general has a huge army. He plans to stay put at Benton Mansion no matter what happens and hold his ground. He said he'll shoot any Yankee that sets foot in his home. But, what about us? What are we going to do?"

Good Lord, the last thing she needed was Ann falling apart. With the way she could carry on hysterically, she'd have the entire household panicked.

She sat up tall and patted her stepmother's hand, affectionately. "Now calm yourself, for heaven's sake. We'll think of something."

A tear dripped down Ann's cheek. She sniffed and gazed into Eden's eyes. "Really? Do you think so?"

"Yes...yes, I promise." Eden stood and guided Ann by the elbow to the entry. "Now you go upstairs and check on Lucy. We'll come up with something when the time comes."

Eden's mind raced in all directions. She had hoped the fighting had settled down since General McClellan's push by sea was no longer a threat. Somehow, his army had managed to continue their pursuit on land and get within a few miles of the Confederate capitol. It was one thing with all the wandering stragglers trespassing on the grounds of Hampton Manor, but to have the massive Yankee army showing up at their doorstep was nothing less than terrifying.

Already, on more nights than she cared to count, deserters and laggards from both armies found their way to the manor under the cover of darkness. All too often, the men would break into the smokehouse or steal a chicken or two from the pens and raid the garden beds, before Daniel or Joseph came out with the shotgun.

Once, during the bright light of midday, while both men were occupied in the fields, a band of Yankees came by and quickly confiscated the cows, pigs, and horses, and if she hadn't run outside with a musket aimed at the captain's groin, they certainly would have taken more. Luckily, there were still some hidden bushels of grains, bacon, and hams in the smokehouse, along with a good supply of root vegetables left in the cellar. With the year's supply of smokehouse meats and chickens dwindling, it was beginning to look like they would soon have to rely on Trinidad's talent for turning just about anything into a hearty meal.

She walked to the front windows and stared blankly outside. *Yes, we'll think of something.*

RAIN had fallen steadily during the past weeks keeping Eden busier than usual. The flooded marshy tidelands had turned small creek beds into toxic swamps. As the humidity climbed with the sizzling Virginia heat, insects, poisonous snakes, and fevers flourished from the stagnant waters. Dysentery, typhoid, and pneumonia were common illnesses along the river, showing little mercy to the young and old.

Once word spread among the field hands, neighbors from nearby farms came in search of her nursing care. The small supply of medical supplies had dwindled to a worrisome level, but Will Benton rummaged through his home and brought her everything he could find. The extra bandages and surgical needles helped with injuries, and the turpentine and quinine aided just about everything else. No chloroform was available, but thanks to the major's interest in spirits, she had a good supply of whiskey and brandy that came in handy as a cough suppressant for the cases of pneumonia she had treated and as a painkiller when Hetty and Daniel's oldest son required his injured knee stitched back together.

Weeks earlier, she had requested Trinidad and Ann stay close to the main house and keep a watchful eye on Lucy, who grew larger and more fatigued each day as her time grew near.

Lucy longed for Isaac and wrote him daily. He managed one short letter in return, and Eden was relieved to learn he and Jimmy were alive, having survived the relentless marching and fighting in the Shenandoah Valley under the resilient General Jackson, with only minor bumps and scrapes.

"Hetty, I need some fresh water. Could you send Daniel down with the pitcher?" Eden asked, having just examined her patient.

"Like I said, Mrs. Lewis, I want you to rest, and I'm going to give you this tonic of herbs, molasses, and vinegar for the cough. The fever should break soon. Also—"

The swift knock at the door caught Eden by surprise.

"Miss Eden!"

Before she could answer, Sarah bolted through the door with brown eyes as round as baby plums, her hands splayed across her chest as she struggled to catch her breath.

"Miss Eden! Mrs. Blair's yellin' at me, she said, 'Fifi, you go and get Miss Eden — now hurry', and Miss Lucy's upstairs hollerin' something about her baby."

"I'll...I'll be right there." Eden's gaze shifted between Mrs. Lewis and Sarah. "Run along and tell them I'm coming."

The servant girl nodded. "Yes'm."

Eden turned back to her patient. "If you have any more trouble, or you're not feeling better within a week, you be sure to call on me again, you hear?"

"Thank you, Miss Blair. I surely will." Mrs. Lewis smiled. "I'll be on my way now. I can see you're mighty busy."

"All right, and you remember what I told you about getting extra rest."

"I certainly will. Goodbye, now."

Daniel assisted Mrs. Lewis to her buggy and driver, while Eden and Hetty headed for the manor.

Ann greeted them at the door and tossed her hands in the air. "Oh, good heavens — there you are. I don't know what's going on with Lucy."

"Has something happened?" Eden hastened past her stepmother to the water bowl and scrubbed her hands with a brush and lard soap.

Ann followed on Eden's heels, chattering like a wet blue jay. "Well, she was in bed, and we were playing cards, like we always do, and I said, 'Lucy, I think you just had some kind of accident because the bed's as wet as a duck's feathered behind.'

And then she said, 'It's too early!' and started yelling at me to go find you."

Eden glanced at Hetty. "Her water must have broken."

Hetty nodded and gave her a linen hand towel.

Eden's pulse quickened, her mind snapping to attention, thinking about the preparation involved in bringing a healthy baby into the world. She turned to Hetty. "Run and fetch a pitcher of fresh water."

Eden dried her hands on the towel, her gaze shifting around the room. She turned to Sarah. "Go fetch a small blanket, clean cloths, and the salve from the outbuilding." She grabbed her stepmother's arm. "Ann, you're coming with me."

"What!" Ann squealed.

Eden snatched her by the dress sleeve and dragged her up the stairs. They entered Lucy's room where Trinidad sat in the bedside chair, her eyes closed, gently stroking Lucy's arm and humming softly. Lucy lay quiet and appeared comforted by the servant's low, mesmerizing voice.

What is it with that woman?

Upon seeing Eden, Lucy snapped back to reality. "Oh, thank heavens you're here — I think something's wrong!"

Eden looked at Trinidad. The servant's composed manner managed to chill the room. "Excuse us, Trinidad. You're dismissed."

The servant lifted her chin and stared directly into Eden's eyes. "If I am dismissed, then I shall prepare dinner." She rose haughtily from the chair. "Let me know if I can be of help."

"What do you suppose is with her?" Ann mumbled.

Eden watched Trinidad exit the room, her gaze narrowing in on the sensual sashay of the woman's willowy hips as she left the room.

"I don't feel the baby moving. I'm so frightened," Lucy whimpered. "Isaac will be heartbroken if the baby's..."

Eden brushed by Ann and knelt at Lucy's bedside. "I'm going to exam you. Now, calm yourself, dear. Let's see what's going on here."

"Oh, must you, now — with me in here?" Ann blurted. "I'm leaving. Holler if you need any—"

"For pity's sake! Stop being a ninny. I may need your help," Eden snapped back. "You stay right there."

Ann sank into the chair, her shoulders wilting against the fabric.

Eden examined Lucy. While it was still a few weeks earlier than expected, Lucy's water had indeed broken.

Lucy held her breath, her fingertips digging into the sheets. "Are you almost done? Is my baby all right?"

A chill traveled the length of Eden's spine. *Oh, Lord...poor Lucy.* This was going to be a problem. "Hang on, Lucy, just a few more moments..."

Lucy squirmed uncomfortably as Eden felt her way around as gently as possible.

An icy chill slithered up Eden's spine. The baby lay in a breech position — a complicated breech position — lying cross-wise, which not only put the life of the baby in peril, but Lucy's life, too.

Hetty and Sarah returned with the supplies and stood silently in the room's shadows.

After finishing the exam, Eden sat on the bed next to Lucy and held her hand.

"I just don't feel anything." Lucy squeezed Eden's hand,

her eyes growing moist. "Why don't I feel my baby? Tell me —
is something wrong?"

Eden turned away from her sister-in-law's pleading eyes.
She needed a full picture of the situation before she told her
the distressing news. "I'm going to listen to the baby's
heartbeat."

She opened her bag and retrieved the stethoscope. While
her hands searched, she fingered around for the other
instruments — the awful tools often needed for a complex,
difficult, and sometimes heartbreaking delivery. *There they are —
the forceps and the hook.* She hoped to God she would not be
forced to use either instrument, but sometimes they were
required.

She had delivered a baby with forceps only twice, and her
mind raced as she tried to recall everything her father had
taught her. For years, she wished she could forget the times she
had watched her father use the horrible iron hook after
stillborn babies died, or during undeliverable breech positions
where the poor mother's life hung by a thread.

The instrument of death.

She pulled out the stethoscope, leaving the forceps and
hook in the bag and out of view from the others.

Not all doctors had stethoscopes and a midwife, almost
never. Thankfully, her father had the latest medical
instruments at the time of his death.

Eden closed her eyes and listened closely. "I hear the
baby's healthy heartbeat." She opened her eyes and looked
directly at Lucy.

Lucy put her hand over her heart. "Oh, thank you, Lord."
Tears slid down her cheeks.

Eden looked evenly into Lucy's eyes. "There's one issue, honey. I don't want to alarm you, but I—"

"Oh, my heavens — what?" Despite her large belly, Lucy scrambled to a sitting position. "What is it?"

There was no way to say it other than to just spit the words out. "The baby's in a difficult position for birth — a very complicated breech position—"

"What the devil is breech?" Ann asked. "Will she and the baby be all right?"

Eden glared at Ann, silently instructing her to shut her mouth.

"I'm frightened," Lucy said in a tiny voice. "What does this mean?"

Eden sighed. "Typically, it means a much longer and more difficult labor. Lucy, we cannot leave the baby positioned the way he or she is right now. The baby would not be able to come out."

Lucy's eyes grew so wide, they looked like they could pop out of her head. She swallowed hard. "What can be done — anything?"

"I need to turn the baby into a better position—"

"Oh, my heavens!" Ann blotted her neck with a handkerchief. "I think I feel a case of the vapors coming on. I need to sit down."

"You *are* sitting down," Eden sneered over her shoulder. She turned back to Lucy and forced a smile. "Honey, we don't have a choice."

Lucy slumped into Eden's arms and cried. "Oh, how I wish Isaac were here. I just can't believe this is happening. I'm paying for my sins, aren't I?" She sniffed and pulled away at arm's length, searching Eden's face. "Please tell me you can do this."

"Yes, we can do this." She smoothed Lucy's hair. "We must do this."

There was no choice. Attempting to let the baby come without intervention would undoubtedly kill them both. Lucy was a slight female with a small pelvis structure. Even if she managed to turn the baby, she worried her sister-in-law might not have the strength and endurance for such a fight.

"I'm going to get you relaxed and then attempt to move the baby into a better position."

Lucy closed her eyes and a tear rolled down her cheek, dripping silently upon the quilt. "I trust you. Do what you must."

"All right, then." Eden scrambled into action. "Hetty, fetch the laudanum and make some raspberry tea. Her pains haven't started yet, and this will help her muscles relax, making it easier when the time comes."

The day had grown hot and muggy, and Eden tossed the curtains aside and opened the windows wide. Trinidad delivered sweet tea, kept chilled in the dark cellar throughout the day, and Hetty and Sarah cooled the women with large peacock feather fans.

Lucy was drifting in and out of sleep. After three long hours, four cups of tea, and a hefty dosage of laudanum, Eden determined the time had come to attempt the tricky procedure and move the baby presenting horizontally into a vertical position. The little hand she had felt at the birth canal earlier would need to be pushed back first.

Eden placed a wet cloth on Lucy's forehead. "It's time,

honey. Are you ready?"

Through half-closed lids, Lucy searched for Eden's hand and squeezed. "We'll do this...together," she whispered.

Doctors often tied a woman's arms down for the risky procedure, but Eden refused to go so far. She retrieved the smooth, rounded wood block from her bag. If she could perform the maneuver swiftly, the biting block, along with as much support as possible, would get Lucy through the torturous pain. God, how she wished she had chloroform!

She bent close to Lucy's face. "I won't lie to you; this is going to hurt." She handed her the wooden bite block. "Use this."

Lucy's eyes paled with resignation as she took hold of the thin block.

Hetty and Ann stood next to Lucy near the headboard. Eden went to the foot of the bed. "You're going to feel my hand now."

Eden moved in slowly, gently, until she reached the tiny hand presenting itself in the birth canal. When she made contact, the baby's little fingers moved. *God give me strength.* "There's going to be more pressure now."

"Use the block now, Mrs. Blair," Hetty insisted.

Lucy did as told, and Hetty and Ann each took one of her hands.

Eden used more force, pushing her way inside, and Lucy cried out. "Bite down hard, Lucy — squeeze their hands — hold tight," she commanded.

She moved the baby's small fist back inside the womb. Once she grasped the little elbow, she moved her fingers higher up to the baby's shoulder.

Lucy arched her back and began huffing and wailing in between biting down on the block of wood. "Oh, Lord!"

Eden glanced at Lucy, who appeared close to passing out. "Hold on tight — almost there." She pushed upward, turning the little shoulder. Slowly, the baby's head began moving up, slipping into a vertical position with the feet nearing the birth canal.

"Eden, look — Lucy!" Ann yelled. "Oh, God in heaven, is she dead?"

Lucy's eyes rolled up in her head, and her body went limp. The block of wood rolled down the side of her cheek, landing quietly on the bed.

"No, but she's passed out from the pain. Hold her hands — I'm almost done."

She had to finish this fast, or she would lose them both.

With Lucy passed out cold, Eden placed one hand above her belly and the other inside. Ever so gently, she maneuvered the baby into a deliverable position. She could do no more without damaging Lucy's delicate tissues, making things worse.

Just as she removed her hand, a stream of amniotic fluid gushed forth, and Lucy woke to a hard contraction. "Oh, Eden...I'm going to die!" she screamed.

Eden swiftly moved around to her bedside and turned Lucy's chin toward her. "You're not going to die — do you hear me? Look at me, Lucy. I won't let you die!"

Ann coughed. "I just don't know why we women have to go through such pain—"

"Ann, hush up!" Eden whispered between pursed lips. She turned back to Lucy.

Another fifteen minutes ticked by and the pains had

clearly gotten worse.

"How much longer?" Lucy asked breathlessly. "I don't know how much vigor I have in me." She smiled weakly and groaned. "Why does this have to hurt so much?"

Eden had always wondered that herself. Why were so many animals able to deliver without so much as a whimper? As a child, she had watched countless animals give birth: pet cats and dogs, horses and pigs and more, and there had always been a clear difference in pain level between a human female and an animal.

She looked into her sweet sister-in-law's eyes and smiled. "I think it's painful so we know how important this moment is for a woman."

Lucy's face suddenly twisted and turned bright red. "I think I need to push. Yes, I definitely need to push."

Eden smiled. "I think it's time, honey. Let me check you first. Try not to push until I say so."

Eden did a quick assessment. Considering the pain, Lucy had handled herself with impressive poise. The baby was coming feet first, but this breech position was nothing compared to the earlier presentation.

"Ayyyyyy!" Lucy yowled.

"You're doing wonderful, honey. Keep squeezing Ann's hand. It helps cut the pain."

"Ha!" Ann squealed. "Cuts whose pain? My lil' ol' hands are bruised."

Ann's comment brought a much-needed smile to Lucy's face. Hetty placed a fresh, cool cloth on Lucy's forehead.

"*Ohhhhh*, here comes another pain...a big one!" Lucy scrunched her eyes shut. "This is a big one — please say I can push — I have to push!"

"You're ready, Lucy. Push away."

Eden, Hetty, and Ann all encouraged Lucy as she yelled and cried in pain. The baby's tiny feet came first, followed by the legs and hips, but the umbilical cord had suddenly become wedged up high.

"I can't!" Lucy thrashed her head against the pillows. I can't..."

Oh, Lord above, NO! Eden reached inside her bag. Just then, Lucy gave a massive push, and within seconds, she had skillfully delivered a healthy baby girl. After cutting the cord, Hetty sponge washed and swaddled the tiny baby and placed her in Lucy's arms.

Eden gazed at Lucy, who looked as beautiful as the Madonna herself, as she lay smiling at her new baby daughter swaddled within her arms. The little girl's blue eyes searched her mother's face and wrapped her perfect tiny hand around Lucy's finger.

"Isaac and I already have names picked out," Lucy whispered, smiling softly. "Please meet little Rebecca Blair."

Eden's chin quivered, her eyes welling with tears. To name the baby after her mother made her heart soar with pride.

Later, with everyone having left the room except for Eden, Lucy snuggled close to her baby and spoke openly. "At night, I close my eyes as tight as I can, and I send good thoughts directly to Isaac's mind. And you know what, Eden? I think sometimes he does that to me, too. I know it must sound silly, but I can feel him thinking of me and the baby right now, and I'm so comforted."

Eden felt a twinge of envy pierce her heart. Lucy and Isaac

had a wonderful connection, everything she had dreamed of for herself, and what she thought she had possessed with Patrick. Cleary, her life with him had been nothing but a lie.

In the distance, the sounds of steady gunfire echoed across the river. Eden scrambled up and pressed her fingertips to the window. Gray ribbons of smoke weaved through the treetops.

"Oh, how I despise that awful sound," Lucy said. "I wonder where Isaac is now. I wish he were here — with us."

"I do, too," Eden said, watching for movement matching the frightening outlying sounds. "I do, too."

"You know, Daniel told me not to worry too much because it won't help. He said he used to worry about Rayce all the time, but just when he'd worry himself silly, the major would show up no worse for the wear."

"Is that right?" Eden muttered, searching the horizon.

"Yes, he said he stopped fretting about him because Trinidad worries enough for the two of them, anyway."

Trinidad again. What power did the mysterious and beautiful Trinidad have over Rayce? In front of others, the formal pretense of master and servant was obvious, but when she spied them alone, they appeared far too comfortable with one another.

Lucy gasped. "Oh, I almost forgot. I received a letter from Aunt Martha earlier today. She's in a terrible way with the Yankees closing in toward Richmond. She said Eliza's by her side and taking good care of her, but her friends had left and headed down south when we evacuated Yorktown. She also mentioned she spotted Rayce walking into the Spotswood Hotel. But, of course, the letter had been written a while ago, and I don't know if anyone's heard from him since."

As much as Eden hated to admit it, at that very moment, she would have liked to have Rayce nearby. Yes, the man was conceited and high-minded, but his masculine presence made her feel safe and secure. She remembered how warm and alive she had felt in his arms.

God help me, I miss his touch.

Lucy's brows knitted together. "You look tired, dear. Perhaps you should get some rest. Do a little something for yourself, honey, you deserve it."

It had been a long day, and Eden felt the unsteady wave of weariness settling in her muscles. "I'll send Hetty up to keep an eye on you and tend to the baby. You rest yourself, Lucy. I'll be back soon."

Eden headed down the portico steps and slowly walked the grounds. She gazed across the sprawling, overgrown lawn; vividly green against the amber sunset. In the distance, field hands, looking like dark dots baking in the heat of the setting sun, busied themselves, tending the crops embarking on their season's journey. She inhaled the rancid aroma of stale gunpowder. Against the charming hues of blooming orchards, the gray clouds of smoke billowed defiantly against the horizon.

Daniel came into view and called out, "We got Yankees a coming, Miss Eden. Yankees be coming up the entry."

"What?" Eden narrowed her gaze, trying to make out the blue uniforms of the men riding up the long path. "Just what we need right now."

"Holy Moses, Miss Eden, what we gonna do?" Daniel asked, breathlessly.

Eden grabbed his shirttail. "Come with me. We're going to stand our ground — that's what we're going to do."

The two stood waiting on the portico as four disheveled Yankee soldiers rode up on horses that looked like they had seen better days. After what felt like an eternity, a tall sergeant, chewing on a sprig of wheat, dismounted from his horse and took a long drink from his canteen. Finally, he trudged up the portico steps, while the other soldiers hung back.

Eden glared at the filthy Yank, reeking of whiskey, without saying a word.

He removed his cap. "Me and my fellers here are tired and hungry. We'd like some food. Likely a chicken or two, and something from your smokehouse will do."

"You Yanks have been here before and taken what you wanted each time." She narrowed her eyes to slits. "I have nothing more for you. I think it's best you leave."

The man took a step forward. Daniel inhaled sharply, about to do the same, but she gestured for him to stay put.

The sergeant surveyed her from head to boot tip and licked his lips. "That a fact?" He took another step toward her. "What I'm saying, pretty lady, is I'm not really asking ya, I'm telling ya. Me and my boys are gonna camp on these grounds tonight, and we're taking what we need."

Eden's gaze darted between him and the three mounted Yankees hanging back.

He thrust a grubby thumb over his shoulder. "One of these boys here ain't feeling so good." He spit the wheat sprig on the porch. "So, don't be trying any funny business neither."

He started back to his men and turned over his shoulder, looking directly at Eden. "You all play your cards right, we'll be outta here at daybreak. Have a great night, now." He snickered.

"Oh, if Lucy wasn't upstairs with a new baby, I'd shoot

that vile man myself!"

Daniel nodded in agreement. "So, what we gonna do, Miss Eden?"

Her pulse quickened and she bolted into action. *The ruffians can't take what they can't find.*

"Daniel, hide what you can while they're setting themselves up. Run to the smokehouse. Gather any chickens and hogs from the pens and run them down to the creek. Hide whatever you can, as fast as you can." She grabbed his sleeve and looked into his dark face. "And don't get caught. These filthy Yanks mean business."

Daniel grinned. "Oh, no. Don't you worry none. I won't get caught. I can be slippery when I need to be." He quickly wobbled away toward the outbuildings.

THE swift knock at the door woke Eden abruptly. She sat up, clutching the coverlet to her chest. "Yes?" she called.

"'Tis me, Miss Blair. I must speak with you."

"Lord above." She rubbed the sleep from her eyes, trying to make out the time on the clock above the mantle. "Come in, Trinidad."

The servant entered and paused at the doorway. "There be trouble with the Yankee men."

She sat up straight. "What kind of trouble?"

Trinidad, whose emotions were always hard to interpret, appeared anxious, making Eden's stomach instantly curdle.

"A Yankee man smelling of whiskey came to the door, and he hold a gun to Daniel's head and told him to fetch a doctor."

"What?"

"'Tis true, Miss. Daniel told him no doctors here at

Hampton Manor anymore. Then the man said he would shoot Daniel dead if he don't find help. Daniel told him he has a wife and children and please not to shoot, but the man said maybe he just shoot Daniel, anyway. Then Daniel told him we have a nurse, and he sent me to get you."

"I have to help this Yankee? What's wrong with him?"

Trinidad lowered her gaze. "I do not know, Miss."

With a shake of her head, Eden forced the distracting nudge for more sleep from her mind. "Where is Daniel now?"

"He be on the portico...with the Yank."

"All right." She sighed. "Tell him I'll be right there."

Eden dressed as fast as she could and made her way down the staircase. Her pulse beat wildly in the hollow of her throat at the thought of helping the Yankee enemy. How she wished Rayce were here!

"Hello there, pretty lady," said the drunken sergeant, "I got me a sick soldier, and this old negro here says you're a nurse who can help him."

Tears pooled in the corners of Daniel's round eyes. "I'm sorry, Miss—"

The Yankee spun his head and faced Daniel. "Who told you to talk, old man?"

"Enough!" The last thing Eden wanted was trouble. She inhaled deeply and glared at the soldier. "Leave him alone, and I'll help you."

The sergeant cocked his head and slowly turned on his boot toward Eden. His top lip curled up at one corner. "Well, that's more like it." He holstered his pistol. "Come with me."

Eden stood firm. No way in hell would she walk alone with this man back to their campsite. "Daniel comes, too. He assists me."

The Yank eyeballed Daniel up and down. "Fine."

The sergeant led the way with Eden following. Daniel ambled behind them, carrying a lantern, while a bright moon in a cloudless sky helped light their way.

They entered the area where the Yanks had set up camp around one of the empty outbuildings. Taking note of the smells emanating from the campfire, Eden realized the men had helped themselves to a couple of loose chickens and a slab of bacon.

She took the lantern Daniel extended, and the three entered the small outbuilding, while the other two Yanks remained outside, tending their confiscated meal on the fire.

The ailing Yankee soldier was lying on his side, crumpled in half. Eden held the lantern out, suspending it above, and the man moaned as the light neared him. His long, sandy-blonde hair and beard glistened with grimy sweat. Judging by the look of his lean, slender build, he appeared to be a young man.

She hiked up her skirt a few inches and crouched low. She touched the back of her hand to his forehead and neck. *Sweltering hot.* "Daniel, go fetch cool water and some cloths."

Daniel hesitated. "No disresptin', Miss, but you sure you wanna be left alone with..." He flashed the sergeant a menacing glance.

She patted Daniel's arm. "I'll be fine."

"Yes'm." Daniel nodded and left.

"So, what's wrong with him?" asked the sergeant.

Eden opened a few buttons of the ailing soldier's shirt at the neck and chest, looking for a rash or swollen glands. "I don't know yet. It could be a number of things. First, I want to see if we can cool him down. These fevers have to break on their own most of the time. Tomorrow morning, first thing, I want you and your men to move him to another area where I can better assist him."

The sergeant nodded. "We can do that."

"Tonight, after I leave, I want you to keep an eye on him. Watch for any changes. Perhaps other symptoms will show up by morning. Then I'll have a better idea." She cast her gaze toward the ill Yank. "How long has he been like this?"

The sergeant rubbed his whiskered chin and looked at the ceiling, contemplating the question. "We've been skirmishing the last few days nearby, and we left yesterday..." His gaze shifted downward, "Uh, with new orders, and such. He'd been talking of feeling poorly this morning. Then, when we were a few miles downriver, it seemed the more we rode, the worse he felt, so we fixed here on your place before it got dark."

Daniel entered with a bucket of fresh water and cloths.

The Yank grabbed his canteen and took a swig. Light amber liquor dribbled down his chin, and he wiped it with his dirt-dusted sleeve. "Then, not long ago, he just started saying he was feeling tired and dizzy and couldn't eat nothin'. Now he's hotter than a musket shootin' uphill."

Eden dipped two cloths in the water several times and wrung them out. "He's very hot, indeed."

She bent low and placed a cool cloth on his forehead and one on his neck. He flinched as if he'd been burned and rolled to his back. Suddenly, his eyelids flew open.

Eden bolted up — staring. Her heart stopped dead, resuming seconds later with a massive thud against her chest, nearly knocking her to the ground. She groped for the bare wooden wall to keep herself from falling to the ground.

Her hands trembled. "You two leave."

"Wha — ?" Both Daniel and the Yankee protested.

"Don't argue with me — go now!" she snarled, startling them both.

The two men shuffled out the door as though their britches had caught fire.

She stared down at the Yankee man whose steel blue eyes gazed back, fixed steadily upon her own.

"Eden," he whispered with a weak smile. His fingers reached up and gently clutched a strand of her long hair hanging to her waist. "I knew...it was you."

She sighed. "Hello, Patrick."

Chapter 11

The merciless weeks of focusing on the missions had been on his mind night and day, but once Rayce hitched the horse and trudged up the portico steps of Hampton Manor, he knew he could leave it all behind for a night or two.

He reached for the entry door, taking note of the lingering scrape on his wrist from the damn Yankee straggler. He'd planned on taking his horse back and simply letting the Yank go, but when the fool whipped out the Bowie knife, it sure made shootin' him all the easier. Too bad the bastard nicked him good before he fell dead on the ground. When the wound got infected, completing the mission with the searing pain and fever had only made the long hours of riding more exhausting than usual. Thank God, the worst of it managed to pass on its own. These days most soldiers weren't as lucky.

Ah, well, he smiled. If he remembered correctly, a certain little nurse would be just down the hallway, should any of his physical needs require proper attention.

He entered the darkened house and removed his filthy

boots at the entry. Finding his way across the moonlit floor, he lit a lamp and went straight to the sideboard in the parlor to pour a brandy before heading to bed. At nearly four in the morning, it was roughly an hour before the roosters started crowing. Best he didn't wake anyone.

With every footstep up the long stairway, the warmth of his comfortable bed seemed to beckon in a hushed whisper along the smooth banister. Finally reaching his bedroom, he washed up quietly, undressed, and climbed into bed with a long sigh. His head no sooner hit the pillow, when he heard the sound of soft snoring followed by stirring near his feet. He reached down, fingering the foot of the bed.

Fur.

Beau. *Damn dog...finds the best place in the house to sleep.*

Too tired to shoo the mutt out, he lay back against the pillow. He shut his eyes, and something moved under the covers next to him.

"What the devil?"

Slowly, he reached across to investigate. Slender arm, petite waist, and the unmistakable long mane.

Now, what have we here?

She was lying on her side, facing the wall. He inched in closer, molding his body against hers, and slid his arm around the curve of her waist. A soft, sleepy sigh escaped her lips, and she curled against him. He breathed in the sweet magnolia fragrance in her hair, pressed against his chin; the scent that called to him each and every lonely night the last weeks.

"Eden," he whispered.

"Mmm-hmm."

"Are you awake?" He gently slid her hair to the side and

kissed the delicate nape of her neck. Christ. He was already growing hard.

"Rayce?"

The sound of her dreamy voice calling his name sent a jolt of heated desire straight to his core. He moved his hips closer and pressed against her warm back. "It's me, Sweetness. As you can tell...I've missed you."

This isn't a dream?

She uncurled her body and stretched her toes. Instantly, her bare leg met with a wall of curly hair as he draped his calf over hers. Part of her wanted to feign sleep and wish him away while she gathered her thoughts. The other part responded to the heated touch of his leg upon hers, the bristly strokes of his mustache grazing the nape of her neck with each soft kiss.

After the madness of yesterday, it seemed as though her world had been turned upside down. Seeing Patrick again jarred memories foreword; memories of the good old days before he left her for the war, before her father died, before Oak Hill burned to ruins. Hearing his soft southern drawl calling her name, his fevered hands on hers, needing her again; no wonder her resolve had softened to churned butter.

She had missed Rayce, but the images of him embracing his tearful servant, smoothing her curly hair with gentle, unhurried hands, would not go away no matter how hard she tried.

With her emotions whirling like a top, she had needed to feel close to him again, to inhale his unique blend of masculine scents, and try to get a grasp of her feelings for each man.

Earlier, with the house quiet and everyone asleep, she had come up with a brilliant plan. She tiptoed down the long, dark hallway at the end of the wing and poked her head inside his bedroom. Immediately, a swift stab of guilt pierced her belly. But once she set a foot inside, she knew it was something she wanted to do. No, something she needed to do.

She had quietly closed the door behind her and fumbled around his bedside table until she found a candle. Once she struck the match, his presence surrounded her like a balmy breeze blowing clear through her soul, enveloping and protecting her.

One of his unlaundered shirts had been lying across a chair. She picked it up and breathed in his scent upon the sleeves, the back, the collar. She shimmied out of her silk chemise, letting it drop to the floor in a puddle, and slipped into the cotton shirt. She rolled up the long sleeves to her elbows and slid between his bedcovers, sinking deep into the soft, down feather mattress.

Now, as if her thoughts had traveled through the whispering spring breeze, Rayce had come home again.

She spooned her backside against his warm, naked body. "I've missed you, too." She rolled over to face him.

He whispered, "You don't know how often I thought of you. Of touching you again."

"Me, too." She reached down, and with a finger as light as a plume, she stroked the tip of his manhood, surprising herself at her boldness. He inhaled sharply, and his body quivered, piquing her interest further.

"Lord, woman...I want you." He inched in closer and drew her head against his neck.

The feel of him, the masculine scent, Lord above, she wanted him, too. She gently took hold of him and moved her hand slowly, rhythmically. He pressed forward, positioning himself deeper, and a husky moan of pleasure escaped his lips.

Having Rayce in her hand, she sensed the power she had over him at that moment, emboldening her further. She bent low and kissed his broad chest, then his neck, trailing her lips up to his welcoming mouth.

The small amount of moonlight left in the waning night sky embraced his silhouette. She pulled the remaining covers from her waist and moved above him, straddling her legs on each side of his hips. Before her, his shaft stood full and erect, and she used both hands to stimulate him. His breath caught, hitching deep in his throat, and the hard muscles in his legs tensed.

He tugged at the shirt she wore. "Pardon me, darlin', but this has got to go."

She bent low and whispered in his ear, "Then take it off, Major."

The power of seducing him felt nothing less than intoxicating. She increased the pace of her movements, and he moaned and groped, trying to unbutton the absurdly tiny buttons on the shirt.

"Forget the damn thing!" He reached under the shirt and gently kneaded a breast in each hand.

Her nipples instantly grew rigid as he caressed her and thumbed the stiff peaks. She grew warmer, wetter, as she moved her hips with the rhythm of her hands stimulating him, arousing him, seducing him.

Rayce grasped her gently rolling hips, guiding her so she rubbed directly against him, without entering her. By God, she felt unbelievably slick and warm as she slowly slid along the length of his shaft. The muscles in his legs and torso tightened, feeling as though they could snap without warning, like the string on an old fiddle.

She paused, and his breath caught in his lungs. He watched in the pale, predawn light as she slowly pulled the shirt over her head and let it slide from her delicate fingertips to the marbled flooring. At the sight of her naked body perched upon his, and her warm, silken treasure pressed against him, he thought he would explode right then and there. He focused on her hair, her breathing, her lovely face.

Her velvety lashes lowered, resting against the top of her cheeks. Captivated, he watched as she slowly leaned down and pressed her breasts against his chest.

She kissed his neck and whispered, "Rayce, I want you inside me."

Dear God. He froze, letting his head clear. As much as he wanted to roll her over and give it to her like there was no tomorrow, a little patience was in order. No doubt, Eden was still an innocent woman.

He kissed her lips gently, tenderly. "I assure you, Sweetness, there's no place I'd rather be."

He eased her over so she lay underneath him. Flickers of rising sunlight poked through the curtains illuminating her golden hair, fanned out in a wide arc across his sheets. Her lithe, ivory legs were sprawled wide beneath him, and the tips of her firm nipples scorched his chest.

"Tell me you're sure, Eden. I refuse to force myself on you."

She gasped the moment his hand moved lower and parted her soft downy hair. Gently, he slid a solitary finger inside of her, taking his time, readying her. "Tell me," he repeated. He slowly withdrew and slid the moistened finger in gentle circles around her small bud.

"Yes," she whispered in jagged breaths, "I'm sure."

His lips lingered against her throat. "There's no turning back after this."

It had been ages since he had been with a virgin, but she was more than ready. Thank God, he probably couldn't have waited any longer, anyway. Having such a lovely creature, lying ripe as a sweet peach beneath him, felt like nothing less than torture.

"Sweetness...If you're ready, I'm going to take you now," he whispered against her neck. He trapped her small, quivering bud between his fingers, waiting for her reply.

Her breath hitched for a split second. "Oh, Rayce," she said, her words soft and breathless against his ear. "I'm ready."

He entered the opening of her slick sweetness. Instinctively, he felt driven to thrust hard and deep inside her with a single selfish plunge, but he knew better and inched his way in, stopping when he felt her thighs tighten. As soon as she loosened them again, he would ease himself in further.

"Rayce, take me," she said against his earlobe, "Take me now."

He felt the precise moment he took her innocence. She gasped in a flash of pain, digging her fingertips into his back, her thighs gripping his hips. He paused, staying perfectly still, until her discomfort passed.

"The worst is over now," he whispered, rising up on his hands. His heart stopped dead in his chest, resuming seconds later after seeing her emerald eyes gazing back at him, burning with desire.

He inched in further, and her thighs suddenly released their firm grip. And like a ripening bloom unveiling its petals for the first time, her lissome legs opened wide for him.

"Eden," he whispered.

This was madness, but she didn't care. "Rayce," she breathed.

His mouth descended down upon hers, his tongue coaxing her lips apart. She slid her hands up his back and over his broad shoulders. Wrapping her arms around him, she kissed him with all she had to offer.

Her heart.

The heat of his breath felt scorching hot upon her neck as he moved in and out, deeper, faster. His lips trailed across her throat, his coarse mustache scratching her skin, hurting her, arousing her, all at the same time. Her insides swelled, gripping the length of him, enveloping him with each powerful thrust.

She trailed her fingernails down the length of his back, digging into his firm buttocks. "Oh, Rayce," she whispered.

"Go with it darlin'," he said, his voice low and husky. He reached down, pulling her bottom up with his hand. He thrust deeper, and she raised her knees higher, meeting his demands.

A low-throated groan of pleasure escaped his lips, sending fiery shivers rushing across her naked skin. He moved inside of her, filling every inch. An energy inside began to rise, her insides shuddering with a desire so deep, her nipples went rock hard with each unyielding plunge.

Suddenly, the room spun and everything around her went white. She cried out as waves of passion seized her body. She writhed beneath him, welcoming his moans of pleasure, and felt the sizzling heat of his desire rain within her.

Their tangled bodies lay framed by the amber sun pouring through the cracks in the curtains. The sounds of songbirds in the high trees outside filled the room as they held each other, welcoming a new morning.

EDEN woke to the voices of Rayce and Ann talking below on the first floor. Fast as a shot, she sat up and listened.

"Major, please calm down," Ann pleaded. "Daniel says one of the boys needed medical attention."

"Let me get this straight. You're telling me there are Yankee stragglers camped on these grounds? Am I hearing you correctly, Mrs. Blair?"

"Oh, no." She had wanted to be the one to tell Rayce about Patrick and the other Yankee soldiers. Now she regretted her earlier decision of waiting until morning, having forgotten what an early riser he tended to be.

"Yes, it's true, Major. Of course, I begged and pleaded with Eden to insist they go elsewhere for care, but she is a handful, as you can imagine. Major...? Where are you going?"

Eden heard him ascend the steps, two at time. He bolted into the bedroom and slammed the door closed so hard the force shook the window casings.

She flinched and slithered to the top of the headboard, clutching the coverlet to her chest. "I...I can explain."

"Well, woman, you had best start!" He moved quickly, rummaging for his clothes. "You had time to tell me about this earlier, and you chose not to? Do you have any idea how serious these situations can be?"

"Well, yes, I guess so, but they needed—"

He glared at her over his shoulder. "For God's sake, Eden — we're at war!"

He marched across the room and planted his hands on her shoulders, his fingertips digging into her skin "You guess so? Now, listen to me. I realize you have no clue what I do when I'm away, and it's better you don't, but I'm telling you there are Yanks who want me dead. There are soldiers who have specific orders to kill me."

His eyes grew dark, wild, and angry as they bored into hers; the kind of eyes she had always imagined the devil himself would possess.

She quickly turned from his frightening glare. "Stop it, you're hurting me. What do you mean — why you?"

He released his grip and rubbed the dark stubble on his chin. After a long pause, he sighed heavily. "The less you know the better, trust me." He walked to his bureau. "You don't know which Yanks are looking for me, and which ones aren't, now, do ya?" he called out over his shoulder.

"Well, no, I suppose I don't, but this one—"

"And, just so you know, I don't give a damn if one of them needs medical attention. I gave you and Daniel instructions how to deal with these situations and where to go, if they won't leave—"

"I know what you said, and I have rid the grounds of stragglers on my own, Rayce. I would have gone to Will Benton's — just like you told us, but I just couldn't. I—"

He tugged his boots on, and Eden's throat went dry when she saw him pull out his gun.

"Rayce, I need to talk to you."

"Later, Eden. I have matters to tend to."

She tossed the covers off and raced to him.

He stopped dead in his tracks, eyeing her from head to toe. "Dammit! Don't go pulling the naked card on me now, woman. I have to go."

She stood fully nude before him, and he followed her every move. Feeling like injured prey about to be devoured by the wolf, she covered herself with the quilt. "Please, don't go. Not until we talk."

The faint sound of a crying baby came from another room. Rayce frowned and tilted his head.

Eden smiled and nodded. "It's exactly what you think it is. Lucy had her baby yesterday."

The small lines around his eyes softened. "Is she all right? Did you deliver...it?"

Eden stifled a giggle. "*It* is a beautiful, healthy, little girl. And, yes, I delivered the baby. It wasn't easy, mind you, but Lucy's doing just fine now."

"Well, that's good." He snapped his gaze from hers. Squinting one eye, he looked down the barrel of his gun.

"Rayce, when the Yankees got here Lucy had just had her baby. And please don't be angry with Daniel. He hid as much food as he could before they set up camp."

"That's all well and good," he said, sifting through a box gathering bullets, "but these men are leaving right now."

He headed for the door, and Eden put her arm out to stop him.

"Let go, Eden," he warned her.

"For heaven's sake, Rayce. If you're going, then I'm going, too." She rushed past him out the door.

She dressed quickly, and by the time she arrived outside,

he was on his horse ready to leave, not even bothering to walk there. "Rayce, wait. I have to tell you something."

"Eden, stay here," he barked. "We'll talk later." He galloped off toward the outbuildings.

Eden ran as fast as she could. She could hear Daniel and Ann calling after her, but she didn't care. She had to get there, and fast.

By the time she neared, choking with breathlessness, Rayce was standing outside talking to two of the Yanks who had just woken up and were relieving themselves on the burning embers of their campfire. She hid behind a tall pile of split logs next to the outbuilding.

"Any of you boys in charge here?" Rayce demanded, fingering the gun at his side.

"Who are you?" asked one of the Yankee privates.

"None of your business, that's who."

"Sarge! A man here wants to see you."

The sergeant came out of the door and narrowed his gaze. "And just who might you be?"

"Never mind that. I'm sending you boys packing." Rayce cocked the gun.

"Whoa there, mister!" The sergeant threw his hands up the moment he heard the click of the gun. "We ain't here for any trouble. We'll be leaving today, anyhows." He pointed a shaky finger at the outbuilding. "But we got a man in there who's mighty ill, and we're gonna need to leave him here unless you can point us to a nearby doctor or that little nurse who—"

Eden stepped away from the woodpile.

"Why, here she is now."

She walked up to the heated conversation and stared into

Rayce's face. If looks could kill, she would already be in a pine box six feet underground, the way he eyeballed her.

Sensing the tension, the sergeant piped up, "As I was saying, your little nurse there has already offered to help him. Ain't that right, Miss?"

The sergeant looked Eden straight in the eyes, a malicious smirk curving the corners of his thin lips. "Turns out they ain't strangers. Sure is a teeny little world when you get sick in the middle of nowhere and land in the very arms of your *fee-on-say*. Don't ya' think?"

She reached out. "Rayce, please listen."

Rayce stepped back. "Now, yes, that would be quite the coincidence," he replied, glaring hard into her eyes. "Let me see this soldier, Sergeant."

Eden followed behind the two men as they entered the building. The small room smelled of fever and grime. Trapped hornets and flies buzzed about, searching for their way out. Eden stood behind Rayce, her head held low, and opened a window.

Lying on top of a bed of thick wool blankets covered by a sheet, Patrick appeared to be asleep. Rayce poked his shoulder with his boot tip. "What's your name, soldier?"

Patrick looked up, trying to focus. "Private Patrick McDowell, sir."

"Huh, you don't say."

Eden could feel Rayce's eyes boring down upon her, bullying her with unspoken anger. Moving past him, she tilted her chin high and bent down next to Patrick. He looked comforted by her presence, his handsome smile curving upward as she felt his head. His fever had abated to some degree, but, clearly, he was still very ill.

"We need to move him to the medical area." She looked around the room. "The air is stifling and foul in here. He needs proper attention."

"Eden." Patrick reached for her hand. "I'm glad you're here, honey. You always were so good at caring for others."

"Christ Almighty" Rayce muttered. "I'm going outside." He marched out the entry and kicked up a wad of dirt with his boot, sending the clod flying past the door.

The sergeant snickered but stopped abruptly with a final awkward snort when he saw the seething gaze he had provoked. "Oh, uh..."

"Sergeant, I'm gonna ask you this once and once only." Rayce pointed the gun at him, aiming right between the eyes. "I want you and your Yankee trash to empty your bags and your pockets in front of me, right now, and then you're gonna hightail it out of here as if your life depends on it, because I assure you, it does."

Patrick's hand in hers felt odd and familiar at the same time, like an old dream she could no longer remember. All those many times they had held hands when they were young, she could never begin to count.

Eden tried to ignore the heated chattering outside. "How are you feeling today, Patrick? Any better?"

Patrick winced. "Not much. But seeing your beautiful face helps."

She managed a stiff smile. "I'll get some fresh water." She rose to leave, but his hand remained on hers.

"How're Isaac and Jimmy? Last I heard they were hoofin' it like marching ants in the valley with Jackson. Any word,

Eden?"

"That's the last I've heard, too." Uncomfortable talking to him while he wore the uniform of the enemy, she pulled her hand from his. "I hope they're all right."

"I do, too. I really do, you gotta believe me." His blue eyes paled, and he bit down on his bottom lip. "Look, Eden, I have something to say...about us."

She swallowed a gasp. *Oh, Lord.* She wasn't sure what he would say or if she could bear to hear it. She snatched the empty pitcher. "I...I'll be right back."

She scurried outside and stopped dead in her tracks, startled to see the Yankee soldiers leaving on their horses in a flurry of red dust and pounding hooves. Littered and strewn about were their guns and haversacks, emptied of their contents of papers, letters, and personal belongings.

She looked up at Rayce. "For pity's sake, what happened?"

"They were looking for trouble, that's what," he said. "They needed to go, and they're lucky I didn't shoot them." He started for his horse, the muscles at his jaw line tensing. "I'll send Hetty and Daniel down to help you with...the other one."

She hurried to his side, putting her arm out to stop him. "Rayce, I don't know what to say. This is who I am — I'm a nurse. I can't leave him like this; surely you understand that. I've known Patrick my entire life, and I just can't turn my back on him now no matter what uniform he's wearing. What would you do?"

What would he do? Rayce stood there, staring down at her sweet face, weighing his options. Hell, there wasn't much to think about. The answer is easy. What he'd do is physically remove the Yankee traitor from his property and away from

184

Eden's heart so he could claim her as his own. Simple as that. This guy had shattered his chance with her long ago, as far as he was concerned.

He looked into her eyes — pleading on behalf of the Yankee lout who broke her heart, no less. Given the situation presented to him now, it wasn't clear where Eden truly stood with the young buck.

Dammit! His stomach twisted in knots. It sure as hell felt like he'd laid claim to her last night when they made love. But what man hasn't been wrong about a woman at least once in his life, right?

Despite trying to remain cool and collected, Rayce faced her with a crushing glare. "You've known that man," he said, pointing a firm finger at the outbuilding, "that man lying in there wearing a Yankee uniform, your whole life, you say? Tell me, Eden, at what point did you know he would run off and join with Virginia's enemy? At what point did you know he wasn't going to marry you?"

Judging by the look in her wide eyes, his harsh words had stung. But what the hell was he supposed to do? If it had been her brother, Isaac, lying there wounded or ill in the Yank uniform, perhaps the situation would have been different. Instead, the man calling to her, reaching for her hand and looking at her as though she were all that existed in his miserable world, was a traitor — a Yankee turncoat bastard who left her wounded and her heart broken. Yes, she was a nurse with a calling to help others, but compassion has boundaries.

"So...so what should we do with him?" she asked in a small, hesitant voice.

Part of him wanted to pull her into his arms and take her

breath away with a passionate kiss, while the other part wanted to tear her to pieces for causing the crushing pain in his chest. He growled and kicked up dust as he walked haughtily toward her. He bent low, his face only inches from hers. "What are we going to do? What are *you* going to do, Eden? Your Yankee admirer is all yours, darlin'."

He turned away, got on his horse, and galloped back toward the stables.

Chapter 12

"Oh, Major, how you do run on," Ann cooed.

Eden looked at all the faces gathered around the dining table. She felt a sense of family for the first time in years. Trinidad had prepared a fine meal of smoked ham and potatoes, candied yams, and assorted baked breads with sweet butter. For dessert, everyone heartily devoured the creamy peanut butter pie. The only thing missing for the table to feel complete were Isaac, sitting next to Lucy, and Mama Claire serving them as usual.

Lucy descended from her bedroom to share in the meal, and the baby lay sweetly swaddled in her arms. Clearly happy to see Rayce, Lucy hung on his every word about the war and any news he had involving Stonewall's Brigade.

Seated between Rayce and Will Benton, Ann laid on her charms as thick as custard, squealing and laughing every time the men spoke. Will glowed with admiration every time Ann talked, and while she ordered him around like her own personal servant, he appeared enchanted to do anything that brought her pleasure.

Rayce was clearly the center of attention, and everyone took turns asking him questions about news from the front, the defense of Richmond, the state of the Confederacy, and more.

Everyone except Eden.

Trinidad presented the large tray of ham and rolls to Ann. "Ham, Mrs. Blair?"

"Heaven's no," Ann snorted. "You know I'll swell up like a tick if I have any more."

Will cleared his throat and caught Rayce's attention. "Do tell, Major. Where do our boys stand right now? Is it as grand as they say about General Jackson's success in the valley?"

"It's true. Jackson is a remarkable general. He and his foot soldiers have taken on the Yanks in the valley and given President Lincoln a big headache, I'm quite sure of that."

Will's eyes lit up. "I've never had the pleasure of meeting General Jackson, have you?"

Rayce smiled. "We have met a time or two."

"Isaac introduced me to him once at the academy," Lucy chimed in. "I'm so proud of him and Jimmy fighting for us alongside that man."

"As well you should be, dear." Rayce winked. "They're a brave and hearty bunch of men. Jackson's making quite the name for himself, and it's well deserved."

Ann's eyes widened. "Do tell us, Major — what's he like? I've heard he has blue eyes that can pierce your soul."

"That I cannot personally vouch for, Mrs. Blair," Rayce said, smiling. "I first met him back in Mexico, when he was a lieutenant. Course, I was just a young buck back then, but I remember him. He's an earnest, unassuming man. I believe he'll prove to be one of our finest generals."

188

"You don't say," Ann mused.

Will patted Ann's hand. "I know I shouldn't ask this in front of the womenfolk, but do we really stand a chance against the North, Major?"

Rayce paused before he spoke. "The Yanks have us outnumbered on the Peninsula, but if we can keep them convinced otherwise, yes, we stand a good chance of keeping them away from Richmond, at least for now."

With so much talk of the war, Eden couldn't keep her mind from wandering. As the day wore on, it became clear Patrick had a case of remittent fever from the attack of malaria he acquired years back. He appeared to be out of the woods and on the mend. Thankfully, Daniel and Hetty were taking turns tending to him.

She gazed out the window, wondering why she had been such a little fool. She should have allowed Patrick to explain himself when he offered to do so. Too many lonely nights had been wasted wondering why he had left her and joined with the North. How could leaving her have been so easy? Today, she had been face-to-face with him, but too cowardly to learn the truth.

After returning to him earlier, Patrick had looked pained when she pressed her finger to his lips and asked him not to speak. "Not now. Later," she had insisted. Now, her unanswered questions scratched inside her belly, like a wicked claw with pointy, vile fingers, urging her to learn the truth once and for all.

She turned and looked at Rayce, sitting in his chair like a great Roman emperor upon his throne, a bounty of delicious foods, fine silver, and wine in crystal goblets surrounding him.

His freshly shaven face looked handsomely weathered, and his neatly trimmed mustache revealed the wicked, white grin she had come to admire. His laugh sounded strong, hearty, and full of life, and he was clearly in his element with everyone laughing and listening to his stories. Without question, he appeared to be having a grand time. Still, throughout the meal, every time he glanced at her across the table, his eyes grew dark and perceptive, and she would fidget with her napkin, unable to meet his gaze.

Rayce rose from his chair. "If you lovely and charming companions will excuse me, I have a few items to tend to around here." He bowed. "Will, perhaps we can meet for cigars and brandy in the parlor and continue our discussion when I'm finished?"

"Of course he will," Anne insisted.

Will smiled and patted her hand. "I'd be delighted, Major."

Trinidad began the long chore of removing the china and silver. Lucy excused herself to retire upstairs, just as Ann and Will announced they were going outside for an after-supper stroll.

With the evening winding down, Eden went upstairs, having decided to take her evening bath early before checking in once again on Patrick. In another day or two, he would likely be well enough to leave.

RAYCE took his time walking to see the soldier. As he approached the open door of the outbuilding, he saw Hetty sitting in a chair, knitting next to Patrick, who appeared asleep on a bed of thick straw and linens.

Hetty rose when he entered. "Master Rayce."

"Evening, Hetty. I believe Trinidad could use some help in the kitchen."

"Yes, sir." She gathered her needles and yarn and left in a flurry of calico.

He grabbed the chair, spun it around, and straddled it backwards, his arms draped over the top.

The sound of the furniture scraping across the wood floor woke the young Yank. Patrick's eyes bolted wide open, clearly surprised to see Rayce glaring at him rather than the kindly, older negro woman.

"Wha — ?" Patrick struggled to sit up.

"Lie back down, son. We're gonna have a little talk. Just you and me."

"Sir?" His brow furrowed. "What about?"

"Well, for starters, how about you tell me why you boys aren't with the rest of your troops. You a deserter, are you? Where you from?"

Patrick squirmed and winced. "No, I'm not desertin'. I'm with the 26th Pennsylvania. We just took a detour, that's all."

"I see. One of General Hooker's men, are ya?" He raised an eyebrow. "Mind if I smoke?"

"Uh, I...I suppose not." Patrick sat up and rubbed his eyes.

"And you're from where exactly in Pennsylvania?" Rayce lit the thin cheroot, dropped the match on the floor, and squashed it out with his boot.

"If you're planning on turning me in, well...then you just go ahead, Mister. I don't much feel like answering your questions neither."

"I don't think you really want me to do that, Patrick.

Armies don't take kindly to deserters."

"Look. I said I'm no deserter." Patrick folded his arms across his chest.

"Uh huh." Rayce inhaled deeply from the cheroot and exhaled a perfect ring of smoke, blowing it in the Yanks face.

He couldn't help but laugh as Patrick waved at the thick, smoky ring surrounding him and coughed.

"All right, fine. Lord Almighty, if you must know, I'm not from Pennsylvania. I'm from Virginia, not too far from here, but I joined up north when the war broke out. There, you happy now?"

"Not quite." Rayce rolled the cheroot between his fingers. "And just what would make a good ol' southern boy from Virginia side with Pennsylvania and the North — Virginia's enemy?"

Patrick sighed and bit down on his bottom lip. Rayce could tell this was something the young man had thought a lot about. Unlike most turncoat abolitionists, Patrick was clearly uncomfortable with his decision.

The Yank took a long drink of water from the glass on the small table. He set it down and stared at Rayce. "Look, it's not like I had a choice, all right? There were some issues — back home, and that's all I want to say about it."

Thick silence stood between them as Rayce glared into Patrick's shifty eyes. "Suppose you tell me if any of those 'issues' has anything to do with that little lady, Eden Blair, I saw you talking to and gawking at."

Patrick's jaw dropped. "I wasn't gawkin'."

"Oh, you were gawkin' all right," Rayce charged. "Tell me."

192

Patrick snorted. "And if I don't?"

"Look at you." Rayce laughed and shot up from the chair, standing above him. "Do you honestly believe you have a chip to bargain with here?"

"No, I reckon' I don't." Patrick lay back down, folded his arms behind his head, and sighed.

"Well, then start talking, young man, and you best be shootin' straight with me, boy, because if you lie to me, I guarantee you, I'm a great shot."

EDEN smoothed the wet sponge dripping with magnolia-scented water down her throat and watched as the sheer window curtains blew gently into the room, nudged by a humid breeze. The light outside had faded to gray, and thunder grumbled across the rolling hills in the distance.

She sat back, resting her head against the smooth rim of the tub, and squeezed the sponge. She tilted her head and watched the small droplets splash like diamonds on the still surface of the bathwater. All the weariness of the last days seemed to drain away, leaving her limbs weak and languid. Another lazy rumble of thunder echoed over the river. She slumped deeper, letting the warm water encircle her up to her neck.

She closed her eyes, and all she could see was Rayce seated across the long dining table, staring at her through the lit candelabras, urging her to face him. She had refused to do so. Lord knows, she could get lost in those eyes, and she dared not tempt herself right now.

Having both Rayce and Patrick on the same grounds was proving to be more than unsettling. The young man she had known since she was a child, who had loved her and kissed her, was ill, asking for her help, and the possibly he could once again be hers — that he needed her — was disturbing, yet equally intriguing.

On the other hand, there's Rayce; the man who had never once proclaimed his love for her, but showed her the beauty in passion and desire. Wrapped within his arms, she felt safe and protected from harm at a time when no one possessed the luxury of such comfort.

The thought of his naked body, hard and lean against hers, instantly gave her goose bumps. She hugged her arms across her chest. "I guess I'm a ruined woman," she murmured. The thunder rumbled across the skies above in seeming agreement. She frowned and flicked her fingers across the bathwater.

Beau scrambled up from his small mat and trotted to the tub whining, his nails clicking like castanets on the hard flooring.

"It's only thunder, boy," she reassured him, scratching him behind the ears. He yawned and dropped down on the rug at the foot of the bathtub.

Why did she feel driven to help Patrick? The lout had left her hurt and humiliated and in fear of ever loving another man. The thought of learning why he had left her had gnawed inside her for so long, she never really weighed her options until now.

Was her injured pride worth her dignity?

The storm moved in quickly, crouching around the house, and the low throaty groan of thunder grew nearly constant. If it got any darker, she would soon need a candle for company.

Lifting a leg from the steamy water, she rotated her foot and flexed it, watching as the silky water beaded down her ankle.

Beau suddenly sprang to his feet at the crackle of lightning. She jumped, sloshing water over the rim of the bathtub and called to him. In a moment, his cold, wet nose poked her outstretched hand. "You're right, boy, it's time to get out."

She pulled herself upright and raised her hands behind her head, running her fingers through her hair and smoothing out the tangles. She twisted the long, silky rope, winding it in a knot on the top of her head, and tucked in the ends.

Beau barked as sheets of rain and hail erupted from the sky, just as the force of wind caught a nearby door and sucked it closed with an enormous slam. She flinched and reached for her towel. "It's all right, boy, I'm coming."

The sky grew dark and spiteful. Wrapped in a thick towel, she scurried around the room to light a lamp, shielding the small flame from the gusts of wind. At the sound of Will and Ann talking below in the parlor, she sighed, relieved they had made their way back to the manor before the sky broke open.

Deciding to join the others, she dressed casually and headed downstairs where she spotted Hetty and Trinidad in the parlor, putting away the polished silver.

Trinidad nodded, acknowledging her entry. "Miss Eden, would you like evening tea?"

"Oh yes, that's fine," Eden murmured. "Hetty, you're back already? Is Daniel tending to the soldier?"

Hetty sat polishing a serving spoon, examining it closely under the candlelight. "No, Miss Eden. The major wanna take over a spell."

Eden's throat went dry. "The…major? Are you sure?"

"Yes'm."

"Oh, all right, then." Eden turned away from the others, her mind racing. "Oh, um, just put my tea in my room, please," she called out over her shoulder.

A huge bolt of lightning hit nearby, slamming into the ground with resounding fury. The old house trembled and groaned in seeming agony. All along the wood paneled walls, family portraits glowed menacingly in the brilliant flashes of light.

A shrieking rush of wind shook the house. The tall windows suddenly flew open, and the candles blew out in an instant. The long draperies twisted in a flurry of fabric as violent gusts of wind and rain ripped through the window, howling like a beast in mourning. Eden groped the arm of the nearby chair for support.

A screeching owl flew by the opened windows. Ann squealed and flung herself on the divan.

Just then, Eden saw an image in her mind of Rayce and Patrick together — just the two of them — in the outbuilding.

That's where he'd gone — the matter he had to tend to.

Rayce was a man she cared for, more than she ever thought possible. But he was clearly capable of doing anything he set his mind to and got whatever he wanted when he wanted it. The very things that drew her to him were also what she instinctively feared.

A sudden, sickening wave of nausea threatened. All at once, the claw residing inside her belly scratched, like a demon emerging from slumber, and she saw her past and future, standing before her like a giant two-headed beast.

Oh, Lord in heaven.

"Miss Eden? Are you all right?" Will asked.

Ann stared at her wide-eyed from the divan. "Eden, what's wrong with you? You look like you've seen a ghost."

A rush of cool air blew an old portrait of Captain Hampton off the wall, sending it crashing to the floor. The wind howled like a wounded animal across the outside eaves. Everything around her — the sounds, the storm, the voices — all appeared to move in slow motion. Beads of moisture formed on her face and neck, and her pulse beat so hard against her throat she thought she would faint. She placed a trembling hand to her chest to calm the frantic beat of her trapped heart and stared at Will and Ann.

Feeling as if the shadowy walls and ceiling were closing in, Eden darted out of the room. Gasping for air, she opened the heavy, wooden entry door. Rain blew in with a giant gust, and hail pelted her face and clothes like shattered liquid glass pouring from the sky.

"Eden! What are you doing?" Ann called out. "What's gotten into you?"

"Miss Blair!" Will cried.

A wild current of air seized the open door. Eden gave the thick knob a forceful yank to shut it behind her. Flying down the portico steps, she ran into the darkness with the wind tearing at her thin cotton dress. Rain hammered her skin, and icy pellets ricocheted off the roof like rapid gunfire. Her hairpins came loose, and her hair fell heavily down her back in a blanket of thick, wet curls.

An explosive crack of lightning pierced the sky in a single brilliant blue flash, striking the giant willow oak tree next to her, splitting it in two. Covering her head, she fell to the ground, screaming, as a blast of sparks rained down around her. The ancient tree began groaning under its own twisted weight.

"Eden!"

Somewhere in the darkness, Rayce called her. She turned her head, side to side, looking for him. A blurry figure came into view, running toward her, then suddenly stopped short in their tracks.

"Eden, get up!" he shouted through the thundering rain. "Get up now and run — dammit — run!"

She scrambled up and scurried as fast as she could, just as a large piece of the once mighty oak slammed into the ground with a tremendous thud, missing her by inches.

"Eden!" Rayce shouted.

"I'm here!" she yelled into the shadowy darkness, the relentless rain hampering her view.

"Eden!" he called again.

She ran toward his voice and slipped in a flow of thick mud. "Oh, no!"

Rayce had heard the lightning strike the massive old tree and ran outside. His heart sank when he saw Eden lying on the ground with sparks spilling all around her and the huge branch about to give way.

He gulped in air, trying to calm the beat of his racing heart as another flash of lightning tore over the river, framing the old manor in a murky yellow hue. Wet strands of hair covered his eyes, obstructing his view, and his clothes were so wet and heavy they stuck to his skin like glue.

Another blast of lighting filled the sky, revealing her

position. He shoved his hands through his slick hair and ran toward her. He crouched down and scooped her in his arms. "What the hell are you doing out in this storm, woman? Have you completely lost your senses?"

He rushed through the rain with Eden in his arms, his boots clomping through the torrent of suctioning mud with each forceful step. With the lightning ripping through the skies all around them, he headed for the nearby grain shed.

He kicked the door open. "This will have to do for now."

The thunder echoed, reverberating off the tall, wooden-planked walls. With Eden in his arms clutching his neck, he grabbed the tarpaulin from a hook by the door and dropped it over a pile of freshly gathered grain as a blanket. After gently placing her down, he stopped to light a lantern.

He lowered himself over her, taking swift assessment. God help him if she wasn't the most beautiful wet mess he'd ever seen. Her long hair was drenched, spreading wide across the tarpaulin in a fan of liquid gold. Her thin dress was soaked through, and her taut nipples looked like ripe cherries through the sheer fabric. "Are you hurt?"

"Oh, Rayce...I..." Her bottom lip quivered, and tears filled her eyes.

He leaned down and kissed her forehead. "Sweetness," he said, sighing, "Damn, you had me worried and..."

She closed her eyes. "And?"

He watched in the dim light as tears ran down her cheeks. He kissed each salty tear. Against her ear he whispered, "And, God help me, but I don't know what I'd ever do without you."

He kissed her, gently, passionately, coaxing her trembling lips apart with his tongue. She wrapped her arms around his neck, clutching thick strands of his wet hair.

She pulled away and looked into his eyes. "Rayce, I've been so—"

"Shhhh, I know." He smoothed her hair. "I understand."

He kissed the drops of rain on her throat and felt her racing pulse against his lips. A flash of lightning sliced through the cracks of the wooden slats, followed by a steady rumble of thunder traversing the skies.

Her wet clothes clung to her skin, her breasts straining against the restricting fabric. Arching her back, she pressed herself against his chest, her fingers tugging at the back of his wet shirt, untucking it from his trousers. She roamed her chilled hands up his back, sending icy jolts rushing across his warmer skin.

"Dear Lord, Eden." He slowly stood up and stared down at her, releasing the rest of his shirt. "Are you hurt?"

"My ankle...a little bit." She offered him a beguiling smile, her green eyes deepening in color within the flashes of light. Leisurely, she sprawled out across the improvised blanket. "But I think I'll live."

"Stay still." He bent down and gently lifted her foot. "Is this the one that's hurt?"

"No," she murmured.

He removed her wet boot and cotton knee stocking and gently massaged the uninjured foot and ankle. He reached for the other foot, held it in his hand, and moved it ever so slightly. "Does this hurt?"

"No. I...I don't think so."

He removed the other boot and stocking and lightly touched her ankle. "And how about here?"

"A little bit." She flexed her foot and turned it slowly about. "It's not too bad."

"Uh huh." He smiled and slid his hands leisurely under the hem of her long dress and gently massaged her bare calves. Her soft skin felt chilled against the heat of his hands. "How about here?" he whispered.

He moved his hands higher, and Eden trembled as his fingers inched their way up to her thighs. He rubbed slowly, his hands gently kneading her supple skin, each time moving closer to her warm, sensitive middle. Having discovered her un-encumbered by the usual myriad of women's undergarments, he gingerly slid a finger toward the velvety soft flesh between her thighs and grinned. "And how about here?"

Eden inhaled his scent, and her body flushed against his large hands. "Rayce," she breathed. His finger penetrated her and moved gently in and out. She rolled her head slowly from side to side against the tarpaulin, her hips moving with a life of their own in a slow, rhythmic dance against his hand. He lifted her dress to her waist and the sudden breeze of cool air made her gasp.

"But—" Instinctively, she moved to protest, but he stopped her, holding both of her wrists in his hand.

"Not tonight, Sweetness," he insisted, letting go of his grasp. "Not this night."

His head moved lower and out of her shadowy view. For a fleeting moment, she wondered where he had gone. Then, she felt her thighs lifted up and his hands underneath her bare bottom, supporting her. She caught a glimpse of his dark eyes as he moved in closer. Before she knew it, his mouth moved down upon her, his tongue circling her small bud.

Her knees instantly quivered. "Oh, Rayce," she breathed.

Then, in an assault of unfathomable dimension, his fingertips dug into the skin of her bottom, and his tongue plunged deep within her. Breathless, she arched her neck back and whispered, "Oh, Rayce, how you torture me."

Like the unyielding storm surrounding them, he showed her no mercy. He moved deeper, faster, causing her pulse to pound like a tribal drum through her body. She reached down and ran her fingers through his thick hair. Fleeting glimpses of sharp wood and metal farming tools dangling from iron hooks above them glinted menacingly with each flash of light slanting through the cracks.

Against her thigh, he whispered, "Eden, my sweet."

A wave of exquisite torment began to rise within her body, building with the energy of the outside storm. Aching with a deep, primitive yearning, she clutched his hair and drove her fingertips into his scalp.

He increased his pace, moving in a dance of wicked seduction, and her body surrendered, helpless against his urgent mouth. Her insides pulsed with desire, and she had to bite down on her bottom lip to keep from crying out.

Without warning, his tongue narrowed in on her sensitive pearl. She squirmed beneath him, crying out as he gripped her writhing bottom, keeping her at his demand.

She lay with her eyes closed, gasping for air when he stood and scooped her in his arms. "Oh, Rayce," she breathed, "don't...don't stop."

He laughed a low throaty growl. "Woman, I wouldn't stop now if you begged me."

He moved her to the smooth-planked wall, hoisted her up,

and lifted her wet dress up to her waist. "Now, wrap your legs around me."

She did as he demanded and straddled his waist. She heard him fumble with his trouser buttons. Wedged firmly between him and the wall, she felt his male strength slide inside her. Instantly, he moaned a husky groan of pleasure.

"Eden, my sweet Eden," he whispered against her throat. He lifted her arms high over her head, holding them firmly. "You're mine, you hear me?"

He moved within her, over and over, deeper, faster, kissing her neck, kissing her mouth.

"Am I yours, Rayce?" Like the churning tide, she felt the swell within her stir once again with each powerful thrust of his hips.

"You know you are," he whispered against her ear. "Say you're mine, Eden. Say it!"

His breathing quickened, and his teeth grazed her neck. He released her arms and cupped her bottom in his hands. He thrust deeper and gazed into her eyes. "Say it now, Eden. Say it, because, so help me God...I'm in love with you."

Lord help me! She kissed him, her tongue exploring his lips, his mouth. She pulled away and looked into his eyes whispering, "I'm yours, Rayce." She buried her nose in his neck, relishing his scent, tasting his throat against her lips. "I'm yours, my darling. I love you."

He moved faster, plunging deeper, his hastened breathing warm and rhythmic against her ear. The tide within her rose to an unbearable height.

"Rayce, I need you. I love you—"

"I love you, Eden, God help me, I do."

His words seared her neck. "And you're mine now, do you hear me?" he demanded, his firm fingertips digging into her bottom.

As if the skies suddenly rained liquid fire, the swell within her burst forth. She gasped, her lips trailing helplessly against his neck, her fingertips digging into his back. He groaned and plunged deeper, and they climaxed together, their sounds of pleasure echoing against the walls of the tall-planked timber.

She struggled to catch her breath. "Please...Rayce."

He smoothed the hair from her forehead, his jagged breathing caressing her neck. "Please what, darlin'?"

"Please...please just tell me you didn't kill him," she choked out. "Just tell me you didn't kill Patrick."

He froze in place, the sound of their quickened breathing echoing in the sudden stillness.

"Rayce?" She grabbed his firm jaw and forced him to look at her. The lightning storm had moved out to sea, but distant flashes poked through the cracks, illuminating his dark, bottomless eyes.

He sighed extravagantly and maneuvered them back to the tarpaulin. "Hell, no, I didn't kill him. Probably should have, though. I suppose I owe your father my gratitude for taking care of the lout himself. Your old beau's a broken man now."

In a flurry of damp fabric, she scrambled up and stared down at him. "What?"

"What do you mean, 'what?'" He reached into the pocket of his shirt, pulled out a cheroot, and lit it. "I'm saying I'm happy your father dealt with him, ran him out of town."

"Ran Patrick out of town? My father?" She rushed about, gathering her boots and stockings. "You don't know what you're talking about." Her fingers suddenly went numb, and she fumbled with the laces on her boot.

His stomach tightened in a stiff knot, like he'd just been socked in the gut. Eden didn't know. She really didn't know why the turncoat bastard had left her.

She stood above him shaking, her arms folded across her chest, staring down at him with a look of contempt. He sat up and reached out to her. "Now, wait—"

"I have to go." She jerked away and smoothed her wet dress, avoiding his gaze.

"Eden, look." He took a puff of his cheroot and squashed it out as if it were a deadly spider. "I thought you knew, honey." He stood up and pulled her in his arms.

She gnawed at her bottom lip, wrenching herself from his embrace. "I...I just have to go, right now."

He faced her. "Now, just hold on, honey. Perhaps we should talk about this first. It's obvious you're upset."

"Upset?" She hastened past him, toward the door. "You can't possibly know what happened, and you make it sound as though my father somehow betrayed me."

"On the contrary, my dear. Your father did you a favor. That I can assure you. You haven't forgotten I was alone for an hour with your old beau, remember?"

"And I'm supposed to believe Patrick would just tell you, a perfect stranger, his tales of woe?"

She pushed the door open wide. With her chin held high, she hiked her dress above her ankles and stepped gingerly across the muddied ground, heading toward the outbuilding.

He rushed out and grabbed hold of her arm. "What are you doing, Eden? Talk to me."

"I'm going to check on Patrick."

"Not now — he's fine. I'll send Hetty to check on him."

She shook her head and pushed his hand away. "Don't try to stop me!" Tears welled in her eyes and her bottom lip quivered. "You don't understand. I need to see him!" She turned away and rummaged through the pocket in her dress.

He sighed and rubbed his chin. "So, you're not going to take my word for it? I can tell you what you need to know, Eden, because, the simpleton that he is, spilled everything to me." He nudged her shoulder.

She turned and snatched the handkerchief he extended, her eyes narrowing in on his. "Who's the simpleton? He could have told you anything, Rayce. What makes you think he'd tell you the truth?"

He smiled. "Well, let's just say the pitiful bastard didn't have much of a choice—"

"Ha! I'll bet. He probably would have told you anything out of fear you'd kill him, you...you brute!"

He took a step toward her. "*Brute?* Now I'm the bad guy?"

She stepped back. "Don't come near me! I...I don't believe any of this. Not for one second do I believe my father was behind Patrick's leaving me. My father held me while I wept in anguish!"

"And I've just made love to you. Why would I lie to you?" he asked, his tone growing angry.

"Made love to me, or had your way with me?" she sneered.

"What? Jesus — you're impossible!" He held his hands up. "Fine. Do what you want."

Eden tilted her chin and turned away. "Fine. I will."

The moon peered through the clouds, lighting her way

toward the outbuilding. With each measured step, half of her told her to stay and talk this out with Rayce, while the other half told her to continue forward toward Patrick. She peered over her shoulder and saw Rayce walking away.

"You just go to him, then!" he yelled over his shoulder, cramming his hands into his trouser pockets.

She spotted the lovely, ebony skinned servant gazing out the parlor window watching Rayce as he hastened his pace toward the manor — toward an awaiting Trinidad.

"Ha! And you can just go find your in-house strumpet!" she yelled, quickening her step toward Patrick.

"What the hell are you babbling about now, woman?" he shouted back. "What strumpet might that be?"

"Trinidad!" she yelled back, dodging a mud puddle. "I suppose you thought I was quite the fool!"

"Damn it all to hell, woman! If that's what you think, then, indeed, you are a fool!" he growled back, his voice echoing across the sprawling grounds. "I'll have you know, that so called 'strumpet' happens to be my sister!"

She stopped dead in her tracks.

Trinidad is...his sister!

She spun around and tried to speak. She cleared her throat. "Rayce...Please, Rayce — wait!" she managed to shriek out, but the moon had shrewdly slipped behind a dark cloud, and he was nowhere to be seen.

Chapter 13

Rayce stomped up the portico steps and bolted into the house.

"Oh, Will," Ann cooed, "Honestly, these freshwater pearl earbobs are positively lovely."

The entry door slammed shut with a monstrous thud. The brass doorknocker banged clumsily as it thumped against the thick wood outside.

"I swear, I have never in my life met such a—" Rayce muttered, stopping short when he entered the parlor and saw the surprised faces staring at him.

Trinidad grabbed Hetty by the sleeve, and the two servants shuffled toward the back of the house, one on the heels of the other.

"Oh, my heavens," Ann breathed. "Whatever is the matter, Major? Is the world coming to an end? First, Eden carries on and runs out in the wicked storm like a woman gone mad, and then you come bolting in looking like a drowned wolf."

She glanced down at his feet and gasped. "Why, look at

those muddy boots." Ann scanned the room. "Trindad?" she called. She spun on her heels and faced Will. "Honestly, where did that woman disappear to now?" She picked up the bell on the end table and called, "Trinidad? Hello? The Major's boots need cleaning."

"Major?" Will asked, frowning, "Is everything all right?

Rayce waved his hand in the air and marched straight to the sideboard. "Oh...er...it's nothing." He inhaled deeply and seized the bottle of brandy, then paused.

No, not tonight.

He exchanged the stylish bottle for the jug of rotgut Kentucky bourbon and poured a full shot.

It's that kind of night.

Ann and Will exchanged glances. Finally, Ann cleared her throat and set the bell on the table. "By chance, Major, did you happen to see Eden? She left in such a fit, and I—"

Rayce grumbled into the shot glass and balled his hand into a fist.

"Oh my," Ann murmured. "Gentleman, perhaps I'll go check on Lucy and the baby and give you men some time for your cigars and...and politickin'."

Will shuffled up from the divan. He waggled his eyebrows and presented Ann with an exaggerated bow. "Mrs. Blair, until we meet again."

Ann smiled and waltzed away, turning over her shoulder to blow him a kiss across the palm of her hand. "Mr. Benton." She nodded at Rayce. "Major Hampton."

Rayce scowled and swallowed the fiery liquid.

Will drifted toward Rayce, his face glowing crimson. "Isn't Mrs. Blair just the best? I must say, I'm absolutely crazy about her."

Rayce stared at Will for a moment, then poured himself another shot and set him up with one, as well.

Will took a healthy taste of the bourbon, swallowed hard, and coughed. "Rayce, you know I'm your friend, and I hope you would confide in me if you ever feel the need to do so."

"And you the same, my friend." Rayce tossed the shot of fiery liquid down his throat and winced. He looked at his love-struck friend and sighed. "Will, how about you take a seat and join me for a couple more, because if you have your mind set on a Blair woman, you're going to need this as much as I do."

AVOIDING the countless puddles, Eden made her way to the medical outbuilding. She paused at the door and inhaled deeply, hoping to calm her racing heart before knocking. She rested her head against the closed door. Finally, she rapped quietly on the wooden entry.

"Come in," Patrick replied.

She entered the dimly lit room and found Patrick sitting in a chair wearing his dusty, Yankee blue trousers, reading a book by candlelight. Several buttons of his muslin shirt were unfastened, exposing the top of his smooth, bare chest, glistening with moisture. His long, sandy blonde hair had been combed since she last saw him. Strands of lighter hair, bleached by the hot Virginia sun, glinted in the firelight, turning his eyes a deeper shade of blue.

She cleared her throat and cast her gaze toward the vacant wall next to him. "I trust you're feeling better?"

"I am." He closed the book and rose slowly from the chair. "Thanks to you."

"Do sit down. You'll need your strength."

He took a step forward and arched his eyebrows. "Heaven's above, Eden, your hair and clothes are soaked." He grabbed a blanket and draped it over her shoulders. "I plan to leave tomorrow."

She gazed up at him and tugged the wool blanket, wrapping the ends tightly around her balled fist. "I see." She sat in the chair. The squeak of the old, wooden legs filled the rooms deafening silence.

He set the book on the small table. Wearing the beguiling smile that used to melt her heart, he walked slowly toward her. "Eden..." he said softly.

She inhaled sharply. "Wait. Don't come any closer, Patrick, I mean it. Say what you need to say and then leave in the morning."

He held his hands up, stepped backwards, and sat on the bedding. "Look, Eden, I know you're sore."

"Sore! You think I've just been sore?" She pursed her lips so tight her jaw hurt.

"I can't begin to make it up to you, honey."

"What?" She glared at him, straight on. "Make it up to me? Patrick, you left me. You left me with our wedding plans in place without so much as a goodbye."

He sighed and lowered his head.

Her hands began to tremble uncontrollably. She quickly hid them in the folds of the blanket. "And if that weren't bad enough, I learned not only did you desert me, you sided with the Yankees. Do I have this correct so far?"

"It's not that I didn't love you, because I did." He lifted his head, his gaze fixed upon hers. "I still love you, Eden."

"Ha!" she choked out. "You love me? Oh, for pity's sake, Patrick. What do you know of love?"

He rubbed his hands through his hair. With a loud, grumbling sigh, he rose from his bedding and took a step toward her.

She put out her arm and looked directly into his steel-blue eyes. "No. Stop right there. I mean it, Patrick."

"Lord above, Eden. I'm just standing up cuz my knees are cramped up, for God's sake."

"Well, fine, then." She stuck out her chin. "But don't come near me."

He paced the floor. "Hell, don't you know how much I've missed you? I got a letter from my mother about the fire and all, and she told me where you were living. So, I decided while I was fighting near these parts I'd pay you a call first chance I got."

"Pay me a call?" she sneered. "Figured you owed me that much, did you?"

He winced. "I just needed to see you again. I was already feeling poorly when I started out to find this place. Now, I'm thinking, I'm lucky I made it here at all."

Eden exhaled slowly, trying to calm the frantic rush of her pulse. "Just tell me why, Patrick. I deserve an explanation."

He rubbed his overgrown whiskers. "Lord, I promised the major I'd come clean and tell you everything. He said I owed it to you, and I reckon' he's right."

"Leave the major out of this," she snapped. "You're lucky he hasn't wrung your neck clean off of your shoulders just for being here."

He snorted. "What's between you and the major, anyhow?

He's one smooth son of a bitch, isn't he?"

She narrowed her gaze. "I said, keep him out of this."

Patrick cleared his throat. "Yes, well, what I want to say is...is that I have always loved you, Eden. I always will. But..." He inhaled and bit down on his bottom lip.

She jutted her chin forward, her gaze narrowing in on his, waiting for an answer. "Go on."

Finally, he exhaled loudly and said, "But, I got myself in some boiling hot water back home. I had no choice but to leave you."

"What? What do you mean by 'no choice'? Of course you had a choice. You had a choice to stay with me, and you chose not to. You had a choice to side with Virginia, and you chose not to. It appears to me you've had plenty of choices."

"Damn." He laced his fingers and cracked each knuckle. "Now this is turning out to be harder than I thought it would be."

She rose from the chair and paced the room. "I can't do this." She started for the door. "Goodbye, Patrick. You're on your own."

"Wait." He grabbed her arm. "You can't leave, Eden. I have to tell you all of it or..."

She raised an eyebrow. "Or?"

"Or the major's gonna turn me in. See that I'm hanged as a deserter."

"Unhand me." She swatted his hand from her arm. "So, what you're saying is you're only telling me this, something I deserve to know, because you face death otherwise? How very noble of you."

Patrick's eyes widened, his brow furrowing into a deep

groove. He moved in swiftly and seized her shoulders. "It's like this, Eden. I'm a son of a bitch, all right?"

Stunned by his sudden movement, she stared into his face, unable to speak.

He looked in her eyes as if searching for something he couldn't find. After a moment, he turned from her gaze, sighed heavily, and dropped his arms to his sides.

He walked to the small window and stared outside. "You remember Jemma — Little Jemmy we called her back home?"

"The little negro girl of your mother's, about fifteen?"He sniffed. "That's her."

Puzzled, Eden frowned and shrugged. "What does she have to do with anything?"

Patrick wedged his hands in his pocket and turned around, avoiding her gaze. He paced the floor. "Well, your father got it into his head I was the father of that little baby of hers."

"You?"

"Yeah. He came to me sayin' I had raped her. Can you believe that?"

Eden felt the warm blood drain from her face. Oh, yes, she remembered Jemma. She and her father had been summoned to the McDowell plantation one morning to confirm Jemma was indeed with child, much to the dismay of Patrick's mother, who had developed a case of dyspepsia upon learning of the girl's impending confinement. She also recalled being ill herself with fever when Jemma's time had come and hearing the urgent knocks at the door, hushed voices, and her father's return in the early hours of the morning.

Think! Eden scrunched her eyes shut, trying to recall the

long night in more detail.

It was late when Jemma's mother had come to the house, begging her father to deliver the baby because her daughter was having such a wicked time. She recalled going downstairs and finding her father tending to the severe wound he had suffered when he fell from his horse on his way home in the wee hours of the morning. The wound she sutured and tended, only to have it fester with insurmountable infection.

Her heart beat wildly as she remembered her father talking to himself that morning, reeking of stale whiskey and muttering incoherently about the "evils of men" and "broken trusts and promises."

He opened her eyes. "Oh, my God. You raped that poor girl, Patrick. Didn't you?" She marched up to him and poked a hard finger in his chest. "You fathered her baby, I know you did."

His mouth hung wide open. "I..."

"I what?"

"Well, she said I raped her, but..."

"But what? Speak up!"

"But she was throwing herself at me," he scoffed.

"Oh, for pity's sake." She turned away from him in disgust. "Damn you, tell the truth, or I'll hang you myself!"

Patrick grabbed her by the arm. "Hell, Eden...lots of men do it."

Lots of men do it. His words echoed in her ears. The muscle in her jaw tensed so tight it throbbed. She looked directly into his eyes, her gaze boring into his.

He released her arm and held his hands up. "All right. Perhaps, I may have wanted it more than she."

"Say it, you coward. You raped her, didn't you? Say it!"

"Eden, stop."

"No. I won't stop. Tell the truth, or so help me I'll—"

"Arrrrrg!" Patrick kicked the wall so hard a shard of wood flew across the room. "Dammit, Eden. Yes, I raped her!" he shouted. "I raped Jemma!"

His evil words echoed across the barren walls.

Eden gasped, her mouth twisting. "My God, Patrick, she was just a girl." She slapped him as hard as she could across the face. "You're a wretched, pathetic excuse for a man. I can't believe I ever loved you."

Thick silence filled every inch of the small room.

Patrick slowly turned to face her. "Be that as it may." He slumped into the chair and rubbed his cheek, red with the imprint of her hand. "Apparently, while the whiny trollop was giving birth, she told your father everything. He delivered the little mulatto bastard."

"Your child," she sneered.

"As I was saying," he continued, ignoring her charge, "your father delivered the baby. He came to my home and found me afterward. Said we needed to talk, man to man. We had whiskey, quite a lot, as I recall, and he told me if I didn't up and leave you he would tell you himself. I told him I wouldn't do it at first, but he was upset and said he wasn't leaving until I agreed. He was stubborn as a mule and stuck to his damn word, by God. There we sat, drinking that whole damn bottle of whiskey. Finally, I agreed just to get him to go home. Then, ol' Isaac had to take matters—"

She gasped. "What? Isaac knew about all of this?"

Patrick cocked his head. "Well, hell yes, he knew." He

fingered his collar. "He damn near killed me an hour later, practically choked me to death in my own bed, making me swear I'd leave and never come back. I left for my cousin's in Pennsylvania the next day." He shook his head. "I swear, the look in Isaac's eyes was like a man gone mad." He reflected a moment and then shrugged. "As I was saying, I agreed to your father's terms, he got on his horse, and that was that."

Her heart beat so hard she could hear the steady waves of blood pounding in her ears. "No, Patrick, that was not that," she said, her jaw clenching painfully. "You may as well have killed my father with your bare hands. I will always hold you responsible for his death."

"What? You can't blame me for his death!"

She stiffened her back. "My father was an expert horseman; you know that. Because of you and your disgusting behavior, he drank heavily that night. It's because of you he fell off his horse on his way home and was wounded. After you left, he died from that wound, Patrick."

She groped the wall behind her for support, tears filling her eyes, and her chin quivering uncontrollably.

He reached for her. "But, I didn't—"

"Don't touch me!" she yelled, swatting hard at his extended arm. "You took more from me than you will ever know."

"Eden, I swear, I never meant to hurt you."

"You left me more than hurt, Patrick. You left me broken — shattered — a slave to my own misery!"

With trembling fingers, she wiped the tears streaming down her cheeks with the edge of the blanket. "But, I'm shattered no longer, do you hear me? With the truth, I've been set free." She laughed at him, mocked him. "You...you, of all people, have freed me."

He frowned. "Freed you?"

She tilted her chin high. "For the first time in so very long, I'm finally free. Free to love again with my whole being."

Patrick sucked in his cheeks before he spoke. "I take it you don't mean you're free to love me again. Should I assume you mean the major? Judging by his questioning, or perhaps I should say his interrogation, and the look in his eyes when he spoke of you, it made me wonder if perhaps he was in love with you."

Eden ignored him, choosing to flick at the mosquito on her sleeve rather than answer.

"I didn't even know who he was at first. He seems like a good man, a straight shooter. I respect that in a man. Hell, Major Hampton's a bit of a legend."

She sniffed and looked at him. "What are you talking about — how do you mean?"

"I heard some officers talkin' at camp not long ago. Seems the major made a name for himself during the war with Mexico. Rumor is, when he was just a young lad at the start of the war, he fought alongside his father. During a bloody battle, his father died in his arms. Apparently, it tore the man up pretty bad, and he was a lost soul after that. They say he didn't care about nobody — not even himself. He feared nothing and nobody." Patrick shrugged. "Because of that, they say he became the best scout that ever was."

Eden furrowed her brow. "Major Hampton? Major Rayce Hampton?"

"Oh, yeah. That's him, all right. I heard the man can slip

in and out of enemy territory, do his business, and nobody ever knows he's been there until it's too late. They said McClellan's face was puckered up red with anger and shoutin' that everything going wrong for him had the markings of 'The Ghost,' but he couldn't prove it. There'd probably be a high price on the major's head right about now, with the war heating up around here, and all."

"You wouldn't dare."

Patrick eyed her sharply. "Of course not. What kind of man do you think I am?"

"You cannot with all seriousness be asking me that," she snapped back.

He nodded. "Fair enough. I suppose I had that coming. But you know how you say you finally feel free? Well, hellfire and damnation, so do I, honey. The major made me a deal, and I'm thinkin' I just might take him up on it."

Eden had to get out of there. If she looked at Patrick one moment longer, she'd retch.

She left Patrick without the blessing of a final farewell and took her time walking back to the manor. The storm had passed and was now nothing more than a gentle rumble over the rolling hills in the distance. The freshly churned river air hung in the breeze, and with each new breath she took, the tremendous weight of fear and resentment seemed to lift from her shoulders.

She strolled up the portico steps, and the front door swung open.

"Great grits and gravy," Ann squawked, "come see this."

Eden followed her into the parlor and found Rayce and Will drunker than a couple of peach orchard boars. Their arms were draped over each other's shoulders in what appeared to be a feeble attempt at holding each other up, singing an out of tune rendering of "I Dream of Jeanie With the Light Brown Hair."

"I dream of Jeanie with the light brown hair,
Borne, like a vapor, on the summer air;
I see her tripping where the bright streams play,
Happy as the daisies that dance on her way.

Many were the wild notes her merry voice would pour,
Many were the blithe birds that warbled them o'er:
Oh! I dream of Jeanie with the light brown hair,
Floating, like a vapor, on the soft summer air."

"Oh, hello, ladies," Will said, teetering while attempting a stately bow. "We'z were jus' singing." He patted Rayce's shoulder, "Right?"

Rayce reached for his shot glass and downed the liquid. "Right you are, ol' boy," he said, slapping Will on the back.

At Will's prompting, they broke into song once again.

"I long for Jeanie with the day dawn smile,
Radiant in gladness, warm with winning guile."

"Major!" Ann screeched. She whisked into the room and took Will by the arm. "What have you done with Mr. Benton? You should be ashamed!"

Will's jaw dropped, and his bleary eyes slowly widened. "Ah, now, we'z just having some fun, right, Rayce?" Meek as a church mouse, he followed behind Ann as she led him by the hand to the divan.

Rayce glanced at Eden glaring at him from the parlor entry, her arms folded across her chest, tapping her boot on the hardwood floor. "Do come in, Miss Blair."

"Yes, Miss Eden, do come join us," Will said merrily, clearly far drunker than Rayce.

Even if Rayce and Will were stinking, falling down drunk, Eden wouldn't have cared tonight. She would happily put up with just about anything to finally be rid of Patrick and his sins.

She entered the room and heaved a sigh of relief. "I could use a nip myself. I'll have whatever you're having."

Whatever we're having? Rayce couldn't help but smirk as he poured her a full shot of the fiery rotgut. "Drink up, m' lady."

Eden took a healthy gulp. "Oh!" She winced. "What is this? It's like liquid fire. Is this what you boys have been drinking tonight?"

Rayce and Will exchanged glances, choking back laughter.

"Go ahead, Mrs. Blair," Will said, giggling and prodding Ann. "Give it a try, too."

Ann raised her chin, clearly offended by the very idea. "Why, Mr. Benton, I've never imbibed whiskey in all my days."

Will's bottom lip jutted out in a pout under his thick mustache. "It's bourbon, actually."

Ann sighed and patted his arm. "Well, I suppose I'll give it a try, but just for you."

Rayce poured a shot and walked to the divan, handing her the glass. *This I've got to see.*

Ann took the shot glass and rose in the most dramatic fashion. "Well, here it goes." She drank the first sip and winced, then held her nose and gulped the rest. "There," she beamed, her eyes watering. "I did it!"

"That's my girl." Will swatted her on the bottom.

"Mr. Benton," Ann squealed, promptly plopping back down on the divan, her blue eyes wide with astonishment.

"Yes, kitten?" he replied.

A demure grin suddenly stretched across Ann's face, and she inched in closer, covering his hand with her own. "Why, Mr. Benton," she purred.

Rayce was trying to decipher Eden's expression, but things were looking a tad blurry. She had gone to the medical building longer than he had expected, and the entire time she was there, it had almost driven him insane wondering what the two had been doing. "So, you up for another?"

Eden sipped her shot glass and shook her head. "Thank you, no. This is actually quite terrible." She set the glass down and slowly walked toward him.

Oh, God, now what?

Expecting the full brunt of her wrath, he stiffened his stance and stood frozen in place. To his surprise, she looped her arm within his and pressed herself against his waist. In his half-inebriated state, it took all of his energy not to snatch her in his arms, toss her over his shoulder in front of the others, and whisk her up the stairs into his bed.

With Will and Ann flirting like eager adolescents on the divan, now would be a good time to escape. He laced his fingers with Eden's and led her up the staircase.

After lighting the bedside candle, he sat in the chair and removed his boots and socks. Sighing deeply, he stood and unrolled the sleeves of his shirt.

"Rayce! Is that a bullet hole in your sleeve?"

"Huh? What?" He looked down. "Oh, that, yes, I have

quite a few of those, I'm afraid. Don't worry, the Yank missed." He unbuttoned his shirt and disappeared behind the rosewood screen. "I'm sorry to have doubted you," Eden called. "I just don't know what came over me. I think I've let my father's death and Patrick's betrayal consume me. And, of course, it never occurred to me the two incidents were intertwined. Did you hear me Rayce? I'm just so thick-headed sometimes."

"Oh, I heard you." He walked into the room in his dressing gown and sat next to her on the bed. "Apology accepted." He lay back and rested his arms behind his head.

She smiled and snuggled next to him, resting her head against his shoulder.

She slid her hand inside the silky fabric, fingering the hair on his chest and buried her nose against his neck.

"What cologne do you have on?" she asked.

"No cologne, just soap. Why?"

She inhaled again and moaned. "Mmm...You smell wonderful tonight. It reminds me of sweet, Virginia dirt mixed with tidewater pine and bark."

He frowned. "Dirt? Hell, woman, I just cleaned up."

"No, it's wonderful, really." She laughed. "I love your scent."

He smiled and plucked at her wet dress plastered against her skin. "Your clothes are still damp, Sweetness, perhaps—"

"I don't care. Just hold me."

He tugged at the coverlet and draped it over her body.

She clicked her tongue. "There's something you mentioned earlier..."

"Trinidad? I figured that wouldn't go unnoticed."

"Tell me about her. How is she your sister? I mean, well,

she's..."

"Black? A negro? That she is, my dear."

He lit a cheroot with the bedside candle and inhaled. Staring at the ceiling, he blew out a thick ring of gray smoke.

"Tell me, Rayce," she whispered into his ear. "Trust me."

He'd kept his life and emotions bottled up inside his gut for so long, he wasn't sure how to lie in a bed next to a woman and talk, really talk. Having a beautiful, willing woman next to him and talking just for the sake of talking completely went against his grain. But the moment her sweet voice said, "trust me," all of that dissolved.

"You've been honest with me," he whispered. "It's time I was honest with you."

"Talk to me, Rayce. I want to know."

"Trinidad is from the West Indies, Barbados to be exact. My family had a sugar cane plantation down there for years. My father traveled frequently before I was born."

"So, she's your older sister?"

"She's my half-sister. Yes, she's five years older."

"Was your father married before he met your mother?"

"No, no." He shook his head. The truth is, while my father was married to my mother, he fell in love with an island woman; a woman whose family had originally been brought to Barbados in ships from Africa many years earlier. Her name was Abena, and she bore my father's child — Trinidad."

"Trinidad's an unusual name."

He inhaled the cheroot, letting the smoke linger against his tongue before exhaling. "I asked Trinidad about her name. She said Abena told her she had accompanied my father to the island of Trinidad on business, and she was conceived during the trip. The name originally comes from the Holy Trinity. I suppose that seemed oddly appropriate to them at the time."

"But doesn't Trinidad have a husband? Children of her own back home?"

"Yes...and no. She had a husband and a daughter. Damn yellow fever epidemic on the island took them both several years back." He inhaled the cheroot and exhaled with a long sigh.

"Rayce, that's terrible. And what about your mother while all of this was going on?"

"When I look back on it, I think my mother knew of my father's infidelity. He must have loved Abena. He spent many months away when I was young. What I don't know to this day is if my mother was aware my father actually loved another woman. I suspect she did."

He paused for a moment, swallowing the lump forming in his throat before continuing. "I grew up seeing such deep sadness in her eyes when my father left on his business travels. I was just a child and suspected nothing, although perhaps I should have."

Eden combed her fingers through his hair. "You couldn't have done anything, Rayce. You were just a child."

"Perhaps. But my father and I were close. It's possible I didn't see the obvious out of my blinded love for him." He inhaled the cigar and frowned. With the flick of his wrist, he tossed the cheroot into the hearth. "While my father lay dying in Mexico during the war, he said he had something important to tell me. He died moments later, writhing in agony in my arms. I never knew what it was he wanted to tell me. His death and those unspoken words of his haunted me for years."

Eden snuggled in closer and pressed her lips to his ear. "I'm so sorry, my darling, that must have been terrible."

"He took a bullet right in the stomach. A bullet meant for me. The man actually dove in front of me, taking the hit himself. The death was horribly painful but mercifully quick."

He paused, trying to push the image from his mind. "It wasn't until my grandfather died, when this manor passed to me, that I found out about Trinidad."

"Your grandfather knew you had a sister all that time and didn't tell you?"

"He knew. But Abena was black. As you can well imagine, this dirty family secret needed to be kept quiet. Besides, the old man had his own inner demons to deal with. His father, Captain Reginald Hampton, had died from what my grandfather had always referred to as 'the misery wrought by trifling with the wrong woman.' The Captain's wife, Faith, had left the captain for another man when my grandfather was just a boy. Grandfather watched the captain wither away into nothing more than a shattered shell of a man. Anyway, before my grandfather died he had an apparent change of heart. Attached to his will was a letter to me with the whole story about my father and Abena and my half-sister."

"How is it she's here now — with you?" Eden tilted her chin, avoiding his gaze. For the first time, he realized just how jealous she had been of Trinidad.

"I thought I was an only child, so I was eager to meet her. I booked ship's passage and found her. After discovering her losses, I brought her here. Abena had passed away years back. The thing is, Trinidad knew about me all those years, but I had no clue she existed."

"So the stories around here about the heartbroken captain are true?"

He sighed. "Oh, and the heartache doesn't end there, I'm afraid."

Eden poked him in the shoulder. "Go on, tell me."

"You really want to hear about all these things?"

"I do — yes."

He tickled her ribs. "I didn't figure you'd be a glutton for such punishment."

"Oh, stop," she chided.

"All right...let's see. Well, with my grandfather's mother gone, and his father, the captain, nothing more than a broken man awaiting the return of his wife Faith, Grandfather just grew into an angry man raised by indifferent servants."

"So, Captain Reginald Hampton married Faith. They had a small son, your grandfather. Faith left the captain for another man." She crinkled her nose. "So, whom did your grandfather marry? He did marry, yes?"

"Another tragedy there, I'm afraid," he said softly. "Grandfather was an educated man. Trained as a lawyer at Harvard, but Christ almighty, he was mean. He fell in love with a woman, but she refused to marry him, even when she found out she was carrying his child. Grandfather urged her to marry him for the sake of propriety, but she rejected the idea. The child was my father. Why she had been with my grandfather in the first place, I'll never know. Within a few years, she was taken by typhoid. She died in this house, in my grandfather's arms, and he never got over the loss."

"And so your poor father was raised by your bitter grandfather, and both of them raised without a mother?"

"I'm afraid so. Beginning with the captain, we Hamptons have been a sorry lot when it comes to relationships and marriage. It's as if a curse descended down upon this place when Faith left the captain." He looked at the captain's portrait above the mantle. "The men in my family have either been devastated by love or left others in emotional ruin. Sadness has festered for years within these walls."

"And whatever became of your mother?"

"She's still alive. We've never talked about any of this. Never. I'm a dreadfully painful reminder to her of a sad time in her life."

She sat up. "Oh, Rayce, tell me that's not true."

"Oh, it's true." He pulled Eden close. "Shortly after my father died, she sold the sugarcane fields in the islands. She remarried my father's business partner. They live in New Orleans. My father had specifically put in his will if he died before her, the business would be sold and the money given to her to build a new life for herself. Perhaps the arrangement was supposed to appease his guilt. I don't know."

She kissed his shoulder. "Do you ever see your mother?"

"I've visited her in New Orleans a few times. When she looks at me, I see the sadness creep into her eyes, and I have to leave. I can't bear the thought of being a burden to her."

"Does your mother know about Trinidad?"

"Out of respect for my mother, I've told her Trinidad is a hired servant."

"Trinidad's a beautiful woman. I think I may have even been jealous of her, but she's terribly spooky, Rayce."

He laughed. "I imagine to others she would appear peculiar. She still adheres to some of her native culture. But I have to say, the woman has surprised me many times. She sees things, Eden. She knows things, often before they happen. I suppose you could call that spooky. I try not to judge. Who am I to judge anyone?" He sat up and stared evenly into Eden's eyes. "This is why I found it easy not to kill that miserable old beau of yours."

Eden sat tall. "Oh, Rayce, the things Patrick did. Obviously, all while he was my beau and we were engaged to be married. Believe me, I thought of killing him myself when he told me everything."

"Slavery is an evil beast, my dear. He's a weak man, and like many weak men before him, he let the evil beast of power cloud his better judgment. Mark my words, sooner or later, the South will break because of this, as well."

"You mean we'll lose this war?"

"Probably." God, he hated to be the one to shatter her naïve views. "Perhaps not as soon as Lincoln would like, but the South is dying, my dear." He sighed. "It's really just a matter of time."

"But, Rayce, you go out and dodge bullets and cannon fire and bayonets daily. Why do you fight for Virginia and the Cause with such passion if you don't believe in your heart we can win?"

He thought about her question for a moment. "Darlin', slavery will die of its own weakness. It has to. But the North's hypocrisy with their insults and raving abolitionists infuriates the hell out of me. It wasn't southern ships that brought the negroes to our shores — it was northern ships. The North stole the slaves from Africa and sold them to us for profit. They're even more responsible for the evil existence of slavery than we are. And now that the North has all the railroads, factories, and urban sprawl, they tear at the very heart and soul of the South they helped create and force her to bend to their will. There simply will be no South with the North thrusting themselves down our throats too fast. Enslaving another human being is a curse, but this war is happening without any regard to our dilemma. And Lincoln, well, don't get me started on him. He's really far more interested in preserving the Union than anything else.

Eden slowly shook her head. "It's so very complicated."

He lay down and pulled her close. "Enough of this talk. I have something else I want to say." He paused. "I'm sorry."

She nuzzled his neck. "Sorry for what?"

"Honey, I was an idiot back at the grain shed. I wasn't thinking clearly. Somehow, I just assumed you knew about Patrick. Of course, I knew you didn't know all of it, but I never meant to hurt you or make you feel your father—"

Eden pressed her finger to his lips. "Enough. Apology accepted."

He encircled her back with his arms, pressing her firmly against his chest. "This dress is still damp. Perhaps you'll catch a chill. Best take it off, don't you agree?"

"I agree, Major." She pinched his side playfully and kissed his cheek. "Mind if I put on one of your shirts?"

"Hell, no, I don't mind. Do you have any idea how good you look in my shirts? Help yourself."

She slipped behind the rosewood screen. "Rayce?" she called out. "When was the happiest time in your life?"

He smiled. "Besides right now? Is this a trick question?"

"No, I'm serious."

He stared up at the ceiling and thought about her question. "The older I get, the more I think back to my years out West. It's so very different from here, Eden. There's a wildness there that can't be tamed. The nights are long and clear and especially dark. The stars look like you could reach up and pluck them right out of the sky; that's how bright they are." He folded his arms behind his head and sighed. "And what about you? When was the happiest time in your life?"

"Besides right now?" She walked out from behind the screen wearing his shirt, trotted back into bed, and lay down next to him.

He smiled and kissed her forehead. "Yes, besides right now."

"Hmm, I think it's when I was a young girl. I never really knew my mother. She died when I was very young, but I adored my father and Isaac and Mama Claire, and I thought the world of Asa, Jeremiah, and Ezekiel. Back then, I never realized evil lurked around familiar corners. There's just a simple and pure nature in the heart of a child before the world and all its shortcomings become apparent. I know it must sound silly to you, a worldly man—"

"Nonsense, woman. I remember well what it's like to be young, too, you know."

With an impish grin, Eden got up, pulled her long hair above her head, and wiggled her bottom in front of him. "Is this how the girls in the saloons out West dance?"

"Get over here, you vixen." He grabbed her by the waist and pulled her on top of him. "Sweetness, I have to leave tomorrow morning, and I don't think I'll be back for a while."

"But I'll miss you." She searched his eyes for an answer he

didn't have. "Oh, Rayce, I'm tired of saying goodbye to you. I want this war to be over soon. I want you and Isaac and Jimmy safe. I just want to close my eyes tonight and wake up with the war over and the South victorious. Is that really too much to ask for?"

His stomach twisted in knots. He wished he could flat-out lie to her. Unable to face those pleading green eyes, he lowered his chin. "Honey, it's not that simple. I hate to tell you this, but the situation on the Peninsula is going to get worse. Much worse."

Chapter 14

"Are you sure, Mr. Benton?" Eden asked.

"Oh, yes, quite sure, Miss Eden. I read it in the *Dispatch*. Richmond is simply abuzz with the news," Will replied, having just returned from the city the day before. He reached for his hat and turned to leave. "Jeb Stuart himself arrived in Richmond and reported to General Lee on the daring ride. Apparently, he and his men rode a hundred miles around Little Mac's huge army. General McClellan is disgraced."

"Disgraced! I can't believe it," Ann yelped. "Of course it couldn't have happened at a better time, either. I've been up every night fretting with worry."

Will rubbed her shoulder and smiled. "Come walk me out, kitten. I've missed you."

Ann smiled and looped her arm with his. "Why, of course. I'd be delighted, Mr. Benton."

Eden sighed with relief. For weeks she had listened to the frightening sounds of gunfire and bursting cannon inching closer. Watching from the windows, the lifeless billows of gray smoke contrasted with the fields awash in hues of green, joining with the mounds of crisp golden wheat. The orchards defied the dreary haze by flaunting their pallet of pastels with the ripening of summer fruits, while vibrant wildflowers bloomed rebelliously in meadows ravaged by marching troops and thick wagons ruts.

She and Lucy sat on the divan in the parlor and turned their attention to the letter Will had just delivered from Rayce. Eden tore at the sealed envelope, and they huddled together, reading the neatly penned missive.

"Oh, no," Lucy whimpered. "Oh no, not Aunt Martha. Oh, Eden can you believe this?"

Eden's heart sunk as she read the letter.

Lucy rested her back against the back of the divan, her eyes glassy and dazed. "I...I can't believe it. Aunty gravely ill and not a single hospital bed to be had in the city. I'm at a loss for words. She's been healthy as a horse her whole life. And poor Rayce. He must be beside himself with worry."

Eden's mind raced. With Aunt Martha fighting for her life and the city in desperate need of trained citizens, perhaps it was time she went where her help would be needed most. From everything she had heard over the past weeks, the incoming wounded soldiers needed more medical help than the city had to offer. And with Rayce's frequent visits to Richmond...

"I'll go!" Eden said louder than she had expected. "I'll tend to Aunt Martha and help our wounded soldiers, too. I can leave as early as tomorrow."

"What?" Lucy's moist eyes widened. "Oh, Eden, you mustn't go to the city now. Aunty needs help, yes, but it could be very dangerous if the Yankees take the city."

"But, honey, with everything we've been hearing, I feel I should go and help but..." Eden sat forward. "I really don't want to leave you alone."

"Alone, heaven's above. The baby and I are fine here with everyone else. It's you I would worry about."

"You needn't worry about me." Eden smiled. "I know my way around the city. I can stay at Aunt Martha's, tend to her, and find time to help at the hospitals. Think about it, Lucy. With so many neighbors having fled these parts, I'm not needed much these days. But Richmond—"

"Eden, you're so brave." Lucy wrapped her in an embrace. "Why, I'd bet my boots you could help poor Aunt Martha and all those wounded boys of ours, single-handedly."

Eden hugged Lucy in return. "Singlehandedly? You give me far too much credit. You know I'll do my very best to help your aunt. I promise."

Lucy's forehead smoothed, and she reached for Eden's hand. "I know you'll do your best. You're not capable of doing anything less. It's who you are; it's your nature, dear. Most of all, I want you to do what your heart tells you to do."

Eden gazed into Lucy's eyes. "My heart is telling me to go to Richmond," she whispered, choking back tears.

"Then that's exactly what you shall do." Lucy sighed and smiled. "Lord knows, if anyone deserves to follow her heart, it's you after all you've been through, even if this war follows so close it singes your skirts."

"Well, let's hope it doesn't come to that." Eden forced a smile.

Lucy inched in and lowered her voice, "I still can't believe it about your father, and Patrick, and-oh, my heavens, even

Isaac knew. Shame on him for never telling me a word." Lucy waved her dainty fingers, fanning her face. "Why, it still gives me the vapors just thinking about it. I'm so happy that evil is behind us."

Eden nodded. "So am I, honey. So am I."

Leading Eden by the hand toward the stairs, Lucy launched into action. "Now, we'll need to get your bags packed. The rest of us will stay put so the armies won't strip this place bare..."

Eden was having a hard time listening. Visions of the vibrant city filled her mind, sending a charge of energy up her spine. Not only would she be able to help with the much-needed nursing care, she would also be at the center of the war, where the current news flew in with a clamor, loud as a flock of wild geese descending from the heavens. She recalled how people scurried into streets, chattered in parks, shops, and depots, determined to hear the very latest word from the battlefields.

"...And we don't dare send you on the train right now. I'm sure Joseph can get you there safely in the carriage. Oh, and you can get the latest news on General Jackson's troops — Isaac and Jimmy. Of course, the rest of us won't leave here unless it becomes absolutely necessary. Those thoughtless armies would take everything they could get their hands on in this lovely place if they had the chance. And Eden, it puts my mind at rest knowing you'll be helping Aunty. I daresay neither Rayce nor I could do without her."

Rayce. There was no doubt in Eden's mind, if given the chance, he would stop by to check on his aunt. Perhaps with a little luck, she would be able to see him when he came into the city.

"My, oh, my. What are you two looking so serious about?" Ann shut the front door and waltzed into the room, her face beaming. "I have delightful news."

"News? Heavens, do tell. We could use some good news around here," Lucy said.

"Well, Mr. Benton," Ann fluttered her lashes. "Will, I mean, has asked for my lil' ol' hand in marriage. Can you believe it?"

"Why, Ann, that's lovely," Lucy gushed.

Eden's mouth flopped open. "Well, I hope you had the sense to say yes. He's a decent man, and he seems very fond of you."

"Of course I said yes, you silly goose." She waved her fingers, making certain her diamond engagement ring flashed brilliantly in their faces. "Why, I've had images in my head for weeks of being mistress of that lovely home of his. It's so very grand it puts my memories of Oak Hill to rest. Little ol' me, mistress of Benton Mansion."

"Let me see that." Lucy snatched Ann's hand. "Oh, my heavens, look at the size of that diamond, Eden."

Eden managed a smile. "Oh, yes...lovely."

She would have loved to slap Ann for her disrespectful comment about Oak Hill, but with the delightful image she had in her mind of Ann packing all of her bags and finally moving away forever, it was worth the moment of swallowing her pride.

"You do love him, yes?" Lucy asked.

Ann turned her blue eyes heavenward, searching the ceiling for an answer. "Well, yes, I suppose. He does have a way of growing on a woman with all that money."

"Then that is wonderful news," Lucy said, wrapping her arm around Eden's waist. "Eden and I were just discussing her trip to Richmond."

"Richmond!" Ann squealed. "Now?"

"Honey, it makes my heart ache to tell you this, but Aunt Martha has taken ill — gravely ill. Eden has offered to tend to her and represent our family by administering to those poor wounded men of ours in the hospitals."

"Oh, how I miss the excitement of the city." Ann turned her eager face toward Eden. "I can go with you."

Lucy walked swiftly to Ann's side, her skirts brushing past Eden, and grabbed Ann's hand. "Dear, the rest of us must stay here and be brave, including you. Besides, Mr. Benton would be heartbroken if you left him now."

"That's true. He is rather attached to me." Ann stuck out her bottom lip. "Yes, I suppose you're right, Lucy."

Lucy looked past Ann's shoulder. "Why, there you are, Trinidad. Miss Blair will be going on an extended trip to Richmond. Please see that her luggage is packed and readied as soon as possible."

Hovering in a dark corner, Trinidad replied with a nod and a stiff curtsy.

Lucy turned to Eden. "I'll speak with Joseph and have him ready the horses and carriage for a morning departure."

Trinidad followed behind Eden as they ascended the staircase. Once inside her bedroom, Eden shut the door behind them with a loud click of the lock. She leaned against the door and inhaled a deep breath. Instantly, the silence between them filled the large bedroom.

"Trinidad," Eden began, "before we pack I'd like for the two of us to talk for a moment." She sat on the bed and gestured for Trinidad to take a seat in the chair.

"Yes'm," she replied softly.

"I'm not sure how to say this, so I'm just going to try my best. The Major…Rayce, I mean, has told me the two of you are siblings, and," she paused, seeking acknowledgment in Trinidad's eyes, but the servant continued to stare blankly at the floor. "Well, what I'm trying to say is that I know you have his best interests at heart. I want you to know, I do, too."

Trinidad slowly peered up, meeting her gaze.

Eden frowned, surprised to see tears pooling in the servant's large brown eyes.

"May I speak my mind, Miss?"

"Yes…yes of course."

"He's my brother, and I love him as only a sister can. But he be a prideful man, and he does not always listen when he should."

Eden found herself creating a mental checklist.

Prideful? *Check.*

Arrogant? *Check.*

Self-absorbed? *Check.*

Doesn't listen? *Check.*

She smiled. "Yes, I know he can certainly be hard-headed."

Rayce had told her about Trinidad's ability to see things, to know certain events ahead of time. She thought back to the night she heard the servant weeping and pleading with him in the parlor.

"Do you mean he doesn't listen to you, Trinidad? Do you

know of something that could cause him harm?"

Trinidad sighed, and Eden watched as the pooled tears, filling her eyes, began dripping down her flawless brown cheeks.

"Yes, Miss. I tell him what I see. But like dust on his coat, he brushes me off. But he knows I be right."

"What are you right about, Trinidad? Tell me, is he in danger?"

"Yes, I sense danger, and the dreams I have are very real. I told him, and he say it is nonsense because he don't want it to be true. Now I feel the time draws near."

Trinidad pulled out a handkerchief from the pocket of her calico dress and dabbed her eyes. She turned her gaze toward the picture of Captain Reginald Hampton over the mantle and jutted her chin forward. "There. Do you see the man, the one in the painting?"

Eden cast her gaze toward the captain's portrait. "Yes."

Trinidad rose from the chair. "Come, please, and look closer."

Puzzled, Eden frowned and followed the woman to the mantel.

Trinidad gazed wistfully at the portrait. "He, too, was a prideful man. Look in his eyes, Miss. Tell me, what do you see?"

Eden placed her hand on her chin and searched the painting. "Well, let's see. I see...a handsome face...dark eyes—"

"No, Miss." Trinidad took Eden's hand in her own. "Now, take your time and look closer...deeper."

Eden wanted to laugh. She had no idea where this nonsense was going, but intrigue pressed her forward. She narrowed her eyes and searched the painting closely. The man was certainly fine looking, and the Hampton family resemblance was striking to this very day, but what was it she was supposed to see?

"Deeper," Trinidad repeated.

She focused on the delicate stokes of the brush on the thick canvas.

"Deeper still, Miss. You must go deeper. Look in the captain's eyes."

Eden gazed into the captain's dark eyes, absorbing herself within the richly tinted oils and the soft, artistic brush strokes made with unhurried hands. Moments later, the captain's mysterious eyes locked with hers.

Trinidad suddenly grasped her firmer, tighter, freezing Eden in place as the walls of the room thinned to dark shadows. The portrait drew her in, deeper...deeper, the captain connecting with her so she no longer looked into his eyes. She was immersed, as though she were part of him and witnessing a scene as it unfolded before him.

In the vision, Eden could see the young captain as he watched from the tall, third-floor window looking out upon the James River. She saw the rolling, green tobacco fields and sprawling lawn joining the shore and wharf below. A tall, wooden ship flying a British flag high upon the main mast departed the dock. She watched as burly men scrambled with the thick lines and heavy canvas sails. And as each cream sail dropped and filled, catching wind on the brisk current, she felt the captain's stabbing anguish build. As though she and Captain Hampton were connected through time, she felt his unbearable pain to the point of near madness, as he waited for Faith's eventual return.

Trinidad's hand tightened, and Eden thought she would cry out. In a flash, the vision was gone, replaced by a tormented, echoing cry coming from somewhere in the back of her mind. What she saw next was a soldier on the bloodied ground attempting to speak as he writhed in pain in the bronzed arms of a tearful, handsome young man who cried out, "I'm so sorry, father!"

"Enough!" She wrenched her hands from Trinidad's firm grasp and slammed her eyes shut. "Enough. I can't watch anymore."

Eden groped for support and stepped back, almost losing her balance. "Trinidad, I don't know what that was, but don't ever do that to me again."

The servant guided her into the chair and crouched down. "The Hampton men be cursed, Miss. They all be cursed, and this curse cannot be broken until the pain in the captain's soul is healed. I tell you, hurt runs deep in the walls here and in each Hampton man. I show you this, because you must know. You must believe me."

Eden took in slow, shallow breaths, trying to steady the frantic beat of her heart. "I don't understand any of this. What is it you want me to do?"

"My dream haunts me, Miss. The major will be in great danger."

"Tell me your dream, Trinidad. I want to know."

Eden admitted it all seemed farfetched, but some unearthly power grabbed hold of her when she stared into the eyes of the captain. There was no denying Trinidad possessed some kind of power, something unique and perceptive others did not.

Trinidad closed her eyes and swallowed hard. "My dream be always the same. I see thick woods of green at sunset. A soft mist, like wet cobwebs, rises over the water next to the major. I see tall oaks in swamp water and snakes swimming around the thick tree trunks and hanging vines. I smell the pine and wet earth. He looks for a way back, but the path has disappeared. He turns to face the water again, but it has turned red...with blood. He looks for something and reaches into the water, but the water has turned thick and black, and he can no longer move. He calls out for help, but the water grows darker, thicker, until he is pulled in deeper and swallowed in death."

Eden slowly shook her head. "Well, what do you suppose it means?"

"It's hard to know dreams, Miss. The mind plays games. But I know in my heart he be in danger. The dream will reveal itself. That I am certain." Trinidad paused and searched Eden's eyes. "You love Rayce, do you not?"

Eden smiled. "Yes...I do. But you already know that, don't you?"

Trinidad rose to her feet and extended her hand to help Eden from the chair. "Let me pack your bags, Miss. I know with my whole being, this trip is your destiny."

"My destiny — that sounds so serious," Eden teased, trying to lighten the moment.

Trinidad's eyes narrowed into dark slits. "Serious, indeed. If you love him, Miss, you must help him, for he and the man in the portrait are one and the same."

Chapter 15

Richmond, Virginia
June 1862

Feeling as though she were boiling with the unbearable heat of summer, Eden blotted her neck and slowly trudged up the porch steps. She opened the door and called, "Eliza, I'm back." Groaning as she sat on the cushioned foyer bench, she sluggishly removed her boots and massaged each aching toe.

"I thought I heard you return, Miss Eden," Eliza said from the top of the staircase.

"How's Aunt Martha doing? Any better?"

Eliza shook her head. "No, she's still feverin', and such. The pneumonia's got her good."

Eden gazed down at the worn leather boots she'd just removed. Having just spent a grueling morning on her feet at Chimborazo Hospital, she couldn't bear to put them on again. She picked up the boots and plodded up the hardwood stairs in her stocking feet.

"Lawd, Almighty, Miss, you look dog-tired today."

Eden waved a limp wrist, "I'm fine, Eliza. I'm going to my room to freshen up. I'll be back to relieve you in just a bit."

She tossed the boots in the corner of her room and stood at the washbasin examining her face in the mirror. "My heavens, I'm as gaunt as a starving waif," she murmured, angling her chin from side to side for a better look.

After dipping a cloth in cool mint water, she lifted her braid and soaked her neck, washing the hospital grime from her face and chest. She placed the cloth around her neck and closed her eyes.

Was it really any wonder why she looked so thin and pale the last weeks? Between caring for Aunt Martha and tending the soldiers at the hospital, she'd had little sleep. The sickening sights, sounds, and foul odors made the reality of war come to life with vivid and disgusting detail, and as each day went by without a word from Rayce, her stomach turned into tighter knots.

Lord knows, from the moment she arrived in Richmond, nothing had gone as imagined. The pleasant capital, with its sense of refined elegance and grace, had been replaced by a city in turmoil. The soft sounds of rustling silk and gentle southern drawls now mingled with the noise of loud-mouthed ruffians and war-weary, disabled soldiers. Women of the night, gamblers, and thieves filled darkened alleys and once cozy side streets, while the steady stream of locomotives rolled into depots at all hours, brimming with wounded soldiers heading to hospitals, big and small. Meanwhile, straddling the nearby Chickahominy River, the Yankees sat like spiders dressed in blue, waiting for the best time to strike.

She heard footsteps clomping up the porch, followed by a swift knock at the door. She patted dry with a linen towel and sighed. "Now what?"

"Hello, Eliza," said the familiar deep voice. "How's she doing?"

Rayce! She ripped the cloth from her neck and dropped it in the water. "And I look such a fright!"

Tugging the ribbon from her braid, she darted to the vanity and brushed her hair in a panicked flurry. Hearing him downstairs talking to Eliza sent a surge of renewed energy right up her backbone. Regardless of Trinidad's warning, never once had she allowed herself to imagine Rayce wounded on a battlefield or hospital bed, or worse, carried home feet-first in a pine coffin. But her daily work at the hospital brought home the reality of how their new love could be shattered in the blink of eye by a swift bullet or the plunge of a bayonet. Diseases ran rampant, like filthy scampering alley rats, going from soldier to soldier. The illnesses took the lives of the men with such ease it left her wondering why God chose to place them on the earth in the first place if they would have to die in such misery.

He's here...and he's safe.

"Miss Eden?" Eliza called, knocking on the bedroom door.

"Uh...yes?"

"Major Hampton's paying a visit. I told him you was here, and he asked to see you."

"I'll...I'll be right there," she called, assessing herself in the mirror. Rather than pin her hair up in an appropriate daytime chignon, she decided to wear it down and long to her waist, the way he liked it.

Rayce is here!

She grabbed her bottle of magnolia oil, dabbed a dot behind each ear and across her throat, and donned a clean, pretty dress.

As she descended the steps, she saw him standing at the bottom near the entry door, leaning on the banister while talking to Eliza. When he saw her, he stopped in mid-sentence and stared up as she walked down the staircase.

For a brief moment, Eliza looked confused, but within seconds, dawning comprehension led her to seek swift refuge. "I have a lil' something to tend to in the kitchen. Back in a jiffy."

Rayce smiled, his dazzling white teeth contrasting fiercely with his deeply bronzed skin and gray jacket.

"Now, what a surprise." He extended his hand as she reached the bottom step. "I came to see my aunt and discover you're here, as well. I must say, I planned on giving you a verbal thrashing for putting yourself in danger coming here, but then I find you..." A single raven eyebrow rose as he slowly appraised her from head to toe, and continued, "I find you looking positively good enough to eat."

She felt as giddy as a young girl in his presence, and the flush rushing to her cheeks was proof.

Eliza entered with glasses of cooled sweet tea. "Thank the Lawd Almighty for keeping that cellar as cool as a melon in the mornin' on these hot summer days."

Rayce cleared his throat. "Shall we have a seat, Miss Blair, and catch up?" he asked in a formal tone.

"Why, yes, of course, Major Hampton." She fanned out her skirt, sat on the horsehair divan, and laced her fingers together across her lap.

Eliza set the silver tray down and left the room, shaking her head. "You two ain't foolin' me none," she muttered, ambling off toward the back of the house. "Not foolin' nobody one bit."

"Eliza's always been a wise, old soul." Rayce scooted in and pulled her close. He took a handful of her hair spilling across the back of the divan. "My God, woman, I've missed you." He smoothed her long bangs from her forehead and gently kissed her lips.

She wrapped her arms around his neck. "Oh, Rayce, I've missed you so much, too."

He breathed in deeply, inhaling the magnolia oil dotted across her throat. She sensed his instant arousal, but now was not the time.

She took his hand and stood. "Let's check on your aunt, shall we? I know she'll be pleased to see you."

"How is she, Eden?" he asked, his voice solemn as he followed behind her up the long, narrow staircase.

"I think she likely would have died had I not come. This is too much for one person to handle."

They reached the top of the staircase, and she squeezed his hand. "I cannot promise anything, my love. I have done all I can. The rest is up to your aunt...and God."

Rayce's breath caught in his lungs the moment he entered the room. The elderly woman lying in bed, fighting for her life, was his mother's sister — his favorite aunt. Each time he thought about the possibility of losing her, it was like a knife in his chest. The older woman had always been healthy, jovial, and energetic, and she had loved him unconditionally his entire life. Unlike the look of sorrow he found whenever he gazed into his mother's eyes, Aunt Martha's blue eyes always glowed with love and understanding. He took a seat next to her in the bedside chair and reached for her hand. "Aunt Martha?"

She lay in her bed asleep, the fluid inside her lungs rumbling between shallow breaths. At the foot of her bed lay a rainbow of colored quilts he remembered her stitching over the years. She opened her eyes, trying to focus on the face calling her name.

"Rayce...my dear Rayce." With a shaky hand, she gingerly fingered her crocheted sleeping cap. "I'm afraid...I've been better, my dear boy."

"What can I do for my sweet ol' girl? You name it and it's yours."

She squeezed his hand and coughed. "You can start...by giving me...a sip of...brandy."

"Let's sit her up," Eden said.

They propped her into a sitting position and wedged the pillows behind her back.

Aunt Martha looked at the two of them, and a small smile tipped upward at the corners of her mouth. She coughed and pointed to her dresser. "There...my flask."

Rayce uncapped the flask and poured a small amount of brandy between her lips. All of his life his aunt had regularly indulged in brandy and other sweet spirits. The funny thing was, she was the only one who thought it a secret.

"Thank you, dear." Her eyes brightened to a lighter shade of blue. "Yes, there is something...you can do for me, my boy. But if I know you...you're not going to like it."

Clearly, some privacy between them was in order. Eden placed her hand on his shoulder. "I'm going to gather some fresh water and cloths." She headed toward the door.

Rayce caught Eden's eye and mouthed, "Thank you."

When he finally ventured down the steps, Eden welcomed

him in the parlor with an embrace. They sat on the divan and drank the sweet tea Eliza had set out.

"I hear the cannon fire every day now, Rayce, and it scares me to death. Even the windows here rattle and shake. How long can you stay?"

"Honey, I wish I could stay longer, but I leave at first light – perhaps earlier. I think it's likely we have most of the night, though." He drew her close, and the words just spilled from his mouth, "Sweetness, I must have you tonight."

She gazed into his eyes and smiled. "I think such an arrangement can be had. I'll have Eliza stay with Aunt Martha tonight."

"I was hoping you'd say that. I'm taking you out for a proper supper." He frowned and rubbed the small of her back. "You've grown thin since I've been away. Perhaps, afterwards, we can go to my room at the hotel for some privacy."

She smiled. "I'd like that."

HE ordered Eden the finest meal the restaurant had to offer, ignoring their overinflated prices thanks to the Federal blockade, but she did little more than pick at her stuffed pheasant and vegetables. Afterward, they went to his room at the five-story Spotswood Hotel, with its lovely, ornate iron façade greeting them as they entered.

"Are you all right, Sweetness? It's not like you to pick at your food. Frankly, I've always admired that about you. I find the Southern rules you women are expected to live by in order to catch a husband absurd. If a woman's hungry, she should eat."

She sighed and waved her hand. "I'm fine. I have you here

now, don't I?"

"You most certainly do." He removed her cloak and draped it over the chair. Instantly, the scent of her magnolia perfume drifted into his nostrils. He pulled her into his arms, and the swell of her firm breasts pressed against his chest sent a jolt of heat straight to his torso. "Lord, woman, you smell wonderful," he whispered against her throat.

With a mischievous grin, she wiggled away from his embrace and stood before him at arm's length.

The naughty vixen was up to something. He grumbled in reply and took a seat, watching as she leisurely pulled the tortoiseshell pins from her hair. Her golden mane tumbled down her back like sweet, creamed honey slowly dripping from a jar. By God, how he'd been waiting for this moment for what felt like an eternity.

All those lonely nights, sleeping in military camps and on damp forest floors, his mind had gone crazy with visions of being with her again. Night after night, he imagined himself lunging forward, tearing her clothes off, and making wild love to her on the spot. Sometimes he imagined it happening under the improvised tent he occupied that night, or on the dirt ground surrounded by thick pines, and sometimes in this very hotel room.

He twisted uncomfortably in his seat. Having her standing before him like his very own Aphrodite, was more than any man should have to bear.

Eden saw the smoldering glow in his eyes when he stood and took a step forward. She shoved her hand out and tried not to smile. "Oh, no, you don't...not just yet, big boy."

He stopped in his tracks, and arched his brows high. "You,

my dear, are the devil in disguise." He plucked a thin cigar from his pocket, lit it, and plopped back down in the chair. "But I must confess, you do have me intrigued."

She stood before him and slowly unfastened the buttons along the front of her dress. Slipping her arms out of the long sleeves, one by one, she let the mass of blue fabric drop in a delicate puddle to the floor.

His gaze drifted leisurely from the discarded dress, wandering up her full length. "Looks like I have the best seat in the house," he mused. "Do continue, Miss Blair."

She looked him square in the eyes and placed her boot upon the chair between his legs.

He cleared his throat and said, "You have my attention."

She smiled, unlaced her right boot, and removed it. Little by little, she rolled her cotton stocking down to her ankle, her fingers gliding gently across her bare legs, then letting the dainty material float to the floor.

She heard the breath catch deep in his throat, emboldening her further. She did the same for the left leg, but this time she tossed the stocking toward him, and he caught it in his hand. His dark gaze glowed, hot as the embers of the burning cigar.

With her eyes fixed upon his, she leisurely unhooked the front of her stays and laid the garment next to her dress. Next, she loosened the petticoat and pantalets, slipping out of them, one foot after another, and dropped them to the floor at his feet. Finally, she stepped back, moving out of his reach, taunting him as she stood in only her skimpy chemise.

His raven eyes narrowed, following her every move. "Woman, if you don't hurry up, I'm going have to pull my gun on you."

"Is that an order, Major?"

"Oh, that's most definitely an order."

She pondered his "order" playfully with her hand upon her chin.

He warned her again with a single raised eyebrow as he tapped his fingers on the holster.

Summoning a teasing smile, she stood in front of him, holding her chin high, ignoring his direct order.

He blew out a ring of smoke and extinguished the cigar. In one fluid move, he rose and scooped her over his shoulder. "If you're the devil, woman, then let me be damned!" He spanked her bottom and tossed her on the bed.

Through the sheer fabric, he could see her pert nipples and the golden triangle between her thighs. Her lithe legs slid across the blanket like silky cream, and she summoned him with a single finger to join her.

"Now it's your turn to wait," he said, removing his holstered gun, and setting it on the bedside table. He unbuttoned his shirt and flung it across the top of the chair. After climbing out of his trousers and drawers, he slipped into bed next to her.

She lay gazing at the portrait over the hearth, gnawing on her bottom lip.

He frowned. "You look deep in thought."

She rolled to her side and faced him. "Oh, I'm…I'm just so happy to see you — to be with you again, Rayce. I've missed you so."

"That makes two of us." He slid his fingers under her chemise, moving his hand across her velvety skin. "You smell wonderful, and you feel divine."

She sighed. "Rayce, promise me something."

The anxious tone in her voice caught him by surprise. He brushed an errand strand of hair from her cheek. "Anything."

"Promise me you'll stay safe," she said. "I don't care what it takes. Just promise me you'll always come back to me."

He cupped her chin and tilted her face toward his. "Why so serious tonight? I've come back to you unscathed for the most part."

Heavy footsteps followed by a swift knock at the door interrupted them.

"Do you have to answer it?" she asked in a choked whisper.

"I do, honey. Stay right where you are. He called toward the door, "Be right there."

He quickly donned his shirt and drawers. As he walked to the door, he glanced back just in time to catch her yanking the blankets over her head and heaving a dramatic sigh.

He opened the door a crack. "This better be important."

The wide-eyed officer blushed. "Uh...yes, sir, I believe it is. The general requested I come get you for an emergency meeting, sir. Here. I have a note."

Rayce read the folded paper. *I knew it.*

"Tell him I'll be there." He closed the door.

Eden tossed the covers from her head and sat up. "You have to go now?"

"Duty calls, Sweetness." He removed his clothes and slipped back into bed. "I don't have long. Perhaps fifteen or twenty minutes at the most. "Let's make it count, shall we, my love?"

He kissed the hollow of her throat and gently slid his hand between her legs, stroking the soft, warm flesh of her inner thighs.

"Oh, Rayce, I…I don't want you to go."

He sat up, trying to ignore the unease in her voice. "Shush now, darlin'. I'll be back. You know I will."

He gently lifted her up so she sat on his lap, straddling him. He gazed into her emerald eyes and ran his fingers through her hair, hanging long and wild down to her curved waist. In a flash, he grew harder than a musket on the battle line. She draped her arms around his neck, and he kissed her, his tongue searching her mouth, feeling her, tasting her.

He slipped his hands under her bottom, hoisting her up just enough to enter her. Slowly, he slid his rigid shaft into her warm slickness, and a deep groan of pleasure involuntarily escaped his lips. "Dammmmit," he moaned against her throat.

She held him tightly, kissing his brow, and he felt the waves of desire rise within her, moistening her instantly.

"Oh, Rayce," she breathed.

She moved rhythmically, her sweet moans of desire, bringing him to the very edge. Being inside her was just as he had remembered each of those lonely nights without her, and every inch of his body responded.

"I'm afraid this isn't going to take long, Sweetness. I've missed you too damn much." He kissed her neck, his teeth grazing her skin. "Lord, I wish I didn't have to leave you."

The moment he spoke against her throat, Eden's body answered with a shuddering climax, practically taking his breath away. Instantly, his body responded to her rising passion. He drove in faster, deeper, sliding against her moist pebble. She moaned and tossed her head back, her long hair brushing against his thighs like silken fingers, just as his body stiffened with spasms of pleasure.

He listened to the seconds tick by on the clock as they held each other in silence, their moist, naked bodies gleaming in the soft glowing candlelight.

"I have to go," he whispered.

She buried her face in his neck and dug her nails into his back, pulling him in closer. "Are you coming back tonight?"

He kissed her forehead. "Most assuredly. Now get some rest. I'll return as soon as I can."

He dressed quietly, listening to the soft sounds of her breathing as she fell asleep. He draped the quilt over her bare shoulders and whispered, "Sleep well, my love."

RETURNING to the room, he tread lightly, trying not to wake her. He stopped in his tracks when she stirred.

"What time is it?" she asked, yawning.

"Go back to sleep, Sweetness. Everything's fine."

He sighed with relief when she instantly fell back asleep. Had she looked into his eyes after the meeting tonight, she would have known everything was not "fine."

After he had been briefed about the meeting held earlier with the generals, it was obvious a grand battle for Richmond was about to unfold.

In his younger days, the thought of impending battle and doing his part for the Cause would have excited him, heightened and stimulated his senses. If he made it through the battle unscathed, great. If not, so be it. But tonight, while coming back to Eden, it felt as though he'd taken a hard blow to the gut. The woman in his bed had changed his life and altered the way he valued his own.

He sat in the bedside chair and watched her sleep. Tonight, for the first time, he realized how much he truly cherished the life he had begun to make with her. There was no use denying it any longer. Falling in love with Eden Blair was the best thing to ever happen to him.

Quietly, he gathered his belongings, and she stirred awake.

"Tell me you don't have to go right now." She sat up, rubbing her eyes.

He adjusted the belt around his waist. "I can tell you that if you'd like, but it wouldn't be the truth."

She rose from the bed and walked toward him. "I don't think I can bear to say goodbye to you again."

God, this is hard.

He pulled her close. "Over the next days and weeks I want you to be mindful of everything around you. Stay at Aunt Martha's. I'll send word to you there as soon as I can."

"You promise?"

He nodded. "I promise."

She looked into his eyes. "What's wrong, Rayce?"

He paused, choosing his words carefully. "Remember I told you this war would get worse before it got better if the South were to have a chance? That time is now, my dear."

"Oh, Rayce, I'm frightened."

"I don't wish to frighten you, quite the contrary. But I do want you safe. You're a smart, resourceful woman, Eden. I want you to trust your instincts."

"What of Isaac? Will he be involved in this, too?"

He lowered his head. "Without a doubt, my dear. Without a doubt."

She sighed, resting her head upon his chest, clutching his thick jacket in her fists.

"I have to go, darlin'. They're waiting for me downstairs." He lifted her chin, turning her face up to his. "Kiss me, sweet Eden. Kiss me as if there's no tomorrow."

"But–"

He silenced her protest with his mouth. She stood on her tiptoes and wrapped her arms around his neck, grasping his hair in her hands.

She pulled back, tears streaming down her cheeks. "Goodbye, my love," she whispered.

His mouth descended upon hers again. He tasted the tears on her lips, and it took all of his energy to leave. He opened the door and looked back. "Goodbye, Sweetness. Until we meet again."

Chapter 16

Eden felt the intense summer heat as a wave of dizzying nausea that came and went throughout much of the day. A soft buzz of steady chatter among the men filled the hospital wards, and nurses and doctors talked in hushed whispers of events rapidly unfolding.

While changing the dressings on an unconscious Rebel soldier, she overheard two women talking about their sons who were local soldiers. They had just been issued two days' rations of baked biscuits and bacon for their haversacks, which usually meant they were preparing for battle. She recalled Rayce's cautionary words.

"It's all gonna be all right, Miss Eden."

Startled by the voice coming from the next bed, she flinched and turned toward the young private, brought in a few days earlier with a bullet wound to his arm.

"Why, you gave me start, Private Tracey. I checked on you only a few moments ago, and you were sound asleep."

"I'm sorry, Miss Eden."

She moved to his bedside. "Let's take a look under those

bandages, shall we?" Gingerly, she lifted the dressing. There was no doubt about it; infection had begun to take hold.

"I was just sayin' I think everything's gonna work out fine soon enough," he offered.

"Well, of course it is." She leaned over to fill his glass with fresh water. "What can I do for you today, Private? Would you like me to write another letter to your mother or perhaps a sweetheart back home?"

"Naw, there ain't nothin' to write home about just yet. But that's all gonna change."

Eden squeezed out a cloth in cool water and placed it on his sweltering forehead. "Well, of course things will change. You're going to get better."

"I don't mean that, Miss. I mean this war is openin' up like a can of corn on the fire about to pop. You can smell it in the air."

"Well, if all the whispering around here is any indication, then I think you might be right. I've been hearing talk all morning myself." She furrowed her brow. "But you shouldn't trouble yourself with such things right now. You need to get better."

"Well, you just looked kinda worried. I don't want you to fret, Miss Eden. I hear tell ol' General Jackson and his men will be behind them Yanks soon." The gangly soldier offered a feeble smile and pointed at his arm. "I just wish I wasn't feeling so poorly. I'd like to give them boys in blue a real Rebel whuppin' myself."

"I'm sure you would. But for now, you need your rest, Private."

"Call me Robert." He paused and tilted his head. "Frankly

speaking, Miss, I thought them big skeeters in the swamps woulda been what got me. Never in my life have I been bitten like that. I itched so bad I thought I was gonna die. It was downright miserable, almost worse than this here arm being shot."

Eden nodded. "If it makes you feel any better, I can tell you a lot of the boys have been saying the same thing. This place is full of soldiers with swamp fever. Some worse off than others."

He smiled. "You got a special someone in the war, Miss Eden?"

"Hey, Robby!" came a voice from the next bed. "What you doin', making a play for Miss Eden? I heard her talking to the other nurse earlier. She's already got a beau, and he's a major in the war — Major Hampton, one of General Stuart's men, so you ain't got a chance."

"Hush yourself, Sam, you durn know it all," Robert sneered, his cheeks flushing red. "That right, Miss Eden? You got a beau already? I guess I shoulda known someone as pretty as you would have been spoken for."

"Oh, you two boys should mind yourselves," Eden chided.

"Ah, come on, Miss Eden, you can tell us," Sam toyed. "We get right bored lying around here all day long. Tell us about your beau."

"Yeah, tell us Miss Eden," said Robert."

She rolled her eyes heavenward and sighed. "I'll tell you more if you both promise me you'll try to get some rest."

The two men nodded.

"Well, yes, I do have a beau, just like Sam overheard. And yes, he's a major in Jeb Stuart's cavalry." For an added touch of entertainment, she placed a splayed hand across her chest and summoned up her most dramatic demeanor. "He's terribly brave and incredibly handsome, and I daresay I'm madly in love with him."

"Ah, shucks, Robby, she's taken, all right," Sam whispered.

Eden couldn't help but smile. "And that's all you boys need to know. Now, get some rest."

"Eden Blair? Why, I thought that was you."

Eden spun around to see her childhood friend, Amelia Honeycutt. Before moving to Richmond, the Honeycutt family had owned a lovely home not far from Oak Hill. Amelia was a few years older and had always been a sight with her clear, bright eyes and vivid shock of red hair contrasting against her marble-like pale skin. Amelia looked especially pretty in her smart dress, and Eden instantly sensed how soiled her hospital apron and gingham dress must appear.

"Amelia Honeycutt, why, don't you look fabulous."

"It's Amelia Wyeth now." She removed a glove and extended her hand, revealing an elegant gold wedding band below a large diamond ring. "I'm an ol' married lady now," she gushed.

"Why, that's wonderful," Eden beamed, truly happy for her friend.

"Thank you, honey." Amelia's smile faded. She leaned in closer, whispering, "Eden, can you believe this war? I'm just sick to death with worry all the time. And I can't sleep a wink with this constant fear and dread upon me."

"Perhaps a nip of spirits before bedtime might help," Eden offered as a solution. "A sip of brandy can work wonders to induce a restful night's sleep." She glanced down at Robert, who appeared to be falling asleep. "I imagine you're terribly worried for your husband. He's in the war?"

"I worry for him, my cousins, even my father enlisted — and practically every boy is off at war now since the conscription." Amelia pursed her pouty lips. "I do so detest bringing this up, but I heard Patrick McDowell joined with the Yankees. Tell me that's not true."

"It's true and I—"

Shots rattled in the distance and everyone in the room paused for a moment to listen.

"Do you know someone in here?" Eden asked, changing the subject.

"Sadly, yes, my sister's husband is over there." Amelia pointed at a nearby bunk. "Lieutenant Wilcox — poor man. The doctor said he's not sure if he'll make it unless his leg comes off. Gangrene, I'm afraid. My sister, Ellen, is beside herself with worry. She has a baby due this month, too. I just feel so helpless."

"Poor thing. It must be mighty hard on her. Now, you be sure to let me know if I can be of help. The doctors are terribly busy these days."

Eden glanced at the clock on the wall and decided a needed break was in order. The hospital shutters were wide open, but the odors and oppressive heat made the room nearly intolerable.

"Let's go outside and talk. I need some air."

"I think that's a good idea," Amelia said, her large blue eyes wide and unblinking. "I do declare, honey, you look a tad green around the gills. I suppose this hospital would do it to anybody, though. Honestly, I don't know how you manage it. I had my little ol' handkerchief to my nose most of the time I was in here." She waved her lace handkerchief in the air. "I do admire what you're doing, helping these poor men. I don't think I have the stomach for it myself. I wish I did. But you always were a good nurse."

"I'm just doing what every other nurse is doing these days." Eden led Amelia by the elbow toward the door.

"Oh, and honey, I was so sorry to hear about your daddy, rest his soul. He was such a kind man."

"Thank you, Amelia. I cherish your kind words, truly I do."

She untied her apron and dropped it in the dirty linen basket near the exit. They walked outside to air so thick and humid it stuck in Eden's throat like a stale biscuit.

Amelia opened her pretty lace parasol, sheltering them from the blinding sun. "My poor sister gets green in the gills, too, but not from any smelly hospital. She gets sick every time she's with child, and it just goes on for months and months."

Eden felt the warm blood draining from her face.

"Eden? Are you all right?"

She gets sick every time she's with child.

While the risk of conceiving a child had always loomed somewhere in the dark recesses of her mind, she had been far too busy caring for others to contemplate her own health. Perhaps it had not been the hospital odors, nor her constant worry about Rayce and Isaac, making her feel nauseated and extra tired. Lord knows, she had completely lost track of time lately, each day and night flowing into the next.

God help me. Not only is it possible I'm with child…it's likely.

"Are you all right?" Amelia repeated, her big eyes bulging with concern.

"Uh, yes, fine," Eden fibbed, "but perhaps I best be getting home."

"My carriage is here. Let me give you a ride home."

She forced a smile. "Yes...yes, all right. Thank you, Amelia."

As they rode toward Aunt Martha's, the two women noticed people scurrying about and deserting the streets, appearing as though they were heading for surrounding hills and moving to the roofs of tall buildings.

Once the carriage turned down cobbled Broad Street, Amelia saw a friend closing up shop at the confectionary. She signaled her driver to stop. "Why, hello, Sarah Lynn!" she called. "Say, do you know what everybody's looking at from the hills and rooftops?"

Her friend talked excitedly of what she had heard. A battle was about to begin, and from the rooftops and tall hills, you could see the white army tents below sprinkling the summer landscape like snowflakes. Everyone she knew was terribly worried they would be forced to swiftly evacuate with their families if the Yankee Army managed to break through our forces and fight their way into the city.

Amelia gasped. "The Yankees here, can you imagine? Let's get you back to your house, honey. I have to get home in a jiffy myself. Oh, I'm so worried." She tapped on the roof with the tip of her closed parasol, and the driver continued on his way.

Eden had a hard time listening. If she were with child, she could already be a few months along. As a midwife, she knew unmarried women gave birth to babies all the time, but the shame and disgrace cast upon the unfortunate women could often be brutal. While Amelia chattered about the enemy closing in on the city, she sank back in the seat, like a turtle returning to the safety of its shell. At the forefront of her mind loomed one question in particular: If she were with child, what would Rayce do when he found out?

She loved Rayce with every ounce of her being, more than she ever thought possible, but their love was new and untested. She was younger, sheltered, and saw the world through a narrower view, while he was older, seasoned, and had been through more in his thirty-four years than she would likely ever see in her lifetime. Obviously, he had been with many women, but she knew of no child of his to exist, and surely, Lucy would have told her if there had been. Had he been through this before? If so, did he flee and leave the woman alone? Would he push her aside? Was his independent nature and freedom held above all else?

With uncertainly flooding her mind, there were two things she had absolutely no doubt about: She would never pay a visit to the back alley butchers in Shockoe, and even if she had to spend her entire confinement in the charred ashes of Oak Hill alone, she would never force Rayce to marry her.

STANDING with Hiram Johnson, who had been kind enough to escort her to Maury Hill after her shopping, Eden watched the musket shots and shells bursting forth. Billowing clouds of dark smoke twisted high above the treetops amidst the pulsing flashes of lights.

She knew Rayce was involved down below, and the rumors surrounding Stonewall Jackson treading on the heels of the enemy made her heart pound with worry for Isaac and Jimmy. The two of them fighting in the Shenandoah Valley had been one thing, but the thought of them entering the barrage of bullets and blasting shells in front of her was another.

Later that night, she lay awake in bed staring at the ceiling, listening to the sounds of wagons clanging down the streets, bringing the wounded into the city. From somewhere deep inside her head, she heard Trinidad's voice say, "This is your destiny," followed by, "If you love him, you must help him."

By daybreak, the steady roar of artillery continued. She rose early and dressed, her mind set on getting to the hospital as soon as possible.

Maneuvering Aunt Martha's buggy through the crowded streets proved challenging, as she dodged ambulances carrying wounded soldiers and worried families hurrying about, frantic for any news of their loved ones. Baggage wagons rattled up and down streets, filled to capacity with trunks and personal belongings, as citizens rushed to the outskirts of the city and away from the fighting.

From the moment she entered Chimborazo Hospital, it was clear the fighting had been fierce. War-torn soldiers were everywhere, moaning in agony; their crimson-stained bandages caked with dried blood and mud. Soldiers lay mutilated, some with missing limbs and near death. In each of the wards, there were more wounded than the eyes could see and not enough beds.

"Miss Blair, I'm glad you're here. We need all the hands we can get," Dr. Radcliff said as he hurried about. "I need you to bathe the wounds of the men in this section of the room. There's extra soap, water, and bandages over on the cart. If a soldier is too far gone, move on to the next. I wish we could save them all, but that's not going to happen."

Despite the heat, a chill ran the length of her spine. More blood and gore than she had ever seen filled the room. Nurses, doctors, and employees scrambled alongside family members looking for their loved ones as volunteers rushed about. The sounds of suffering, moaning men, filling every inch along the rough-planked floors, echoed in her ears.

"Don't just gawk, my dear. I know it's hard, but you have to be strong," the doctor said before hurrying off to a nearby bed.

"Yes...of course," she replied, her voice nothing more than a choked whisper.

She moved from bed to bed, doing what she could to help. Several of the men were traumatized beyond words. For others, their stories flowed out in fits and starts, tales from the battlefield oozing from their very souls.

A soldier lying motionless with his back to her caught her eye. His muslin shirt and gray trousers were torn and bloodied. As she slowly inched her feet toward him, the room narrowed, thinning to shadows. She reached down and gently touched his shoulder. He moaned and rolled toward her.

She gasped and dropped to his side. Judging by the bloodied bullet holes in his clothing, it appeared he had been shot multiple times, but the blast to his cheek made him almost unrecognizable.

"Is it bad, Miss?" he whispered.

"Oh, Patrick...it's...it's Eden, I..." She instantly felt her long-held anger evaporate as she stared at him, wearing the gray uniform of the Confederacy. She clasped his hand. "What happened, Patrick? What can I do?" Her eyes filled to brimming at the broken sight of him.

"Eden." His dark pupils narrowed. "It is you. I thought I'd died and gone to heaven with the sound of your sweet voice again." He swatted at his bloodied face.

"No — don't touch it. Let me help you." She scrambled up and dashed to the cart for water, fresh cloths, and bandages. With her hands full, she returned and crouched beside his bed. As she cleaned and dressed the wound on his face, he stiffened and bit down on his lip until it bled. Tears dripped down her cheeks. "I'm so sorry I'm hurting you."

He sighed. "There ain't no use, Eden. I took one in the face, another in the leg. One in the shoulder, too. I don't think I'm gonna make it outta this scrape."

"Don't say that. I've seen worse." She took a wet cloth and gently rubbed the mud out of his long hair and picked out the pieces of pine and wood chips.

He closed his eyes. "Guess you're wondering what...what I'm doing in gray?"

"Yes, well, the thought did enter my mind." Her tears fell as small droplets on his bloodied shirt, but she forced a smile. "You seemed to think you looked better in blue, last I remember."

He opened his eyes and attempted a feeble smile, but only the left side of his lower face moved. "That Major Hampton of yours...he's quite a man, honey."

She froze at the mention of Rayce's name. "How so?"

"Back at that manor of his, he made me realize I hadn't been living the life of the man I truly could be...the man he knew I wanted to be. He told me all men are worthy of a second chance. If I didn't make things right, I'd rot away inside a Rebel prison; he'd see to it. So, I guess you could say I didn't have a choice. But I knew in my heart it was the right thing to do. He said there had to be some good inside me somewhere." He winced and clenched his jaw.

"Patrick, stay with me, I'm listening," she said, smoothing his hair from his forehead.

"Where was I? Oh yes, the major. He had me believing in myself. When he brought me to camp, I joined with the Rebs right then and there, where I belong."

Patrick closed his eyes and a soft snore escaped his mouth.

"Patrick." She squeezed his hand. "Please, when was the last time you saw Major Hampton? I need to know."

He squirmed in a sudden fit of pain and clenched his fists.

"Oh, Patrick — please. Stay calm, you'll only make it worse." She smoothed his hair, and he settled down. "Please think, when did you last see the major?"

He sighed. "I'm all confused, honey, not feeling myself. Forgive me. I really should have told you about him first thing. Last I saw, the major wasn't doing so well."

Her heart sank like a stone in water. "Tell me, Patrick. Please, tell me everything you can remember."

His blue eyes paled. "I went back to the river where I was to meet him. He was there, but his face looked tinged with fever, and he was talking crazy, like a fever can do to you. We were down along swamps of the Chickahominy, the closest place to hell you can imagine, Eden." He shivered and snapped his eyes closed as if reliving the nightmare.

"Go on, you're doing fine," she said calmly, though her heart raced like a baby bird trapped inside her chest.

"Damn poisonous snakes in the water. Hanging vines. All those mosquitoes...it was horrible. The major brushed off being sick, saying he'd be fine, but I knew better. I've had swamp fever, and I knew I needed to find help."

Eden's stomach twisted. *Trinidad's dream.* "Go on, what happened? Did he get help back at camp? Oh, my Lord, is he in here with you?" Her gaze darted about the room.

"I wish I could tell you, honey. There'd been firing all around us in those thick woods all day. He told me to get back to the regiment. He'd complete his mission. Mark my words, Eden, if we win these rounds of brutal battles, it's due to Major Hampton." He paused. "You know, once I joined up with the Rebs, I was told by General Stuart himself I was to take orders directly from Major Hampton. So, when he told me to leave and head back to camp...I did. But I left knowing I'd get him help. I was moving through those woods, when out of nowhere, damn Yanks fired from inside the thickets." He heaved a deep sigh and pointed to his face. "They shot me up good, as you can see."

"And the major?" she asked in a strangled voice.

"Last I saw, he was on the banks of the Chickahominy looking like he could fall over dead any minute and...well, I know you love him, Eden, so I can trust you with this."

Patrick hesitated, his gaze shifting, surveying the room. He gestured with a curled finger for her to come closer.

She moved in toward his face.

"There's more," he whispered. "He wasn't just sick and talkin' crazy, he was also dressed in a Yankee captain's blue uniform near the raging battle lines."

Chapter 17

After leaving Patrick's side, Eden searched the wards for Rayce in the event he had been transported to the hospital. Cannon fire roared in the distance, while wounded men lying shoulder-to-shoulder on the floor pleaded for help as she skirted by.

She spotted Amelia heading toward her. "Amelia, how's your brother-in-law?"

"The same, I'm afraid." She held her handkerchief to her nose and sniffed. "I hear the fighting's been horrible. Now I'm worried about the rest of my family. Last I heard, General Lee attacked the Yankees, and more fighting's going on near Gaines Mill."

"What have you heard on General Jackson's troops — anything?"

"Just that they're not far away, and I must say, hearing Stonewall Jackson is nearby just gives me an extra dash of hope. I do pray they'll keep those filthy Yanks from occupying our city like that wretched General Butler did in New Orleans. I shake at the very thought."

"I'm sure our men are doing their very best, and we can't ask them for more than that," Eden reassured her.

"I'm sick with worry for my husband, Eden. I don't know what I'd do if anything happened to him. When I visit my brother-in-law and look around at all these boys piling in here like injured cattle, I know the very same thing could happen to him — maybe even worse." She dabbed the corners of her eyes with a lace handkerchief.

Eden looped her arm with Amelia's and said the appropriate things one person says to another to comfort them. She put on a brave face for her friend's sake, but all she could think about was Rayce.

There had been no news from him. *Nothing.* He had promised he would get word to her as soon as possible, and after the recent series of nearby battles, he would have wanted to put her mind at rest.

She knew Rayce was in serious trouble. Every time she thought of him now, she imagined him ill, lying prostrate on the banks of the sluggish Chickahominy — barely conscious, perhaps dying. To complicate matters further, he had last been seen dressed in the uniform of a Yankee near the fighting lines and at the mercy of either army. The possibility of a horrible outcome was very real.

Finally home after the long, draining day, she trudged up the stairs. Eliza met her at the top.

"How's she doing?" Eden asked.

"Take a look for yourself, Miss."

She entered the bedroom and saw Aunt Martha sitting up and drinking tea. "Well, look at you. I must say you're looking like a woman on the mend." She placed her hand on Aunt

Martha's forehead. "And you're considerably cooler."

"This may sound most unladylike, but I woke up in a pool of my own sweat this morning. I looked like an old mare after a ten-mile run. I've felt better ever since." The older woman coughed and leaned her head against the propped-up pillow behind her. "The coughing is still a mean bear, but I do feel better."

"The cough will likely last a while. The breaking fever is a sure sign you're not getting any worse, though, so we should all count our blessings."

Eliza nodded in agreement.

"Eden?" Aunt Martha jutted out her bottom lip. "I have something to ask you."

"Yes, Aunt Martha?"

"Heavens, child! Call me Aunty like Lucy does."

Eden smiled. "Yes, Aunty."

"Eliza tells me you've taken to driving the buggy out alone to the hospitals. Is this true?"

Eden flashed the servant a sharp glance, and Eliza's shoulders instantly shrank against the flowered wallpaper.

"It's true, but—"

"A woman alone must be careful of rumors and innuendo, my dear. Traveling without a companion just isn't safe, anyway."

Eden swallowed a threatening chuckle. Like all good Southern women, Aunt Martha still held her honored principals in high regard, even if the world was shattering to pieces around her.

"What's the latest on our boys? Eliza here hasn't told me a thing — said I didn't need to worry my ol' gray hairs about it until I was feeling better. But I hear the cannon fire. I hear those rattletrap ambulances rolling down the streets. What's been happening?"

Eden relayed all she had heard from the soldiers in the hospitals and Amelia's latest news about recent battles. She told her about citizens taking to rooftops and hills, and the scenes of anguish and bloody gore at the hospitals. She chose not to mention what Patrick had told her about Rayce. To put Aunt Martha in a tizzy at this point of her recovery would be risky.

"Bless his heart, General Jackson's coming. Well, hallelujah!" Aunt Martha cocked her head and studied Eden's face. "What of Isaac — anything? Lucy must be beside herself with worry."

"Nothing."

"Jimmy?"

"No. And I've asked around everywhere. I pray they stay safe." Eden started for the door.

"And what do you know about Rayce?"

She stiffened and turned around to face Aunty's eyes, hinting of mischief. She wondered if the older woman knew more about their relationship than she had let on. Perhaps Eliza shared her own thoughts on the subject.

She sighed and looked away. "The truth is, I don't know," she said. "I truly just don't know."

The room fell silent, and Eden could feel the older woman's watchful gaze upon her.

Aunty exhaled noisily. After a long pause, she instructed Eliza to go downstairs to do her chores and shut the door behind her.

"Now, my dear," the older woman said firmly. "I think you should share this heavy burden you're carrying. Not only can I see it in your face, I can feel it consuming you. If it's about my nephew, Rayce, whom I love more than myself, then I deserve to know, too. Please give it to me straight up, and don't spare me, child, there's nothing this ol' bird can't handle."

Eden immediately felt the heavy weight of veiled secrecy lift from her shoulders. As if a dam had suddenly burst forth, she told Aunty of their relationship — how it had grown over the months. She talked about Trinidad's worrisome dream she could not ignore. She told her about Patrick lying in the hospital bed and his recent change of heart for the Rebel cause. While it still worried her to do so, she went ahead and told her what Patrick had reported about Rayce being ill. What she couldn't bring herself to mention was the news about Rayce having last been seen wearing a Yankee uniform or the possibility she carried his child.

"That's it." Aunt Martha bolted upright and adjusted her nightcap. "Hand me my flask while I ponder all this."

Eden snapped to and retrieved the flask from the top of the dresser where Eliza cleverly kept it out of the older woman's reach.

Aunty took a healthy swig, and then another. "Ah, there, that's better. That's for the coughing fit I was about to have." She twisted the top back on. "Now, I wasn't going to say anything to you about this because it involved a private conversation I had with my nephew the last time I saw him but..." She clicked her tongue, contemplating her words.

"But..." Eden repeated.

"Well, what I'm trying to say is Rayce has never been one

to talk about the women in his life, and mind you, I've been told by reputable sources there have been many. Hearts are likely still breaking all over the South. Do you know why he's never spoken of them?"

Eden tilted her chin high. "Well...no—"

"Because none of them really mattered to him, not a one of them...until you came along. Trust me, my dear, I heard it from the ol' boy's mouth myself." She smiled and patted Eden's leg. "Now, I'm thinking you feel the same way he does, am I right?"

"Absolutely." Eden's eyes pooled with tears. She reached for the old woman's hand. "Absolutely, I love him — I do. He's the one."

"All right, my dear." Aunt Martha sighed, and the deep lines around her eyes softened. "You look tired. We'll wait patiently for word from him. If we don't hear anything in the next few days, we'll come up with something. Between the two of us, we'll figure this out."

Eden held back her stinging tears and gave Aunty a hug. Silently, she gave thanks to God for sparing the older woman's life. Now, if only the same could be done for Rayce.

Later that evening, Eliza brought pails of hot water for Eden's evening bath. As an added touch, the kindly woman sprinkled fragrant rose petals from the garden into the bathwater. While she felt instantly refreshed the moment she slid into the warm water, it did nothing to soothe her worries. After the water cooled, she dried herself, donned a thin nightdress, and slid between her sheets, eager for a decent night of sleep.

Minutes slowly turned into hours as she tossed and turned

in bed. Finally, her body gave in to the overwhelming exhaustion, and she fell sound asleep. At some point in the dead of night, she woke to the sound of sorrowful weeping, coming from outside.

She scurried out of bed and pressed her nose to the window. Two men on horseback had just ridden up to the house next door and were standing on the porch. She dressed swiftly and went outside to investigate.

Following the mournful sounds, she walked up the steps next door and found Aunt Martha's neighbor, Mrs. Withers, sitting on her front porch, her arms wrapped tightly around her knees, sobbing. She explained to Eden she had just been informed two of her sons had perished during the battle at Mechanicsville.

Eden watched as the two men mounted their horses and left. The steady trot of the iron-hoofed horses echoed in the dark night as they proceeded down the street, presumably to the next home on their list.

She sat on the step next to the elderly woman and wrapped her arms around her heaving shoulders. "I'm terribly sorry, Mrs. Withers. I'm so very sorry for your loss." She hardly knew the petite, older woman, but that mattered little these days. Every family was in the same terrible predicament — never knowing from one day to the next if loved ones were alive or dead. Open displays of affection for anyone in obvious pain were commonplace these days, day or night.

After helping Mrs. Withers back into the house and tucking her into bed, Eden returned home completely exhausted and slept soundly the rest of the night. The next day she woke nauseated and asked Eliza for tea with her breakfast.

As the nausea continued and her breasts became fuller, little doubt remained in her mind she carried Rayce's child. As much as she wanted to help him — even saddle a horse and ride off to find him herself, she knew for the safety of their unborn child, she could not put herself in harm's way. Nor would Rayce ever want her to — that she knew. But what should she do?

She heard Trinidad's words of warning. *If you love him, you must help him.*

"Curse you, Trinidad!" She set her cup down hastily, spilling the hot tea over the rim. Sighing heavily, she wiped up the mess with her cloth napkin.

It wasn't Trinidad's fault Rayce was in such a mess. She certainly didn't make all of this happen — she just knew in advance he would be in some kind of trouble, leaving Eden to wonder; *Is it a gift or a curse Trinidad possesses?*

Nor was it Patrick's fault simply for being the bearer of bad news, she countered. If it were not for the two of them, perhaps Rayce wouldn't even stand a chance.

AFTER hitching the buggy, Eden made her way to Chimborazo Hospital to visit Patrick and look for Rayce. With the extra rest and medical care, perhaps Patrick could recall more details.

The moment she entered the ward, the contents in her stomach churned. The odors resonating from the wards reeked with death, disease, and infections. She spotted Dr. Radcliff hurrying about in a flurry with a scowl of determination fixed upon his haggard face.

She lifted her thick skirts and stepped gingerly over the wounded men on the floor as she made her way to Patrick's bunk. As she drew near, she saw an older soldier with a bloodied, bandaged stump for a leg now occupied the bed.

"Excuse me, Dr. Radcliff." Eden grabbed his sleeve. "I'm looking for a soldier—"

"Miss Blair, I'm glad you're here. The men coming in today — as you can see...it's horrific. I think you—"

"Doctor! Come quick!" a panicked nurse called for him.

"Pardon me." He eyed her tight grip upon his arm.

Eden reluctantly let go, and he dashed away.

A negro worker entered with a rolling tray of bread and coffee for the patients.

"Excuse me, could you tell me what happened to Private Patrick McDowell?" She pointed toward the bed he had occupied.

"Oh, yeah, I remember him." The black man's eyes narrowed in thought. "Three bullet wounds — one to the face — that the one?"

"Yes, that's him. Has he been moved?"

"Naw, Miss, he died in the middle of the night. Sorry...did you know him well?"

Eden thought about the question as a sob wedged deep within in her throat. *Did she know him well?*

"No...No, I suppose I never really knew him at all," she managed to choke out.

"Miss, you all right?" he asked, "You need some water?"

"I'm...I'm..." Her throat tightened with a threatening scream. Upon seeing the cracked door at the rear of the room, she hurried toward the exit, gasping for air.

She heard the man calling after her. "Miss, are you all right? Miss, don't go out there!"

She ran outside and shut the door behind her. Leaning upright against the outdoor wall, she closed her eyes and tried to catch her breath. Right away, the most offensive and unimaginable stench drifted up her nose. Slowly, she opened her eyes. To her right, standing at least five feet wide and just as deep stood a pile of mangled and bloodied amputated limbs. The scene before her was of such unbelievable carnage, she began shaking, and her vision dimmed as if she were about to faint.

Holding her hand across her throat, she ran as fast as she could toward the end of the long building. Turning the corner, she stumbled and reached out, groping the walls with shaky fingers trying to steady herself. Breathless, she pressed her back against the whitewashed wall and slowly slid to the ground. *Lord help me.* With trembling hands, she covered her face and cried.

After the extended break, she slowly walked back inside to check on Robert and Sam. Robert told her the doctor had given him a fifty-fifty chance of losing his arm. While she sat listening to his sad news, she kept her private pain to herself and read the Bible verses he had requested. After their meals, she wrote a letter for Sam to his mother and sisters in North Carolina. Robert managed to scribble a letter by himself to his cousin in the city, hoping to find a place to stay once he received his discharge from the hospital.

The rest of the day, Eden kept busy tending to the boys in gray, but her heart belonged elsewhere. There had still been no sign of Rayce.

EDEN fingered her collar and fanned herself. "This heat is

unbearable. Honestly, I don't know how much more of this I can take."

Aunt Martha's fingers paused on her needlework. She looked up over the rim of her reading glasses. "You're right, dear." She called over her shoulder. "Eliza, pull the curtains and let's open these windows all the way. We're not running a Turkish steam room here."

Eliza drew the lace curtains aside and thrust the windows open. The sound of a clomping horse pausing at the walkway caught their attention.

"There's a man out front hitchin' his horse," Eliza said. "Looks like he's heading up the porch."

Aunt Martha set her embroidery on the divan, and she and Eden slowly rose from their chairs.

Eden's stood frozen in place, her stomach twisting in knots.

"Dear, you must stay strong." Aunt Martha took hold of her elbow, guiding her toward the door.

"Oh, no. I just...I just don't know if I can bear this. What if it's bad news?"

"Let's pray it isn't," Aunt Martha said. "Open the door, Eliza."

The tall man removed his hat when the door opened. "Is this the residence of Mrs. Martha Meadows?"

Aunt Martha stepped forward and raised her quivering chin.

"It is, and you're speaking to her."

"Ma'am, I have a message for you and a Miss Blair from, let's see here...from Captain Isaac Blair."

"Isaac! Is he all right?" Eden covered her heart with a

trembling hand.

"I don't rightly know, Miss. Here."

Eden snatched the envelope from his fingers in a flash, tore open the envelope, and began reading. "Oh, no...oh, dear."

Aunt Martha gnawed on her bottom lip. "For heaven's sake! Don't leave me hanging, what does it say?"

"It's Jimmy McDowell. He's been wounded, and they've transported him to Chimborazo Hospital. Isaac wants me to get to him and make sure he's tended to properly."

Eden had a terrible thought. Given all the fighting going on, Jimmy probably had no idea his brother, Patrick, had passed away. She would likely have to deliver the horrible news herself.

"I need the buggy to get to the hospital, Aunty, right away."

"Yes, dear, absolutely. I'll have Eliza go with you."

"No, please, I'm fine. I don't know how long I'll be there."

Aunt Martha bit on her fingernails in a fit of nervousness.

Eden sighed. "Oh, all right, fine, you win. Eliza can take me today. But will you be all right alone?"

"Of course, honey. I'm fine. Now go!"

Once inside the hospital office, Eden asked for the location of Lieutenant James McDowell. A kindly plump woman left briefly and then returned.

"You're in luck. Normally it takes a lot longer to find the newly admitted boys. I'll take you to him."

Eden followed the woman and looked around the ward, wondering how much more of this she could take. Each day the scene was exactly the same. Some soldiers lingered for weeks while others died shortly upon arrival, their beds filled swiftly with another sick or wounded soldier.

"He's over there," the woman said.

Had the woman not pointed him out, she would have known it was Jimmy, anyway. He and Isaac had always looked like they were brothers, sharing the same sandy blonde hair and playful blue eyes ever since they were children. All around him, soldiers were resting, so she walked quietly to his bedside.

His eyes were closed. "Jimmy," she whispered. It's me — Eden." She noticed the large bloodied bandage on his foot and lower leg. His hair was covered with thick dust, and he looked so still...like a corpse. "Oh no, Jimmy." She bent down.

"Can't a guy get any sleep around here?" He opened his eyes wide and grinned.

She flinched. "Jimmy! Lord above, you scared me half to death!"

"Yeah, I always was good at that, remember?"

"Oh, I remember all too well, you rat."

"Yep, the matron told me I had a visitor, and after her description, I knew it had to be you. I just wanted to play with you a bit — for old time's sake. I can't tell you how happy I am to see you, honey." He winced with a sudden flash of pain.

"What happened, Jimmy? How badly are you wounded?" She surveyed his bandages.

"Well, I think three of my toes are gone. The lower leg's pretty well shot up, too. I was charging with my bayonet and jumped over a log. Then, I thought my whole foot had been shot off in midair. Durn Yank got me good. Hurt like hell. The good news is the doc says my wounds shouldn't be life-threatening as long as no infection sets in. I'm just trying to work through the pain best I can."

"You must stay strong, Jimmy. How's Isaac? Please tell me—"

"Now, now, don't worry your pretty little head. Last I saw, he was just fine. No major scrapes on the ol' boy, and let's hope it stays that way."

She reached for his hand. "I say my prayers for you boys every night — truly I do."

"And I thank you kindly for those prayers, honey."

Jimmy shifted position and growled in pain between clenched teeth. He paused, waiting for the discomfort to subside before he spoke. "I hate to ask you this because I know it's uncomfortable. Any chance you've heard anything about that Yankee turncoat brother of mine? I haven't heard diddly and neither have Mama and the girls. 'Course, we still worry about him, and all."

And there it was. He didn't know, and she would have to be the one to tell him.

She took the handkerchief from her pocket and blotted the moisture forming at her throat. She spotted an unoccupied stool next to a nearby bunk. She brought it close to Jimmy's side and sat.

His eyes followed her every move. "Hey, is something wrong?"

She took his hand in hers. "I'm so sorry, Jimmy. Patrick, well, he died a few days ago—"

"Died! Patrick's dead? Oh, Lord, you're serious — you're not pulling my leg?"

"It's true. You know I wouldn't joke about something like that. And Jimmy, he joined up with the Rebs weeks before and tried to right his wrongs. Truth be told, he died right here in this very hospital."

Jimmy swallowed hard, and he brought a balled up fist to his mouth as he fought back tears. "I'm sure Mama and the girls have been told by now. Oh, Lord, my poor Mama must be beside herself." He placed his arm over his eyes and shook his head. "I wasn't expecting this."

"I'm so sorry," she said, choking back tears.

"I know you are." His arm fell limp to his side, and he looked at her with moist eyes. "Now don't go chewin' yourself up about giving me the bad news. I'm thankful it was you who told me and not some stranger."

"Is there anything I can do for you, Jimmy?"

"I don't know...I just don't know anymore." He sighed. "Well, maybe. Any chance the next time you visit you can bring me something decent to read? I miss reading. Hell, Eden, I miss all the simple pleasures we used to take for granted. I suppose this is rather unpatriotic of me, but I'm sick to death of this damned bloody war."

Jimmy frowned, and the lines around his eyes deepened to dark crevasses. Clearly, the news she had delivered about his brother had already sunk in.

THE scorching midday sun did little to dry the humidity in the air. Eden loosened the ties on her bonnet and dabbed at the moisture along her neck. Eliza steered the horse through the cobblestone street while dodging potholes, carriages, marching troops, and pedestrians. The two women heard shouting, and Eliza slowed the buggy.

"Hey there, Yanks! Look at ye now!" one man yelled.

"If these are the officers, imagine what Lincoln's army must look like!" a woman hollered, laughing.

"Where are your big guns now, Yanks?" another man chimed in.

A long line of Yankee prisoners were being marched single file toward the river. Young boys followed behind them, hooting and hollering and calling them names. While some of the prisoners appeared in good shape, others, toward the back of the line, looked shocked and weary, and some seemed downright ill.

"Let's go, Eliza. Just hurry past these Yanks."

Eliza clicked her tongue and swatted the horse's behind with the buggy whip. "Come on, git goin', girl," she ordered.

Some of the soldiers glanced at them as they rode by. Others marched with their heads held low, while a few simply looked too dazed and confused to notice anything.

Eden felt the blood suddenly drain from her face. There, near the back of the line, dressed in a Yankee uniform, was none other than Major Rayce Hampton.

Chapter 18

Eliza craned her neck and stared at the long line of prisoners they had just passed. "Lawd almighty, Miss Eden, you see what I see? That sure looked like Major Hampton."

He's alive! Eden gripped the side of the buggy so tight her hands went numb. "Pull over, Eliza. I...I need to think a minute." She sat back, steadying herself, and rubbed her hands together to draw the blood back into them.

"But that *can't* be him, Miss Eden. He ain't no Yankee."

"Don't be silly — of course he's not." She twisted in her seat, looking back at the line of men as they faded from view. "That was Major Hampton, right — you saw him, too?"

"Oh, yes. It surely was him, and he was dressed in blue, sure enough. I couldn't take my eyes off his worn out, handsome face."

Shielding her eyes from the sun, Eden placed her hand below the brim of her bonnet. "I heard they take the Yankees to Libby Prison for processing. Looks like that's where they're headed."

"What we gonna do, Miss Eden...Miss Eden?"

Rayce is alive! Still, she had seen him look better than he did moments earlier — much better, in fact. But, if he's sick with swamp fever, she could help. He was strong and healthy, and with the proper care and treatment, he could recover soon. She would see to it herself. At last, the sleepless nights, staring vacantly at the walls and ceiling, picturing him lying dead along the banks of the Chickahominy would finally vanish.

"Let's head home, Eliza. I'm going to freshen up and pack some of the berry pie you made earlier. We're going to Libby Prison. I'm going to spring Rayce Hampton from the Yankee jail — now hurry home."

Eliza's jaw dropped. "You gonna what?"

"You heard me, I'm going to get that man out of there if it's the last thing I do!"

"Make tracks, girl." Eliza snapped the buggy whip. "Lawd Almighty, I ain't never heard of such a thing," she mumbled, shaking her head.

EDEN ran up the steps, two at time, and bolted into Aunt Martha's bedroom completely out of breath. "He's here...and he's alive!"

"Who...You mean — Rayce?" Aunt Martha sat up like a shot, squirming as though someone had just poured ice down the back of her nightdress. "Are you talking about Rayce — you saw him?"

"Yes." Eden gave Aunty a big, squishy hug. "We saw him, didn't we, Eliza?"

"Oh, we saw him, sure enough, but he looked like he was feeling kinda...blue."

Eden eyed Eliza sharply. "What Eliza simply means is, yes, we saw him, he's alive, but there's a small wrinkle, you might say, that needs to be ironed out. But don't you get yourself in a fit. I'm handling the situation."

Aunt Martha frowned. "What's going on, Eden? What 'wrinkle' needs to be 'ironed out'?"

Eden waved her fingers, trying not to over worry the older woman. "Well, we were coming back from Chimborazo after seeing Jimmy. He'd been shot in the foot and lower leg."

"My stars, is he going to make it?"

Eden nodded. "He's doing well, should be fine with proper mending. I'll check on him each day to be sure, don't you worry. Anyway, as I was saying, we were coming back from the hospital when we saw a long line of Yankee prisoners. People were yelling all sorts of things at them — not nice things — hateful things, of course."

Aunt Martha nodded. "Of course."

"We were riding past the line, and there, near the end and trudging away in the hot sun, marched Rayce."

"Dressed as a Yankee? Oh, my heavens! He's been taken where — Libby Prison?"

"I think so," Eden replied. "And he wasn't looking well."

"But that's a dreadful place. I hear it's filled with rats, and the men are crowded wall-to-wall with no beds or even blankets. Mind you, I didn't think too much about it before because our enemies are in there. But now, it's my nephew. Well, we know he's no Yank." Aunt Martha paused and shook her head. "All his life, he's lived on the edge. I swear I used to wonder if he had a death wish. And perhaps he did after his father died in his arms way back when, and he took off for so many years."

She looked straight into Eden's eyes. "Lord help you keeping up with him. Danger should have been that man's middle name."

Eden sprang up from the bed. "Well, wish me luck. I'm sure they'll let him out within the hour when he explains who he is, or I'll just have to do it for him." She dashed out the door toward her own room, yelling behind her, "Either way, we're going to see him soon, and I'm beside myself with joy!"

"MISS Eden, it sure ain't fittin' for us two womenfolk to be down here near the docks. My own mama, bless her soul, would have taken the switch to my backside for coming down here."

"Hush, Eliza, we don't have a choice. I only had you come in case I need help getting him into the buggy."

Eden looked at the daunting four-story, brick building facing Cary Street. The imposing structure, with its whitewashed peeling outer walls, had once been the warehouse of Libby & Sons, Ship-Chandlers. As they drew closer, they saw a crowd of sloppily dressed guards pacing on the sidewalk, their hair and whiskers long and unwashed. When they saw the women in the approaching buggy, a group of about a dozen men came toward them carrying their muskets.

Eliza reined in the horse and pulled the buggy to a stop.

A tall, older guard moved to the front of the group. "What can we do for you, Miss?"

Eden stepped out of the buggy. "I'm here about a prisoner. I believe he was brought to this place within the last hour or so."

"Hmm…well, we did get some fresh meat in here just a bit

ago, didn't we boys?" The men behind him chuckled. "There ain't nothing we can do to help you, Miss. No visitors allowed."

"Then I need to see the person in charge."

The older man paused, removed his hat, and wiped his forehead with a dirty handkerchief. "Well, then you need to be talking to Lieutenant Turner."

Eden cupped her hands together in an attempt to stop their shaking. "Then take me to him, please."

"As you wish. Follow me." He paused and pointed a bony finger at Eliza. "She coming?"

Eden glared directly into his eyes. "Yes, of course. Why wouldn't she?"

"Oh, uh...I was just asking, Miss."

The women followed him into the building. He led them down a flight of stairs, and Eden noted the walls below looked just as dingy as they had outside.

They came to a closed door. The guard knocked. "Lieutenant Turner, sir?"

The sound of shuffling papers filled the silence. "Yes, what is it, I'm busy," said a deep voice from behind the door.

"Sir, there's a lady here, a Miss...Miss..." He looked at Eden for guidance.

"A Miss Eden Blair," she replied louder than she had expected, drawing a grimace from the guard.

More shuffling of paper.

Behind the closed door came the grating sound of furniture scraping across the floor, causing Eden to wince. Finally, a voice called. "Come in."

The guard opened the door and held his hand out, gesturing for her to go inside. She entered the room while Eliza and the guard waited in the hallway.

Before her stood a stout man with a prickly scowl. She instantly felt the air in the room chill from the icy stare in his dark eyes. He gestured toward a small chair. She smoothed her skirts and sat. His gaze followed her every move. Finally, he turned and walked in front of a large desk and took a seat in an armchair opposite her.

"What may I do for you today, Miss Blair?"

"Lieutenant," her voice cracked. She cleared her throat. "Lieutenant, I have reason to believe you have imprisoned an innocent man."

He cocked his head and laughed. "Have you any idea how many times I've heard that?"

"Sir, this...this is not a laughing matter." She felt the heat of her flushing cheeks. "What I mean to say is a certain prisoner, whom I believe you may have just placed within the confines of your prison today, is actually a Rebel officer."

He slowly rose from his chair, walked to the front of the desk, and stood in front of her. He sighed as though thoroughly bored and glared down at her. "And just how did you make this determination?"

"Why, I saw him myself. He was marching toward this prison in a Yankee uniform."

The lieutenant bent forward and looked her squarely in the eyes. She could feel the callous insincerity running through his veins.

"And how do you know this Rebel officer, who you just happen to have seen dressed in a Federal uniform, didn't turn Yank himself?"

"Because...well, because he wouldn't do that, sir. That's

how I know."

He laughed in a villainous manner, and she felt the tiny hairs on the back of her neck stand.

"Not good enough. You should leave now." He walked behind his desk and sank back in his chair, busying himself with the stack of papers.

Eden's knees trembled, but she rose from her chair, anyway. "Major, I...I demand to see the officers just brought in. I can point him out to you."

"You are in no position to demand anything!"

She flinched and swiftly sank back in the chair. "Sir, can you at least look in your ledger for your most recently admitted prisoners?" She loosened the bow of her bonnet tied across her throat.

He stared at her for a moment, his eyes unblinking, boring into hers. "Please, I'm a busy man."

She narrowed her gaze and glared into his eyes, searching the dark depths for even the smallest amount of compassion. "Sir, please. Please check your records."

Finally, he sighed and opened a large ledger sitting on the desk in front of him. "Just whom am I looking for?"

That's a good question.

"Umm ...check Hampton. Rayce Hampton."

His brow furrowed deeper as his thick finger moved down the page. "No. Not here. Now, please, there's nothing more I can—"

"May I look for myself?"

"You absolutely may not! Now, I'm going to have to ask you to leave."

"Please, wait." She cringed at the pleading tone in her

voice. Her mind scrambled as she tried to remember what Patrick had told her. What was it? Last he saw him he had been on the banks of the Chickahominy in...a captain's uniform.

"I believe he may have been dressed as a captain – yes, a Yankee captain. Can you look for a prisoner newly admitted with the rank of captain?"

He fingered the ledger again. "There are two."

"May I see them?"

"The only way to see a prisoner is to apply for a permit with the Provost Marshal."

"But that could take days – perhaps weeks!"

"Those are the rules, and I abide by those rules, Miss Blair. I'm sorry, but there's nothing more I can do for you. Good day." He rose to escort her to the door.

Eden started for the door, her skirts brushing past him. "I'll show myself out, sir." She tilted her chin high. "Come, Eliza, we're leaving."

The heavy door behind her promptly closed with an echoing thud.

"Why, that man not help us any? He sounds like a mean man to me, like the devil got him good."

"I don't know, but he couldn't be better suited for running an enemy prison. I almost feel sorry for the Yankees in there. I certainly feel bad for Rayce. Don't worry, Eliza, I'll figure out something – just you wait and see."

Eden heard a soft whisper in the back of her mind. "*If you love him you must help him.*"

As they exited the building, a young guard approached. "Miss Eden, is that you?"

She stared at the familiar curly-haired man standing in

front of her.

"It's me, Miss Eden, Tommy Brewster — from back home."

Eden remembered him now, one of ol' man Brewster's unfortunate sons. Tommy had a wild crush on her for years when they were young children. In Sunday school, he used to stare at her during their lessons, and she would slug him in the arm and tell him to stop. Unlike his father, Tommy had always been a shy but pleasant young man.

"Why, of course, Tommy Brewster. How's life been treating you?"

"Oh, all right, I reckon," he gushed. "I'm posted here for now, but I hope to see battle one of these days."

Eden frowned. "Be careful what you wish for, Tommy. I'm at the hospital regularly, and some of the men there once thought like you. Many of them feel differently now."

"I was sorry to hear Oak Hill burned."

"And I was sorry to hear about your father," she lied.

"Some say he had it coming. But, he was my pa, so, it's hard." His solemn face suddenly brightened. "Say, what brings you here — a Yank prison of all places?"

Perhaps an opportunity presents itself.

"Oh, Tommy, I'm just beside myself with...with..." She pulled a handkerchief from her pocket and dabbed the corner of her eye.

He took a step forward. "Oh, Miss Eden, don't cry. Can I help?"

Eliza's brown eyes narrowed. "Miss Eden, we best get back to Aunt Martha's, I know she—"

"Go on back to the buggy and wait for me," Eden said, between pursed lips.

Eliza scratched her head and hesitated. Finally, she turned and walked back to the buggy, mumbling.

Tommy drew closer. "Tell me, what can I do to help?"

Eden sighed and fluttered her lashes as quick as butterfly wings. "Well, that mean ol' Lieutenant Turner told me I couldn't see a dear friend of mine who's been imprisoned as a Yankee in there." She sniffed and jutted her chin toward the prison. "He's not one bit a Yank — he's a very dear old friend and a Rebel major."

Tommy scuffed his feet and thrust his hands into his pockets. "Well, heck, Miss Eden, they got rules in here — stiff rules, and they don't let no visitors in. I wish I could get you in, but I can't." He looked up with a hopeful gaze, saying, "You know I would if I could."

Eden could hear Eliza's trumped-up coughing coming from behind her. "Oh, my, Tommy...whatever shall I do?" She turned away and felt his eyes upon her back. "I just feel so tired of this war and tired of the rules and...well, I'm just liable to do something foolish." She dabbed her eyes with the handkerchief.

Tommy touched her arm, and she turned around to face him. "Don't go talking like that, now, Miss Eden. You're not going to do anything crazy, are you?"

Eden smiled. "Why, Tommy, I just had an idea; maybe you can help me. Could you fetch me some clothes so I can pass as a guard? Why, I can go in and find him myself and make sure he's doing all right. Last I heard he was terribly ill."

"Now you are talking crazy. Lord above, Eden — no, I won't get you any guard clothes!"

"Oh, Tommy!" She turned away and blubbered into the

handkerchief.

"Now, hold on, hold on, wait a minute here...stop your sniffling. You're not going in there, especially dressed as a man — that is crazy talk. But perhaps..."

"Yes?" she asked in a choked whisper, turning to face him again.

"Well, perhaps I can check on him. I could make up some dumb excuse, like a problem with the window, or something I saw from down here. You wait in the buggy, and I'll return shortly."

Walking back to the buggy, Eden thrust the dry handkerchief into her pocket and smiled.

Tommy returned twenty minutes later. "I asked around to find out who the new Yank fellows are. There's one guy in there who's a chatter monkey. I asked him where the newly arrived captains were. A captain raised his hand; he was right there in the same room. He told me a second captain named Captain Nimrod Collins of the 61st Pennsylvania was sent right to the prison hospital section 'cuz of swamp fever."

"Oh, that must be him," she said. *Nimrod. Only Rayce would be stuck with such a name.*

She fluttered her lashes, and Tommy's face softened.

"Tommy, you've done me proud. I thank you from the bottom of my lil' ol' heart, and I want to repay you for your kindness."

He beamed with a bright smile.

"Come here. I'd like to give you a little something."

"Oh...all right, if you insist." He inched closer to the side of the buggy.

"I do insist — here." She reached down on the floor and

brought up a wrapped package. "It's a berry pie Eliza made just this morning. I want you to have it."

"Oh!" He flushed as red as rhubarb wine and held out his hands. "Umm...thank you."

Eden waved as Eliza urged the horse forward. "Goodbye now, Tommy, and thank you again."

"My, oh my," Eliza chuckled. "I never seen such a love-struck boy in all my days. He thought you was gonna kiss him."

Eden would have laughed, too, but her mind kept turning back to Rayce. How would she get him out of there? So many deaths had been attributed to malarial fevers coming from the toxic black swamps of the Chickahominy and other stagnant waters on the Peninsula. With the extra rains and flooding, it had already proven to be a particularly deadly year. The chance Rayce would get the proper care needed to stay alive while he remained in prison was probably zero.

"How the major get himself in this mess, anyhow? Lawd Almighty!"

"Swamp fever, Eliza."

As the buggy rattled down the road, they saw a group of cavalry soldiers riding through. Eden mumbled, "I doubt Jeb and his boys would be here, given all the fighting—"

The thought came to her so suddenly it was as though a bolt of lightning struck her upside the head. "Oh, Eliza, let's get home quickly. I have an urgent message to send!"

Chapter 19

Eden watched as another funeral cart passed, loaded with a simple pine coffin, followed by a muffled drum thudding the mournful "Death March."

"Come away from the window, honey. You're just making yourself sick with worry," Aunt Martha said, as she took a seat in the parlor.

"I know...you're right." Eden pulled away from the window to join in the afternoon tea.

"How was your visit with Jimmy today?"

"He's doing better than most of the wounded. With this heat, infections and gangrene are flourishing. It's terrible."

"And what about Robert, Sam, and the other boys?"

Eden forced a smile. "Private Tracey is doing better, too. He told me he'll be released soon. Some of the other boys there aren't doing as well. And what I saw outside was simply, awful, Aunty. Stragglers are wandering the streets — thousands of them — without guns or coats, tired, wet and hungry, their uniforms riddled with holes and stained with blood."

"But we must be thankful the Yankees pulled back after

Malvern Hill, honey, remember that. I can't even begin to imagine what could have happened."

Being thankful was difficult with soldiers lying sick and wounded on the wet battlefields. By the hundreds, local citizens were sent in buggies and carts loaded with bread, water, and wine to help the ailing soldiers. After emptying the goods, long lines of buggies returned bringing back the dead and wounded.

"I'm glad Jimmy's doing better. Still, he must be suffering with the loss of Patrick."

Both women turned toward the sound of heavy footsteps coming up the porch.

Aunt Martha gasped and froze in place. "Get Eliza to answer it. I'm too frightened to open the door. There's not a house in the city where someone hasn't perished. I can't bear the thought."

Eden's own terror instantly vaporized with the onset of Aunt Martha's sudden panic, giving her the needed courage.

After the soft knock, she opened the door. A young uniformed courier slowly removed his hat.

"Are you Miss Eden Blair?"

Oh, God. "I am."

"I have a message for you." He handed her the sealed envelope.

With the expression on his face indecipherable, Eden's pulse quickened.

"Good day," he said.

Eden stood frozen as she watched him mount his horse and ride off as quickly as he had arrived. With her fingers feeling stiff and useless, she tore awkwardly at the envelope with her fingernails and yanked out the folded paper.

Aunt Martha scrambled up from her seat to Eden's side. "Oh, Lord, what does it say?"

Eden read it aloud: "Dear Miss Blair. I'm pleased to inform you the soldier you inquired about, Major Rayce Hampton, has been removed from the confines of Libby Prison at the order of General James Ewell Brown Stuart. Major Hampton has been transferred to Chimborazo Hospital for treatment of his condition. My sincerest apologies. Lieutenant Thomas P. Turner, Commandant. Libby Prison."

"I knew Jeb would come through." Eden scrambled around the room, darting from one side to the next, looking for her bonnet and gloves. "Oh, the snake in the grass. That man Turner would have just let him rot in there rather than check this out himself. Thank heavens for Jeb." She stopped in her tracks and faced Aunt Martha. "I know this must sound silly given the circumstances, but do I look all right, Aunty?"

"You look beautiful. Now, run along. I'm so worried about him. I'll yell for Eliza to fetch the buggy."

"No, I'm going alone. And don't you dare fuss at me, this is far too important."

Eden entered the hospital, rushing from ward to ward, only to find the place looking as though the battle must have happened on the infirmary's grounds. Soldiers with fresh, life-threatening wounds were crammed wall-to-wall and shoulder-to-shoulder, moaning in agony in beds and on the floors. Medical staff treaded lightly, moving from one soldier to the next, and local women wiped fevered brows, dressed wounds, and offered soft words of encouragement. With everyone exceedingly busy, she ventured cautiously through the wards, looking for Rayce.

A sudden gust of warm air howled across the river, rushing

through the opened windows as though calling her name. She turned around and recognized him instantly.

Her gaze darted around the room, trying to find the best route to his bedside. She lifted her skirts above her ankles and stepped carefully in the impossibly small spaces between the men lying on the floor.

"Help me, Miss," A young soldier whispered. "Help me."

"I think I'm dying," another man murmured as she tiptoed near his head.

Tears obscured her view. "I'm so, so sorry," she whispered, moving as fast as she could to get to Rayce.

She wiped her tears with the back of her hand. Up ahead, lying on his back without a shirt, Rayce wore the blue trousers she had seen him in days before. Thankfully, he had a bed, perhaps in part to General Stuart's influence and prompting.

As she drew near, the tears she had reserved for Rayce dripped down her cheeks. Once at his bedside, she stared for what felt like an eternity at his still, seemingly lifeless body. With her knees trembling beneath her, she crouched down and held his hand.

"Rayce...I'm here," she whispered in his ear.

Nothing.

His head felt searingly hot, so hot she thought it could blister her palm. Quickly, she reached for the pitcher next to his bed and dipped her hands in the water. She drenched both hands fully, and then held one to his forehead and the other to his neck. He began to mumble garbled words.

"Rayce, my love, I'm here."

Appearing as though he recognized her words, his eyes opened for a split moment, but the fever still had him in its evil grip. Just as quickly, he closed his eyes, and he lay still and quiet once again.

She had no idea how long she had been there, for she fell asleep sitting on the floor next to him, her head on his leg, waiting.

She woke to a gentle tap upon her shoulder. "Miss Blair, I thought it was you," said Dr. Radcliff.

Eden glanced up, automatically tidying her hair with her fingers. "Oh, Doctor. I..." She blushed, embarrassed to have fallen asleep on the floor, but he of all people, who worked long hours day and night, would likely understand.

A gentle smile lifted the corner of his thin lips. "It's all right." He jutted his chin forward. "I take it he's someone special?" He looked down at his notes. "Major Hampton. Swamp fever — and a bad case, I'm afraid. I've seen a lot of it from the soldiers who've been around the Chickahominy. This one has an extremely high fever, causing delirium and unconsciousness. Says here he's been in and out of it for days."

"What can be done?" she asked, her voice cracking.

"We've given him whiskey and quinine. If he's going to get better this fever needs to break, and soon. His body can't hold out much longer."

A nurse called for the doctor.

"I'm sorry. Excuse me, Miss Blair."

Hours ticked by, yet she barely noticed. Her head hurt, and her nostrils stung from the steady smell of disease and infected wounds. Having decided to get a moment of fresh air, she slowly rose and let go of his hand. She turned to leave and heard a whisper so faint it could have been the passing of a soul.

She spun around and dropped to the floor beside him. "Rayce!" Drips of moisture had begun to dot his forehead, neck, and chest. She smoothed his hair away from his brow. "Oh, Rayce, did you say something?" She hemmed in and brought her ear close to his mouth. "Talk to me, darling, please."

"If you...wanted me...on my back...you could...have just asked," he whispered. His eyes slowly opened, his dark pupils struggling against the light, and she could see the smallest curve of a smile tip the corners of his parched lips.

"Rayce! Oh, Rayce, the fever is breaking," she whispered against his weathered cheek. "You're going to be fine, my darling." Relief flooded through her, tears of joy streaming down her cheeks, landing upon the hollow of his tanned neck.

"Has he...left?" Rayce asked, his voice a gravelly whisper.

"Has who left — the doctor?"

"No...McClellan."

The fever — *he didn't know.* "Yes, Rayce, we're safe."

"McClellan," he repeated. "The Young Napoleon...what a fool...I knew he'd retreat."

"Oh, my darling, he's heading back to Washington as we speak." Eden inched in closer and whispered into his ear. "I know, my love. I know it was you, Patrick told me. I don't know the details, but this I do know: However you managed such a feat, you have changed the winds of this war, and Richmond and the Confederacy can breathe yet another day."

He smiled and closed his eyes.

"Rest, my love," she said, "the fever is breaking, and all will be well."

Chapter 20

Two Weeks Later

Eden woke to a room as dark as the devil himself. Her heart raced as she ran her hands under the smooth sheets, searching for the body next to her.

He was there; warm, healthy, asleep.

He stirred. "What is it, Sweetness — another nightmare?"

"Yes," she whispered, "another nightmare."

She felt him move toward the edge of the bed, followed by the sound of a coarse strike of a match. He cupped the small yellow flame and lit the tallow candle in the lantern next to the bed. The glowing light fluttered softly against the walls of the bedroom. He slid under the sheets beside her and pulled her warm, naked body against his.

"I was just so frightened, Rayce," she whispered.

He inched closer, aligning his hips with hers, and gently drew her head to his chest. A temperate night breeze drifted through the open window, and his musky scent mingled with her sweet magnolia oil, heightening her senses.

His lips brushed the top of her head. "Perhaps I can be of assistance."

With a single finger, he tilted her chin to meet his gaze, his firm manhood pressed against the swell of her small belly, adding to her arousal. She looked into his eyes, rich as dark velvet and as seductive as smooth silk. "Yes, I think perhaps you can."

She sat up, and he rolled to his back. Leisurely, she lay on top of him, forming the gentle curves of her body against his.

His broad hands moved with precision as he massaged the tension in her muscles along the base of her spine. Roaming higher, he smoothed the tight muscles in her back and shoulders. He gathered her hair, gently pulling the thick bundle away from her neck, and his firm fingertips kneaded the small knots of stiffness at her nape until her body completely relaxed.

"Feeling better?"

"Much better," she said, relishing the feel of his fingers slowly moving through her hair.

As if he were determined to erase every trace of her frightening nightmare, he rotated his fingertips firmly across her scalp. Her breasts grew warm, and her nipples turned hard as tiny pebbles pressed against his chest. A hoarse moan escaped his throat when his lips sought the tender skin of her neck.

She pulled away and looked into his eyes. "I want you, Rayce."

She slid her hand down the side of his long torso, feeling the warm skin over his firm muscles underneath her palm. She heard his sharp inhale when she placed her hands under his solid buttocks, pressed against the smooth sheets, and pulled him closer. "I want all of you," she said.

He kneaded the curves of her hips. "I can never get

enough of you, woman."

A finger trailed down her spine, stroking the back of her bare thigh and bottom. She felt the thread of passion in his hand, sending a warm serpentine dance of pleasure slithering up her backbone.

He paused. "Care for a nightcap, my sweet?" He lifted her in his arms and laid her back down on the bed. He walked to the bureau and poured two small glasses of brandy. When he turned back to face her, he stood in full view of her appreciative gaze.

His hair hung long, wavy, and as dark as his raven eyes; his chest tanned, broad, and matted with thick curls snaking down his lean torso, tapering to his groin. He stood next to the bedside, full and erect, and she instantly felt the sleek warmth between her legs intensify.

Rayce looked down, holding her gaze, and the passion in her emerald eyes hit him like a body blow, sucking the air out of his lungs. Her fan of golden hair lay sprawled across the feather pillows, framing her lovely face. When her full lips parted and her tongue moistened her bottom lip, his body instantly responded, his shaft turning stiffer than a ramrod in the heat of battle. Her creamy breasts and ripe hips beckoned him with the promise of more, as she lay before him like a silky treasure awaiting his discovery. Was this enchanting beauty his for the taking? *Absolutely.*

Ready to slide back into bed, he set the glasses down on the side table and turned to face her. With a beguiling smile, she leisurely rose on her hands and knees. Her eyes grew wildly green against the soft light. He froze in place, watching as she slowly slithered like a serpent against the sheets to the side of the bed. Before he knew it, he was inside her warm mouth.

Her hands and lips consumed him. Every muscle in his body grew taut. Through half-closed lids, he could see their large shadows flickering against the dark walls, adding to his desire.

He reached forward and clasped her smooth backside in both hands, kneading the sleek mounds with his palms and fingertips, moving in closer — closer to her silky middle. "Dear God, Eden. The things I want to do to you."

She stopped and smiled, her full lips glistening in the candlelight, and gazed up at him. He cupped her chin in his hand. "I'm going to explode, woman."

In one fluid move, he scooped her up by her waist and gently flipped her over on the bed. With her lying flat on her back, her legs dangling over the edge, he slowly knelt down, lifted her knees, and penetrated her warmth with a single deep plunge of his tongue.

She gasped and clawed at the sheets, her fingernails scraping across the soft fabric. Slowly, he probed in and out, circling every square inch of her sensitive pearl.

"Rayce, oh, my heavens…I beg of you, this is so naughty, she breathed. "You must stop — no, don't stop."

He increased his pace. She writhed beneath him as he plunged deeper, faster; tasting her as though she were a sinful delight kept from his needy reach for so very long.

She raked her hands through his hair, tugging thick stands and wrapping them around her fingers. She gripped his scalp, pulling him closer. Her soft moans sent a shock of heated desire sweeping across his skin. Her muscles tightened and she began squirming.

The curve of her desire rose to such a height, Eden felt her body quivering with the need for a release against his ravenous mouth. "Rayce, I neeeeeed you."

He stopped, but only for a moment. He flashed a wicked smile and reached to the side table for a glass of brandy. Puzzled, she frowned, watching as he took a drink, his eyes flashing devilishly in the candlelight. He held the glass above her chest and tilted it precariously so the liquid hugged the rim, threatening to pour over her. Instinctively, her muscles tightened until they trembled, waiting for the inevitable spill. He smiled and slowly let the drops of brandy drip, one by one, upon her breasts.

Each delicate drip sent a jolt of desire straight to her core. She inhaled in jagged breaths as each droplet fell against her heated flesh.

His dark eyes flashed, capturing the dancing flame as each drip hit her nipples and lazily trickled down the sides of her breasts. She arched up when his mouth came down upon her and devoured the soft skin of her breasts.

He set the glass down and dipped a finger in the amber liquid. Slowly, he trailed his finger from the pulsing hollow of her neck, down between her breasts, until he reached her navel. The cool liquid felt like ice against her warmer flesh, sending shivers rushing across her skin.

He slowly circled each breasts with the damp finger. "These are mine," he said smiling.

Eden giggled and trembled all at the same time. "Is that so?"

He kissed each peaked breast and whispered, "I, Major Rayce Hampton, declare Eden Blair's lovely breasts are forever mine — all mine. Amen"

His eyes narrowed, and a smile curved beneath his mustache. He reached over and dipped his finger in the brandy once again. Before she knew what was happening, he slid the moistened finger inside of her. The cool, wet feel against her warm center sent her head into a dizzying spin of desire. Then, his mouth came down upon her once again, teasing and taunting her. Without warning, she cried out as waves of carnal yearning brought her to the very edge of ultimate seduction.

Trembling beneath him, he had brought her to the very brink of heated ecstasy. He stood and looked at the incredible creature he had claimed — the beautiful woman he wanted like no other he had ever known before. With a single smile, Eden was every woman he had ever fantasized about.

He slid her back on the bed and lay above her. Instantly, he found her warm center again with his hand, and she gasped. He nudged her legs apart, spreading them wide. Slowly, he entered her, relishing the feel of his hard shaft against her slick velvet walls that felt like they'd been made for him and him alone.

She moaned and slowly joined his rhythm.

He increased his pace and reached for her wrists. Holding them high above her head, he pressed them hard against the soft sheets. He looked into her eyes and plunged deeper. "You're mine, Eden. You hear me, woman?"

"Yes, Rayce," she whispered, "I love you so much. I'm yours."

The rising passion within her came to an intense crescendo. Her body tightened and pulsated against his; her nipples warm and firm against his chest. He felt her insides rock with spasms of intense pleasure.

She pulled and tugged at her clasped wrists, but he held on with a vice grip. She nipped at his shoulder and grazed her teeth across his neck.

He had held out as long as he could, but the taste of her — the feel of her — the pulsing ripeness streaming from her made the physical yearning nearly unbearable. He moaned against her throat, his tongue and mouth ravishing her neck. "I love you. God help you, Eden, I do."

He gently slid his tongue across the small hollow of her neck and kissed the skin between each breast. He captured her nipple in his mouth, licking the pink peak, nibbling and sucking until his body stiffened in jolts of desire, and he poured within her warmth a torrent streaming from his very core.

He released her wrists, and she held him tightly as he gasped and panted against her neck, his body quivering with spasms of pleasure.

He moved first, slowly rolling off of her. He scooped her up, moved her up to the headboard, and they both lay down together, side-by-side against the thick pillows. Like a puzzle of flesh, their bodies fit together perfectly as they lay tangled against the rumpled sheets.

"What are you thinking about, Sweetness?"

Eden smiled, put her finger to his lips, and he kissed it. "I'm thinking you are the man of my dreams, Rayce Hampton, and I'm the luckiest girl in the world."

"That's funny, because I'm feeling pretty lucky myself." He trailed a finger down her chest, circling her breasts. "I'm thinking perhaps we should go another round, what do you think?"

She laughed and tossed a pillow at him. "You do not, you rat. Besides, I think we should get some sleep. We have a lot to do tomorrow to get ready to leave for Hampton Manor. Honestly, I can't wait to get there."

"Yes, yes, all right, my love." He yawned. "Would you mind blowing out the candle next to you?"

"I will. But first, I'm going downstairs to find some food — I'm absolutely famished."

EDEN sighed wistfully as she opened the wooden trunk. While she felt an undeniable calling to stay and help the sick and wounded soldiers in Richmond, she was being pulled by a larger force — a force urging her to flee the filthy city and protect the child she carried. Diseases flourished in the overpopulated capital, and long lines of coffins swelled in the cemeteries, often popping open while awaiting burial by the overworked gravediggers. Each day, she reminded herself she needed the safe, peaceful environment Hampton Manor provided. After everything Rayce had done for the Confederacy, she was overjoyed he had been granted an extended furlough. He deserved a break, and she looked forward to spending each and every moment with him.

She had not told Rayce about the baby. Everything had been so perfect since he had come to Aunt Martha's after his initial care at the hospital. *Not now...maybe tomorrow*, she would always tell herself. Then each tomorrow turned into another one...and another.

"I made lunch and brung you some tea, too." Eliza brought the tray into the bedroom and set it on the small table. She lingered in the doorway. "I'm gonna miss seeing you around here, Miss Eden."

"Thank you, Eliza. We sure have been through some wild events together, haven't we?"

"Lawdy, yes, we surely have." Eliza cleared her throat. "Uh...I wanna thank you for helpin' me with Miz Martha. While it might not be fittin' for me to say this, in many ways she's like a sister to me — both of us widowed and without our husbands, and all. I don't know what I ever woulda done without her. Lawd, I thought she was gonna up and die for sure before you came."

"I'm glad I came, too."

Aunt Martha joined them in the bedroom. "When do you and Rayce plan to depart for the manor?"

Eden set her neatly folded lace shawls in the trunk. "Tomorrow morning at first light. Today I'm going to the hospital to say goodbye to Jimmy and the other boys."

"Has Rayce already left for his meetings?"

Eden nodded. "You know him. He left bright and early." She glanced up and saw tears welling in the corners of Aunt Martha's blue eyes. She walked swiftly toward the older woman and put her arms around her thick shoulders. "Oh, I'm going to miss you, too, Aunty. Now you promise me you'll come as soon as you can for a nice long visit."

"I will...I promise," she sniffed. "And now, dear, I need you to promise me something."

"Anything...you know I will."

Eliza slipped out of the room and headed downstairs.

Aunt Martha sighed and paused before speaking. "You must take good care of yourself, Eden. You care for others without regard for yourself, and while that may be a blessing for everyone else, sometimes a woman needs to know when it's time to put herself first."

Aunty was an observant woman with keen senses when it came to others. Eden wondered if she had guessed about the baby. "I will, I promise."

By afternoon, she had finished her packing. With everything finally in order, she went out back to the carriage house, hitched the buggy, and headed off to the hospital to say her farewells.

"I can't tell you how relieved I am you're doing so much better, Jimmy. The doctors here are very good." She gingerly lifted the bandages and looked at his wounds, which were healing nicely. While three of his toes were gone, the bullet wound to his lower leg had gone straight through, missing the bone, and no infection had set in.

"Compared to most of these boys in here, I can't complain, honey," he said. "Still, I don't think I'll be much help with these missing toes. I'm gonna have to figure out how to walk without them, I suppose. I hate this damn war, but I'm not ready to go back home to Mama and the girls and just sit around."

"I'm sure as long as you can walk, the army can use your help."

"Yeah, but then again, without Patrick out there anymore, I'm the only man in the family." Jimmy looked around the ward. "Lord, Eden, did we ever think it would come to this? All of us men had waited around eagerly, hoping and praying Virginia would split from the Union so we could go off and fight the Yankees, and look at this sad mess all around us."

She sat on the stool next to his bed. "No, we surely never

did, and I pray this war ends swiftly for everybody's sake. I just don't know what will become of us all if the South falls in the end."

He smiled. "Something tells me by the content look in your eyes, you're going to be just fine no matter what happens to the rest of us." He sat up, and winced. "Eden, I'd like to apologize for the pain my brother put you through. I swear, I never knew what he was doing to little Jemmy. And I never would have imagined he was involved in your father's death, either. Perhaps I should have figured things out — maybe paid better attention, but I had been caught up in my own life."

Eden shook her head. "Don't you dare blame yourself, do you hear me? Patrick's the only one to blame, and he knew it in the end."

"Perhaps so...perhaps so," he said, his voice trailing off.

"I must be going. I wanted to make sure you're all right. I'll be leaving for Hampton Manor in the morning. I'm so looking forward to seeing Lucy and the baby again. You must tell Isaac his baby girl is so sweet and lovely when you see him."

"And you tell everybody I said hello." He fingered a small tear in his shirt. "Is Ann there — at the manor? Perhaps I'll have a chance to visit."

Eden looked into his jovial eyes and smiled. "Oh, my heavens, Jimmy, you're sweet on Ann."

"Well, maybe a little bit," he laughed. "I was just thinking if I have the chance to come by I'd like to pay her a visit, too." His eyebrows arched high. "Oh, you can stop looking at me like that; I know she's already spoken for."

"I'm just surprised you've looked at her in that way, is all." She crinkled her nose.

He laughed. "Oh, and I know all too well the way the two of you spar like wild cats, and I even understand why. She's nothing like you, of course, but she does have a certain way about her; well, I always found rather...alluring, I must say."

"Alluring? Oh, stop, Jimmy, I can't even imagine." She stood, giggling. "Now, you take care of yourself. You know I love you like a brother." She kissed the top of his head. "Please stay safe."

"And I love you, too, honey." He flashed a dazzling grin. "Now, you'll be sure to tell Ann I said hello, right?"

"Oh, you're incorrigible. Yes, I'll mention it. Well, I'd best get going. I need to check on some of the other boys. Good bye, Jimmy."

Before heading to the other wards, Eden walked outside to take a break. The afternoon sun had slipped low in the sky, and the moist humidity felt like a warm, wet rag against her skin. She looked out over the massive grounds toward the James River and the wide ravine, Bloody Run Gully, below. Soon, she would be looking at the very same river from Hampton Manor with the man she loved by her side.

Upon arrival in the next ward, she quickly learned one of the more severely wounded boys she regularly tended to had died from infection during the night. The other boys were happy to see her and wish her well on her journey. The thought of leaving her favorite patients behind — likely never seeing any of them ever again — tore at her heart. The least she could do was wish them all well and offer words of encouragement before she left.

Private Sam Hollack was doing dandy, and Eden wrote another letter for him to his family in North Carolina.

"Thank ya kindly, Miss Eden," Sam said, "I'm sure going to miss your smiling face. I hope it won't be too long before I'm back on the lines. It's mighty hard being laid up like this when you wanna be helping."

"And you be sure to take good care of yourself, Sam." Eden waved a finger at him for emphasis. "The army's lucky to have such a devoted soldier. Oh, and I almost forgot — I brought you some of Eliza's gingersnaps you like so much."

She extended the cookies she had placed in her pocket before she left. Each small package she had wrapped in paper and tied with a tiny ribbon.

He unwrapped the cookies and took a bite. "Mmm-mmm. I adore these. My mama makes 'em, too." He pointed at Robert. "Look at ol' Robby over there; he's so lucky. After all his beggin' and pleadin', Doc told him he can get outta here today. Where'd you say you gonna go, Robby?"

Eden turned to Robert, who sat quietly on his bed flipping through an old, tattered magazine.

"Doc just needs to fill out my papers, then I'm finally on my way. Gonna go to my cousin's place around here for a few days before I head back."

"Well, you are the lucky one. Getting out of here and on the mend. I'm happy for you, Robert." Eden offered him a cookie.

"Thank you, Miss Eden."

At Dr. Radcliff's insistence, Eden spent the rest of the afternoon tending to some of the newly admitted soldiers, one after the other. Many of the men were in terrible shape, coming in from battlegrounds all over Virginia. She spoke words of support, wiped fevered brows, and cleaned wounds. The gratitude expressed from the men overwhelmed her, bringing fresh tears with each injury she cleaned and bandaged.

"Oh, my, look at the time." She had stayed far longer than expected. When she went outside, she was surprised to see the stirring wind bending the tops of trees and the clouds darkening, signaling a brewing summer thunderstorm. Her skirt whipped wildly in the wind, and she wrangled with the reins as she tried to untie them from the post.

"Hello, Miss Eden," a voice said from behind. "Let me get those for you."

Eden gasped. "Oh, my, you scared me, Robert." She caught her breath and looked him over from head to toe. "Why, look at you. Finally out of that place, are you?"

He handed her the freed reins. "And I couldn't be happier about it. Time to get back to the war," he said, smiling. "And timing sure is everything these days."

"I agree." She placed a hand on her hip. "Look at you, all mended up. And to think you almost lost your arm. I said my prayers for you every night, I did."

He extended a hand and helped her into the buggy. "And I thank you kindly for those prayers." He smiled. "Looks like your prayers worked. Say, Miss Eden, you headed home?"

"I surely am." She put on her bonnet, tucked in the loose tendrils, and tied it securely. "And I best get moving with this sky turning all dark and spiteful."

He pulled out a crumpled piece of paper. "Say, could you tell me where this here address is? I don't know this city much at all. It's my cousin's place, and I need to get there."

She looked at the paper. The address was down near the water not too terribly far away, but certainly not within walking distance for a man who had just left the hospital. She glanced at the threatening sky above, then down at Robert. "You do have a way there, yes?"

"No...no, I surely don't. My cousin's at war." He scuffed his feet and looked around. "Don't think I can walk it, neither. Lost my vigor after being laid up so long."

It would only be a short detour from her planned path. "Well, I suppose I could give you a ride. It's not too far off my route, and it's certainly the least I can do after all you've been through. Without you boys fighting on our behalf, Richmond would surely have fallen to the Yankees." She patted the empty seat next to her. "Come on up here, Private Tracey."

They wound their way through the crowded streets toward the old wood and brick buildings a few blocks from the docks. As Eden had feared, the storm was rapidly approaching, with rumbling thunder rolling across the dark sky in the distance. People scurried about, slipping hurriedly into homes and shops as the clouds gathered force and the wind picked up. The ribbons on her bonnet swirled wildly, smacking her in the cheeks and coming untied. She struggled to hold the reins and keep her bonnet in place.

"Let me take those reins, Miss Eden. It's getting mighty fierce out here, and my arm's well enough."

"Oh, thank you, Robert." He scooted closer, and she handed him the leather reins. "This storm is coming up fast, and I need to get back to the house soon."

"I'll get us there as quickly as possible so you can get home in a jiffy." He urged the horse to a faster clip. "Hmm...with all these people scurrying around, I think we best try this turn — should be faster." He smacked the horse and turned sharply around a corner, entering an alley.

"But, Robert, are you sure?" Eden looked around at the piles of garbage in the narrow alleyway and large rats scurrying about crawling over heaps of trash. Butts of old cigars, molded wads of chewing tobacco, and broken liquor bottles littered the ground. Loud music blasted from nearby gambling houses around the corner. The smell of thick tobacco smoke mixing with stale alcohol and raw garbage make her stomach turn.

They curved around another corner toward a boarded up warehouse on the docks, and she turned her head when they passed what she was sure were several prostitutes loitering outside.

"Robert, I'm quite sure we've made a wrong turn. This isn't even close to the address. We need to head back up that way a bit." She pointed in the opposite direction.

He pulled the buggy to a sudden stop, and Eden lurched forward. "My goodness!" She faced him. "Did you hear me? We need—"

Eden's gaze met with eyes as dark and determined as the approaching storm. Instantly, she felt a sudden stab of pain in her side. A cold tremor ran the length of her spine when she saw the shiny pistol Robert had pointed in her ribs.

RAYCE opened the door to the house, and the wind whirled like a spinning top through the door. "Damn," he swore under his breath as he forced the door shut.

A steady growl of thunder echoed across the skies, shaking the window casings. He saw Aunt Martha scurrying up from the parlor divan, rushing toward him.

"Oh, Rayce…my dear boy, I'm so worried!"

He smiled. "Good grief, it's just an evening thunderstorm. You'll be fine, Aunty." He rubbed her shoulder. "Where's Eden?"

"Good Heavens, boy. It's not the storm — it's Eden I'm worried about!"

"What do you mean?" He frowned and walked swiftly past her, his gaze darting around the room. "Where is she?"

His aunt shook her head. "That's what I'm trying to tell you. She's not here, and she was due back hours ago."

"Well, where'd she go?"

"You know how she is. She went to the hospital to check on Jimmy and some of the other patients one last time and say goodbye."

"Alone?" He glared at Eliza, who instantly shrank like a wilting lily near the front door.

Aunt Martha put her hand on his arm. "Oh, Rayce, I've tried to tell her it's not proper — or safe for that matter — to take the buggy out by herself, but you know her, she's so strong-willed. I can't tell you how many times I've offered for Eliza to take her; I've even insisted upon it." She flopped down on the divan. "It's after dark, there's a storm, and I'm just so worried about her. She should have been back a long time ago."

Rayce sat next to his aunt. "Now, take a deep breath and calm yourself. There must be some explanation."

She nodded and inhaled steadying breaths.

"Now, I want you to think...where exactly did she say she was going?"

"Well, let me see...all I remember her saying was she planned to see Jimmy at Chimborazo. Yes." She looked into his eyes. "Yes, she was headed to Chimborazo Hospital."

"Then I'll go there and—"

"Wait. Sometimes she goes to Winder Hospital to help out, but I don't think she mentioned going there today." She squeezed her eyes shut. "I wish I could remember!"

Lord. The hospitals were a long way across town from each other. She could be at either hospital or anywhere in between.

"All right," he said, his mind racing. "Joseph and I will go first to Chimborazo and search there. If I don't find her, I'll go to Winder and look for her."

He could see his aunt working herself into a frenzy with worry. He put his hand over hers. "Now, calm down, I'll find her — I promise. She may even be back before I return."

He stood up to leave and headed for the front door.

"I'm just so upset. I never should have let her go to those filthy hospitals. Not in her condition. But, you see, she never personally confided in me about it." She rose and walked toward him.

His hand slipped from the brass doorknob, as his aunt's words registered in his head with the subtlety of a bolt of lightning. He spun on the heel of his boot and faced her. "Confide in you about what condition?"

Aunt Martha's eyes grew so wide they looked like they could pop right out of her head. "You mean you don't know?" She leaned against the wall and moaned. "Oh, Rayce, I hate to be the one to tell you this, but she must have had some reason to keep it from you. Eden...well, she's with child, I'm sure of it."

Her words came at him in slow motion. *She's with child.* "What?" he mouthed.

"You told me you planned to make an honest woman of her after you both returned to the manor, but honey, that time is *now*. She's with child, my boy, and I'll tell you, that poor girl has had a time of it with queasiness. She thought Eliza and I didn't hear her all those mornings and sometimes even at night, but we did. She's out there now, Lord knows where in this storm at night, and she's with child, Rayce, and I'm worried sick!"

He thought back to Eden's exhaustion, her loss of weight, and how she'd only pick at her food. Now, she felt lusciously ripe and curvy, her breasts full and firm, and she ate like a horse.

Oh, Lord, how did he not see this himself? More importantly, why hadn't she told him? The ring in his coat pocket he had purchased earlier in the day suddenly felt a lot heavier. For now, the questions he had for Eden would need to be pushed aside.

He put his hands on Aunt Martha's shoulders. "I will find her," he said decisively. "Can you think of anything else — any other details?"

"No, nothing important. I know she was excited to see a couple of the other soldiers she'd grown fond of. She was bringing some of Eliza's cookies to Private Sam Hollack and." She paused and tapped her chin in thought, then went on. "Oh, yes, and to Private Robert Tracey, and I think—"

"Did you say Robert Tracey? Private Robert Tracey — from North Carolina?" He dropped his arms to his sides.

"Yes...yes, that's him. Yes, from North Carolina. I can't remember what company and regiment she said he's with. But he'd been so kind to her and loved listening to her stories. Rayce, dear, what's wrong? You look as white as a ghost."

That son of a bitch!

Chapter 21

"Quit squirming — you're just making it worse on yourself," Robert barked, pacing around the room. "I don't want to hurt you, but don't test me."

Eden wrangled with the ropes on her wrists and lower legs, keeping her bound to the wooden chair in the center of the basement room.

"I told you, stop that squirming. You're going to give yourself some wicked rope burns."

"You'll never get away with this," she sneered, glaring back at him. Her wrists were already beginning to burn where the rope had dug into her skin, slicing like a dull knife.

"And don't even think about screaming, or I'll cover your mouth, too."

Eden's gaze darted around the large, near-empty basement in the old warehouse. The room felt cold and damp, and she could hear a steady drip of water on the dirt floor from a nearby leak. Old wooden crates stood stacked in the corner, and empty liquor bottles littered the ground. A tall spittoon and another wooden chair next to a small table were all that filled the room.

"He's bound to find me eventually, you know."

Robert marched over to her and bent down, looking directly into her eyes. "I know. And like I told you already, you're going be the bait that helps me capture that big fish of yours."

"How can you be so sure he'll know to find me here, anyway?"

His eyes narrowed. "Because both sides are very aware of each other; that's how good we are at what we do. It's like a game of chess, Miss Eden."

"It's Miss Blair to you!" she snapped. "How can you compare what you do to a game of chess? I can't believe I thought fondly of you — you traitor."

His faced turned beet red. "Being a traitor depends on what side of the war you're on, wouldn't you say?"

"Abducting a woman and holding her captive is a crime, you swine. I hope when this is over you rot in jail. Better yet, I hope you're hanged."

He gnawed on his bottom lip and sighed. "I changed my mind, little lady. Feel free to scream when you see him. That way the poor bastard will be distracted, and I can take care of him without him seeing it coming." He pulled a knife from the back of his trousers and began cleaning his fingernails.

"Just who are you?" She glared at him from head to toe. "Your accent is suddenly gone, Private Robert Tracey," she said, exaggerating each syllable in his name. "You have the sharp tongue of a vulgar Yankee."

"Let's just say, I'm your major's counterpart, from the opposite side."

"Well, you're nothing like him. There's no way you could

ever be the man he is. If it weren't for him, this war would have been over and the city taken over by the likes of you filthy Yanks."

He bent low and placed his fists on both sides of the chair next to her skirt, his hateful eyes only inches from hers. She could feel the deep anger stirring within him from her harsh, accusatory words.

"You go ahead and tell yourself that, Miss Blair. I assure you, your Major Hampton is no saint, either. There's more to him than you'll ever know." He stood up and rubbed at the tension in his fists. "He does what he must to complete his missions, and I do what I must."

"So, you're saying your mission is to kidnap a woman? Tie her up and hold her captive? He would never need to stoop so low."

"My mission is to stop Major Rayce Hampton, at all costs!" he shouted.

"You're a coward, and you'll never be a hero to anyone."

He raised a hand in the air, ready to slap her face. She flinched in anticipation of the impact, when they suddenly heard footsteps coming down the stairwell. The basement door opened and in walked a disheveled soldier in a Confederate uniform. When he saw her, he took off his cap and smoothed his oily hair with his chubby paw.

"Ah, so you got her? Good job, Archie." The man plodded in and set some papers on the table.

"Yeah, I got her," Archie said, annoyed. "She's feisty, with a hot temper; so keep your eyes on her. She'd slice you open if given the chance."

The man scratched his head. "Too bad she's a hostage. I

like my women like that." Both men laughed as they turned to talk in private.

Eden listened and was able to make out bits and pieces of their conversation. "McClellan furious. Pinkerton's men. Spies." She wiggled her legs, trying to loosen the ropes while they talked. "Must take him out once and for all." Their words were like a blow to her chest, and a wave of nausea threatened. "They're going to kill him," she whispered.

She turned her head from side to side, searching the room. *What to do.* The only option she could think of would be to somehow loosen the ropes and flee.

I can't let this happen to him.

She could hear rain falling outside and the low rumbles of thunder echoing against the desolate streets. In between the sporadic flashes of lightning, she could see darkness outside from an alley window to the basement. By now, Rayce likely knew she was missing, and Eliza and Aunt Martha would be beside themselves with worry. She rubbed her calves together, feeling a little give in the knot while she tried to loosen the rope on her wrists.

"Yeah, she's a hellcat for sure, that one. I can tell by those scorching green eyes," the man said, peering around the corner. He waved a finger at her. "Now, you behave yourself. No funny business, you hear?"

Eden glared back at him, her fingernails digging into the rope binding her wrists.

"Well, Archie, or I mean, 'Robert Tracey'." He snickered and looked back at Eden. "I'll check in with the men who've been tailing him and be back in a bit. The guy's been all over the city today, but last I heard he stopped in at the Spotswood.

Just keep a watch out in case he gets here before I get back."

"I got it covered."

The man replaced his cap, trudged up the stairs, and was gone.

"So, your real name is Archie, is it?" Eden asked.

"Mmm-hmm," Archie mumbled absently, busy unfolding the papers the other man had left.

She wiggled her wrists and ankles while his eyes were fixed on what appeared to be maps of some kind. She felt the rope on her lower legs loosen, and she had to catch herself to keep from gasping aloud.

Oh, Lord. She had to keep him distracted. If the rope slipped far enough down her boot, he would see it under the hem of her skirt.

"Excuse me, Archie...it is Archie, yes?"

"What?" He looked at her with vague interest. "Yeah, what of it?"

"I'm in need of some water. I'm afraid I'm very parched and feel rather dizzy." She coughed.

He cocked his head and studied her for a long moment. "I don't trust you, Miss Blair. Wish I did; but I don't. When the others get here, I'll get you some water." He turned away, studying the papers again.

"If I don't get some water, I daresay I might just faint." She felt a lump form in her throat as she tried her best to stay perfectly still. If the loosened rope around her legs slipped any more, it could fall to the dirt with a heavy thud.

Archie rapped his fingernails on the table and sighed in exasperation. "Good Lord, fine. Anything to stop your chattering. Can't you see I'm busy?"

He marched over to her and bent low — his lips so close to hers she could feel the scratch of his stiff mustache on her upper lip. She slammed her eyes shut.

"And if you try anything — ANYTHING at all, I promise, you won't live to tell about it."

Her eyes bolted wide when she heard his departing footsteps. Quickly, she let the rope slide from her calves and drop on her boot tips. She wiggled her feet until she was free of the rope, and with her heel, she swiftly brushed it underneath the chair and out of view.

NO need to go to Chimborazo or Winder Hospitals. Rayce knew right where she would be.

Everything that had happened today was beginning to make sense. He had spotted the usual tails on him at various times throughout recent days, but today they had been more persistent. Finding a way to lose them proved more challenging, demanding more of his attention than ever before.

After changing out of his uniform at the Spotswood Hotel, he had been careful to exit through the rear and out of their view, but getting back to Joseph and the carriage took more time than he had planned. He had not seen them for hours and now he knew why.

Clearly, the traitors had figured out a different approach. Archibald Cox, masquerading as Private Robert Tracey. Apparently, after winning her trust, the perfect opportunity had presented itself when he found Eden alone.

Rayce hoped the note he had left at his first stop would get to the appropriate party in time. If not, he would likely have to take care of the situation himself. He'd done just that many times before — improvise, but never had the life of the woman he loved been on the line — the life of his woman and his child.

Lord. He shook his head at the thought. He had certainly never been in this mess before. As crazy as everything was with the wretched, lingering war, and the threat presented to him now, he had never been happier in his life, and he owed it all to Eden. He'd be damned to Hell if he would let anyone harm a hair on her beautiful head or that of their unborn child.

He raised the collar on his coat and walked swiftly toward the boarded up building.

A provocatively dressed woman with smudged pink circles for cheeks exited an alley door in front of him. Loud music blasted through the door, then died out when the door slammed shut behind her. She cocked her head and watched as he approached. He tugged the brim of his hat over his brows and lowered his head as he quickly passed by.

"Hey ya Mister, I won't bite. How's about you buy a girl a drink?"

Two drunken soldiers passed by at the top of the alleyway. One stopped abruptly, took a drink of a bottle, and then tossed it in the street where it crashed into dozens of echoing pieces of shattered glass.

He quickly turned the last corner and stood in the dark, rainy alley behind the pile of crates, waiting...waiting for the kidnapping Yankee bastards to lead him to where they were keeping her inside the building.

He hunched low when he heard a deep voice coming from the basement below.

"I GOT you something better than water. Brought you sweet

tea. Miss Babette's bawdyhouse makes the best around, and she's just a few doors down. She even had ice." Archie held the glass to her mouth. "I told her I'd be back for a poke later."

She jerked her head away. "You mean to tell me you brought me a drink from a house of ill repute — from a prostitute? You're even more revolting than I thought. No, thank you."

A dark shadow caught her attention. She narrowed her eyes. Rayce peered at her from outside the small basement window leading to the alley.

"I thought you said you needed a drink of—"

Her gaze snapped back to Archie. "Oh, my...yes, what am I thinking? Yes, I'm absolutely parched."

Archie placed the glass to her lips. She slowly sipped the tea while stealing unnoticed glances toward the window. Rayce pressed his finger to his lips, gesturing for her to keep quiet.

"There, Miss Blair. No longer parched." He took the glass away and headed back to the table. "Now, I need to read over these before my men get back. You just close your eyes or something, perhaps try a little nap."

With Archie standing a few feet away, Eden quietly continued working the knot at her wrists. Rayce suddenly disappeared from the window, and her pulse quickened. Her heart pounded so forcefully she wondered if it would beat right out of her chest. The sensation became so strong and frightening the only thing she could hear was the sound of her heart beating in her ears.

Stay calm.

She glanced at the ground, distracted by a small shimmer near her feet. The sprinkle of light flickered again for a split second against a flash of lightning. She looked up at Archie who appeared occupied with the papers. Slowly, she slid her boot over the object and realized it was a shard of glass covered in dirt. The thought of this vile man killing Rayce was something she would not — could not consider.

If I can get the glass and cut the ropes...

She sat staring at the dirt, trying to figure out how to get the sharp glass shard from point A to point B, when she heard harsh voices and scuffling outside the window.

Even with all his apparent planning, Archie snapped to with an awkward start, clearly surprised. He drew his gun, and Eden caught sight of the Bowie knife he used to clean his fingernails tucked into the back of his trousers.

Archie's eyes twitched as he slowly walked to the window, his gun cocked and ready.

Suddenly, the window broke in a piercing crash of shattered shards, and in flew a crate falling to the ground with a heavy thump on the dirt floor. The glass spilled all around, hitting Archie in the face, missing Eden by only a few feet.

"What the hell!" Archie screeched, scratching wildly at his bloodied face with one hand, his gun pointed aimlessly in the other.

Eden twisted in her seat toward the loud sounds of scuffing boots and deep voices descending the stairway. Within the blink of an eye, Rayce stood at the bottom of the steps with one hand around the neck of the man who had left the basement earlier, and a gun in the other hand pointed at his head.

"Dammit!" Archie yelled.

"You have two choices here, Archie, live or die," Rayce announced.

Eden didn't dare say a word and distract him from this terrifying situation. The way she saw it, Rayce had the same choices, given Archie's gun was pointed at him, too.

"Don't let him shoot me, Archie," the other man begged. "Come on, now, I don't wanna die!"

Archie stood next to Eden, his cheeks and jaw embedded with sharp shards of glass, his gun aimed at Rayce.

"You haven't a pot to piss in, Major. I have your girl here, remember?" He reached behind and pulled the Bowie knife from his belt at his back.

Eden gasped and gnawed on her lower lip. Archie appeared to have the advantage with two weapons.

"You all right, Eden? He hurt you?" Rayce called. He began moving slowly toward her with his captive.

"I'm fine," she answered.

"Stay right where you are, Major." Archie smiled as he walked in front of Eden. "Looks like you're the loser here. The way I see it, you have no choice but to lay your gun down and let my man go."

"And what makes you think I'd do that?"

"Because with one shot I can take you out." He wielded the gun in front of Eden's face. "Or I could take your little lady out instead — your choice."

Rayce stopped and looked at Archie as though he were excrement on the sole of his boot. "So you've had to resort to kidnapping innocent women, have you, Archbibald?" He laughed in a low throaty growl. "What makes you think I can't take you and your partner out before you have a chance to fire a single bullet?"

Archie looked perplexed, as if debating whether Rayce

had such a plan or was simply bluffing. Eden could see in Rayce's dark eyes he sensed Archie's nervousness — smelled the fear in his enemy.

"For Christ's sake, Archibald," Rayce said. "Be a man — let her go."

The man being held by his scruff chimed in, "Yeah, maybe we better forget this and—"

Rayce grabbed the man's collar and shook him to shut him up, and turned his attention back to Archie. "Look, if you're going to kill one of us, it has to be me. I'm who you want, so let her go. Do you really want to have the death of this woman and her unborn child on your pathetic conscience?"

He knows. Her breath caught, and she looked at Rayce, her eyes welling with tears. He glanced at her for a brief moment, his eyes acknowledging hers, and she saw the corner of his mustache curl up in a small smile.

Oh, what a mess. In her womb grew Rayce's child, and here they were, her small family, at death's door. She had to think of something.

"I didn't know she was with child, for shit's sake...but just the same, I have my mission, Major."

As if the sun had come out in a dark moonless night to light her way, Eden saw the path in front of her. Without so much as a second thought, she readied herself for just the right moment.

Closer. Closer. Archie moved toward her and in a flash, she kicked her boot tip as hard as she could, landing straight between his legs.

"Umph!" Archie bent over, his body folding in half. His gun went off, shooting a bullet through the ceiling. Eden shrieked as he fell to the ground.

Quickly, she extended her leg as far out as she could and kicked the gun out of Archie's hand, sending it brushing against the dirt into a dark corner.

The man in Rayce's grasp tried to pull free from his clutches. "Stop it, you bastard!" Rayce shouted.

"That's it! I've had enough of these games," Archie said, wincing, his face red and pinched with pain and fury. He scrambled to his knees and held the sharp knife against Eden's throat. "Enough! I don't care if she's with child — you hear me?" he yelled. "I have my damn orders. I won't let you get away this time."

Rayce appeared to be weighing his options carefully while Archie looked insane — capable of doing anything.

"All right, Archie...Now, just leave her alone. Don't do anything you're going to regret," he said calmly.

Archie's large eyes looked as wild as his desperate need for recognition. "The only regret I'd have is if I didn't take your life when I finally had the chance. Drop your gun, Major — now."

Eden felt the shiny blade slice her neck. She cried out in pain as drops of blood dribbled down her neck.

"You filthy bastard!" Rayce shouted.

In a move faster than anything Eden had ever seen, Rayce hit the man he'd been holding over the head with his gun, knocking him out cold, and then lunged full-force tackling Archie to the ground in front of her feet. They tangled and fought, wrestling against the dirt.

At one moment, she could see Rayce's gun in the twisting and turning of bodies, and in the next moment she saw the blood-tinged blade of the knife in between both men's hands as they wrangled, fighting to the death.

"Rayce!" she shrieked. "Get him, Rayce!"

"Go to Hell!" Archie roared in Rayce's face.

"You first!" Rayce hissed back.

All at once, she heard the deafening blast from a gun, and both men went still and limp on the ground.

"Oh, my God, Rayce. Oh, please get up!"

For a moment, the room went completely silent. Somewhere in the back of her mind, she thought she heard the soft sound of her tears as they dripped down her cheeks, landing upon her skirt.

"You all right there, Rayce?" a voice called from the broken window.

Rayce pushed the dead man away from him and pulled the knife from his lifeless hands. "I'm fine," Rayce called as he slowly stood and cut the rope on Eden's wrists.

Eden stood and turned toward the window, "Mr. Johnson?"

Rayce brushed the dirt from his clothes. "Say hello to the best shot in Richmond, Sweetness. I believe you two have already met."

Hiram Johnson crouched at the window outside and gave Eden an awkward wave. "You two hurry up and get out of here. I'll get this mess taken care of."

Eden fingered the blood on her neck, and her knees suddenly buckled beneath her. Rayce lifted her up, swallowing her in his arms. "I was so scared," she said, going limp, tears flowing down her cheeks. "I thought you were going to die."

He tilted her chin high, evaluating the wound. "You're

going to be fine, my love. It's just a scratch. He gazed into her moist eyes. "I'll never let you out of my sight again, woman. Remember? You're mine...forever."

"Forever?"

"Forever, Sweetness." His mouth descended upon hers, and Eden knew the love they shared would indeed last forever.

Chapter 22

Eden woke from her nap with a start when the carriage made a quick turn. "Are we here?"

"Almost, my love."

She sank back against the plush seat and snuggled closer to Rayce. He put his arm around her, drawing her head upon his chest.

He gently brushed a loose tendril from her cheek. "Happy, my darling?"

"So very happy." She held up her hand, admiring the exquisite diamond and emerald engagement ring he had presented to her when he asked for her hand in marriage before they left Richmond. A ray of sunlight captured the elegant stones, and brilliant flutters of light danced against the dark walls of the carriage. "It's so beautiful, Rayce."

He tilted her chin and looked into her eyes. "Nothing but the best for you from now on, Sweetness." Softly, he kissed her lips. "We're almost there, and then I'll have you all to myself."

She stared at his handsome, chiseled profile as he gazed out the window. *Life is full of irony.* The man she once loathed would soon be her husband, the father of her child…the man of her dreams.

As they entered the grand iron gates of Hampton Manor, she heard Joseph's gentle command as he pulled on the leather reins, urging the horses to a slower tempo. She looked out at the tall, imposing tulip poplar and oak trees blowing gently in the soft breeze drifting across the river. Dotted with working field hands, the sprawling green fields swayed in the wind with each small gust.

Standing tall before her was the grand manor in all its splendid glory. With the exception of a lone cannon ball wedged in an outer wall, the large home stood unscathed, having survived the brutal campaign that had consumed much of the Peninsula.

It all seemed so long ago.

The orange glow of the setting sun reflected off the large windows, and Eden raised her hand to shield her eyes. The front portico held clay pots of blooming summer flowers, and the fields and orchards were awash with the rich hues of seasoned crops. As if beckoning her, the giant house with its majestic brick chimneys, resonated with the promise of long-awaited happiness, and she felt a warm glow surge across her skin.

The tall third-floor window stood wide open, its view obscured by the bright light of the setting sun. She narrowed her eyes and saw the outline of a figure looking out upon the river.

"Rayce. Who's that at the window?"

"Which window?"

"Why, the third floor window, darling." She pointed. "Up

there. I saw someone looking out toward the river."

Rayce leaned over and looked out of her window. "I don't see anyone, Sweetness. Nobody ever goes up there anymore." He placed his hand over hers. "The sun has always had a way of casting shadows up there. I'm sure that's all it was."

She cast her gaze toward the window again, but the mysterious image had disappeared. "I suppose you're right."

The large front door opened and out walked Lucy. Will followed behind, with Ann holding baby Rebecca in her arms. They all stood smiling and waving, greeting the carriage as it made its way up to the entry.

Eden smiled. "Ann's holding the baby. Lord above, I never thought I'd see the day."

The front door nudged wider, and out walked Mama Claire, followed by Uncle Asa and Jeremiah.

Eden gasped and squeezed Rayce's hand. "Oh, my darling. What a surprise — you did this."

"They're your family, Eden, and soon they'll be mine, too. This is their new home."

THEY stood watching as the dark carriage entered the graceful, tree-lined entryway to the manor. Trinidad placed a gentle hand upon his shoulder. "It's time," she said, turning away from the large window facing out toward the river.

She picked up the aged oil portrait propped upon the worn divan. She looked at the beautiful, young woman painted on the canvas one last time before covering it in cloth and storing it away forever. The emerald eyes framed by long, honey-blonde hair adorned with a delicate magnolia blossom, stared back.

"You rest your weary soul, Captain, for she carries within her womb a son...a son who will grow to be a fine, strong man and rule the manor himself one day."

A sudden gust of warm, fresh air, gentle as a soft sigh, filled the old, musty room.

"That's right. Come away from the window and rest yourself, Captain. She has finally come home."

The End

A word about the author . . .

Diana grew up in Virginia where her love of American History began. Living near an abandoned Civil War graveyard as a child sparked her active imagination with tales of honor, romance and things that go bump in the night. She enjoys writing about strong heroines up to the challenge of fighting harsh circumstances while taming the heart of the man she loves.

Diana resides in Nevada. Visit her at www.dianaballew.com

Also from Diana Ballew

Immortal Prey — Evernight Publishing

Bound by Glory — Coming 2016 — Trifecta Publishing House

Recipes from Hampton Manor and Richmond

(Converted for modern-day living.)

Trinidad's Virginia Ham and Brandied Peaches

Virginia Ham (10-12 lbs. cooked)

2 Tablespoons light brown sugar

1 Tablespoon bread crumbs

1 teaspoon ground cloves

3 Tablespoons honey

Garnish with brandied peaches.

Preheat oven to 375 degrees. Combine brown sugar, bread crumbs and cloves and press mixture over ham. Place ham in shallow baking pan and bake 15 minutes or until sugar melts. Remove from oven and drizzle honey over the ham. Return to oven 15 minutes. Serve with brandied peaches.

Brandied Peaches

2 cans (1 lb. 13 oz. each) peach halves

½ cup brandy, preferably peach brandy

½ cup sugar

4 drops almond extract

Drain peaches and reserve 1 cup of juice. Boil the reserved peach juice until it measures about ½ cup. Add ½ cup sugar and ½ cup brandy to the juice. Mix well. Add the almond extract. Cool. Pour brandy syrup over the peaches and serve.

Mama Claire's Baked Egg Custard

4 eggs

1 quart milk, scalded

½ cup sugar

¼ teaspoon salt

1 teaspoon vanilla

Mix well-beaten eggs, sugar and salt. Pour over this the scalded milk slowly until sugar is dissolved, stirring constantly. Add vanilla and pour into 8 greased custard cups. Place cups into a pan containing 1 inch of hot water. Bake in moderate oven 350 degrees for 30 minutes or until a knife inserted comes out clean.

Eliza's Molasses Cake

2 cups all purpose flour

1 teaspoon baking powder

1 teaspoon ginger

1 cup molasses

2 eggs

½ cup soft shortening

¼ cup milk

Mix the first three ingredients. In a separate bowl beat together the remaining ingredients. Combine the two mixtures, stirring well. (Add a little more milk if needed to make a thick but pourable batter.) Pour into a greased 9 x 13 inch pan. Bake at 375 degrees for about 50 minutes or until done.

Enjoy!

www.ingramcontent.com/pod-product-compliance
Lightning Source LLC
Chambersburg PA
CBHW061623210726
48287CB00001B/257